MW00986121

ONE FOR THE AGES

A DCI JACK LOGAN NOVEL

JD KIRK

ONE FOR THE AGES

ISBN: 978-1-912767-72-4

Published worldwide by Zertex Media Ltd.
This edition published in 2023.

2

www.jdkirk.com
www.zertexmedia.com

BOOKS BY J.D. KIRK

A Litter of Bones

Thicker Than Water

The Killing Code

Blood & Treachery

The Last Bloody Straw

A Whisper of Sorrows

The Big Man Upstairs

A Death Most Monumental

A Snowball's Chance in Hell

Ahead of the Game

An Isolated Incident

Colder Than the Grave

Come Hell or High Water

City of Scars

Here Lie the Dead

Northwind: A Robert Hoon Thriller

Southpaw: A Robert Hoon Thriller

Westward: A Robert Hoon Thriller

Eastgate: A Robert Hoon Thriller

For the Super Special Chums!

CHAPTER ONE

THE CORD around her neck was making a liar of her.

She'd told herself she was ready for death. She'd cited it to others like a mantra.

I've had a good innings. I've lived a long life.

When it came, she'd said, she wasn't going to fight it.

But there, on the floor, blood on her face and her nightdress riding up around her waist, she fought with everything she had, her liver-spotted hands grasping like claws at the belt of a dressing gown as it dug into the loose skin of her throat, and bit hard on the windpipe below.

Her feet slid back and forth on the floor, one bare, the other with a fur-lined slipper still hooked onto her toes. Her bare legs kicked as best they could, but most of their strength had left them years before, and they just rubbed on the threadbare carpet, chafing her skin.

She couldn't remember falling. She couldn't recall why she was on the floor, or why there was so much blood on her hands. Her white floral nightdress—the pattern turned near-invisible by a few hundred laundry cycles—was stained with a spray of crimson that would never wash out.

Her recollection hadn't been good for a few years, but the lack of oxygen was devouring her memories now, chewing through them, so she couldn't remember why this was happening. Couldn't remember what she had done.

Because she must've done something, surely? She must've done something to deserve this. Here. Now. She must've done something to have earned such a punishment.

Whatever it was—whatever she'd done—she wanted to scream that she was sorry, to crawl, to beg, to make it all stop.

She wanted to be in bed. Or at the library. Or at the lunch club. Anywhere but here. On this floor. With the cord around her neck making a liar of her.

There was a grunt. The pressure on her throat intensified until she could see flickering shadows circling her, closing in from the corners of the room, a pulsing strobe of dark shapes and twisted figures.

Her fingers were no longer her own. They weren't responding. Weren't obeying. They clung limply to the belt of the robe, no longer pulling at it. No longer fighting. No longer able.

Pressure built in her head, and behind her eyes, until she was sure she was going to pop right open. Her chest heaved, her lungs spasming their last.

The panic of the last few moments floated away like her childhood kite, like her brother's blue balloon, like the dandelion clocks she once blew with her mother.

She watched them drifting off now. All of them. As the confusion of panic lifted, it took the fog of old age with it, leaving her free to relive those moments, and a million others, all at once. All in one brief, brilliant instant.

And when death finally came for her, half-naked on the living room floor, she was no longer of a mind to fight it.

CHAPTER TWO

THE DRIVE TO Glasgow had taken forever. Rain had battered the BMW almost from the moment Logan had left Inverness, and a bank of damp mist had cocooned the car all the way down the A9, before lifting at Perth to reveal a sky overcast with brooding grey clouds.

It was a journey that had quite accurately reflected his mood, and done absolutely nothing to lighten it.

And the day had been destined to be all downhill from there.

"Jack."

The cheap plastic seat shoogled beneath him as Logan looked up from the floor. He'd been staring at the few inches of vinyl tile visible between his size thirteens for the past several minutes, yet wouldn't have been able to tell you what colour it was.

He blinked, like he was coming out of a hypnotist's thrall, then nodded at the man with the shiny brass buttons who'd just stepped into the room.

"Gordon."

The lines of the other man's face tightened. A finger was raised, though he stopped short of giving it a reproachful wag.

"I know you don't like this any more than I do, Jack, but the Deputy Chief Constable is in there, so let's be professional, eh?"

Logan hid his sigh by rising to his feet. "Sorry. *Detective Superintendent Mackenzie.*"

"Better. But if you could maybe say it with a bit less contempt..."

Logan shot a withering look at his old boss. "You asked me to be a professional. No' a bloody miracle worker."

The senior officer smiled at that, and both men shook hands. "Good to see you haven't changed, Jack." He withdrew his hand and tucked them both behind his back. "Once an arsehole, always an arsehole, eh?"

"Why change the habit of a lifetime, eh?"

"Ha! Aye. Quite."

The detective superintendent glanced back at the door behind him, then pulled it closed all the way and motioned for Logan to follow him a few paces further into the waiting room.

Logan might not have changed, but he couldn't help but notice that his old boss had. The flat top haircut that had once earned him the nickname *the Gozer*, after one of the villains from the *Ghostbusters* movie franchise, had thinned away to nothing. What little hair was left was cropped in tight to his scalp, possibly in an attempt to disguise quite how grey he was going.

He'd always been what those in the ranks below had described as 'an uptight prick.' He'd mostly played fair, though, and even if very few people actively liked the man, they generally had a level of respect for him.

Even Logan, which was saying something.

The Gozer stole another look at the door, then lowered his voice to a murmur. "Sorry it's not under better circumstances, Jack. This whole thing, it's... Well, it's a rough one."

Logan nodded. "How is she?"

"She's doing OK. I think. You know how she is."

"Aye."

"I mean, you more than most, I suppose."

Logan didn't grace the remark with a response.

"What about the bastard she pummelled?" he asked

"Allegedly pummelled. And he's fine. Bugger all wrong with him. No lasting damage done."

Logan grunted. "Shame."

"You read his file, then?"

"Just the highlights."

"Hmm. Yes. I don't blame you. Quite an epic bloody tome, otherwise."

The Gozer checked his watch, confirmed it against the clock on the wall, then leaned in a little closer and beckoned for the towering DCI to bring an ear down nearer to mouth level.

"Listen, Jack, I know this is out of the blue, but if things go... the way they might in here. Well... There's going to be an opening."

"No," Logan told him.

"I don't want an answer now."

"Well, I'm giving you an answer now, Gordon. It's no. I'm happy where I am."

"Just think about it. That's all I'm saying," the detective superintendent urged. "Hopefully it won't come to that, but if it does..."

"I don't need to think about it. I don't want to move."

The Gozer breathed out slowly through both nostrils, straightened up, then nodded curtly. "Fine. OK, Jack, that's fine. You've made your position clear."

He returned to the door, placed his hand on the handle, then looked back over his shoulder.

"Of course, we both know that in this job we don't always get what we want."

He let that hang there in the air between them, then he turned the handle, opened the door, and gestured for Logan to lead the way.

Gary Hawthorne's testicles had never had it so good.

He'd be the first to admit that, generally speaking, he didn't pay them enough attention. They just sort of hung there most of the time, minding their own business, doing their own thing. He only really thought about them if there was a problem. And, mercifully, such problems were rare.

They were a bit like the oil boiler in the back garden, in that respect. As long as it continued to produce heat and hot water, he generally forgot it even existed.

Today, though, was different. Today was special, and he'd given both bollocks an extra helping of care and attention.

They'd been soaped with a menthol and eucalyptus body wash that had made them positively *zing,* then vigorously yet tenderly dried off with one of the good towels.

After that—partly as a special treat, and partly to ease the burning sensation the body wash had ignited along the whole length of his arse crack—Gary had given them a thorough dusting of talcum powder, before tucking them safely away inside a pair of brand new, never-before-worn, cotton boxer shorts.

He wasn't sure if it was possible for testicles to feel *minty fresh,* but if it was, then his did. They very much did.

They *too much* did, it could be argued, but hopefully the talc would soon sort that out.

Even if it didn't, it would still be worth it. Sandra had been away at her mother's in Thurso for almost a fortnight. Before that, she'd been run ragged on night shifts for weeks.

Tonight, though, she'd be back with him. Tonight, they'd

share a bed. Tonight, if he played his cards right, his freshly trimmed and scrubbed genitalia might be emerging from their almost six-week-long hibernation.

And, after last night's excitement, he was all fired up and ready to go.

Wriggling into his jeans, Gary spotted the little envelope icon on his phone notifying him that a message had come in while he'd been in the shower.

He didn't pick the phone up. Not yet. Not right away. Better to not know for a few moments longer. Better to hold onto the hope.

He unhooked his shirt from the back of the door, where he'd been letting the steam work away at the creases. The water hadn't been as hot as it usually got, though, so the shirt didn't look all that different.

He pulled it on, regardless, and eyed his phone screen as he fastened all but the topmost button.

She wouldn't. Surely not. She'd promised.

He sat on the edge of the bath and wrestled his damp feet into his socks, his gaze still fixed on his mobile. It sat there on the toilet cistern, slightly propped up on a slim pack of wet wipes. Just sat there. Waiting. Smug as fuck that it knew something he didn't.

But he did know. That was the worst of it. He didn't need to open the message to know what it was going to say.

The only question was how it would be worded. The general contents of the message, he could guess, but the specifics were still a mystery.

Maggie, Sandra's mum, could've suffered a setback. That was an obvious one.

Or maybe the old bastard had passed on the flu that had made it necessary for Sandra to drop everything and rush to her side in the first place. Maybe Sandra was now stuck in bed, head spinning, nose streaming, vomit threatening to put in an appearance.

Or maybe she just didn't want to see him. Maybe she'd finally followed through on all those threats to leave him.

Whatever. The details weren't important. There'd be some excuse or other waiting there for him. Some *lie*, probably.

Gary's wife wouldn't be joining him in the bedroom this evening.

All that grooming had been for nothing.

He finished putting on his socks, stood up, and looked down at the sodden carpet of pubic hair lining the bottom of the bath. It had seemed like a good idea at the time, but the sight of it there, all matted and full of suds, suddenly made him want to gag. And, he was sure, he could already feel the itching starting.

Shoving his hand down the front of his jeans and scratching at his stubbly skin, he knew he couldn't put it off any longer. He picked up the phone and angrily jabbed a thumb against the screen.

His eyebrows crept halfway up his head as he read the waiting message.

Be home about 2. Get wine and dig out massage oil. Need to unwind!!!

"Oh! Shit!" he heard himself say out loud, and suddenly his crotch no longer felt like he'd been dragged knob-first through a jaggy bush. Suddenly, the wet wad of pubes was a carpet of rose petals.

The text had more or less confirmed it. He'd been on the benches for over a month, but tonight, Little Gary Junior was back in the game.

Tonight, he was getting his end away!

"Daaaad?"

The call from downstairs came just as Gary started to tap out a reply to the message. Rory, the younger of his and Sandra's two sons, sounded wary. Nervous, even.

Christ, what had he done this time?

Gary's thumbs reared back from the screen and hung there, like cobras ready to strike.

"What is it, Roar? Don't tell me you've broken something."

"*Daaaad!*"

The shout was louder now. It came from the foot of the stairs, and there was a suggestion of panic to it that made Gary shove his phone into his pocket and pull open the bathroom door.

Both boys stood at the bottom of the stairs, looking out through the window that ran the full height of the front door. They were only four years apart—thirteen and seventeen—but while puberty was just starting to cause Rory problems, it had already spat Edgar out the other side as a smelly, hairy adult.

Both boys' backs were to him, their attention fixed on something outside.

"What is it?" Gary asked. "What's the matter?"

It was Edgar who answered in his usual dull monotone.

"There's a man."

"What?" Gary hesitated at the top step. "What do you mean?"

"In the garden," said Rory. "There's a man."

Gary's feet made no move to carry him down the steps. "What?" he asked, all but scoffing at the suggestion. "What do you mean? Who? What man?"

"I think it's Mr Hall," Edgar said, looking back and up over his shoulder at where his father still stood motionless at the top of the narrow staircase.

"What, old Mr Hall?" Gary asked. "From down the road?"

"I think he's been hurt," said Rory. He cupped his hands around his eyes and pressed them against the glass, like he was wildlife watching with a pair of binoculars. "He looks like he's hurt himself."

Gary tutted twice on the way down the stairs, and was

shaking his head when he reached the bottom. "If this is a joke, guys, it's not very... Ooh, fuck."

He stopped when he saw the old man in the garden, and felt an overwhelming urge to duck, like they were the ones who'd been caught somewhere they shouldn't be.

Old Mr Hall from down the road stood in the middle of the lawn, turned side-on so he wasn't looking at the house, or at the gate that stood open at the end of the path. Instead, he seemed transfixed by the washing line, and the blue carer's apron that twitched idly on the morning breeze.

"He's got blood on him," Edgar remarked.

The old man was dressed in a dark blue blazer over a white shirt. Gary had never seen him without his tie. Today was no exception, though it was looser around his neck, like he'd taken less time and care over the knot.

The collar of the shirt was spotted with red. Possibly the blazer, too, though it was hard to be sure from that distance.

There was no mistaking the blood on his trembling hands, though. It had coated them, clogging up the creases and drying in the wrinkles. He held them in front of him, fingertips close together but not quite touching, like he was carefully carrying a ball only he could see.

"Shit."

Rory looked up. "Dad?"

"What? Oh." Gary shook his head. "Nothing. Just... Something must've happened to him. Stay here, alright? Both of you."

"Should we call an ambulance?" Edgar asked. For all the growing he'd done in the last few years, he looked even more anxious than his younger brother. "Or, I don't know, the police?"

"Police? No. No, no need for that," Gary said. "Anyway, by the time they get here..."

He didn't finish that sentence, and instead wriggled his feet into the battered old gardening trainers that lived under the radiator in the hall.

"Just hang off here, OK? I'll go check he's alright. Alright?"

The boys swapped looks, then both nodded.

"Alright," they confirmed.

"Alright. Good," Gary said. He reached for the door handle, then stopped when Edgar called to him.

"Dad!" The older boy shifted nervously on the spot as he looked through the glass at the blood-stained figure in the garden. "Be careful."

"Don't worry. It's Mr Hall. He's a harmless old man," Gary said. He offered a comforting smile as he opened the door. "What's the worst he could do?"

CHAPTER THREE

LOGAN CLIMBED into the front seat of his BMW, pulled on his seatbelt, then laid the flats of his hands on the top of the steering wheel. He let out a low, almost imperceptible groan as he stretched his fingers, trying to work out some of the tension that his clenched fists had built up during the interrogation.

Not that they'd called it that, of course. It was just a chat to give them a bit of background. That was all. Just an informal, but one-hundred-percent on the record wee blether to help them make their decision.

Or, more likely, to help them justify a decision they'd already made.

He'd played his part as best he could. He'd answered honestly—or as honestly as he'd been comfortable with—and had made his personal feelings on the matter very clear.

It was the Gozer who requested that, "The nasty wee fucker had it coming," was stricken from the record. Logan had insisted on keeping it in.

"Well?"

There was nothing particularly alarming about the voice

that came from behind him, aside from the fact that he hadn't been expecting it.

He jumped, his fingers tightening on the wheel, a hissed, "Jesus Christ!" bursting from his lips as he twisted in his seat to look behind him.

Heather Filson sat staring at him from the back seat. Her hair was lank and matted, and the bags under her eyes were large enough for a fortnight's holiday in Marbella. If Logan hadn't looked in the back of the car before leaving Inverness, he'd have been convinced she'd been sleeping there for weeks.

"How the hell did you get in?" he demanded. "Did you break into my bloody car?"

"Course I didn't break in," Heather retorted. She sniffed and wriggled in the seat, getting comfy. "I got a key made when I was up in Inverness."

Logan's eyes widened and his mouth fell open. "What the fuck did you do that for?"

"In case I needed to get in," Heather said, like this should be patently obvious. She sat forward. Logan caught a whiff of cigarette smoke, and just a suggestion of something alcoholic. "Well?" she asked. "Am I fucked?"

Logan considered his response. "Maybe," he admitted, then he shrugged. "I don't know. For once, I don't think they've already made their minds up, and I get the impression the Gozer's working damage limitation. He knows you're a good copper."

Heather laughed drily. "He knows we're short-staffed more like."

"Same result either way."

"Arse might not be out the window, then?"

"Maybe not all the way," Logan said. He faced front, sighed like a disappointed parent, then met her eye in the mirror. "What were you thinking?"

Heather slumped back against the seat. Perhaps in response

to his tone, there was something of the petulant teenager about it.

"Got a bit carried away, that's all. And he's fine. No lasting damage done."

"Fortunately."

Heather shrugged. "Maybe." She chewed her bottom lip for a moment, and looked out through the side window of the car. "He laughed, Jack."

Logan watched her in the mirror. "What? What do you mean?"

"Outside the court. After the bastard got off. He stood there, in front of her, in front of her mum and her old man, and he fucking laughed. Told them she'd wanted it. Told them she'd begged for it. Said now it was down on record what a slut she was."

The steering wheel creaked beneath the strength of Logan's grip. "Bastard."

"He was trying to get her dad to take a swing at him. Goading him into it. Egging him on."

Heather continued to look out through the side window, her gaze following the police cars pulling in and out of the station car park, like she half-expected one of them to be coming to arrest her.

"Her dad, he's a teacher. Primary school. An assault charge —because that's what the fucker was pushing for—would've ruined him."

"So you intervened."

Heather's eyes flicked forward and met his in the mirror. "Aye. Sure. Let's call it that," she said, a smile tugging at one corner of her mouth.

Logan failed to see the funny side, which only broadened the smile of the woman behind him.

"Don't worry, Jack. I'll be fine."

"Are you, though?" Logan asked her. "You look—"

She jumped in before he had a chance to finish the sentence. "It's been a rough few days. But, yeah, I'm dandy."

"You can talk to me."

Her lips pursed together, and she rolled her tongue around in her mouth, like she was trying to chase down a reply that didn't want to be caught.

Finally, she managed a curt, "I'm grand. Honest," then went back to gazing out of the side window. "They're like bees. Aren't they?"

Logan turned in his seat and shot a frown back over his shoulder. "Eh?"

Heather nodded at the comings and goings of the police cars. "In and out. Back and forth," she said. "All day, every day. Bzzzz."

Logan followed her gaze, but found it hard to share her interest. "Aye. Well. Always something happening."

Heather nodded slowly. "Always something," she mumbled, then she gave herself a shake, leaned forward, and patted Logan on the shoulder. "Anyway. Cheers for that, big fella. You better get off. Tell your missus I said hello."

Logan managed a half smile at that. "She'll be delighted."

"She up the duff yet?"

"Fuck off!" The words fell from his mouth so quickly they surprised even him. "No. Been there, done that. No plans on it happening again."

"Right. Fair enough." Heather patted him on the shoulder again, then reached for the door handle. "You told her that?"

"What?"

It was Heather's turn to sigh.

"Jesus, Jack. You're one of the smartest guys I know." She opened the door, and the sound of the passing police vehicles filled the inside of the car. "But you're also the biggest fucking idiot."

She flicked his ear with a finger, laughed at the back of her throat, then jumped out of the car and went marching off towards the station.

"Ow," Logan said, somewhat belatedly.

He wound down his window to call after her, but the right words wouldn't come.

From the pocket of his coat, his phone buzzed. He reached for it, clocked DI Ben Forde's name on the screen, then looked up to find Heather gone.

"Bollocks," he muttered, then he tapped his phone screen. "Ben. What's up?"

Logan listened to Ben's response in stony silence. Outside, beyond the window, police cars buzzed in and out, coming and going, back and forth.

Always something.

"Keiss? Where the hell's that?" he asked. His eyes crawled higher up his forehead as he listened to the reply. "A hundred and ten miles north of Inverness? Is that no' the Arctic bloody Circle?"

While Ben laid out the directions, Logan jabbed the button that started the engine, and felt the rumble of the car coming to life.

"Right, well, that's going to take a while, then," he finally said. "But, I'll be there as soon as I can. So, you know, a week on Tuesday."

Without waiting for a response, he removed the phone from his ear to end the call. A shout from the other end stopped him before he could thumb the button.

"Sorry, missed that. What did you say?" As he listened to the response, his face tightened into a frown. "What?" he asked. "What do you mean, *helicopter*?"

CHAPTER FOUR

A LITTLE OVER three hours later, Logan strode away from the chopper, bent almost double for fear of being decapitated by the still-spinning blades. He clutched an *Asda* carrier bag in one hand, the top all bunched together in his fist like he was worried the contents might escape.

The 'landing pad' was a muddy field, and by the time Logan had reached the car that sat parked up and waiting for him by the gate, his shoes were caked in the stuff, and his socks were damp.

There were socks in the bag. Underwear, and a shirt, too. He'd had time to grab it before boarding the helicopter, since he had no idea how long he was going to be away from home, and what the shopping situation was like this far north.

Based on what he'd seen on the flight in, 'non-existent' would be a pretty accurate way of describing it.

What he hadn't thought to buy was a new pair of trousers. Shame, really, given that the bottoms of the legs of the pair he was wearing had started to succumb to the mud.

As he approached the car, the driver's window slid down. A grin emerged, followed by the rest of the face it belonged to.

"Alright, boss?"

"No' particularly," Logan grunted. He strode around to the passenger side and tried the handle of the rear door. It refused to open.

"Oops. Sorry, boss," said DC Tyler Neish, stretching across from the front until he was just able to hook a finger over the door handle. He gave a tug, and the door *clunked* open. "Got the child safety locks on."

Logan opened the door the rest of the way and met the eye of the man inside. "Child safety locks?"

"Can't be too careful, boss."

"They're no' even bloody born yet," Logan reminded him. "I don't think you need worry too much about them pissing about with the doors."

"Aye. That's what Sinead said," Tyler admitted. "But, I just thought, better safe than sorry."

"And hang on..." Logan looked from the door to Tyler, then back again. "They don't work like that, do they? Child safety locks. They're no' to stop you opening it from the outside, they're to stop the kids opening the door from the inside and falling out."

Tyler looked up at the DCI for quite a long time, his lips moving silently.

"Shite, aye," he eventually said. "Sorry, boss. I must've just locked it normally."

Logan horsed the bag into the back seat, fixed Tyler with a look that said he was going to pretend this conversation had never happened, then shut the door with a slam.

He climbed into the front without a word and pulled on his seatbelt. Tyler kept watching him, the same smile fixed on his face. His eyes darted downward, just for a moment.

"I see your shoes are quite muddy, boss."

"What?" Logan checked out his feet and winced. "Oh. Aye. Sorry."

"No worries. It's a rubber mat. Easy clean. They recommend that when you've got kids."

"*Nearly* got kids," Logan corrected.

"Aye. Well—"

"Better safe than sorry," Logan said, guessing the end of the sentence.

Tyler's smile widened. He wound up his window, then started the engine. "How was the flight?"

"Totally unnecessary," Logan replied.

Granted, it would've taken a good five to six hours to drive from Glasgow all the way up here, if not longer, and apparently there was a police chopper based not far out of Wick, just a few miles away from where Logan was headed, so it was a relatively easy run.

But, from what he'd been told before take-off, they were dealing with one dead pensioner and a blood-soaked husband. Half his team had already been dispatched from Inverness. It didn't exactly strike him as an emergency.

"Oh, I don't know about that, boss," Tyler said. He checked his mirrors, indicated to nobody, then pulled out onto the long, narrow road. "Something about this one feels pretty damn weird..."

"Jesus."

The sight of her sitting there caught Logan off-guard. He hadn't been expecting her to be sitting. Nor had he expected her eyes to be quite so wide open, her head tilted onto one shoulder so she seemed to be staring straight at him as he entered the living room of the small, one-bedroomed terraced house.

He'd kicked the worst of the mud off his shoes outside, before covering his feet with a pair of protective plastic slip-ons designed to reduce the risk of crime scene contamination. They rustled underfoot as he stepped into the room.

"Disconcerting, isn't it?" came a voice from Logan's left.

The DCI turned sharply and found the Scene of Crime team's Geoff Palmer standing in the corner of the room, fully kitted out in his white protective suit. His hood was up, so the only part of Palmer visible was the perfect circle of his face surrounded by the hood's elastic trim.

The wall behind him was a similar colour to the outfit, so the pudgy red features of the SOC man appeared at first glance to be floating five-and-a-half feet off the floor.

"No' as disconcerting as you, you creepy bastard," Logan said, looking Palmer up and down. "What are you doing, haunting the place?"

"That's funny," Palmer told him, though the bunched-up ball that was his face said otherwise. "And no, I'm doing my job, *actually*. Some of us have been here for a good couple of hours now." A snidey little smirk tugged at the corners of his mouth. "I even offered Shona a lift up. In your absence."

"Well done," Logan said, turning his attention back to the body. "I'm guessing she said no."

The smirk left as quickly as it had arrived, and Palmer quickly changed the subject.

"She's been in and done her bit," was all he had to say on the matter.

Logan managed to hide his surprise. Usually, once Shona had attended a body, she'd have closed the eyes, and yet the dead woman was still staring at him. That suggested she'd been dead long enough for the thin skin of her eyelids to start constricting.

"Shona still around?" Logan asked, trying to keep his interest sounding exclusively professional.

"What? Don't you know?" Palmer asked, seizing on the question. "Why, you two not talking or something?"

"We're not, actually," Logan said. From the corner of his eye, he saw Palmer's whole body become erect. "Don't get excited. No phone signal," he explained, and he enjoyed the way the SOC man deflated again. "So. What's the story?"

Palmer frowned, like he was struggling to understand the question. Then, with a start, he seemed to remember the body sitting propped up in the armchair.

"Oh. Yes. Right. Well, we've built up a picture, but that's about it. Any forensic evidence has been well and truly compromised before we got here, between paramedics, and plods, and nosybody bloody neighbours. We'll be lucky to get anything at all."

"But you've built a picture...?" Logan prompted.

"Yes. Shona and I did. Between us." There was just the hint of a suggestive eyebrow waggle before he continued. "Time of death is looking like last night. Between ten and midnight, Shona thinks. No sign of forced entry. Windows and back door locked, so the killer either came and went through the front door, or, if you ask me, was here the whole time."

"You're thinking the husband?"

"Seems likely," Palmer confirmed.

Logan kept his distance from the body, but bent forward at the waist so he could get a better look. She was dressed in a blouse with a cardigan over the top of it. A pair of mustard-coloured slacks covered her bottom half. It all looked a bit dishevelled and mismatched.

"Strangled," he remarked.

"Yes. Seems that way," Palmer confirmed, though it hadn't been a question.

The red, raw-looking burn marks on her throat, and the burst blood vessels in both eyes had quickly told the DCI what they were dealing with.

"Not there, though," Logan said, gesturing to where the

woman sat. The back of the chair was against the wall. "No room for anyone to get behind her."

Palmer appeared a little put out by the observation, like he'd been hoping to do some big reveal.

"Aye. Well," he said, tucking his hands behind his back. "Bet you can't guess where she was killed, can you?"

Logan looked around the room, then pointed to the miniature campsite of tent-shaped evidence markers on the floor beside a coffee table. "There?"

Geoff scraped his top teeth across his bottom lip, presumably realising that it had, on reflection, been a stupid bloody question.

"Yes. But you wouldn't have known without all that pointing it out," he said, desperately grasping for some sort of win.

"Fine. OK. Well done," Logan said. He turned to the other man, then tutted. "For God's sake, Geoff, take the hood down. I feel like I'm talking to the fucking moon."

"No can do. Protocol," Palmer replied. "Now, do you want to know what happened, or would you rather keep having a go at my appearance?"

Logan appeared to give this some thought, then turned back to the dead woman.

"She was strangled on the floor, then moved to the chair?" he guessed.

"Oh, if only it were that simple..." Palmer said. He pointed, rather smugly, to the corner of the coffee table, where a solitary evidence marker stood.

"Blood," Logan remarked.

"*Finally*, he spots it. And there, on the carpet. Hard to see, because it's so dark, but it's there. Believe me," Palmer said. He rocked back on his heels, delighting in some imagined minor victory. "Nothing gets past us lot."

Logan squatted and studied the carpet. The stains weren't

easy to see, but now that he knew what he was looking for, they were unmistakable. He raised his head until he was looking at the woman in the chair again. Other than the markings on her neck, there were no obvious injuries.

"Not hers?"

"Oh, it's hers," Palmer said. He removed a hand from behind his back again, and this time pointed to a waste-paper basket down beside the dead woman's armchair.

Logan took the long way around so as not to step on any of the bloodstains, then leaned over and peered down into the bin. A nest of bloodied tissues lay wadded up inside, filling the receptacle more than halfway.

This close to the body, the DCI could see a light crusting of dried blood around both of the dead woman's nostrils.

"She cleaned herself up?"

"Someone did," Palmer replied. "There's a cloth in the bathroom that they used too, along with a pair of blood-stained pyjamas, and her nightdress."

"Nightdress?" Logan asked, looking from the Scene of Crime man to the body and back again. "She got changed?"

"*Was* changed, more likely. Buttons of her blouse are done up wrong. And, I mean, that cardigan? With those trousers?"

Logan glanced around the room. It was small and sparsely furnished, but with a lifetime's worth of old clocks, gaudy ornaments, and other clutter covering most of the surfaces.

"I doubt she was that bothered about making a fashion statement."

"Well, Shona agrees with me," Geoff said, and he rocked back on his heels again like the balance of power had physically shifted towards him. "We put our heads together, the two of us, and we reckon the victim was attacked while wearing her nightdress, fell and hit the table on the way down, then was strangled where she landed."

"So, someone moved her, changed her, and cleaned her up

after death?" Logan asked. His mind raced, thinking it through, searching for the *why*, but not finding it. Not yet. "They must've known we'd see through that. I mean, Christ, if *you* can figure it out..."

"With your girlfriend's very kind assistance," Palmer said. He gave a self-satisfied little sneer, like he was deflecting the DCI's insult onto Shona.

It wasn't the *gotcha* he thought it was.

"True. You did have help, right enough," Logan said. He shot the other man a thin smile of reassurance. "Chin up, though, Geoff. I'm sure you'd have got there on your own, eventually."

He turned on the spot, took another look around the room, then returned to the door. He was keen to get out of there—to get away from that hollow-eyed, lifeless cadaver as soon as he possibly could.

And he'd seen quite enough of the dead body, too.

"Got anything else to tell me?" he asked.

Palmer put his hands on his hips, blew out his cheeks, then shook his head. "Think that's the main headlines," he said. "Although..."

Logan stopped mid-turn towards the exit.

"Although?"

"I've been given a few tickets. Got some going spare."

"Tickets?"

Palmer nodded. "For a gig."

"A gig?"

"There a bloody echo in here?" the Scene of Crime man asked. "Yes. I've been given a few tickets for a gig."

"What gig?"

"My gig."

Logan stared at him, making no attempt to hide his confusion. Nor, for that matter, his obvious disinterest.

"My next stand-up gig!" Palmer clarified.

"You do stand-up?" Logan asked. "As in stand-up comedy?"

"Yes! Of course, I... What?" Geoff blustered. "You know I do stand-up. You know this. We've gone over this!"

Logan's gaze somehow became even more blank. "I don't think we have."

"Yes! We have! Loads of times!" Palmer insisted. He shook his head. Although, given that the hood didn't move much, it was more like he shook his face inside the elasticated circle. "Doesn't matter. The deal with the venue is I'll shift some tickets."

"How many tickets?" Logan asked.

"Not many," Palmer said. "Just, like, I don't know... One to two hundred."

Logan frowned. "One to two hundred? That's quite a wide range."

"One hundred to two hundred, I mean."

"Ah. Right. Got you. That's quite a lot to shift."

"It won't be a problem," Geoff said, though his expression said otherwise. "So, you want a few? Nine, or ten, or whatever?"

"Ten? Jesus. Who am I meant to be bringing with me? *Showaddywaddy?*"

"Or even just half a dozen," Geoff said, a pleading note to his voice. "I could do you some really good ones. Right down the front."

Logan narrowed his eyes and chewed on his bottom lip, considering the offer. "Are they free?"

"They are, aye! Completely free."

Logan thought for another moment, then nodded, coming to a decision.

"No. You're alright," he said. He smiled, and gave the shorter man a hearty slap on the shoulder. "But good luck with that."

And then, before Palmer could say a word to stop him, Logan went striding out of the room, through the hallway, and into the chill of a cloudy mid-January in the far north of Scotland.

CHAPTER FIVE

A COLD WINTER'S wind assaulted Logan as he stepped out of the terraced house and into the garden. The victim's house stood on what was the village's High Street, though there was a distinct lack of shopping facilities.

Or, for that matter, facilities of any other kind.

What was there was some grass. Two decent-sized patches of it, in fact, just about the right size for kids to have a wee kick about with a football.

There were no houses directly across from the victim's, which would reduce the likelihood of the neighbours having seen anyone coming and going to the house.

Mind you, in a place this size, you quite often got lucky. In Logan's experience, small villages like this one seemed to harbour a disproportionate share of the world's nosy bastards.

Beyond the grassy areas, off to the left, lay the North Sea. The wind carved charging white horses across its surface, before heading inland and swirling icily around Logan as he marched along the path and out onto the cordoned-off street.

Still, at least it wasn't raining.

Further along to the left, facing the water, stood a row of

old-looking, traditional stone-built houses. The row the victim's house was on was more modern than those, with insulated cladding on the outside, and a sixties or seventies feel to the architecture.

Clearly, the street was a later addition to the village, though the place didn't seem to have grown very much since then.

Tyler's car stood just inside the fluttering cordon tape, where he'd parked it after picking Logan up from the chopper. There were a couple of polis cars there—one in front and one behind him—and an ambulance parked a little further along the road.

Geoff had parked the SOC van directly in front of the house, because of course he bloody had. Logan watched four white-clad members of Palmer's team walking in a line across one of the grassy areas, eyes on the ground in front of them as they shuffled along in perfect step with each other, like the world's dullest dance troupe.

Shona's car was nowhere to be seen. Nor, for that matter, was anyone else's.

"Is this it?" Logan asked, joining Tyler and a young uniformed constable, who stood chatting outside the next garden along.

At the sight of the DCI, the constable practically leaped into the air. His face arranged itself into a look of wild panic, and he made Logan think of a schoolboy who'd just been caught smoking behind the bike sheds by the headmaster.

"Is this everyone?"

"How do you mean, boss?"

Logan stopped beside the two younger men and tutted. "It's no' a trick question, son. I mean is this everyone? You and me, and Constable…"

He looked expectantly at the uniformed officer, who just stared back at him, wide-eyed with fear.

"Your name, Constable. What's your name?"

"Oh! Sorry!" the man in the uniform said. His eyes made a series of tiny and increasingly panicky darting motions, like he was rifling through his memory banks but finding them empty. At last, though, he ejected, "John!" then seemed genuinely relieved to have remembered.

"Constable *John?*" Logan said, then he sighed and shook his head. "Sod it, that'll do. You, me, and Constable John. Is that all of us?"

"Oh no, boss." Tyler shook his head. "There's another uniform, too. They're away in there."

Logan followed Tyler's finger as he pointed towards the house next door to the one where the murder had taken place.

"What's he doing? Talking to witnesses?"

"*She,* boss," Tyler corrected. The look on his face and the tone of his voice both suggested he'd just taught the DCI a valuable lesson about the dangers of casual sexism in the workplace. "And no, she's making us tea. It's her house."

Logan let a look linger on the DC for a moment, then he blew out his cheeks and shook his head.

"Right. Fine. So, us three and the Tea Jenny. That's it?" he asked. "I know Sinead's stuck in the office, but what about Hamza?"

"He's on his way, boss. Bringing up a new recruit."

Logan, who had turned to watch the synchronised shuffling of the Scene of Crime bods, now spun back.

"What? What do you mean? What new recruit? No bugger's told me anything about a new recruit."

"Haven't they? Oh. She's Sinead's replacement for when she's off on maternity leave," Tyler explained.

Logan's shoulders rose up to meet his ears, and his fingers curled into claws, the very thought of a newcomer to the team—particularly one he hadn't been given the chance to choose himself—making his body contort involuntarily.

"Christ. Who is she? Do we know?"

"Don't know much about her, boss, no. I think her name's Tammi-Jo. With an *i*. Swanney, I think. Tammi-Jo Swanney."

Logan's shoulders jerked higher at that, and he ejected a sharp *nng* sound from his nose, like he was in physical pain.

"Jesus Christ, what was she before this? A Nashville cabaret act?"

Tyler blinked. "Sorry, boss?"

"Where's she come from?" Logan asked. "What's her background?"

Tyler wrinkled his nose, thinking back. This, Logan knew, meant that he'd been given all the information, but hadn't really been paying that much attention at the time, and was now having to work hard to fill in the gaps.

Beside them, the constable who'd identified himself as John, quietly cleared his throat, then pointed to his car. "I'll just..." he began, sidling off, then he stopped dead when Logan fixed him with a glare.

"You stay where you bloody are," the DCI instructed. "I might need you for something."

"Right, sir. Sorry, sir," John said, puffing out his chest like a soldier standing to attention before the King.

"Think she's from Aberdeen, boss," said Tyler, dredging the information up from the foaming slurry of his memory. "I'm sure Detective Superintendent Mitchell said Snecky rated her highly."

Logan sighed, then rubbed his eyes with a thumb and a forefinger. He hadn't been particularly happy at the direction the conversation was going, and the mention of DCI Samuel 'Snecky' Grant could only ever make things worse.

"Well, that doesn't exactly say much, does it? She could be a balloon on a stick and she'd still show promise next to that useless bastard."

Tyler smiled. "Pretty sure she's not a balloon on a stick, boss. I reckoned I'd have remembered that being mentioned."

"Sometimes I have my doubts, son," Logan muttered. "Sometimes, I have my doubts."

Before anything else could be said, the door of the house they were standing outside opened, and a female constable emerged carrying three mismatched mugs. She hesitated when she saw Logan, but then continued along the path, and smiled at the other two men as she passed them their tea.

"Cheers," she mumbled, then she took a sip from her own cup, and furtively eyed Logan over the rim.

Tyler and John both slurped at their drinks, neither one meeting the DCI's eye. It was left to the newcomer to break the silence.

"Sorry, who are you?" she asked, softening the bluntness of the question with a big, friendly smile.

Tyler coughed, almost choking on his tea. "This is, uh, this is Detective Chief Inspector Logan," he explained, once he'd recovered. "Boss, this is Constable, um..."

Unlike her male counterpart, the female officer picked up the cue right away.

"Clarke. Constable Clarke. Gemma. And God! Sorry!" she gushed. "I just thought you were some, you know, just a randomer." Her eyes flitted between the cups. "Did, eh, did you want tea or anything?"

"I wouldn't say no," Logan conceded. His coat was a long, heavy thing, but even it was proving ineffectual against the cold wind blowing up from the shore.

"Right. OK," Constable Clarke replied. She looked back over her shoulder at her front door, then winced. "Are you able to wait five minutes? It's just, I've only got the three mugs."

Logan chose not to question that. In the years after his divorce, he'd owned just one mug, and it was only since getting in tow with Shona that he'd splashed out on a full set. Who was he to judge her three-mug lifestyle, which was positively lavish in comparison?

"It's fine," he said, though his disappointment wasn't hard to spot.

Constable Clarke suddenly perked up. "Oh! I could ask Granny!" she cried, then she winced and shook her head. "Wait. No. Forgot. She's dead."

"Granny?" Logan looked over at the house next door. "You're related?"

"What? Oh, no. That's just what everyone called her. *Granny*. She was everyone's gran round here. Always baking cakes. Apple pies. Scones. All that sort of stuff."

"And pancakes," John added.

Gemma's mouth formed into a little letter O of pleasure. "Oh, God, yeah. The pancakes. They were always so nice, and—"

"Round," John said.

His uniformed colleague pulled a face and gave a tilt of her head that suggested this wasn't quite where she'd been going with the sentence, but she went along with it, all the same.

"Nice and round, aye," she said. "I mean, obviously she's not done any recently."

"How come?" Logan asked.

"Cos she's deid," said the man in uniform.

"No, John," Constable Clarke replied, and she shot him a withering look, which saved Logan the bother. "She's not been well for a while. Nothing specific, I don't think. Just old age, really. I tried to get in and help her and Albert out when I could. We all did. And she had a carer coming in a few times a week."

During the explanation, Logan's ears had all but twitched like a dog's at the mention of the name. "Albert? Who's that?"

"He's her husband. Lovely man," Gemma said. A look of uncertainty crept across her face. "I mean, I always thought he was, anyway, but if he's done this..."

"What makes you think he did it?" Logan pressed.

He'd been told before his flight up that this was the current working theory, but it was always good to hear it firsthand from someone who actually knew the people involved.

Gemma looked surprised to have been asked the question.

"Well, I mean, I don't know," she admitted. "But I think he was home at the time, wasn't he? And he was covered in blood when Gary found him."

"Gary?"

John pointed along the street. "Gary Hawthorne. Lives a few houses down."

"His boys saw Albert wandering around outside earlier this morning," Gemma explained. "He was in their garden, just standing there, hands and clothes all bloodied." She shuddered, the thought of it horrifying her. "Goes to show, you don't really know anyone, do you?"

Logan nodded slowly, filing all the information away. "And where is he now?"

"Gary? Probably in his house," John said. "How come?"

"No, not bloody... The old man, I mean. The husband," Logan said. "Where have you put him?"

"He's down at the station in Wick, boss," Tyler said. "DI Forde and Shona took him down."

Logan tutted. "Right. So there *are* more of us here, then? Why didn't you say that when I asked?"

Tyler smiled sheepishly. "Sorry, boss, I thought you meant *here* here. Like..." He pointed to the pavement beneath his feet. "*Here.*"

Logan hadn't bothered to stick around for the answer. He was already over at Tyler's car, trying the handle of the front passenger-side door.

Locked.

"Tyler, get this open and let's get going," he instructed, then he nodded to the uniformed constables. "You pair hang around here. Talk to the other neighbours. See if anyone's seen anything. Wait until Scene of Crime's done their stuff and the ambulance is away, then lock up and come meet us."

"Will do, sir," said John, tucking his thumbs into his stab-proof vest and puffing himself up like he'd just been injected with 20CCs of pure authority. "Leave it to us."

Logan muttered something under his breath, then glared at Tyler as he rattled the door handle again.

"Sorry, boss. Just coming," Tyler said, searching his pockets for his keys as he came scurrying over to the car.

"Eh, Detective Constable?"

Tyler almost tripped over his feet as he looked back over his shoulder. Constable Clarke smiled awkwardly at him, then her gaze dipped to look down at his right hand.

"Any chance you could leave my mug?"

CHAPTER SIX

"IT'S ANOTHER OF THESE, THEN," Logan grimly intoned, as Tyler pulled up outside Wick Police Station.

He always appreciated a station that felt like it'd been properly broken in. One where you could immediately smell the polish for the brass, and see the impact scuffs on the staircases.

God knew, he didn't have a romantic view of the polis, but standing in an old station like that, with history seeping from the walls of the maze-like corridors, he sometimes came to within spitting distance.

The newer stations didn't have anything like that effect on him. They felt too corporate, their business centre styling a world away from a good, old-fashioned *nick*.

The station at Wick was a typical modern build—an uninteresting rectangle of grey brick and darkened glass, with a slanted roof that made it look like a shoe box with the lid propped open.

The colours were a little different, but it reminded Logan of the new station down in Fort William, which he'd always found completely soulless.

The former station, located slap bang in the middle of the

town centre, had been much better. It was a hotel and restaurant now, though. This, apparently, qualified as *progress*.

Just like in Fort William, the Wick station sat right at the very edge of the town, like it didn't want to be a nuisance, or impose itself unduly upon the rest of the place. Logan had never seen the point in building stations out of the way like this. As far as he was concerned, the polis's entire *raison d'être* was to make its presence well and truly felt.

"How do you mean, boss?" asked Tyler, as they both climbed out of the car. He squinted up at the station. "Another one of what?"

Logan shoved his hands deep down into his coat pockets, suddenly feeling very old. Tyler's generation had come onto the job long after identikit stations like this one had become the norm. Any discussion on the matter would be a waste of breath.

Although, to be fair, he felt that way about a lot of conversations he had with the detective constable.

"Forget it. Doesn't matter," Logan said, setting off towards the station's glass and steel entrance. "I just hope this one doesn't have an officious old arsehole on door duty, too."

They were lucky on the *crabbit old bastard* front. As it turned out, there was no Caithness area equivalent of Moira Corson lying in wait for them inside the station. Instead, after they'd scribbled their signatures on the sign-in form, a uniformed sergeant whisked Logan and Tyler through to the room that had been given over for the investigation.

DI Forde was already installed behind a desk, three biscuits deep into a packet of *Jammy Dodgers*. He was slurping from a mug of tea when the door opened, and raised it in greeting as the two detectives entered.

"Aha! Afternoon, Jack. You made it, then," Ben said. With

his free hand, he swept some biscuit crumbs off the desk and onto the floor, and then immediately pretended that he hadn't. "How was the helicopter?"

"Noisy," Logan told him.

"Still, quicker than driving," Ben pointed out. "Glasgow to here, that'd have been a good, what? Five, six hours?"

"Aye. But at least I'd have had a bloody car," Logan pointed out.

"You can use mine," Ben told him. "With Sinead in the office, Mitchell's let me come up here to play, but on the understanding that I don't actually do anything."

"Aye, well, why change the habit of a lifetime?" Logan asked.

He caught the car keys that Ben tossed to him, then shoved them into a coat pocket.

"Cheers. I'll try and no' destroy it."

"Why the hell do you think I'm giving it to you?" Ben asked. "I want one of them fancy new ones, like yours. If it means I get heated seats, by all means, destroy away."

Logan grunted out something that was meant to call to mind a laugh, without actually being one, then looked around the room.

There were fourteen desks in total, arranged into one big rectangle—four on the longer sides, three each at the top and bottom. This left a lot of wasted space in the middle of the room, with no obvious reason as to why.

A digital whiteboard was fixed to the wall at the far end, and had Ben not perfectly positioned himself in their line of sight, the board's glowing white pixels would've been the first thing the detectives saw as they entered.

The room felt less like a place to solve a murder, and more like somewhere to study Higher Maths. The cheap metal and plastic chairs sitting tucked beneath the desks only added to the whole classroom vibe.

"Shona around?" Logan asked, turning back to the DI in time to see him cramming another biscuit into his mouth.

He knew the answer to the question already. He'd spotted her car parked out front.

"Mmf?" Ben asked, exhaling some light gold-coloured crumbs. He chewed until the biscuit had reduced down enough for him to be able to talk properly. "Oh! Aye. Shona. Sorry, she's in the canteen grabbing a bite to eat before she heads down the road. Said I was to let you know when you got in." He peeled the plastic wrapping of the biscuit packet down a little, exposing another *Jammy Dodger*. "Which I now have."

"Right. I'll go check in," Logan said.

Tyler shrugged off his jacket, looked around for somewhere to hang it, then draped it over the back of a chair, staking his claim to a desk near the door.

"What should I do, boss?" he asked.

"Have you no' got a *Game Boy* you can keep yourself out of trouble with or something?"

Tyler grinned. "Oh, if only, boss."

"Right. Well, I'm sure DI Forde will find you something to do." He glanced over at Ben. "Though, at the rate he's going, it'll probably be going out to buy more biscuits."

Ben raised another *Jammy Dodger* in salute, then shoved it in his mouth.

"Mind if I give Sinead a call first, boss?" Tyler ventured. "See how she's getting on in the office? I could check how the dog's doing, too," he suggested, like he was trying to sweeten the deal.

"Aye, fine. But don't bother asking about the dog. That bloody idiot of a thing'll be fine," Logan said, as he headed for the door. He opened it, then stopped, but didn't look back. "Although," he said, gruffly. "I don't suppose it'd do any harm to check..."

CHAPTER SEVEN

WHEN LOGAN ENTERED THE CANTEEN, he found
Shona sitting alone at a table right in the middle of the room, her
fingers pecking away at a bowl of chips like the beak of a hungry
bird. There was a can of *Irn Bru* open beside the bowl and, next
to that, a chipped white plate held an interesting-looking
sandwich.

The moment she saw him, Shona's eyes lit up and a smile
hitched up her cheeks. Foregoing another chip, she clicked her
fingers and pointed at him with both hands, then let out a long,
loud, "Eeeeeeey!" like she was channelling The Fonz from
Happy Days.

It was clear from the subsequent wince and shifty sideways
look that she immediately regretted this, and she seemed
relieved that none of the uniformed officers sitting at the other
tables appeared to have noticed.

They had noticed Logan, though. Given the size of him, this
wasn't a surprise. As front-line officers, everyone there had been
taught to identify the biggest threat in any situation. Generally
speaking, that was usually Jack Logan.

The canteen wasn't particularly large, and wasn't especially busy. Just half a dozen sets of eyes watched him cross to the table where Shona was sitting, and by the time he reached it, everyone had concluded that he wasn't there to cause trouble. They all went back to picking at their food, silently dreading the shift they were about to go on, or ruminating on the one they'd just come off.

Shona didn't get up from her seat, and instead just gestured to the chair across the table. Neither one of them was big on public displays of affection at the best of times, let alone when on the job.

"You made it then," she said, right before she filled her mouth with a sizeable bite of a sandwich. As she bit, some of the contents slopped out of the back, and Logan watched as it splattered onto her plate.

"Aye," he confirmed. "Is that..." He leaned in closer to check, for fear he might be about to make a fool of himself. "Is that a baked bean sandwich?"

Shona's mouth was too full to reply, but not too full to grin happily at him. She answered the question with a nod and a raised thumb.

Logan looked past her to where a surly-looking man almost as tall as he was, and broader still across the shoulders, leaned over the serving counter, staring idly into space.

A quick scan of the menu board behind the counter confirmed his suspicions.

"They don't do that here, do they? That's not a thing."

Shona shook her head, then forced down a swallow. "Not as standard, no," she admitted. "But the guy was up for experimenting. He seemed pretty bored, so I thought I'd shake things up a bit and set him a challenge." She leaned in and lowered her voice to a whisper. "I think if I hadn't, he might well have killed himself. I just got that vibe off him. You know?" She pointed at the rest of the piece still lying on the plate. "This might've saved a man's life."

Logan regarded what was left of the sandwich. The bread was thin, cheap, and white—the only bread Shona actually liked, despite her insistence on filling the bread bin with seeded wholemeals, oaty cobs, and others of that ilk.

Or, the bread *had* been white, at least, before the sauce from a big dollop of baked beans had started turning it into a soft, mushy shade of orange. It was already disintegrating around where her fingers made contact with it, and he watched as she hurriedly stuffed the bit she was holding into her mouth before all structural integrity could be lost.

While chewing, she gestured to the other half still sitting on the plate, and made a mumbling sound that he worked out meant, "Want a bit?"

"I think I'll pass," Logan said, though he helped himself to a couple of chips and waited for her to finish what was in her mouth.

She pushed the plate away then, deciding against the other half of the sandwich, at least for the moment. She then began the tricky process of cleaning her fingers, mouth, and chin with the solitary paper napkin that had been provided by the man at the counter.

"How did it go this morning?" she asked. "How's the She-Devil?"

Logan blew out his cheeks and shook his head. "Christ knows. Not great, I'd say. Been drinking, I think."

Shona paused, mid-wipe of her mouth. "Shite. That's not good."

"No. But I did my bit. I put in a good word. All I can really do." His chair creaked as he adjusted his weight in it. "The Gozer asked if I could be persuaded to go back to Glasgow."

"The Gozer?" Shona's eyebrows arched with interest. "From *Ghostbusters*?"

Logan nodded. "Aye. That's right. From *Ghostbusters*."

The eyebrows dropped rapidly, confusion etching itself

across Shona's face. She hung off for a second or two, waiting for a further explanation that didn't come.

"The Gozer? From *Ghostbusters*?" she asked, incredulously. "Gozer. *Gozer the Gozerian* asked if you could be persuaded to go back to Glasgow? *The* Gozer the Gozerian from the movie *Ghostbusters* invited you back to Glasgow?"

Logan hesitated, not quite sure if she was taking the piss. "It's not actually the thing from the film. It's just a nickname."

Shona flopped back into her chair, put a hand on her chest, and sighed. "Oh, thank Christ for that. I thought you were having some sort of psychotic episode." She leaned forward again, quite suddenly. "Wait. Glasgow? They want you back in Glasgow?"

"I said no," Logan told her. "Told him I wasn't interested."

She relaxed again at that, though not all the way. "Right. OK," she said. "Well... right. Wow."

Logan reached across the table and rested a hand on top of one of hers. "I'm not going," he assured her. "I'm staying right here."

She smiled at that, then she shot another furtive glance at the nearest few officers. "What, here? In Wick? Jesus. To be honest, I think I'd prefer you being in Glasgow. At least they've got decent shops."

Logan chuckled. "Aye, well, maybe we'll split the difference and I'll stay in Inverness."

"Sure, I'll drink to that," Shona said.

She lifted her can of *Irn Bru,* then looked disappointed when she found it was empty. She picked up another chip, held it so it was sticking straight up, made a noise like a lightsaber from *Star Wars*, and then ate it in two big bites.

That done, she fidgeted with her hands, smiled awkwardly, and shrugged.

"I have no idea what that was," she confessed. "It just felt like, you know, I should mark the moment somehow."

"Aye. Well, you did that alright," Logan told her.

Then, just as he was about to steer the conversation onto the topic of the dead woman in the armchair, his phone buzzed in his pocket. Checking the screen, he found a message from Ben that simply read:

Get here quick.

"Shite," Logan grunted, rising from the table.

"What? What's wrong?" Shona asked, pushing back her chair and jumping to her feet.

"Not sure," he said, showing her the text.

"Sounds ominous. You want me to wait here?"

Logan shoved the phone back into his pocket. "No. Come up to the room. We can do the work chat up there."

"But, Ben's message. What if there's a problem?" Shona asked.

"Why do you think I'm bringing you?" Logan asked, pushing his chair back under the table. "If there's a problem, I'm leaving you to fix it."

DS Hamza Khaled was there in the Incident Room when Logan and Shona arrived. He sat at the desk nearest the far corner of the room, massaging his temples with his fingertips. His shoulders were hunched and he barely looked up from the desk when the DCI and pathologist entered the room.

Logan had seen that look plenty of times before. Usually, right before someone slung a blanket over the person's shoulders, and told them help was on the way.

Though the sight of him was enough to make Shona let out a little gasp of shock, the cause of Hamza's misery was not immediately obvious.

"God. What is it? What's happened?" Logan asked.

Hamza's voice was a croak at the back of his throat. "It was horrible, sir. It was just... It was awful."

"What was?"

"That journey, sir," Hamza continued. "It was nearly the end of me."

"Shite. What happened? Did you crash or something?"

"What? No. No, nothing like that," Hamza said. "Don't get me wrong, I was tempted a couple of times, but... no. It's the new lassie. She just doesn't stop talking. She's like that bunny from the adverts. Just on and on and on. Just like, I don't know, not even like a stream of consciousness, more like a river of shit." He raised a shaky finger and pointed to Tyler. "I mean, we think he's bad."

"Oh, cheers for that, mate," Tyler replied.

"But—and I don't swear often, sir—but fuck me. Compared to her, he's pretty much silent. He's like one of them French mime artists. Still annoying, like, but not even in the same league. Just a whole different beast."

"Oh, great," Logan groaned. "And where is she now?"

"You didn't kill her, did you?" asked Shona. She smirked, safe in the knowledge that, however irritating the new recruit was, she'd rarely have cause to deal with her.

Hamza shook his head. "No point. I doubt even that'd stop her. She'd just immediately reanimate and carry on where she left off. She went to the toilet when we got in." He went back to rubbing his temples again. "I swear, my ears are actually ringing. I feel like I've been at an *AC/DC* gig for the last two hours, only an *AC/DC* gig that, for reasons best known to themselves, they've decided to hold in my car."

"Apparently, Snecky speaks very highly of her," Ben said, feeling the need to offer some sort of defence for the lassie, albeit a half-hearted one.

"Well, of course he bloody does. He'll have wanted to shift

her onto us, so he doesn't have to put up with her," Logan replied. "He's a fly bastard."

"Aye. Aye, he is that, right enough," Ben conceded. He'd worked under Snecky for a few years, so knew the man better than most, and far more than he'd like to. "Useless copper, though."

Everyone in the room had dealt with Snecky at some point in their careers, and all of them nodded in silent agreement at this assessment of the man's abilities.

"I just can't get a handle on her," Hamza said. "One minute, I think she's just nervous, so she's babbling, but then she's so overconfident about it. It's like she's actively made a plan to just talk endless amounts of shit without stopping for breath."

"Pah! Wow. *Tch*," Shona said, shaking her head and not quite meeting anyone's eye. "That would be a weird thing for someone to do..."

Hamza raised his head a little, and briefly looked guilty. "Oh, no. I mean, don't get me wrong, we can all do it," he said. "But not like this. This is another level. I've never met anyone who can talk so much and say absolutely nothing. And I've got a *child*."

Before Hamza had a chance to work through his trauma any further, the door opened behind Logan. Unfortunately, he hadn't yet moved fully out of the way, so it struck off the back of his right foot and rebounded.

The person on the other side let out an, "Oof!" then immediately tried the door two more times before Logan had a chance to step out of the way.

Some real welly was put into the fourth and final attempt. Unfortunately, because Logan was no longer blocking it, this meant the door was flung all the way open, and a young woman with bobbed blonde hair came stumbling into the room and straight into the DCI's arms.

"Yikes! Good catch there, Bigfoot!" she said, gazing up at him with eyes that positively delighted in their own blueness.

The words sounded wrong coming from her mouth. Her accent was a cut above everyone else's on the team—Scottish, still, but plummy enough that Logan made a few subconscious judgement calls about her family's level of wealth and her experience of the private education system.

She gave him a couple of friendly pats on the chest, then stepped away.

It was only then that it seemed to occur to her who the man whose embrace she'd just flung herself into might be.

"Wait. Oh! So, hang on," she said. She rapped her knuckles against her forehead like her brain was misfiring, then smiled, showing the sort of teeth you generally only saw on toothpaste adverts, and even then they were usually digitally enhanced. "You're him. Aren't you? Bound to be. Big. They said you were big. But I didn't think, you know, like *big* big. I thought fat. I'll be honest. And I know that's wrong. Because people can't help it, can they? Well, sometimes they can. Pies, and that. But it's an illness, isn't it? We shouldn't be fat shaming. Not in this day and age."

She put her hands on her hips, swallowed, looked around the room, then pointed to the door that was still swinging slowly closed behind her.

"There's something wrong with that. They should really get that looked at."

Shona leaned in closer to Logan, a smile curving up the corners of her mouth.

"I think I like her," she whispered.

"Logan! That's it!" the newcomer announced. She clenched her hands into fists, jerked them up to shoulder height, then made a sound that could best be described as *snikt.*

When nobody responded, she let her hands flop back to her sides again.

"It's Wolverine's name. You know? The guy with the metal claws. From the *X-Men*. The films. And comics. Not that I'm into that sort of thing. I'm not. Well, not really, but I've got two brothers who're both total geeks. And, you know, Hugh Jackman? Am I right?"

She held a hand up in Shona's direction, hoping for a high-five that Shona was only too happy to supply.

"You're *so* right," the pathologist confirmed.

"Preach!" the blonde woman sang, then she returned her hands to her hips and looked around at the others. "So, I'm Tammi-Jo. With an *i*. Like, the letter, I mean. Not for looking out of. Obviously I've got two—Oh! There he is!" she cried, pointing to Hamza, then giving him a little wave. He returned it, half-heartedly. "The old chauffeur there. The designated driver. I mean, not that he's actually a chauffeur, obviously. I know he's like a, like, you know. Police."

"Aye," confirmed Tyler, who was quite enjoying Hamza's obvious discomfort. "He's definitely *a police*, right enough."

At this, Tammi-Jo shot him a little smile, then returned her attention to Logan.

A moment later, though, she gasped and turned fully to face the detective constable.

"Wait. Hang on. Are you who I think you are?"

Tyler appeared worried by the question. "Eh... depends."

"DC Tyler Neish?" Tammi-Jo asked. "Is that you? Are you him?"

Tyler replied with quite a non-committal sounding, "Yes," like he was concerned what he might be about to be accused of.

"Holy heck! Oh my *God!* Seriously? *The* DC Tyler Neish? You're a total legend!"

Logan bristled, his brow furrowing. "What fresh hell is this now?" he muttered.

"Am I?" Tyler asked, perking up.

"Absolutely! Everyone I know, everyone coming up, we all think you're great!"

This time, Tyler perked up so much he was practically on his tiptoes. "Do you? How come?"

Tammi-Jo laughed. It was a melodious sort of sound that echoed around the room like music. "*'How come?'* he says!" She fired an incredulous smile at Logan and the others before swiftly switching focus back to Tyler. "You're like the greatest DC that's ever been. You cracked that case with the dead comedy guy all on your own!"

Tyler deliberately avoided the looks this earned him from the other members of the team.

"Well, I wouldn't say it was exactly *on my own...*"

"Modest, too!" Tammi-Jo said. "And that time you saved that girl's life. You know, on the railway bridge. You were nearly hit by a train!"

"I was!" Tyler chirped. "I *was* nearly hit by a train."

"She'd have been dead if it wasn't for you," Tammi-Jo continued. "We all talk about that, even now."

Though he'd started the conversation with some trepidation, Tyler was fully engaged in it now, and loving every minute.

"Do they, aye? Bloody hell! I had no idea!"

"Do they still talk about the time he dressed up as a big squirrel and ran away from a big dug?" Logan asked. "Or threw up all over my car upholstery?"

Tammi-Jo's impeccable smile remained fixed in place, but one of her carefully sculpted eyebrows dipped in confusion.

"Sorry?"

Logan glanced over at Tyler and, in a moment of weakness, felt bad about raining on the DC's parade.

"Nothing. Doesn't matter," he said. He turned on the professionalism, though didn't quite manage the charm to make it sound all the way convincing. "Detective Constable Neish is a valuable member of the team, and I'm sure you'll be the same for the short time you'll be with us, DC..."

"Swanney," she promptly replied. "As in the river. Well, as in the song about the river. But it's spelled differently. And, I don't know, the song might be racist. That blackface guy did it, I think, so I'm not sure. What's his name? You know the guy?" She waved her hands, jazz-style, then let loose with a startlingly loud, "'*Mammy*!' You know? Him."

Everyone in the room just stood there, staring at her in silence. Tammi-Jo cleared her throat, smoothed down the front of her navy blue blazer, and threw a thumb back over her shoulder.

She smiled weakly. "Would anyone mind if I go out and come back in? Because, I don't know about anyone else, but to me, this whole thing feels pretty irredeemable at this point. I'm aware that sometimes I talk too much. It's like my dad used to always say..."

"Was it, 'Shut the fuck up'?" Logan guessed.

The young DC's eyes went wide. "Yes! Exactly that!" She gasped. "How did you know?"

"Lucky guess," Logan told her. "And, listen, everyone in this room has been a pain in my arse at some point. Some more so than others. But we're a team here, for better or worse." He held out a hand to her. "Keep that in mind, and I think you're going to fit in just fine."

Tammi-Jo stared at the hand for a moment like she couldn't quite believe this was happening. Then, she latched onto it with both hands and shook it gratefully.

"Thanks! I won't let you down. I know first impressions might suggest otherwise, but I do actually know what I'm doing. Honest. So, thank you. Seriously."

"I'm sure you do," Logan said, watching his hand being enthusiastically pumped up and down. "And it's fine. You're welcome."

"Maybe I could shadow you, sir?" she suggested. "Just until I get up to speed."

Logan almost choked on the idea. "Christ, no!" he said, then the pinpricks of hurt in the newcomer's eyes compelled him to soften the blow. "I mean, I generally just sort of stalk around on my own, growling at folk. That's sort of my whole thing. If we want to get you up to speed, you'll be much better off with..."

He shot a sideways look at Hamza, saw the panicky shake of the detective sergeant's head, then locked eyes with Tyler.

"DC Neish," he announced. "A living legend like him'll have all sorts of wisdom to impart."

"Seriously?!" Tammi-Jo asked. She discarded Logan's hand like it was last night's fish supper, and spun to face Tyler. "I mean, I *hoped*, obviously. But I didn't dare ask. I didn't think it'd actually happen! That I'd actually get to work with DC Tyler Neish!"

"Have I slipped into a parallel world or something?" asked Ben from his seat.

"I'm starting to wonder the same thing myself," Logan told him.

Tammi-Jo hurried around the desks, shook Tyler's hand with even more enthusiasm than she had Logan's, then pulled out a chair and motioned for him to sit.

"Eh... cheers," Tyler said.

He kept his eye on the seat all the way until his arse was on it, like he was worried she was going to pull it away at the last moment, and reveal that everything she'd said was all one big wind-up.

It didn't happen, though. Instead, once he was sitting down, she pulled out the chair right next to him and shimmied herself in close to the desk.

She clapped her hands together, rubbed them vigorously, then flashed her immaculate smile at the rest of the room.

"Right then, team," she said. "What have we got?"

"I know what we've not got," Logan said. He raised a hand, like he was clutching an invisible mug, and tipped it towards his mouth.

Tyler, suddenly excited, thrust both hands in the air. "Wait! There's a new person! That means I'm not the tea bitch!"

"Don't get ahead of yourself, son," Logan replied. He removed his jacket, and used it to lay claim to a desk. "DC Swanney's excited to learn from you. So, the pair of you go and get the kettle on."

Groaning, Tyler got to his feet. "I don't even know where the kettle is, though, boss."

"You're DC Tyler Neish," Logan reminded him. "World's greatest detective. I'm sure you'll crack the case."

"Right. Aye. Fine. Will do, boss," Tyler said. He trudged over to the door, then looked back at the other DC when he realised he wasn't being followed. "You coming, then?"

"Oh! Right. Sorry. Yes. Did you mean...? OK!" Tammi-Jo bounded to her feet, rushed to his side, and hooked an arm through his. "Lead the way!"

Hamza waited until they'd left the room, and the door had closed behind them, before letting out a sigh he'd been holding in for some time.

"See?" he muttered. "Told you."

CHAPTER EIGHT

TEN MINUTES LATER, the team had all been supplied with their teas and coffees, and Hamza had set up a video link on the big digital board. Everyone sat gathered round in their plastic chairs, then Tyler let out a little yelp of laughter when Sinead appeared on the screen.

"Here, check you out. You're huge!" he declared.

On-screen, a slightly pixelated version of DC Sinead Bell pulled back, looking offended, then glanced at the pregnancy bump tucked below the camera's line of sight.

"Thanks a lot."

"No! Not that. Your head, I mean," Tyler hurriedly clarified. "Your head's huge."

"How's that better?" Sinead asked him. "My head's not the bit that's pregnant."

"You're on a big screen," Logan explained.

"It's like being at the pictures," Ben added. "I was half expecting them to play a load of trailers before you came on." His tongue flitted across his lips. "God, I could just go some popcorn now."

Sinead's face peered down at them in silence for a moment.

"Eh, right. OK."

Suddenly, there was a frantic scrabbling sound from Sinead's end of the call. She looked down, then drew back just as Taggart managed to launch himself up onto the desk.

The picture became a blurry extreme close-up of the dog's nose, his nostrils narrowing as he tried to sniff out the voices on the other end.

"Aw, a puppy!" Tammi-Jo cried. Her face crinkled up like the sight of those canine nasal cavities was the most adorable thing she'd ever seen.

Over the sound of snuffling, they heard Sinead call out an apology. The nose withdrew, and the rest of Taggart appeared briefly in the frame as Sinead lifted him away from the camera.

His legs kicked in the air like he was trying to swim, then Sinead groaned with the effort of bending as she returned him to the floor. She exhaled slowly, composing herself, then rolled her chair back in closer to the screen.

"Sorry about that. He must've heard your voices," she explained.

"You alright?" asked Tyler.

Sinead flashed a smile at the camera, though it wasn't the most convincing one any of the detectives had ever seen.

"Fine. I'm grand," she said.

"The Wizard of Oz!" Tammi-Jo cried, shunting the conversation in an entirely new direction.

Everyone else, Sinead included, stared at her.

"Sorry?" Logan asked.

"I was thinking who she reminded me of up there. It's the Wizard of Oz!" Tammi-Jo explained, appearing to delight in this realisation. "I don't mean weird old man Wizard of Oz. Obviously, I don't mean that. I mean big face Wizard of Oz. '*I am Oz, the great and powerful!*' That one." She waved at the screen. "Hi there, by the way. We haven't met. I'm DC Swanney. I guess I'm the new you!"

Something about the look on Sinead's face made Tyler realise quite how close Tammi-Jo's chair was to his own. He shifted his a little to the left, trying—but failing—to disguise the movement with a cough.

"Um... congratulations," Sinead said, but it came out sounding like a question.

"I've heard all about you," Tammi-Jo continued. "I'm going to have to really up my game, because you've left me with some seriously big boots to fill!"

"I'm sure—" Sinead began, but the new detective constable cut her off.

"Not as big as your head, though!" she cried.

She laughed, not in a cruel way, but with something bordering on genuine joy. Then, she looked around at the team, searching for confirmation that everyone else had found this as hilarious as she had.

Nobody seemed to see the funny side, and her laughter dried up in her throat.

"Sorry," she said, much more quietly. "I know your head's not *actually* that size."

"So, *any*way," Logan said, cutting in before things had a chance to turn ugly. "I know you've only got a few days before you go swanning off on your extended paid holiday, but we wanted you in the loop on this. We thought we could use your insight."

Sinead raised her eyebrows at him. "You mean you want me to do the Big Board?"

"And that. That would also be helpful," Logan confirmed.

"Question."

Everyone looked round to see Tammi-Jo raising her hand, all bright-eyed and inquisitive. Clearly, it hadn't taken her long to recover from her previous moment of awkwardness.

She had crossed her legs, and now had a notebook balanced on one knee, ready to scribble down anything of interest.

"Yes?" Logan asked.

"What's a Big Board?"

Tyler leaned a little closer to her, though not too close, for fear that Sinead might have something to say about it.

"The boss, he, eh, he likes to use a big corkboard to keep track of stuff. Suspects. Witnesses. Timeline. That sort of thing."

"Oh. Like in the olden days? Wow. OK." Tammi-Jo clicked the top of her pen, wrote a short note, then said, "Gotcha. Please continue."

Logan looked past the newcomer to where Shona was sitting at the back of the room, making a valiant attempt not to laugh.

"I don't mind doing the board, sir," Sinead told him. "But is it going to be a lot of use with it down here, if you're all up there? I mean, wouldn't it be better doing one up there so you can all refer to it?"

"She's got a point, Jack," Ben said. "We don't want to have to..." He gestured vaguely at the screen. "*Face Dial* through to Inverness on this bloody thing every time we want to get a look at it."

Logan shifted in his chair, his huge frame drawing creaks of complaint from the flimsy metal and plastic. "Well, I mean, aye. There is that, I suppose, but I still think—"

"You don't have to try and make me feel useful, sir," Sinead said, and the smirk on her face told Logan he'd been well and truly rumbled. "I've got plenty to be going on with here."

She held up a plastic tub of *Cadbury's Roses*, and tilted it towards the camera, revealing a fifty-fifty mix of chocolates and empty wrappers.

"These are going to take me another hour to get through, for a start. So, see? It's all go here, sir."

Logan chuckled, then nodded. "Fine. We'll set up a board here, and send you pictures. Hamza, can you...?"

"No bother, sir," DS Khaled replied. "I'll get it sorted."

"Don't mess it up," Sinead warned him.

Hamza tapped a pen to his forehead in salute. "I'll do my best."

"Right," Logan said, looking around the room. "Who's first."

Tyler, who had been the first member of the team to attend the scene, took the lead.

The 999 call had come in shortly after ten o'clock that morning, and Constable Gemma Clarke had been given it, due to her closeness—in every sense—to the occupants of the address the shout-out was for.

She'd arrived at the scene to find half a dozen neighbours standing around in the garden, and a couple of others inside the house with the victim and her husband.

Tyler had to double-check the notes he'd been given at that point.

"Albert Hall? That can't be right, can it?" he asked.

"What about it, son?" asked Ben.

"That's the husband's name, boss," Tyler explained. "That's what that constable who lives next door's written down, anyway. But that seems a bit, you know?"

"Cruel of the parents?" Hamza guessed.

"Maybe it wasn't deliberate," Tammi-Jo said. "Maybe he was born first. Maybe *he's* the original!"

She crossed her arms and sat back in her chair, nodding sagely, like she'd given them some real food for thought.

"Maybe," Logan conceded. "Although, I think the Albert Hall was built in the eighteen-seventies, which would make him at least a hundred and fifty years old."

"Oh. Right." The new DC uncrossed her arms again. "I didn't do history."

Logan briefly considered asking what subjects, if any, she *did* do, but thought better of it. He turned his attention back to Tyler, instead.

"No wonder Palmer was moaning about the place being

compromised. Sounds like half the bloody village was through there."

"Aye. A lot of the people outside had already been in, boss," Tyler confirmed. "The victim, Greta, was well thought of."

Logan thought back to the conversation they'd had outside the house. "Everyone's Granny," he muttered.

"Seemed to be popular with everyone," Tyler confirmed.

The obvious response to that remained unspoken. Clearly, given what had happened to her, she wasn't popular with *everyone*.

"Anything else?" Logan prompted.

Tyler glanced down at his notes again. "Not really, boss. Uniforms chased everyone out. The husband was taken to the hospital down here to be checked over."

"The one across the road?" Hamza asked. "Passed that on the way in."

"Place this size, I can't imagine there's more than one," said Ben.

On-screen, Sinead's fingers tapped away at an off-screen keyboard. "Actually, I'm seeing two," she told them. "Caithness General, across the road from you, and another one. Town & County. That seems to be much smaller, though." They all heard a mouse being clicked a couple of times. "Looks like more of a care home than an actual hospital, I think. So he's probably at the one beside you."

"Thanks for that," Logan said. "Why was he brought in?"

Tyler looked to Sinead for the answer, then realised the question had been addressed to him. "Oh! Me? Um, just a general check, I think, boss. She mentioned that he had a lot of blood on him, and that he seemed to be in shock."

"Someone went to the hospital with him to make sure the evidence was preserved, aye?" asked Ben.

"I think so, boss, but I'd need to check on that."

"The constable. The next-door-neighbour. Clarke, was it?"

Tyler confirmed this was right.

"She said the husband was found in a garden along the street."

"Shortly after nine, boss, aye."

"Fully dressed?"

Tyler's eyes darted down to the notes. "Nothing about him being naked..."

"I mean in outdoor clothes. Palmer's team found bloodied pyjamas along with the victim's nightdress. We'll need to talk to him, but I'm guessing he dressed her and dragged her up into the chair. Sounds like he got himself changed, too, then went back to the scene."

"He was with the body a while, then," Hamza said.

"Aye. All night, maybe," Logan said. "Given the first time anyone saw him was after nine this morning."

"Do we know when she died?" Ben asked.

Logan chose, at that point, to defer to the expert in the room. Shona, who didn't usually sit in on this sort of thing, made a few awkward, embarrassed mumbling sounds, before finding her voice.

"Uh, last night. I'm thinking between ten and twelve," she said. "She was strangled from behind, though we don't know with what yet. Going by the marks on her throat, it was something thick, though, like a rope, not a cord or a cable."

"And have we found anything like that in the house?" Logan asked. "Anything that would fit?"

Shona shook her head. "Not that I saw, no. But it's possible Geoff's team has. You'd need to ask him."

Logan baulked at the very suggestion. "Tyler. Deferring that one to you. You can talk to Palmer."

"Aw, boss!" the DC protested. "Talk to that arsehole? Can we not just wait for his report to come in?"

Logan considered the request. Subjecting anyone to *Palmer Duty* always felt like a particularly spiteful form of punishment.

But sometimes, it had to be done.

"No. Sorry. I want to know sooner than that. There's a lot it could tell us," Logan said. "You don't have to go see the bastard, just give him a call. But be warned, he might try and punt you tickets for his next stand-up show."

"Christ!" Tyler winced. "Right. Well, thanks for the heads-up on that at least, I suppose. I'll think of an excuse."

Logan shrugged. "I find just telling the bastard you think he's an insufferable, unfunny arsehole is a pretty decent one," he suggested. "But whatever you think yourself."

"And maybe don't rush into saying no," Hamza suggested. "Once you have kids, any excuse to get away from them for a few hours is not to be sneezed at."

With the spotlight off her, Shona had begun to sink back against the rigid plastic of her chair. She sat forwards again when Ben caught her eye.

"Anything else you can tell us, Shona?" he prompted.

"Not much yet. Sorry. Although, I get the impression she didn't go down easy. Her face was hit off the coffee table. Maybe to soften her up, if she was putting up a fight. Or, she might've just fallen and hit the table on the way down. Either way, there's an injury there to be looked at." She wrung her hands together, the scrutiny making her awkward. "I'm going to head down the road in a minute to prep for the PM. I'll be able to tell you a lot more once that's out of the way." She checked her watch, then got to her feet. "Actually, I should be setting off now."

Logan nodded, then rose to his feet. "Right. Aye. OK. Sounds like a plan. I'll see you out, then go see if the husband's up for a chat in the hospital."

"Oh. Aye. About that, boss," Tyler said. "Something you should know. Albert. He's deaf."

"Deaf?"

"Aye. And not just, like, hard of hearing, old man sort of deaf. *Deaf* deaf. You know, like full-on sign language, and that?"

Logan groaned. "Well, that's no' going to make things any easier. Have we got someone we can bring in?"

"Bound to be someone, Jack, aye," Ben confirmed. "Not sure who it'll be, but I'll put in a call to Mitchell and see who we've got."

Up on the screen, Sinead was looking off to her left, listening to a male voice that those in the room in Wick could only just hear.

"Uh, Dave says there's someone here he knows," she said, turning back to the screen. "A constable. Friend of his. She knows BSL."

"Right. Fine. Ben'll talk to Mitchell and get it authorised. I want him up here, anyway, to handle exhibits, so he can bring her with him."

He picked up his coat and pulled it on, then pointed to each of the team in turn.

"Tyler, talk to Palmer. Hamza, Big Board. Ben, clear Dave and his friend with Mitchell. Sinead, get digging around. Get me everything you can on the victim and her husband. I'll see Shona out, then head over to the hospital."

Tammi-Jo held up a hand. "You forgot me, sir. What should I do?"

"Oh. God. Aye." Logan ran a hand through his hair.

"I'm happy sticking with Tyler," she said. "I'm sure I'll learn a lot."

Shona, who had been the only one to spot the flicker of concern crossing Sinead's enormous face, jumped in.

"You should go with Jack," she suggested. "With DCI Logan, I mean."

"What?" Logan stared at her like she'd just stabbed him in the back. "Why?"

Shona tried very hard to think of a convincing argument. "So you can see her in action," was what she settled on. "New recruit, and all that. Knowing you, you'll want to get the measure of her."

"Oh, God. Is it a test?" Tammi-Jo fretted. "I don't really do well on tests."

Logan was still staring at Shona. He hadn't quite picked up on what it was, but she had a reason for doing this, and he was pretty sure it wasn't because she hated him.

"Aye. Fine. Good call," he said. "DC Swanney, give me two minutes, then meet me out front," he ordered. "Then we'll go find out what you're made of."

CHAPTER NINE

"HAVE I done something to offend you?" Logan asked once he and Shona reached the car park.

The pathologist shot an inquisitive look back over her shoulder, and shook her head. "Not that I noticed, no. Why do you ask?"

"Saddling me with the new lassie. What did I do to deserve that?"

Shona's laugh was a light trill of a thing, but something about it suggested it could just as easily become a cackle.

"Ah, it'll be good for the pair of you," she said. "And, sure, you know it makes sense."

It did, of course. He was the leader of the team, and it was his duty to get to know the strengths and weaknesses of everyone on it.

Even if they were a pain in the arse.

"Any word about the She-Devil?" Shona asked, as they made their way over to her car.

"Nothing more yet, no," Logan replied. "Not sure I'll hear anything for a while. Not from her, anyway. She didn't seem in the best headspace when I saw her."

"Oh. Right. Sorry," Shona said.

Her relationship with DCI Heather Filson had got off to quite a rocky start. And, to be fair, it had then continued in much the same way. Shona wasn't the woman's biggest fan—she'd be surprised if anyone on earth fell into that category, in fact—but she reckoned that, beneath all the bravado and innuendo, Heather was decent enough.

Logan nodded, then shrugged, as the rest of the conversation he'd had with Heather in the car rushed to make itself a priority.

"Sinead's, eh..." he began. He hadn't had an ending in mind for the sentence before he started, though, and it fell at the first hurdle.

"She's what?" Shona asked, stopping by the driver's door of her car.

"Pregnant," Logan said, then he grimaced and hurried to clarify. "Nearly due, I mean."

"She is that, alright," Shona confirmed. "She's looking well for it, though. You know, giant head aside."

"Had quite a rough time, though," Logan said. "Her morning sickness fair dragged on. Back problems. Mood swings."

Shona shook her head. "Women don't have mood swings during pregnancy," she said. "It's everyone else in the world who becomes an irritating arsehole. That's just medical fact."

Logan laughed, but then quickly got back on topic.

"It's been rough, though, either way," he said. He blew out his cheeks. "And that's just the start, isn't it? It's going to be hard for them. Sleepless nights. Endless stress. No social life."

"Aren't you just describing being in the police?" Shona asked.

Logan laughed again, but even less convincingly than before. "No, but, aye, but, it's a thankless task they've got ahead of them. I don't envy them."

"Oh, I don't know," Shona said. "I mean, it's got its upsides, hasn't it? I mean, look at you and Maddie. You might go back and change things, if you could, but you wouldn't change her, would you? You wouldn't change the fact she was born."

"Eh, no. No, I suppose not," Logan conceded. He could feel his grasp on the discussion slipping, and tried another approach. "But, I mean, I suppose that's it, isn't it? Maybe it's a young person's game. Kids. You don't need as much sleep when you're in your twenties, do you? Your patience is pretty much limitless. Everything's exciting then."

Shona looked up at him, searching his face. For the first time in as far back as she could remember, he was doing his best to avoid direct eye contact.

"What do you mean, Jack?" she asked. "What are you saying?"

"Oi-oi!"

Logan and Shona both turned to see Tammi-Jo striding across the car park like a power walker, all swinging hips and pointy elbows.

She stopped beside them, her smile showing off her world championship standard teeth.

"Sir," she said, nodding to Logan. "Ma'am."

Shona returned the smile, quite forcefully. This time, she was the one avoiding Logan's eye. "I'm not a ma'am. I'm not police. Sorry, we weren't introduced. Shona Maguire. I'm the pathologist."

"Oh! Yes! That's you?" cried Tammi-Jo. "Oh, so you and him are...? Bloody hell! You're punching above your weight there, sir, eh?" Panic flitted across her face as her brain caught up with the words tumbling out of her mouth. "Not in a bad way, though. I don't mean like you're ugly or anything, you're not. And you're big. Tall, I mean, not... So that's a bonus, you know? I'm just saying..."

"What are you saying, Detective Constable?"

"I don't know what I'm saying, sir," Tammi-Jo admitted. "But I wish I'd stop saying it."

By the time Logan turned back to Shona, she had the driver's door open, and one foot inside the car.

"I'll, eh, I'll talk to you later," she told him. "Good luck with it all."

"Right, aye," Logan said.

He should've said more. He wanted to. But the words weren't there yet.

"Nice to meet you, Detective Constable," Shona said, getting into the car. "Don't let him boss you around too much. His bark is worse than his bite."

"Thanks. I'll keep that in mind!" Tammi-Jo said.

She waved enthusiastically when Shona closed the door and fired up the engine, and continued to do so until her car had pulled out of the car park, and disappeared out of sight around a corner.

"Aw. She seems lovely," the DC declared. "You're a lucky man, sir."

Logan, who had been watching the car the whole way, now looked down at the upturned face of the newest member of his team. With her wide blue eyes and blonde curls, there was something childlike about her. She looked like she should be investigating missing puppies or sweetie shop break-ins, not cold-blooded murders.

Twenty-four hours. That was how long he gave her. Twenty-four hours, and she'd be requesting a transfer back east.

Fingers crossed, anyway.

"Right, then," Logan grunted. He turned until he was facing the hospital across the road from the station, and set off at a march. "Let's go get this over with."

By the time they reached the hospital, Logan's head was thumping. Hamza hadn't been kidding, the new DC could talk the hind legs off a donkey. If 'Wittering Shit' was an Olympic event, Detective Constable Tammi-Jo Swanney would come back with the gold every time.

To her credit, she seemed to be acutely aware of this fact. This only made things worse, though, as after any particularly verbose outpourings of nonsense, she'd profusely apologise and talk herself down.

She'd do so to such an extent, in fact, that Logan felt compelled to reassure her that it was fine, at which point she'd launch into some other meandering monologue about Christ alone knew what.

He'd always prided himself on being a man of few words, and so Tammi-Jo should be everything he hated in another human being. And yet, despite her endless babbling and chirpy, full-throttle enthusiasm, he had to admit that there was something ever so slightly endearing about her.

Not that he *would* ever admit that, of course.

It wasn't her looks, either, striking as those were. She was about the same age as his daughter, if even that. Younger women, with the exception of Shona, and one other ill-advised fling he'd rather forget about, had never been his cup of tea.

"Right, OK. Stop talking," Logan intoned, when they reached the door to the nurse's station.

DC Swanney nodded quickly, then gave the faintest little sigh of relief, like she'd been looking for an excuse to shut up, but hadn't been able to find one.

They'd been directed to the relevant ward by a woman at the front desk, and now stood at one end of a long corridor lined with doors. Nurses zipped back and forth, crisscrossing the corridor carrying bedpans, and trays, and blankets, wheeling trolleys and drip stands, and escorting patients to and from various rooms.

It was almost like an elaborate dance, and no cubic foot of space in the corridor was ever unoccupied for more than a few seconds.

"Busy, isn't it?" Tammi-Jo said, which felt like something of an understatement.

"Seems to be, aye," Logan agreed, then he rapped his knuckles on the door beside them, and stepped back, listening to the tutting and movement from within.

"Yes?"

The nurse who appeared at the door was halfway through a bowl of cereal. She clutched it under her chin, spoon poised to take another scoop, a dribble of milk visible at one corner of her mouth.

"Eh, hello. I'm—"

"God. OK. *OK*." The nurse chewed her cereal, then grimaced as she forced down a swallow before it was ready. "Police, is it? Albert, you're here for, is it?"

"That's—"

"Bloody awful the way you're treating that man. Bloody awful. He's in his eighties," the nurse said. Her expression couldn't have been colder if it was sculpted out of ice. "I don't know what's happened, or what he's meant to have done, but he's an old man. He deserves a bit of bloody dignity. Not to be treated like some hardened bloody criminal."

Tammi-Jo leaned forwards, clutching her hands together and speaking with absolute, heartfelt sincerity. "Of course. We couldn't agree more."

The nurse spared her just a momentary look. "Aye, you stay out of this, Tinkerbell. Grown-ups are talking." She shoved another spoonful of cereal into her mouth, chewed it frantically, then set the bowl down on a shelf just inside the door. "Right, follow me," she commanded, and more milk went dribbling down her chin. "But if either of you upsets him, you'll have me to bloody answer to."

She set off down the corridor at a clip, forcing the detectives to hurry to keep up. If the movement of the other nurses was a dance, then she knew all the steps. She seemed to cut through all the chaos without missing a beat, turning her shoulders to avoid one collision, then taking a perfectly timed side-step in the opposite direction to dodge past a slow-moving patient.

By the time she reached a door at the far end of the corridor, Logan and Tammi-Jo were half the ward away.

"Well, get a bloody move on!" the nurse called to them. "None of us is getting any younger." She pointed to DC Swanney. "Except maybe her. No idea what her story is."

The activity thinned out a little towards the end of the corridor, and the detectives were able to pick up the pace. When they were half a dozen paces away, the nurse knocked sharply on the door of the private room, then entered without waiting for a response.

A surly-looking uniformed sergeant stepped into her path, blocking her way.

"Whoa, whoa, whoa. Hang on there," he warned, eyes narrowing and shoulders pulling back. "You can't just walk in here without warning."

"I gave a warning. I knocked," the nurse shot back. She was several inches shorter than the sergeant, but she made up the difference in attitude. "See what I'm dealing with?" she said, turning as Logan filled the doorway behind her.

The Uniform's eyes became slits, and he puffed himself up —an Alpha defending its territory from a potential rival.

"I wouldn't waste your breath, Sergeant," Logan said, flashing his warrant card. He gestured to the hospital bed, where a frail old man sat propped up, drowning in the big marshmallow of a pillow. "What the hell's this?"

"Suspect, sir," said the sergeant, snapping to attention. "Name's Albert Hall, sir. I thought it best to stand guard, sir, until the SIO arrived to advise next steps. I'm assuming that's you, sir?"

"I meant what the hell is *this*?" Logan demanded, indicating the old man's wrist. It was attached to the bed frame by two loops of metal. "Why's he been handcuffed?"

"In case he tried to escape, sir. Couldn't be having that."

The old man in the bed had his eyes open, but he wasn't paying any attention to anything happening in front of them. He shared the same dead-eyed stare as his wife had back in the house, and if it wasn't for the bleeping of the heart monitor, and the faint rise and fall of his narrow chest, you'd be forgiven for thinking he'd gone to join her.

"I mean, Christ Almighty, son. Have you seen him? What do you think he's going to do? Climb out the window and vault the bloody fence?"

The sergeant rocked back on his heels a little, like the glower from the DCI had physically rocked him.

"It's just... Well, I mean, there's procedure, sir, isn't there?"

"Never mind procedure. How about using some common bloody sense?" Logan said. "Would you tape up a prisoner's mouth?"

"What? No! No, that would be... You're not allowed."

"Well, that's what you've done here, isn't it?"

The sergeant stole a sideways glance at the old man's face. "No. No, he's not—"

"He's deaf. He communicates with his hands," Logan barked.

There was a moment—a dangerous one—where it looked like the sergeant might continue to argue.

In the end, though, he just said, "Oh. I didn't... I hadn't thought of that."

"Get him uncuffed," Logan ordered. "Now."

"Right, sir. Yes, sir. Sorry, sir."

They all watched as the sergeant dug out his keys and unfastened the old man's wrist. It fell immediately onto the bed, like there was nothing left inside him to hold the arm up.

"Right, now go wait outside," Logan barked.

The Uniform hesitated. "Do you mean out in the corridor, sir, or...?"

"Out. Side," Logan said. "If anyone needs you, they'll come and get you."

"Uh. OK. Sure. Right you are, sir."

Logan waited until the other man had opened the door. "Oh, and Sergeant?"

"Sir?"

"We're guests here. In fact, no. We're worse than that. We're an inconvenience. You remember that next time."

The sergeant nodded, his cheeks flushing red, then he went scurrying out of the room.

"I take it back," said the nurse, once he'd left. "Maybe you're not *all* arseholes."

"You didn't say we were," Logan told her.

The nurse smirked. "I didn't say it to you," she replied.

Logan and DC Swanney waited in silence while the nurse checked the old man over, then stepped out of her path when she headed for the door.

"Five minutes. That's it. He needs his rest."

"Deal," Logan said.

She tapped her watch to emphasise her point, then stepped out into the corridor, and was swallowed up by the chaos of the ward.

"Wow!" Tammi-Jo breathed, once the nurse had gone. "That was *intense*. The way you just told that sergeant how it was going to be. No messing. Just eye-to-eye, not taking any shit. Wow. DCI Grant never did that sort of thing."

"Snecky? No, can't imagine he did," Logan said.

"He was more of a..." Tammi-Jo's smooth brow furrowed as she tried to think of a suitable term.

"Sleekit wee weasel-eyed bastard?" Logan hazarded.

Tammi-Jo blinked in surprise, then smiled. It was a mischievous sort of smile, like she thought they might get into trouble, and was excited by the prospect.

"I didn't say that! That was you, not me," she replied. "But that's the sort of neck of the woods I was aiming for, yeah."

That won her some brownie points from the DCI. Though it didn't take a genius to see through DCI Samuel 'Snecky' Grant, those who did were alright in Logan's book.

"Hello, Mr Hall," Logan said, raising his voice and going a little overboard on the enunciation.

He had no idea why. If the man really was completely deaf, no amount of bellowing was going to make a difference. His gaze was still fixed dead ahead, too, so lip reading was out of the question.

Pulling a chair up to the end of the bed, Logan took a seat, inserting himself directly into Albert's eye line. The old man, however, didn't seem to notice. The focus of his gaze didn't change.

Even sitting there, right in the way of it, it wasn't piercing or direct. It was the opposite of those things. It was nothing. It was lifeless. It was empty.

"Albert, can you hear me?" Logan asked, though this time he didn't bother turning the volume up.

When the old man didn't respond, Logan sat back, ran a hand down his face, and then looked over his shoulder at Tammi-Jo. Seated, he was only a half-inch shorter than her, so they were basically eye to eye.

"Any thoughts, Detective Constable?"

Tammi-Jo's shoulders jerked back and a number of expressions all danced their way across her fine features, mostly from the 'shock and horror' end of the spectrum.

"He didn't do it," she said.

"Bloody hell. No messing around," Logan said, after a moment's pause. "What makes you say that?"

"Your girlfrie..." All the air escaped her like she was a deflating balloon, and she tried again. "The pathologist, I mean. She said the marks on the throat were thick. Like a rope."

Logan nodded. "So?"

"So, no way he had the strength to pull hard enough to leave marks."

"I wouldn't be so sure about that," Logan said. "Some of these old fellas are stronger than they look."

"Yeah, but check out his hands," Tammi-Jo said.

Logan turned back in his chair and studied Albert's hands. They both lay on top of the covers, palm downwards, so the fingers looked like the legs of spiders.

Not healthy spiders, either. The knuckles were so swollen and inflamed that the fingers had begun to twist out of shape.

"I noticed when he was cuffed," Tammi-Jo continued. "Rheumatoid arthritis, I'd say. I mean, I'm not an expert on the subject, but my granddad has it. *Had* it," she corrected. She shook her head. "That sounds like he got better. He didn't. He died. It was sad. We were all upset. But he'd had a good run of it. He always said that himself."

It occurred to her that she may have slipped back into wittering mode, so she cleared her throat and tried to steer herself back on track.

"So, yes. At his age, and with his hands in that condition, I really can't see how he could've strangled anyone. Just holding onto the rope would've been agony, let alone pulling it hard enough to leave a mark."

Her eyes darted between the old man and—from her perspective—the slightly less old man, and the surprised look on Logan's face made her fingers start fidgeting nervously.

"Sorry, sir. Did I say something wrong?" she asked.

Logan got to his feet. Her neck craned back as she followed him all the way up.

"Quite the opposite, Detective Constable," he said. "Good observation. Totally agree, by the way. I think the odds of Mr Hall here having killed his wife are up there with him winning *Strictly Come Dancing*."

He rested a hand on the old man's arm, and gave it a squeeze. If he was in there, even if he couldn't communicate, Logan wanted him to know he wasn't alone.

"I'm sorry for what's happened, Albert. We're going to take care of it. Alright?" Logan waited for a response he knew wouldn't come, then nodded. "Alright."

He turned away from the bed, and ushered Tammi-Jo out into the corridor.

"What should I do now, sir?" the DC asked, once they had closed the door to Albert's room. "Want me just to head back to the station? I'm sure your head's probably thumping with me already."

She let out a little self-deprecating laugh, but then glanced down, averting her eyes.

"Aye, it is a bit," Logan admitted. "But that's why God gave us painkillers. You up for a house call, Detective Constable?"

Tammi-Jo froze, like something in her head had seized up. As usual, though, her silence didn't last for long.

"Yes, sir. Totally. Thanks, sir," she gushed, falling into step with Logan as he weaved his way along the ward. "DCI Grant, he didn't like 'letting me loose' as he called it. Generally just kept me in the office doing paperwork, where he could keep an eye on me through his window."

Logan glanced back at the young, blonde-haired, blue-eyed officer.

"Aye, I bet he bloody did," he muttered. "Thankfully, for all concerned, I'm no' Snecky. When you're on this team, you work for it. Aye, sometimes that might mean paperwork, but you'll be getting your hands dirty, too."

They made it to the end of the corridor. Logan pushed the swing door open with the flat of a hand, and stepped aside to allow the younger officer through.

"That sound alright to you?"

Tammi-Jo's smile bordered on the blinding. "Sounds great to me, sir!"

"Good," Logan said, following her out into the adjoining corridor. "Then how about you and me go poke our noses into some other bugger's business?"

CHAPTER TEN

TYLER WALKED in slow circles around the car park, his phone pressed to his ear, a cup of tepid coffee held in the other hand. It had been too hot to drink when he'd put the call in to Palmer, and hadn't noticed it cooling while he'd been kept on hold.

Now that call was over and he was chatting to Sinead, he'd missed his window of opportunity, and the coffee was unpleasantly cold.

"Seriously, she doesn't stop," he said. "Hamza's head was about fit to bursting with her. Just endlessly chattering on. Like one of them pull-string dolls, only the string's stuck out, so it won't stop talking."

"Looks pretty, though," Sinead said.

Tyler frowned *very* deeply, and made a series of short exhalations, like he was struggling to process this information.

"Is she? Didn't notice," he said.

Sinead laughed at that. "Bollocks you didn't," she said. "She's gorgeous. God, even I quite fancied her, and she said I looked like the Wizard of Oz. It's fine. You can say it. I'm not going to think you're going to run off with her or anything."

Tyler smiled. "No danger. And aye, OK, I suppose she's alright. If you like that sort of thing."

The line went quiet. Deathly so.

Tyler felt his heart sink down towards his toes. It had been a trap. It had been a trap, and he'd walked right into it.

"Sinead? I'm just winding you up. She's not my cup of tea at all. I don't think she's—"

He heard her sniggering, and almost collapsed onto the tarmac.

"You absolute cow!" he cried.

"Sorry. Too easy," Sinead replied. "You walk right into these things."

Tyler was forced to admit that, aye, he did.

"I mean, don't get me wrong, I don't want her getting too comfy," Sinead continued. "I want my spot back sooner rather than later. But... I know what it's like to be the new girl. Fresh into the job, surrounded by all these men that seem to know exactly what they're doing. And you, of course. Thank God you were there."

"The hell's that supposed to mean?" Tyler demanded, all mock outrage and bluster.

"I just mean, stunningly attractive or not, she's going to be scared. She's going to feel like she's way out of her depth."

Sinead hesitated, and for a moment it sounded like she was reconsidering what she was about to say. In the end, she forced it out.

"Just keep an eye on her. Make sure she's OK."

"Keep an eye. Make sure she's OK. Don't run away with her," Tyler said, speaking the words slowly. "Sorry, just writing this down."

"You're a dick," Sinead laughed. "And give her my number. In case she wants to talk to someone who's not, you know, a man. Or a boy, in your case."

"Here! I was man enough to knock you up!" Tyler

protested, and he could practically hear his wife recoiling on the other end of the line.

"Ugh. God. I think that's the worst thing you've ever said."

Tyler grinned. "It's the worst thing I've ever said *to you*. I've said way worse than that, believe me. I've even said swear words."

"Wow. What a stud," Sinead said. "I'm one lucky woman."

"Don't you forget it."

Tyler stopped pacing when he reached a low wall, and took a seat on it. The stone was rough and cold against his backside.

"How you doing, anyway?" he asked. "Any more twinges?"

"Nah. Nothing more. Think this morning was just the wee buggers fighting."

Tyler laughed. "Aye. Probably. But that's good. If we keep them fighting each other, they won't think to gang up against us."

"Oh, I'm sure they'll figure that out soon enough."

They both fell silent then. Not awkwardly. Not uncomfortably. They just shared a moment of reflection, considering how much their lives were going to change just a few weeks from now.

"Aye," Tyler finally declared. "We're screwed, aren't we?"

"Pretty much," Sinead confirmed.

There was a loud and insistent bleeping in Tyler's ear. He pulled the phone away long enough to check the name of the incoming caller, endured a whole-body shudder, then went back to his call.

"Sorry, sweetheart, that's Palmer calling me back. I better go."

"Aye, I'd better get back to it here, too," Sinead said. "Love you."

"Love you, too," Tyler replied. Unfortunately, he was halfway through thumbing the icon that switched calls, and the voice that replied was the nasal whine of the Scene of Crime team leader.

"Well, I didn't know you felt that way, Detective Constable," Palmer sneered. "But I've got bad news for you. I'm not into that sort of thing. I like women."

He paused then, as if leaving a break for laughter. Tyler just sat on the wall, looking confused.

"Fair enough," he said.

"That was a joke," Palmer clarified.

This only deepened the DC's confusion. "Oh. Right. So... you don't like women?"

"What? No. I mean, yes," Palmer said. "Yes, I like women. Of course I like women. I mean, not all of them. Have you seen the state of some of them?"

"How's it a joke, then?" Tyler asked.

There was silence while Palmer tried to formulate a response. In the end, he just bluffed through it.

"Obviously too highbrow for you, lad. *Whoosh.* Right over your head," he said. "By the way, what are you doing next—"

"I'm busy," Tyler said, jumping in quickly before Geoff had a chance to offer him tickets. Better to nip the whole thing in the bud as quickly as possible.

"You don't know when I was going to say."

Tyler winced. "Oh. Right. Aye. When is it?"

"The twenty-third," Palmer said.

"Aye. I'm busy then."

"Wait. No. My mistake." There was a note of triumph in Palmer's voice. "The twenty-*fourth.*"

"I'm also busy then," Tyler replied. "In fact, that whole week's out."

Down the line, Palmer muttered an almost silent, "Shite," as he realised he'd been outwitted by a superior opponent.

And, considering who that opponent was, he was rightly dismayed about it.

"Fine. Doesn't matter. It's going to be jam-packed, anyway," the SOC man finally said. "Standing room only."

"Right, OK, good. Well, anyway, moving on. About that rope you were going to look into for me, Geoff? Any sign?"

"No. There was nothing in the house that fits the description."

Tyler sat his coffee mug down on the wall, and fished around in his pockets until he found his notebook and pencil.

"Nothing? Nothing at all? So, what are we saying? It was taken?"

"Well, I doubt it got up and walked out on its own accord," Palmer replied, and from the rising inflection in his voice, it was clear he was going to somehow work that line into his next open mic spot. "So, yes, I'd say it was taken."

Tyler scribbled a note in his pad. "Right. OK. Anything else you can tell me?"

"About what? About a thing that isn't there?" Palmer asked. "What do you want me to do, describe the spot where it wasn't?"

Tyler removed the phone from the side of his head and pointed it away from him, counting slowly so he didn't say one of those 'worse things' he'd been talking to Sinead about.

When sufficient time had passed, he returned the phone to his ear, just in time to hear Palmer say, "...and everything else will be in the report. Which I could be working on now, if I wasn't being interrupted."

Tyler saw the way out, and leapt for it. "Aye, fair enough, Geoff. I'll let you crack on, then."

"Finally!" Palmer said, throwing in a theatrical sigh for good measure. "Oh! But, before you go!"

Tyler rested the tip of his pencil on his notepad, ready to start writing.

"Yeah? What is it?"

"The other one. Your pal. The detective sergeant."

"DS Khaled?"

"That's the one! He might like tickets," Palmer said, then he appeared to immediately have second thoughts about the idea. "Although... I'm not sure, so maybe you can tell me. Do Asians like comedy? Like, proper comedy, not all that Bollywood slapstick stuff."

Tyler looked down at his pad and realised that, while Geoff had been talking, he'd unconsciously drawn a penis at the top of the page. For something so juvenile and inappropriate, it seemed entirely on the money.

"Goodbye, Geoff," he said. Then, with no small amount of satisfaction, he ended the call, and in the silence of the car park, he added, "Ya wank."

CHAPTER ELEVEN

THE DETECTIVES WATCHED in silence as a pair of balls went bouncing along the path, *thacking* on the slabs as they slowed to a gradual roll.

The owners of the balls stood at the opposite end of the garden, their eyes wide and their mouths hanging open.

Logan was used to being stared at. He'd come to expect it, in fact. When a man of his height and girth turned up out of the blue, it was perfectly normal for people to experience a state of temporary catatonia.

Today, though, he wasn't the star attraction. Neither of the two teenage boys who had, until recently, been doing keepie-uppies in their front garden, had even appeared to have noticed him.

"I think I'll go ahead and leave this one to you, Detective Constable," Logan whispered, opening the gate for Tammi-Jo to lead the way.

She sprang into action like an actor stepping out onto the stage, flashing a big beamer of a smile and hailing the boys with a friendly wave.

"Alright, lads? Having a wee kick about, are we?"

She hooked the toe of a shoe under one of the footballs, flicked it into the air, and managed an impressive three-and-a-half bounces on her knees before losing control.

"Come on, that wasn't too bad, was it?" she declared, after the ball had gone bouncing onto the grass. "I could do better in different shoes."

The younger of the two boys had noticed the performance and gave her a nod of admiration. The older one—his brother, Logan guessed, given their similarity—continued to stare at the vision of beauty currently standing there in his garden.

The poor bugger looked smitten. It was only a matter of time before the lad's tongue rolled out onto the grass and his eyes turned into twin love hearts, Logan reckoned, so he decided to put him out of his misery.

"We're looking for Gary Hawthorne, lads," he said, stepping in front of the DC. This seemed to break her spell on the older boy, and he blinked rapidly as he came back down to Earth. "Is that your dad?"

"Eh, aye. Are you the police?" asked the younger brother.

"Is this about what happened to Granny?" asked the older.

Logan nodded. "Aye. Aye, I'm afraid so." He nodded past them to the house. "He in? Your dad?"

"Yeah," they both answered, then they stepped in opposite directions onto the grass as Logan carried on up the path, and drummed his big polis knock on the front door.

Tammi-Jo scooped up one of the balls, passed it from hand to hand like it was a basketball, then held it out to the older brother.

He gawped at it in wonder for a moment, like it was some sort of gift from the gods. Then, with shaking hands and reddening cheeks, he reached for it.

"Too slow!" The DC laughed, tossing the ball back over her shoulder for the younger boy to catch.

At least, that was the intention. The throw was far too hard, though, and the ball went sailing through the air, cleared the next garden completely, and landed in the next one along from that.

The confused silence that followed was broken only by the sound of the front door opening.

"Sorry about that," Tammi-Jo said, wincing. "I didn't... That wasn't meant to..." She cleared her throat and pointed along the path, to where Logan was stepping inside the house. "I'll just..."

Both brothers watched her as she followed Logan inside. They stood there, saying nothing, until after the door was closed.

"You well fancy her," said the younger.

"Shut up. No, I don't," said the older. He bent to hide his blushing cheeks, grabbed the one remaining football, then tucked it under his arm. "Now, hurry up and get your ball back, so I can kick your ass again."

Even as he ran for a gate, the younger boy launched some derisory laughter back over his shoulder. "Yeah," he said. "In your dreams!"

Logan and Tammi-Jo were shown into an open-plan living and dining area and urged to take a seat on one of the two matching couches. The room felt modern, with light grey walls, matching laminate flooring, and a big round light fitting that reminded the DCI of the transporter bay from *Star Trek*.

He found himself sitting directly beneath it, and tried to ignore the feeling that he might, at any moment, be beamed up.

It was clear that a family lived here. The walls were adorned with big canvas-style portraits that showed the two boys they'd met out front at various stages of development. There were smaller framed pictures between these, and those tended to show either the boys and one parent, or all four family members together.

They looked happy. But then, most people did in these things. Why the hell would anyone hang a shower of miserable-looking bastards on the living room wall?

"Are you OK for tea, coffee...?" Gary asked.

He had remained standing while the detectives had taken up the offered spots on one of the couches, and danced from foot to foot like he had a bothersome rash spreading misery somewhere south of his waistline.

"No. I think we're fine," Logan said. "We don't want to take up any more of your time than we have to, Mr Hawthorne."

"Please, call me Gary. Gary's fine."

Logan gave a curt nod of thanks. "Gary. OK. Well, as I said out front, I'm DCI Jack Logan. Jack's fine. This is Detective Constable Swanney."

"Tammi-Jo," she said. She offered him a hand to shake, and he stared at it in much the same way as his son had stared at the football.

"Uh, hi. Hello. Nice to meet you," he said.

He shook the hand for a little longer than was necessary, then quickly released it like it had fired out an electrical charge.

"You sure you don't want tea or anything?" he asked, sidling towards the door.

"Honestly, Gary, we're fine," Logan said. He nodded to the couch standing at a right angle to the one he and Tammi-Jo sat in. "Take a seat. We've just got a few questions about what happened this morning."

"Right. Yeah. Yeah. Course." Gary perched himself on the arm of the couch like he didn't want to fully commit to sitting. "I did tell Gemma everything that had happened. You know? Gemma Clarke? She's in the police."

"We've met," Logan said. "And thanks for that, but I'd like to hear it firsthand, if you don't mind? In your own words."

"Yeah. Course. Yeah, yeah." Gary rubbed one hand on his thigh, like he was trying to use the denim to scratch a nasty itch. "So. I was... Where was I? Bathroom. Yes. I was in the bathroom. Upstairs. I'd just had a shower."

Logan stole a glance at DC Swanney, and found her sitting with one leg crossed over the other, listening intently.

"Sorry, Gary, one second. Could you write this down for me, Detective Constable?" he asked.

"Oh! Right, yes! Sorry!"

Both men watched as Tammi-Jo patted all her pockets, her movements becoming increasingly frantic before suddenly stopping altogether.

"I think I've left my notebook back in the office, sir. Have you got one?"

Logan, to his credit, resisted the urge to sigh as he reached into his pocket, retrieved his own pad, and handed it over.

"Thanks, sir. I've got my own pen."

"Glad to hear it."

"Wait." The DC searched her pockets again, then shook her head.

Logan held out a pen before she had a chance to ask for it. She accepted it sheepishly, nodded her thanks, then they both turned their attention back to the man on the other couch.

"Sorry, Gary. You were saying?"

"Uh..." Gary's gaze shifted from Logan to the woman beside him. "I've got a pen you could have."

Tammi-Jo smiled. "Where were you ten seconds ago?" she teased. She clicked the button on the end of Logan's pen, and gave it a little wave. "I'm fine, thanks. Just you carry on."

"Right..." Gary's eyes lingered on her for a second or two, then he directed his attention back towards Logan. "Sorry. What was I...?"

"You were in the bathroom."

"Right! Yes! Bathroom. So... I was up there. I'd had a

shower. I'd got dried." He shook his head, annoyed at himself. "Sorry, that's too much detail. Sandra texted."

"Sandra?" Tammi-Jo asked.

"My, uh, my wife," Gary replied, and he almost sounded apologetic. "She, um, she texted to say she'd be home later today."

"She been away?" Logan asked.

"Yes. Looking after her mum. In Thurso. Been gone a wee while. But she'd texted to say she was coming back today."

He stopped there. His mouth formed into a thin smile and his eyebrows raised, like he'd reached the end of the story.

Logan gave him a moment before prompting him. "And then what?"

"Hm? Oh! Yes, sorry. So, I was reading her text." He tapped himself on the side of the head. "Wait. No. I was *replying* to the message when Rory shouted. Or was it Edgar? No. Rory, I think." He shrugged. "I'm not sure. One of the boys shouted, anyway. And I could tell that... It was Rory. I remember now. I could tell there was something wrong, you know? I thought maybe he'd broken something. Kicked a ball through a window again. Something like that. But I knew there was something."

He slid down from the arm so he was sitting on the couch, and leaned backwards, sinking into the cushions.

"So, I come downstairs, and there's someone out front. There's someone in the garden," he continued, his voice lowering in volume like he didn't want the boys to hear. "Just right out front. Just standing there. Large as life."

"And this was Albert Hall?" Logan asked.

"It was. Old Albert. From down the road. Just standing there in his shirt and tie. Jacket on. Just standing there. In the garden. And I thought, 'Aye, aye, what's this?' He's wandered before. Couple of times, Sandra said. Dementia, or what have you. So I thought, you know, that's just this. This is that. He's just wandered."

Gary sat forwards, glanced around the room, then lowered his voice all the way down to a whisper.

"But that was when I saw it."

"Saw what?" Logan asked.

"The *blood*." Gary's face paled, like the thought of it was making him feel faint. "That's when I saw the blood."

"On Albert?"

"Yes. On his shirt, mostly. But his hands, too. Spots everywhere."

Tammi-Jo raised her borrowed pen to interject. "Spots?" she asked. "Like spray, would you say, or smudges?"

Gary frowned, like he didn't understand the question.

"I mean, like were they lots of little individual dots, or could he have got it on his hands and accidentally spread it around? Touched his face, adjusted his collar, whatever?"

"Does it matter?" Gary asked.

The DC nodded, quite firmly. "It does."

"Right. Well... sorry. I'm not sure. I didn't really notice the details."

Tammi-Jo smiled encouragingly. "That's OK. Don't worry about it."

She waved him on with her pen, then returned to her note-taking as he continued.

"Uh, OK. So, I told the boys to stay in the house while I went out to see what the story was. They didn't, of course, because they're teenagers, but they kept their distance. I asked Albert if he was alright—stupid, really, because I know he's deaf, but I didn't know what else to do. I don't think he even heard me, though." Gary tutted, annoyed at himself. "Obviously. But, I mean, I don't even think he knew I was there, sort of thing? You know? It was like he was sleepwalking, or something. But with his eyes open."

"Did you call an ambulance?" Logan asked.

"I was going to. I got one of the boys to go get my phone, but then Albert, he just started walking off. Not quickly—he's not exactly nippy on his feet at the best of times—but deliberately, you know? Like he was on a mission," Gary explained. "I tried to get him to wait, to have a seat, or something, but he just kept going."

"Going where?"

"Home. He, eh, he went home." Gary was fidgeting so much now that his fingers were practically interwoven. He coughed quietly, then looked at each of the detectives in turn. "You sure I can't get you something to drink? There's juice, too."

"We're fine," Logan reiterated. "What then? What happened next?"

Gary squirmed. Clearly, this was the part he'd been dreading.

"One of the other neighbours came out. From across the way. Patrick."

"Patrick...?" Tammi-Jo prompted.

"Um, Parkes. Patrick Parkes. He sort of followed along to see what was what."

"He followed you to the house?"

"Yeah," Gary confirmed. "We, um, we took Albert inside. Patrick and me. We wanted to make sure he was OK. That he wasn't, you know, like, going to just go wandering off again. And I wanted to make sure he wasn't too badly hurt. I couldn't see an injury, but I thought the blood had to be his." His gaze flitted to the ceiling, and he took a moment to compose himself. "I thought that then, anyway. Before we went in. Before I saw..."

A movement at the window caught his eye. Both boys were peeking in through the glass, watching his conversation with the detectives.

"Bugger off, you pair," he said, jerking a thumb to indicate his buggering off direction of choice. "Get back to your practising."

The two lads ducked down out of sight. A moment later,

Logan and the others heard the distinctive *thunk* of a football being hoofed along the garden.

"Sorry. They both really liked Granny. She used to watch them playing football on the grass out front. She'd call them into the garden for juice and sweets," Gary said. He ran a hand through his hair and gripped the top of his head, the stress of the day sitting heavily on him. "They saw her, too. Earlier, I mean. Today. I told them to stay. Not to come in. But they saw her. Sitting there. Sitting there just staring like that." He met Logan's eye, and said, "Dead," like he was delivering some sort of big revelation.

Sighing, Gary flopped back into the couch's embrace.

"Do you think they'll need counselling? Seeing something like that? At their age."

"How old are they?" DC Swanney asked.

It took Gary almost a full second to settle on the numbers. "Seventeen and thirteen."

Tammi-Jo scribbled the numbers down in the margin of her notes, and left it to Logan to offer a response to the question the boys' father had asked.

"Kids that age, they're pretty resilient," he said. "But, if you have concerns, your GP should be able to advise about mental health support."

Gary laughed at that. It was a sharp, sarcastic thing, with a seam of bitterness running through it. "Aye. Maybe in three-to-five years." He shook his head. "Disgrace what they've done to the health service, isn't it? Cut it to the bone so they can sell it off in chunks to their rich pals. Makes me sick."

Logan glanced down at Tammi-Jo's pad to see if she was making a note of that outburst, but he couldn't make heads or tails of anything she'd written, so he jotted it down mentally, then got back on topic.

"Sorry. My wife's a carer," Gary said, realising he'd gone off on one. "Granny's one of her clients, actually. We get to see the effects of the cutbacks up close."

"I understand," Logan said. "Going back for a moment, she was dead when you found her?"

"Granny? Yeah. I mean, I wasn't sure right away. I thought so. Patrick did, too. She looked dead. But I had to check, you know? So, I felt for a pulse, and I listened for her breathing. I didn't have a wee mirror. They say you should do that, don't they? A wee mirror over the mouth, see if it fogs up. I didn't have one, so I didn't do that." Gary sounded genuinely contrite about his failures on the wee mirror front. "But, I mean, I don't even know why I bothered doing any of it," he continued. "She was clearly dead."

"She was," Logan confirmed. "There was nothing you could've done. She was gone long before you got there."

Gary let out a long, shaky breath, like these were the words he'd been waiting to hear. He ran his sleeve across his eyes, his voice cracking as he spoke.

"That's... Because I didn't know. What to do, I mean. I didn't know if I should've been doing CPR, or... or... I just didn't know what to do. And Patrick, he was just watching, like he was... I don't know. Like he was frozen. And the boys were there. And Albert, he was just standing there, just standing there looking at me. For the first time that day, he was just... He was looking at me, like I should be doing something. Like I should be helping her. And I didn't know. I didn't. I didn't know what to do."

"There was nothing you could do," Logan assured him again. "You did everything right, Gary. There was nothing anyone could've done differently."

Gary lowered his head and nodded. His shoulders heaved as he struggled to stifle his sobs.

"Actually, Gary," Logan said, offering the poor guy a lifeline. "I think maybe we will have that cup of tea, after all..."

CHAPTER TWELVE

SINEAD REACHED for the box of *Cadbury's Chocolate Fingers* that sat next to her monitor, fumbled blindly in the packaging while she scrolled through the information on the screen, then frowned when her fingertip search proved fruitless.

She tore her eyes from the screen and looked at the clear plastic tray on the desk. Surely she hadn't eaten all of them? She'd only opened the packet twenty minutes ago. She couldn't have unconsciously grazed her way through the whole thing in that time, could she?

Wheeling herself back in her chair, she looked under the desk. Taggart was curled up, fast asleep, where he'd been since shortly after the call with Logan and the others. One eye had opened, and an ear had pricked up when she'd opened the packet, but she'd been slow and careful enough with it not to waken the dog all the way.

He hadn't eaten them, then. Dave was away. It didn't take much in the way of deductive prowess, then, to conclude that, yes, she'd gobbled up the lot.

Sighing, she ran both hands across the vast expanse of her belly.

"I blame you pair," she said, and most of her guilt evaporated, just like that.

It was, she'd discovered, one of the few benefits of being pregnant, the ability to transfer blame for any accidental chocolate binges. Or cake binges. Or biscuits, pastries, ice cream, and anything else packed densely with fat and sugar.

She'd never really had much of a sweet tooth before getting pregnant. Sure, she enjoyed the odd caramel wafer, and who could say no to a few squares of chocolate? By and large, though, she'd been more a fan of savoury foods than sweet ones.

Those days, however, as the empty packet on her desk could attest, were gone. With the amount she was packing away, when the twins finally came out, they'd be bouncing off the walls on a sugar high.

She tipped the packet up in case there was a solitary chocolate finger stuck in close to the narrow end, hidden by the folds of the plastic.

There wasn't.

Damn it.

The door to the Incident Room swung open, and Sinead began the slow process of wheeling herself around to face it. There hadn't been a knock before the door was opened, which suggested only a couple of possible visitors—one who made the rules, and another who thought they didn't apply to him.

To Sinead's relief, it was the former she saw standing there when she finally completed her one-eighty in the chair.

"Detective Superintendent," she said. She made a bit of a show of starting to stand up, and then stopped when Det Supt Mitchell waved her back down into the chair.

"Don't stand up on my account," Mitchell said.

Sinead smiled. "Thanks, ma'am. Takes me about twenty minutes these days."

"Yes. I'll bet," Mitchell said. "And then, I'd imagine you're counting the seconds until you can sit down again."

"Yes! Bang on," Sinead said. "It's just one thing after another. Apparently, you start glowing at some point, but I've yet to hit that stage."

Mitchell shuddered. "This is why I stick with women," she said. "Far less chance of this sort of thing happening."

Sinead's laugh was a little awkward. Detective Superintendent Mitchell was usually something of a closed book. Her sexuality was no secret—Sinead had briefly met her partner once, at some after-work do—but talking about it like this was unusual.

It was made even more so by the fact that Mitchell was dressed in full uniform, like she was about to head out on some official parade. The formal nature of her outfit jarred with the way she was talking.

"You picked names yet?" the detective superintendent asked, picking up a stapler from a desk.

"We've got a list. Well, two lists," Sinead said. "Boys and girls."

Mitchell idly turned the stapler over in her hands, then set it back down again.

"You don't know what you're having?" she asked. "Or is it one of each?"

"We don't know. We decided not to find out." Sinead's brow creased, just a little. "Can't remember why we decided that. Tyler was desperate to know, but I think I might've been in a bad mood, so I overruled him." She smiled. "I blame the hormones."

"God, no. Don't do that. We're all allowed days like those. No excuses necessary."

Sinead watched as Mitchell ran a finger across the top of a monitor, like she was checking it for dust. The detective superintendent then looked up at the ceiling, eyes flitting across it as if counting all the tiles.

"Is, eh, is everything alright, ma'am?" Sinead asked.

"Fine. Yes. Yes, fine," Mitchell said. She folded her hands

crisply behind her back, suddenly aware of her fidgeting. "The two constables get off OK?"

"They did, yes," Sinead confirmed.

"Right. Good. And you're feeling OK? You know..." Her gaze flitted to Sinead's midsection. "Considering?"

"Yes, ma'am."

"Good. Good. All good, then," Mitchell said. "I'm, uh, I'm going to be away for the rest of the day. Possibly tomorrow, too."

Sinead blinked. This wasn't the sort of information she was usually privy to. "OK..." She smiled, a little uncomfortably. "Going anywhere nice?"

"Ha! No. Glasgow. I mean, nothing against the place, but it's a work thing." She clicked her tongue against the back of her teeth. "It's very much a work thing."

"Is it about Heather?" Sinead asked. "Sorry, DCI Filson, I mean?"

"I'm not at liberty to say," Mitchell replied, though her hesitation suggested she had been close to doing so.

"Right. No. No, I suppose not. Sorry, ma'am, shouldn't have asked. Is there anything you need me to do for it? Help you prepare, or...?"

"No. No, no. No. Nothing like that," Mitchell said. "You concentrate on..." She waved vaguely at the monitor. At least, Sinead hoped it was at the monitor, and not the empty packet of chocolate fingers. "I just... I know you've not got long left before you go on leave, and in case I'm down there longer than I plan to be, I wanted to wish you all the best."

"Oh. Oh, well, thank you, ma'am. That's really kind of you."

Mitchell nodded, just once. Her cheeks puffed out, like she had a lot more she wanted to say, but was fighting to keep herself from doing so.

"Right. OK. Well, all the best, Detective Constable," she said. She wasted a few more moments looking around the room again, then about-turned to face the door.

She didn't take a step, though. Not yet.

"Sorry, ma'am," Sinead said. "I know you said... But, are you sure you're OK?"

Mitchell's silence was telling. Her hands were folded behind her back again, and Sinead watched all the fingers twitching, one by one.

"DCI Logan," Mitchell began. "How vital would you say he is to the running of this team?"

"What?" The word came out as a gasp. "Very. I mean, completely. No disrespect to DI Forde, or... well, to any of us, but without DCI Logan, I don't know what we'd do."

Mitchell still hadn't turned back. Her shoulder straightened, and while she wasn't tall, she drew herself up to her full height.

"Yes," she said. "That's what I thought. I'm glad we're in agreement."

She did turn then, twisting at the waist, and firing a nod back over her shoulder. Her expressions were never easy to read, but there was something like gratitude hidden somewhere in this one.

"Thank you, Sinead. You've been very helpful," she said. She began to walk off, then thought better of it and turned back one more time. "And, for what it's worth, I can see you glowing from here."

With that, she left the Incident Room. Sinead watched the door swinging closed, and waited until the sound of the detective superintendent's footsteps had faded into silence.

"Well," she muttered, opening her desk drawer and reaching for a second packet of chocolate fingers. "That was a bit weird."

Using her feet, she steered her chair back to face her screen. She was almost there when the pain struck—a sharp, stabbing sensation shooting up from her pelvis that made her grimace and hiss, and clamp both hands down on her belly.

Down on the floor, Taggart's head lifted from where it'd

been resting on his paws. He let out an inquisitive wee whine while Sinead breathed slowly in and out through her nose.

She sat there, her legs half under her desk, her bump resting against the edge, waiting for the pain to come again.

It had been a sore one, she thought, though the fact it had come and gone so quickly made it hard to tell. Maybe it hadn't been that bad. Maybe it was just the unexpectedness of it that had made it seem worse.

If it came again, she'd be ready for it. She'd be able to gauge it properly.

She'd know whether the time had come to panic.

She was still sitting there two minutes later, same spot, same position. Still waiting.

Taggart's head had lowered, and he'd closed his eyes again, like he'd concluded the excitement was over. Sinead was starting to think he was right.

It had been a random twinge, that was all. Nothing to worry about.

"Not a problem," she whispered, like she was trying to convince herself, or perhaps to bend the Universe to her will.

No way she was going into labour. Not now. Not today. Not without Tyler here.

Not on her own.

She finished turning herself into position at the desk.

She opened the box of chocolate fingers, and this time only slid the plastic tray halfway out.

"Not a problem," she said again.

And with that, she got to work.

CHAPTER THIRTEEN

DCI LOGAN AND DC SWANNEY stood at the gate of Granny and Albert's house, heads tucked into their shoulders to fend off a light but icy cold drizzle that had started a campaign of harassment against them.

They hadn't stuck around long at Gary Hawthorne's house after their tea. He'd told them everything he knew, and while it all helped to paint a general picture of how the morning had gone, none of it was particularly enlightening.

Logan was hoping that the crime scene itself might shed more light on things. There was just one thing holding that up.

"Tyler! Where the hell are you?" Logan barked into his phone.

The reply crackled from the mobile's earpiece. "Right around the corner, boss. Be right there."

Logan ended the call, and then heard the sound of an approaching engine. For a young lad with several police driving qualifications under his belt, he drove like someone's elderly aunt. The DCI and the DC both stood watching as Tyler's car trundled cautiously along the street, then eased to a stop at the kerb beside them.

There was a bit of faffing while Tyler shut off the engine, checked his lights were off, and unclipped his seatbelt, then he stepped out into the rain, all big smiles and bluster.

"Sorry for the holdup, boss. I got a bit lost," he announced.

"Lost? It's one road in and the same road back out again. How could you possibly get lost?"

"No, I mean in the station," Tyler said, and he didn't appear remotely embarrassed to admit this. "Couldn't find my way off the second floor. Just kept ending up back in the same place. Thought I was caught in a time loop or something."

"That happened to me once," Tammi-Jo told him. "Aye, not the time loop. I've never had that happen. But getting lost in a station. Up in Aberdeen."

"It's so easily done," Tyler said. "They make all the doors—"

"Look the same!" DC Swanney laughed, and the melody of it danced between the raindrops. "That's what I keep saying. Like, go for colours or something. Make it easier for people."

"Exactly!" Tyler agreed. "Or just, you know, bold suggestion, put signs on the doors."

"I *know!*" Tammi-Jo cried. "How hard is that?"

Logan didn't mean to groan, but it just sort of happened, regardless. On their own, the DCs had the potential to bug the living shite out of him. Together, their powers would be limitless.

"God help me," he muttered, heading through the gate and up the path. "What have I done?"

The house had lost some of its eeriness now that the body had been removed and, more importantly, now that Geoff Palmer was no longer lingering like a bad smell in the living room.

All the forensic evidence the Scene of Crime team had found

would now be in the process of being recorded down the road in Inverness. This seemed a bit pointless to Logan, since most of it would then make its way back to Wick station for his team to log, but Palmer had a routine, and he didn't like to deviate from it—especially if doing so might make Logan's life even incrementally easier.

There was a hole in the carpet where a square had been removed. It had been lifted from the area where the blood spray had been found, so tests could be done, and the blood type determined. Logan fully expected it to be a match for the victim, but there'd be no saying for sure until the results came through. If it wasn't, it wouldn't be the first time that he'd been surprised by the lab's findings, and it might make the investigation that much easier.

Which is why he knew it would be the victim's. Wins like that rarely fell into his lap.

"What is it we're looking for, boss?" Tyler asked.

"Not sure yet," Logan told him. "Just keep your eyes peeled. See if anything looks out of place."

He turned his attention to the walls. They'd been covered a long time ago with a green and white patterned wallpaper he assumed had fallen out of fashion before it'd ever had a chance to fall into it. The white parts were slightly yellowed by age, and by years of nicotine staining.

Someone in the house was a smoker, then.

The lack of photographs was interesting. Had he not just come from Gary Hawthorne's house, he might not have noticed, but there were no pictures of Granny or Albert—or of anyone else for that matter—anywhere in the room.

Ornaments, yes. God, were there ornaments. But not a single photograph. Not a wedding picture. Not a holiday snap. Nothing.

It wasn't wholly unusual, he supposed. Since his divorce, he'd lived in a variety of places—some better than others—and hadn't bothered putting pictures up in any of them but his current house.

But that was because all those places had felt temporary. They'd been buildings that he spent some of his non-working hours in. None of them had been a home in the way this place had been.

"Something's been taken. Look."

DC Swanney pointed to a spot in the middle of the mantelpiece.

"What do you mean?" Logan asked. "How can you tell?"

"Well, just look. There should be something there," Tammi-Jo insisted.

Logan shot a look at DC Neish, who just shrugged.

"What are you, psychic or something?" Tyler asked.

"No! It's just... It's obvious," Tammi-Jo said. She pointed to the spot again. "Look! See? There was something there."

Logan decided to bite. He leaned in closer and studied the spot where she was pointing. It was, at first glance, just an empty space, but from the right angle it was possible to see a clean rectangle in the fine layer of dust that had accumulated on the mantelpiece.

"Aye. I think you're right," Logan agreed.

"I knew there was something up as soon as we came in," Tammi-Jo told him. "It was bothering me. It's like an ADHD thing. Or maybe an OCD thing. I'm not sure which. Either way, it's like a radar or something. It just niggles until I spot what it is that's not right."

She gestured along the mantelpiece with an open hand. This was mostly for Tyler's benefit, as he still looked a bit confused.

"Then I noticed. Ornaments on both sides, nothing in the middle. Just a space that doesn't fit."

"How can a space not fit?" Tyler wondered.

"You know, it's just like... Like there's a lack of something."

"You're talking to the right man about having a lack of something," Logan remarked. "Tyler's got a list a mile long."

"I just... I just sort of knew there had to have been something there at some point. I just didn't spot it right away."

"Aye, very good," Logan said. Now, he decided, was not the time to try and unravel anything of what the DC had just said.

"You're right, though. It is slap-bang in the middle," Tyler said, peering down at the clean mark in the dust. "A clock, maybe?"

"Could be. Then again, it could be just about anything," Logan replied. "Can't say I remember seeing anything there earlier. When we're done here, check in with Palmer and see if he took anything from there."

Tyler groaned, but this time didn't bother to offer an objection.

"Good spot, Detective Constable," Logan told Tammi-Jo, then he gestured to the living room door. "No point us all searching in here, though. You two go search the rest of the house. Take your time. Check everywhere. Something might jump out."

"On it, boss," Tyler said. He held the door open for Tammi-Jo, and they both headed out into the hallway.

Once there, he pointed upwards to the floor above.

"You want to do upstairs or downstairs?"

Tammi-Jo's eyes practically popped out of her head. "You're asking me? God. I don't know. I mean, you're the one with all the experience," she said, wringing her hands together. "What do you think?"

Tyler's eyebrows rose. "Uh, I, eh, I don't really think it matters," he concluded, after a momentary struggle. "I could do upstairs. You could do down here. If you want? I don't mind."

"If you think that's best," DC Swanney said. "Yeah. Let's do that, then. If I get stuck or anything, I'll shout. I mean, not literally stuck. I'm not going to get my head jammed in a kitchen cupboard or anything. *No way, José.* I learned that lesson last time."

Tyler's eyebrows lowered again, then continued far beyond their starting point.

Tammi-Jo smiled. "That was a joke." She chewed her lip. "Kind of. I wasn't really stuck. Well, no, technically I *was* stuck, but not for long. And it wasn't a cupboard. Well, it wasn't a *kitchen* cupboard."

She was babbling, and she knew it. Tyler could see the panic spreading across her face like a rash as she tried to find an exit from the conversation.

He thought back to what Sinead had told him, about offering support and helping her settle in.

He wasn't entirely sure what that entailed, though, so he made a fist, very lightly punched her on the shoulder, and made a clicking noise at the corner of his mouth like a cowboy summoning his horse.

While probably not quite what Sinead had had in mind, it seemed to do the trick. Tammi-Jo stopped talking, looked at her shoulder where he'd touched her, then said, "Thanks for that," in a somewhat puzzled tone.

"No bother," Tyler said.

And then, basking in the feeling of a job well done, he plodded on up the stairs.

CHAPTER FOURTEEN

DISAPPOINTINGLY, Hamza hadn't been able to source a corkboard from anywhere in the station.

A sergeant downstairs had suggested that one of the local supermarkets might have one. He'd conceded, though, that they were unlikely to be large enough to qualify as a Big Board, and that a Small Board wasn't going to be of any benefit to anyone.

It could all be done digitally, of course. It would've taken Hamza just a few minutes to put together a virtual Big Board that could've been projected onto the screen for all to see.

But he could well imagine what DCI Logan would have to say about that. Also, the thought of having to explain how it worked to DI Forde every five minutes made the idea significantly less appealing.

In the end, he'd found a large whiteboard mounted on a set of wheels, and had staked a claim to that. It wasn't quite the same—they'd have to attach things to it with Blu-Tack or magnets rather than pins, for example—but nor was it a million miles away.

Once he'd found that, and navigated the station corridors with it, he'd set to work adding the information they had. He'd seen Sinead do it plenty of times, and had tried to replicate her approach, with a timeline at the very top, and information on all the key players below that.

As of that moment, the key players consisted of the victim and her husband. Hamza had been planning to mark the husband up as a suspect, but a call from Logan earlier had more or less relegated him to potential witness status.

This was great news for him, of course, but not so good for the investigation, as it reduced their list of suspects to zero.

He'd just finished writing in the old couple's names when the door opened and DI Forde came in carrying a cup of tea in each hand, and with a cardboard file folder pinned to his side by one arm.

"I assumed you wouldn't say no," he announced, setting the mug down on the desk closest to the Big Board.

"Thanks," Hamza said, immediately picking it up again.

He blew on it to cool it a little, then took a sip. Only then did he question the folder.

"Got something, sir?"

"Hmm?" A moment of confusion came and went, then Ben realised what the DS was getting at. "Oh! Aye. Witness statements from the door-to-door." He tossed the folder onto the desk, where it landed with a *thack*. "I'm going to go right ahead and spoil the ending for you, though. No bugger saw or heard anything."

Hamza shot the folder a dirty look, like it was somehow responsible for the bad news.

"I'm guessing, village that size, CCTV coverage isn't exactly great, either?"

"Non-existent," Ben said. "Uniform even checked if anyone has any of them fancy camera doorbell things. They don't."

"Can't imagine there's a lot of passing traffic at that time of night, either, so dashcam footage is unlikely."

Ben took a glug of his tea, then nodded. "Aye," he confirmed. "That's pretty much the size of it."

Both men turned and regarded the Big Board.

"So, this is about all we have so far, then," Hamza said. "I mean, we've got cause of death and all that to add, but I thought I'd wait until the pathology report came through, so we're sure what we're dealing with."

"Good call," Ben said. "But, you know, good work. It's a start."

Hamza snorted. "Thanks, sir. And aye, it is. But just barely."

Ben brought his mug to his mouth again, but didn't drink. "Well, who knows?" he said. "Maybe Jack and the others are having more luck than we are..."

After wasting a few seconds *Eenie, Meenie, Miney, Mo*ing at the top of the stairs, Tyler picked a room to search first. It was a bedroom, with two single beds positioned side by side, just a couple of feet apart.

The blankets, sheets, and pillows had been removed, leaving just two plastic covers on yellowing mattresses that were probably old enough to be his parents.

If, indeed, mattresses were capable of such a thing.

The rest of the room wasn't much better. With its mismatched, old-fashioned furniture and wood-panelled walls, it would almost have felt like time had stopped in here several decades previously, had everything not been so faded and worn down by age.

The same smell seemed to seep from every surface—a faintly cabbagey sort of aroma with sour and bitter notes that made their presence felt at the back of the throat.

At first glance, Tyler thought the carpet was patterned, but then realised it was just marked and stained by decades of wear and tear. A patch right in front of a big dressing table had been so badly worn away that Tyler could see snatches of newsprint through the fibres.

Given how old the carpet looked, the newspaper underlay must've been there forever. Tyler wondered what the headlines on them would be, and reckoned that 'Wheel Invented' would be a pretty safe bet.

There wasn't a lot else of note in the room. The top of the dressing table was dusty, and while it might once have held hair products and makeup, it was now just a resting place for a big box of a TV with a metal hoop for an aerial fixed to the top.

The television was just one more thing in the room that predated Tyler's existence. He could just vaguely recall TVs that weren't flatscreen from his childhood, but he'd never seen one so square, or with big chunky buttons and a dial on the front. Not outside of old sitcoms, or the *Back to the Future* trilogy, at least.

The screen of the telly that time forgot was thick with dust. The controls, too. It had been a couple of years, he thought, since the analogue signal had been switched off, so it was unlikely that this TV would've functioned at all since then.

There were three bedside tables in the room, all of them different, all of them in various states of disrepair. One of them —the largest, and most knackered-looking—was positioned between the beds, while the other two were on either side, so each bed had access to an individual table, and a shared one.

Tyler pulled open the drawer of the middle one, and listened to the *brrrr* of something rolling forward from the back.

He stared in mute, horrified silence as a discrete, yet impressively lifelike sex toy thudded to a stop against the inside of the drawer front.

The colour was all wrong—it was bright green—but otherwise, the thing looked very much like a miniature version of a real penis, from the bulging veins to the curve of its head.

He stood there staring at it for a while, and couldn't shake the feeling that it was somehow staring back.

"Jesus," he eventually whispered, then he quickly slammed the drawer closed again, and tried to convince himself that he'd imagined the whole thing.

The sex toy, however, had other ideas.

The force with which Tyler closed the drawer sent the thing hurtling towards the back. The impact with the rear wall of the drawer somehow woke the device up, and a thunderous droning filled the room, the buzzing of the vibrator massively amplified through the walls of the otherwise empty cabinet.

"Shit, shit, shit, *shhh*, shut up!" Tyler hissed, pulling the drawer open again. The sex toy rattled around inside the drawer, its high-speed buzzing dragging it around in circles, so it appeared to be running laps.

Tyler didn't want to touch it. In fact, if he had the time to draw up a list of things he had no desire of ever doing, interacting with a dead pensioner's dildo would've been right at the top of the list.

But he couldn't just leave the bloody thing going. The noise of it against the drawer bottom was like a pneumatic drill. Pretty soon, Logan and DC Swanney would come running, and what the hell was he going to tell them?!

They'd think he'd been messing about with it. They'd think he'd done this on purpose!

No. He couldn't be having that. The rest of the team would never let him live it down.

"Jesus!" he groaned. Why did this sort of thing always happen to him?

He took a moment to compose himself, then he made a grab for the vibrator like a bear trying to snatch a salmon from a fast-flowing river.

The moment his fingers made contact with the silky rubberised coating, he recoiled in revulsion, leaving the dildo free to pull another few noisy three-sixties while he watched helplessly on.

He wiped his hands on his trousers, had a word with himself below his breath, then he tried again. This time, his hand was like a striking cobra, plucking a mouse from its hole.

Tyler let out a little cry of triumph, but he'd spoken too soon. The vibrator, still buzzing, leapt out of his hand, and he spent a frantic few moments juggling the bloody thing before he was able to get a proper grip.

It took him a few horrifying moments to find the button that switched it off, then he dropped it back into the drawer and then, much more carefully than last time, he slid the drawer closed.

"Bloody hell," he whispered, wiping his hands on his trousers again. He followed the remark with a whole-body convulsion. "Frisky old buggers."

Satisfied that the sex toy was once again dormant, he turned his attention to the rest of the room. He'd never been great at this stuff. The actual *detecting* part of being a detective had never really been his strong point.

He saw his role as more making tea, chasing people, and providing light relief in times of high stress.

Sometimes, he could even stretch to charming women, although this usually relied on them being over a certain age, and having a particularly strong mothering instinct.

Sinead, on the other hand, was great at this sort of thing, and had a real gift for the observational part of the job. She was good with little details, while Tyler considered himself more of a 'big picture' sort of guy.

Still, he couldn't exactly go back downstairs empty-handed. Sure, there were other rooms still to check, and maybe he'd find something in there, but this was obviously the victim's bedroom. If there was anything waiting to be discovered, this was the most likely place to find it.

Tyler narrowed his eyes, set his jaw, and concentrated, trying to spot some tiny out-of-place detail, like the new girl had done downstairs with the outline on the mantelpiece. That had been a belter. Tyler would've loved to have spotted that. He'd be telling the story for weeks.

He was concentrating so hard on trying to spot some such detail that he almost failed to notice the much bigger details of the built-in wardrobe in the corner of the room. It had narrow, slatted doors, with little copper-coloured handles on the fronts.

It was remiss of him not to spot it right away, and he was glad that nobody else was around to notice. To be fair, the whole thing was half-hidden by a couple of ancient Terry Towelling dressing gowns that draped from a set of hooks hung over the top of one of the doors.

"Please no more sex toys," he whispered, approaching the wardrobe.

One motorised phallus, he could just about deal with. If he should stumble upon a big box full of the buggers, though... Well, that would be another matter entirely.

At the doors, he took a breath, steeling himself, then he gripped the handles and pulled.

The doors creaked open, letting the light from the window flood in. Dresses, shirts, and suits were jammed in side by side on hangers, some of them covered by bags to protect them from the ravages of time, and the appetites of hungry moths.

He looked down at the floor, and was relieved that there wasn't a motorised sexual aid in sight. There were just shoes. A lot of shoes. All sorts, and shapes, and sizes. High heels. Sturdy boots. Scuffed old brogues.

One pair in particular caught his eye. They were much newer than the others. Trainers. A bit beaten up, but still in decent nick.

Unlike the others, which were pointing towards the back wall of the wardrobe, these were facing him.

Unlike the others, which were empty, these were not.

Tyler followed the legs for a split second, then his head snapped up. He saw an eye in the shadows behind the clothing.

He opened his mouth to shout, but the figure in the wardrobe exploded out at him, fists flying, eyes blazing like something from a horror movie. Knuckles cracked across Tyler's jaw, snapping his mouth shut and rattling his teeth. Spots flashed before his eyes, so he had no chance to avoid the second punch that sent him spinning towards the floor.

He found a bed, instead, landed sideways on the plastic sheeting, then slid off and thumped onto the fraying carpet.

A foot passed him. He grabbed for it, fingers clawing at the trainer, trying to use the laces for purchase.

Rather than pulling away, though, it came at him. Quickly, too. It slammed into his sternum, knocking the air from his lungs until they shrivelled in his chest.

He tried to cry out, to shout, to warn the others, but there was nothing left in him to force the words out.

Tyler grabbed again, but caught only air. The door was wide open, and he was the only one left in the room.

He heard footsteps thundering down the stairs. Two shouts, one male, one female, then the front door was opened and slammed with enough force that the whole house seemed to tremble on its foundations.

"Tyler?" Logan's bellow rose up through the floor.

Before Tyler could wheeze out a response, he heard the door opening again.

"I'm after him!" DC Swanney cried.

"What? No. Wait," Logan's voice came from halfway up the stairs.

"I've got this, sir," Tammi-Jo insisted. "I can do it."

There was a moment of silence that ended in a groan. "Go," Logan said. Everything else he had to say on the matter was shouted, so the DC could hear it from outside. "But be bloody careful!"

Tyler tried to drag himself up, but the waterproof mattress covers were too slippery for him to find purchase. He used the bedside cabinet, instead, and was almost back on his feet when Logan came bursting into the room with his phone in his hand.

"I'm fine, boss," Tyler managed to wheeze. "Just need a sec."

Logan quickly looked him up and down, checking for damage, then nodded.

"Call it in," he instructed.

And then, DCI Logan did something he'd been desperately trying to avoid of late. Something he hadn't enjoyed doing as a young man, and had grown to positively despise in recent years.

He ran.

CHAPTER FIFTEEN

SHONA SAT on one of the tall stools by the counter of the mortuary office, reading the note that had been left for her.

Then, once she'd done that, she read it again.

Beside her, the kettle clicked off as the water inside it rolled to a boil. She didn't notice, and the *Bombay Bad Boy Pot Noodle* sitting open and ready on the counter beside her remained inedibly dry.

"Wait, what?" she said out loud, then she adjusted her sitting position and read the note again.

The words were becoming familiar by this point, though they were no less unexpected.

"An assistant?" she said.

She turned the note over in case there was more information on the back. Or, perhaps, a punchline.

She found neither.

"An assistant?" she said again, and this time she aimed the question at the wall in front of her. It elected not to answer her. "What do they mean, I'm getting an assistant?"

She let the note fall onto the counter, then leaned back. At the last possible moment, before gravity took hold, she realised she was sitting on a stool, and only a quick grab for the under-side of the countertop stopped her from toppling backwards onto the floor.

Such was the effect the note had on her.

She was getting an assistant. Full-time, too.

This was bad. She didn't want an assistant. She wanted a fully qualified pathologist to share some of the workload, and who wouldn't be hanging around the place while she was.

And that would almost certainly have suited the other pathologist just fine, too. Generally speaking, they got into working with dead people because they were uncomfortable around most living ones. Another pathologist would just nod and smile at her as they passed, and then leave her to get on with things.

An assistant, though? An assistant was going to be here while she was. An assistant was going to get in her way.

An assistant was the last thing she bloody needed.

Shona hadn't been in the best of moods since her conversa-tion with Logan, and the note hadn't helped. The thought of an assistant coming to work with her not only made her anxious, but it completely robbed her of her appetite, so she could barely eat two-thirds of the *Pot Noodle* once she'd finished preparing it.

There were no further details on the note to let her know who the assistant was, or when they'd be arriving. Hopefully, that meant it wasn't imminent.

She decided the best thing to do was to put it out of her mind and get to work. So, once she'd finished the last third of the *Pot Noodle*—because she wasn't a believer in wasting food—she scrubbed up, gloved up, and entered the mortuary proper.

The body had been delivered straight to the slab from the ambulance. Greta Hall—Granny, to those who'd known her—lay waiting as Shona entered.

"Hey. Sorry to keep you," the pathologist announced. "One

of those days." She looked down at the corpse and winced. "Mind you, not in the same league as yours, I suppose."

She stopped beside the dead woman, rested a hand on her arm, then gave it a comforting squeeze.

"I'm so sorry for what happened to you," she whispered. "And for what I need to do."

She gave the arm another squeeze, then slid open a drawer, revealing her neatly stacked and lined-up tools.

"If it's any consolation," she said, reaching for the surgical steel. "I promise it isn't going to hurt a..."

Something on the body caught her eye. A wound. A distinctive one, at that.

"Well now," Shona muttered. She bent to take a closer look. "What do we have here?"

CHAPTER SIXTEEN

LOGAN'S OPINION of running had not improved by the time he went clattering around the corner of Granny Hall's street, and was immediately assaulted by the cold, salty air blowing in off the North Sea.

By the time he'd made it out into the garden, there was no sign of either DC Swanney or the man she was chasing, but a broken length of the cordon tape that had been blocking the pavement and part of the road on either side of the garden had at least indicated which direction they'd gone.

Logan staggered to a stop when he rounded the corner, pain already shooting up his legs. His boots weren't made for running. Nor, for that matter, was the rest of him. He'd barely gone fifty yards, but could already feel his lungs turning raw with the effort.

It was a good job Shona wasn't here to see this, or she'd have him taking up jogging again.

From where he'd stopped, there were only a couple of possible routes Tammi-Jo and her target could've taken. One was down an incline towards the harbour, but that would be a dead end, unless he happened to have a boat waiting to whisk him out to sea.

The other direction was much more likely. It banked back up behind the High Street, and would leave various escape routes open to the man being chased. There were a couple of ruined buildings up there, too, by the looks of things. Plenty of hiding places.

Before deciding, Logan shouted out DC Swanney's name. Even his mighty lung capacity couldn't match the North Sea wind, though, and the words were whipped out of his mouth and quickly lost to the whims of the weather.

"Bollocks!"

The back road was the best bet. Logan wasted half a second talking his feet into it, then set off in a lumbering dash, puffing his way up the shallow incline that led back towards the heart of the village.

The lapping of the water at the harbour's edge was proving distracting. DC Swanney tried to block out the sound of its sloshing as she crept along the front of the large, brick-built harbour building.

It was old-looking. A couple of hundred years or so, she'd guess, though she had nothing to base that on but guesswork.

Or she didn't until a moment later, when a large, rusting plaque on the front revealed the place had been built in 1833. Not quite the two hundred years, then, but not a kick in the arse off it.

There were several doors set into the building's front—all heavy, wooden things with no obvious way of opening them from the outside. She considered knocking on one of them, but decided that announcing herself like that probably wasn't the best idea.

The guy she'd been chasing hadn't been too far ahead. He'd know she was coming, but he didn't necessarily know she was already here. She wasn't ready to give away the element of surprise yet, however slight it might be.

A few small boats were bobbing around in the harbour. She looked inside them as she passed, but saw no signs of life within.

He could've jumped in the water, but that would seem extreme. Given the temperature and the time of year, she reckoned she'd have heard him squealing the moment his testicles met the icy kiss of the water.

So, the harbour building, then. It had to be.

A set of crude stone steps led up the side of it and joined a sloping track that ran along the back. With no way in through the harbour-side doors, Tammi-Jo took the steps two at a time, peeked around the corner, then checked for a back entrance.

She passed a darkened window and saw her reflection staring back at her from the glass. She was disappointed to note quite how scared she looked. Although, given how quickly her heart was beating, it should have come as no surprise.

"Come on. Get a grip," she whispered, glaring at her mirror image. "You've trained for this. This is what you always said you wanted."

Her reflection neither confirmed nor denied this, so she walked on, and soon found another door at the top of a short flight of stairs.

And this one, unlike the others, had a handle.

She didn't bother to knock. Being in close pursuit of a fleeing suspect gave her a lot of leeway, warrant-wise.

Of course, she had no idea if the guy she was chasing was inside. She'd lost sight of him when he'd gone sliding down the hillside leading down to the harbour, but unless he'd vanished into thin air, this was his most likely hiding place.

The door was heavy, but she threw it wide open and charged inside, drawing a yelp of fright from a young man wearing dark clothes and a shocked expression, who had been lurking just inside the doorway.

He brought his hands up like he was making to grab for her, and the world cranked down into slow motion.

She remembered her breathing. She remembered her stance, and her core, and everything else she'd ever been taught. She remembered it all, and so, when she saw those hands coming up, she was able to catch a wrist, to twist, to yank, and to force the bastard's arm up his back as she slammed him, face-first, against the wall.

"That's quite enough from you, sir. I'd advise you not to struggle," she said, slapping a metal cuff over his trapped wrist. "Because you..." She paused, savouring the moment. "Are under arrest!"

"Aye. That's not him."

DC Swanney and DCI Logan both looked at the man standing handcuffed between them, then back at Tyler, who was sitting on the front step of the victim's house.

Tammi-Jo smiled, but it was very much edging towards a grimace.

"What do you mean?" she asked.

"I mean, it's not him. It was a different guy," Tyler said. He reached up and used the handles on either side of the door to hoist himself onto his feet. "That's not the man who jumped out of the cupboard. I don't know who this guy is."

"I tried to tell you that," the man in the cuffs protested. His accent was from somewhere around the North East of England, though not particularly strong. "I said I wasn't whoever it was you were looking for."

"You tried to grab me," DC Swanney said.

"What? I did not! I got a fright when you came barging in, that was all. And, to be honest, you looked a bit scared."

Tammi-Jo scoffed. "I wasn't scared."

"Well, you looked it. I put my hands up to try and reassure you, but then you nearly broke my bloody arm and arrested me!"

Logan, who had come running back down the hill when he'd seen the DC leading who he believed to be the suspect up from the harbour, was still suffering the side effects of all that exercise. He ran a hand through his damp hair then rested it on the back of his neck, massaging the aching knot that was forming there between his shoulders.

"You sure?" he asked Tyler. "You wouldn't have got a good look at him."

"Definitely not him, boss," Tyler insisted. "The guy in the cupboard was older. Forties, maybe."

"He could be in his forties," Tammi-Jo said, still not wanting to face up to the fact that she'd made a mistake.

"Shut up! *Forties.* I'm twenty-six!" her prisoner cried.

"He was a bit shorter, too, I think," Tyler said. "And, you know, he had a different face."

"Why were you creeping about, then, if you weren't up to something?" Tammi-Jo demanded. "Explain that."

"I wasn't 'creeping about'. It's a holiday rental. I'm here on my own. I was just heading out for a walk along the shore."

"On your own?" Tammi-Jo seized on the remark, though even she knew she was clutching at straws. "That's a bit weird, isn't it?"

"Not really. I like my own company," the prisoner replied. He shifted his weight from one foot to the other and fidgeted his hands behind his back. "Although... If you fancied joining me for a walk, I'm told it's really nice."

"Oh, for God's sake," Logan muttered. "Uncuff him. Let

him go. Sorry for the inconvenience, sir. Genuine mistake. I'm sure you appreciate that these things happen."

"Uh, yeah. I'm sure they do. It's fine," he said. "Fun story to tell when I'm back home."

He waited until Tammi-Jo had removed the handcuffs, then rubbed his wrists where the metal had been cutting into them.

"I, eh, I mean it, though," he said, blushing a little. He came across as the kind of guy who'd have no problem asking a woman out, but the two male detectives watching on were making things a bit more awkward. "The walk's supposed to be amazing. If you wanted to come with me, I could wait until you're—"

"Jog on, son," Logan said, pointing back the way they'd come just a few minutes before.

The wrongly accused man looked a bit crushed, but then nodded and started to walk away. He only made it a few steps before he turned back.

"Eh, sorry. Just checking. Am I unarrested now?"

Logan frowned. "What?"

"She arrested me. Do I need to be unarrested or anything? Is there, like, an official thing you need to say? Or can I just go?"

"You can just go," Tammi-Jo said, now desperate to be rid of him. The longer he hung about, the more humiliating the whole thing was.

"Right. OK. If you change your mind about that walk..."

She *shooed* him away. Then, with skelping red cheeks, she turned back to face the music.

"I'm really sorry, sir," she said. "I thought it was him. The other guy must have given me the slip."

Logan drew in a breath so deep it made his nostrils flare all the way open. For a moment, it looked like he was about to deliver a bollocking, but then he exhaled, and the threat evaporated.

"It happens. And I lost the pair of you, so I'm not one to talk.

We didn't get the guy, but it could've gone a lot worse," he said. "Nobody's hurt."

"I got kicked in the chest, boss," Tyler reminded him.

"Well, aye, but we expect that sort of thing with you," Logan replied. "With your track record, you're lucky it was just a guy that kicked you and no' a horse."

Tyler conceded this with a nod. "Fair point, boss, aye."

"Are you alright?" DC Swanney asked, grateful for the opportunity to move on from her cock-up. "Do you need to go get checked out or anything?"

"Nah. I'm fine," Tyler said.

"What you'll discover, Detective Constable, is that Tyler here is a bit like a rubber ball," Logan explained. "You can bounce him off anything, and anything off him, and he somehow emerges more or less unscathed."

Tyler grinned. "Aye. I mean, mentally, I'm in absolute ruins. I still have nightmares about that train. And that high speed crash. And that time I was hit by a car."

"And that big dug," Logan reminded him.

"God. Aye. Don't remind me about the big dog, boss," Tyler said. "That thing nearly chewed my arse off."

Tammi-Jo found herself laughing along with them, her own embarrassment fading.

"So, you see why we think he's pretty much indestructible at this point," Logan said, once Tyler had finished rattling off his list of catastrophes. "And why you're not alone in making the odd error of judgement."

"I suppose not, sir," DC Swanney said. "Thank you, sir."

"No need for that," Logan told her. Then, with a nod towards the house, he got back to business. "Anyone find anything?"

"What, apart from a middle-aged man in a cupboard, boss? Not really, no," Tyler said. The memory of the bedside cabinet propelled itself to the forefront of his mind. "Just..."

He stopped then, and grimaced, realising that he'd caught himself just a moment too late.

Logan turned to him, an eyebrow raised.

"Just what?"

"Eh, nothing, boss. Nothing really."

"Which is it? Nothing really, or nothing?" Logan asked.

Tyler's shoes creaked as he redistributed his weight. He avoided Tammi-Jo's eye, but didn't quite manage to meet Logan's either. Instead, he stared past them, scratching the back of his head.

"Just... It wasn't much. Just, in the bedroom, I found a thing."

"A thing?"

"Aye, boss."

"What kind of thing?"

Tyler's throat suddenly felt quite dry. "Like a... Like a lady's thing, boss. You know, like a thing for ladies."

"No, Tyler, I don't know," Logan said. "What the hell are you on about?"

"Was it hair straighteners?" Tammi-Jo asked.

"What? No." Tyler shook his head. He wished it had been hair straighteners. He wouldn't have any problem telling them he'd found hair straighteners. "It's more of a... private lady's thing. Literally. For, you know, ladies' privates."

"Tampons?" Tammi-Jo asked. She frowned. "What's a woman that age doing with tampons? That *is* suspicious."

Tyler shook his head again. There was a weariness to it, as he finally accepted his fate.

"It was a sex toy," he said, blurting out the words. He made two letter Cs with his thumbs and forefingers, pressed them together at the tips, then pulled them apart a few inches while making a noise like a slide whistle.

He considered the size of the imaginary phallus he'd created in the air, then brought his hands a little closer together again.

"Wait, no. It wasn't that big."

"A dildo?" DC Swanney cried. It was so shrill and piercing a shout that Logan and Tyler found themselves looking around to make sure nobody was standing within earshot.

"Alright, keep it down, Detective Constable," Logan said.

Tammi-Jo looked momentarily confused, then her eyes widened in horror when she realised she must've said the words out loud.

"Sorry, sir. Just... I'm shocked."

"Not half as bloody shocked as I was," Tyler said, and he shuddered again at the thought of it. He looked up at Logan, his expression both haunted, and tormented by questions. "Do people still do that sort of thing at that age?"

"What are you asking me for? How the hell should I know?" Logan replied.

"Sorry, boss. No offence. I just thought, you know, you're a bit older..."

"I'm no' in my bloody eighties!"

Logan's protests were cut short when he realised someone was shouting in the middle distance. The other detectives noticed it, too, and they all looked around to try and find the source of the sound.

"Aye, aye, boss. Ten o'clock," Tyler said.

Logan turned to his left, but saw nothing. Tyler pointed off to the right, across the grass, to where a portly man in a shapeless grey vest was marching towards them.

"How's that ten o'clock for anyone?" Logan muttered, but Tyler just shot him a confused grin, like he had absolutely no idea what the DCI was on about.

The man who had been charging across the grass stopped when the detectives all turned to look at him. He seemed to have come from one of the houses a little further up the street, across the other side of the grass, facing onto Granny Hall's row.

He was shouting. Ranting, in fact, judging by the way he

was waving a clenched fist. The wind blowing up from the sea made it hard to tell exactly what the rant was about, but a few key words managed to slip through.

"Did he...? Did he just tell us to piss off, boss?" Tyler asked.

"Aye. Aye, I think he might've done." Logan rolled his shoulders, flexed his fingers, and nodded. "So, I think maybe the cheeky bastard and I should have a wee word..."

CHAPTER SEVENTEEN

"HAVE NO FEAR, DAVE IS HERE!"

Constable Dave Davidson sat in his chair in the open door-way, hands raised like a messiah greeting his flock. He remained there like that, grinning broadly, then grimaced when the doors he had flung open so dramatically came swinging back towards him.

"Fuck."

There was a clatter and a thump, and Dave's big entrance became marred by the fact he was now wedged between both doors.

Hamza and Ben, who were both sitting at their desks, drinking yet another cup of tea, watched him impassively.

"Need a hand there, Dave?" Hamza asked.

"No. No, I've got it," the constable insisted.

He elbowed one of the doors, shouldered the other, then gave them both as big a shove as he could before frantically wheeling himself through the already narrowing opening and into the room beyond.

"There we go," he announced, slightly breathlessly. "How's it going? You caught them yet?"

"Not yet, no," Ben told him.

"Thank Christ for that. Right waste of a drive that would've been." He pointed to a large desk that stood apart from the others. There was a lockable cabinet beside it, just right for storing the exhibits. "This me?"

"Aye, if you like," Ben said. His gaze went to the doors, which had now settled back into place. "Haven't you forgotten someone?"

"Nidds? I mean, Bea? I mean, *Constable Niddrie?*" Dave began wheeling himself over to his desk. "She's away for a pish."

"Oh," Ben said, suddenly wishing he hadn't asked.

"She's got the bladder of a child. Had to stop twice on the way up here."

"That might just have been your driving," said Hamza, who'd had the misfortune of being driven around in Dave's car before.

"Ha! Aye, might've been that, right enough," the constable agreed. "She *was* usually screaming at the time..."

"Aye, and no wonder!"

The three men turned to see one of the doors standing half open again. A constable in her early thirties stood there, decked out in her full uniform, with her hat held under one arm.

There was nothing particularly remarkable about her— average height, average build, with a sort of dirty blonde hair that stopped just above shoulder level. Her only real defining feature was the galaxy of freckles that covered most of her face.

"Talk of the devil," Dave said, and neither of the other two detectives failed to note how he straightened in his chair when he realised she was there. "Detective Inspector Forde, Detective Sergeant Khaled, meet Constable Beatrice Niddrie." He shrugged. "Or Nidds, depending on who you ask."

Ben and Hamza rose from their chairs and approached the new arrival.

"Ah, yes. I know you," Ben said, and the constable's head

immediately turned to look at him, like some sort of laser targeting system. "You do the internal mail sometimes, don't you?"

"Sometimes, sir," Nidds confirmed. "But I wasn't always that. I was on the beat. With Dave, in fact. Before he got, you know, mangled."

Ben and Hamza both winced at the word choice, but Dave let out a snort of laughter.

"Oh. I see," Ben said. He tried to phrase his question with a little more tact than the constable had just demonstrated. "So, what happened? Was it...?" He pointed to one of his ears, and hoped this would be enough.

"No, sir. Not that. I've been deaf since I was young." She brushed her hair back to reveal a hearing implant attached to the side of her skull, then let the hair fall back in place again, hiding it from sight.

Ben cursed himself. He should've realised. If he'd been paying attention, he might've picked up just the slightest suggestion of something in her voice that would've told him her hearing development had not been a normal one.

"I see," he said. Then, though he wasn't entirely sure why, he added, "I'm very sorry."

"Not your fault, sir. Plus, I was lucky enough to have rich parents who were keen to get me fixed up."

"Right. Well, that's good," Ben said.

Although, given how she'd said it, he wasn't entirely sure that was the appropriate response. He tried to lead them back onto safer ground.

"So, how come you're not public facing now?" he asked.

The constable adjusted her hat beneath her arm. "It was... Uh, a temper issue, sir. I lost mine while dealing with a suspect."

"I'm sure we've all been there," Hamza said, and Nidds jerked her head around to stare at him before he'd made it past the first few words.

"On six separate occasions," she added. Her nose furrowed up and her mouth went small, then she shrugged. "Technically seven, but one was the same guy twice."

"Oh," said Hamza.

He looked to Ben, hoping he would have something to add, but all the DI could say was, "Right."

"I had to go to a panel. Two, actually. Disciplinary and medical," Nidds continued. She smiled broadly. "Anyway, long story short, they don't let me out to play with people these days. So, it's nice to get out and about." She fired Dave a sideways look. "Even with his driving."

"*Especially* with my driving," Dave corrected.

Nidds smirked, then turned her attention back to the detectives. "So, uh, sirs. I'm told you need my help with something?"

"Aye. Aye, that's right," Ben said. "You need a wee break after that journey?"

Nidds shook her head. "No, sir. Ready when you are."

"Right. OK, then," Ben gave Hamza a nod, and the DS reached for his coat. "No time like the present, I suppose."

Sinead stood by the window of the Incident Room, looking out over the car park, across the dual carriageway, and towards Inverness City Centre. The evening was rolling relentlessly towards nighttime, and the lights of cars and buildings blurred in the raindrops on the glass.

She noticed none of it. Instead, she gripped the windowsill until her knuckles went white, ran through a few of the more obvious breathing techniques, and waited for the discomfort to pass.

That was all it was, she told herself. Not pain. Just discomfort. Just things getting ready so nature could take its course.

Not today, though. Not a chance. Not without Tyler here. Nature could keep holding its bloody horses.

Once everything had settled down, she peered down through the rain to the car park. The Uniform who'd delivered the files she'd asked for stood out there in his hi-vis rain jacket, shuffling impatiently while Taggart sniffed around the patch of grass up near the road's end.

She felt a pang of guilt, but then considered the effort that would've been involved in her taking the dog out herself, and immediately felt absolutely fine about it.

Turning away from the window, she waddled over to her desk and, with some difficulty, lowered herself into her chair.

The stack of information she'd requested lay piled on her desk. The Scene of Crime report was in there. Preliminary findings, anyway. The full report would take longer, depending on what tests they had to run.

There were other documents in the pile along with the report. Birth certificates. Marriage, too. There were two of those for Albert, in fact, one from the early seventies, the other from eight years later.

Sinead flicked through the rest of the pile, but found nothing to indicate how the first marriage had ended. She made a note of it, set those documents aside, and moved on.

There were a few old newspaper stories about the couple that looked like they'd been printed off from one of the local weeklies' websites. One was about them giving five grand to a children's charity. There was no date on the article, but the couple looked to be in their late sixties at the time.

Another article was about Greta Hall being the millionth customer of one of the supermarkets in Wick. There wasn't much of a story, just a caption below a big picture of Greta looking bewildered as a grinning man in an ill-fitting suit presented her with a bottle of champagne, and two staff members in uniform shared the responsibility of handing over a big bunch of flowers.

The other cutting was more interesting. It was a request for anyone who'd seen Greta and Albert's downstairs windows being smashed to get in touch with the police. This story had a date on it. February the third. Two years ago, give or take a couple of weeks.

She noted the date and investigating officer named in the article, returned the printout to the pile, and booted up her laptop.

While she waited for the login screen to load, something else in the stack of documents caught her eye. It was sticking out from the folder containing Geoff Palmer's report, just one corner visible where it hadn't lined up with the rest of the paperwork properly.

There were numbers on it. A bank statement, she realised.

While the laptop chimed to announce it was all fired up and raring to go, Sinead dug her fingers into the pile, and slid out the Scene of Crime folder.

She opened it to the bank statement.

She stared down at the numbers.

A whistle slipped out through her teeth.

"Ho-lee shit," she mumbled.

And then, she reached for the phone.

CHAPTER EIGHTEEN

THE MAN who'd ranted at the detectives from across the grass had not lost much of his indignation when Logan had flashed his police ID. There had been no immediate apology, or even a de-escalation of hostilities. Instead, the man had swollen himself up like a human pufferfish, and made a show of standing his ground.

He was in his fifties, though it was hard to say which end he was closest to. His hairline had beat a retreat to the very top of his head, but his bushy black eyebrows were doing their best to compensate, and to draw attention away from the sheer abundance of his forehead.

His natural skin colour was the same deathly pale shade of white as most people's in the far north of Scotland, but it was coloured with patches of red, like he'd been going at it with sandpaper. This also wasn't a particularly unusual look up here, given how brutal the wind could be, but his seemed worse than most.

The bulb of his nose was the same reddish colour, and pitted with blackheads. It was the sort of nose Logan had encountered in pubs and back alleys the length and breadth of the country, and which had been an everyday sight back in his own heavy drinking days. Sometimes in the mirror.

"Correct me if I'm wrong, sir, but it sounded a lot like you shouted at us to, 'Piss off,' a moment ago," Logan said. "I'm assuming we misheard?"

"Oh, no, you heard right, alright! That's exactly what I said. That's exactly it!"

He grunted out the words, his breathing erratic, like he was trying to chew through a mouthful of food at the same time. His accent wasn't local. It was from somewhere south of the border. Midlands sort of area, Logan reckoned. Moneyed background.

"I didn't know you were police then, though, did I?" he continued. "Thought you were just busybodies, or worse—some bastards from the bloody tabloids!"

This last remark won the man a few brownie points in Logan's book. Anyone with such obvious disdain for the men and women of the tabloid press couldn't be *all* bad, after all.

Still, brownie points or not, he was still coming across as an insufferable, loudmouthed pain in the arse.

"Why would that bother you, Mr...?"

"Parkes. Mr Parkes." He didn't offer a first name, but he didn't have to.

"Parkes?" said Logan. "Patrick Parkes?"

The man looked taken aback for a moment, but then nodded. "Yes. That's right. How do you know that?"

"Gary Hawthorne mentioned you. Said you'd helped him get Albert home, and that you were there when he found—"

"Yes. Well, I rather wish he hadn't done that," Patrick grumbled. "That's nobody's business."

"I'm afraid it is, Mr Parkes," Logan said. He tapped himself in the centre of the chest. "It's my business. Most things round here are at the moment, in fact. Until we find out who killed Greta."

"Granny," Patrick corrected, through teeth that were just

gritted enough for the detective to notice. "Round here, we called her Granny. And, to answer your previous question, having the press snooping around would bother me because this is a close community, and a quiet village, and the last thing any of us wants is a load of well-fed Central Belt bastards coming up here looking for muck to rake up."

"About Greta and Albert?"

"About anyone!" Patrick cried. "Are we not entitled to our privacy? Can we not be against being flashed all over the front of the *Sun* or whatever shitrag decides it wants to publish our pictures on the front page?"

"Why would they want to publish your pictures?" Logan asked.

"Why do they do anything? To sell more bloody papers!"

Logan wasn't quite sure how having a portly, balding, middle-aged heavy drinker on the front cover of a newspaper would entice more readers to buy it, but he just nodded understandingly.

"So, you're police?" Patrick asked. He put his hands on his hips. They were quite wide hips, so this really pushed up his shoulders. "How is Albert doing? Have you seen him? Is he alright?"

"He's doing about as well as can be expected."

"Well, what does that even mean?" the other man cried. "I tried to get in to see him, but they won't let me." He ran his tongue around inside his mouth, like he was trying to rid himself of a bad taste. "'Family only,' they said. No one else is allowed."

"Aye. Well, they're just doing what's in his best interests," Logan reasoned.

Patrick's grunt suggested he didn't agree, but his attention shifted to other matters.

"What are those two up to?" he demanded.

He jabbed a pudgy finger past Logan to where Tyler and

Tammi-Jo were still waiting outside the front of the house for the now largely unnecessary uniformed backup to arrive.

"Nothing for you to worry about, Mr Parkes," Logan said.

"Is it about that man? The one who was snooping around at the house?"

"You saw him?"

"I did more than bloody see him. I shouted at him. Told him to piss off. Gave me quite a bloody mouthful in return, I can tell you. Language that would've made a whore blush. *Effing* this, and *effing* that. Calling me a, 'Nosy effing C,'" and all sorts. Foul stuff. Proper vile stuff."

"I see. When was this?"

"An hour ago. Thereabouts," Patrick said. "He soon cleared off when I told him I was going to call the police, though. Although, not without a few more choice words. 'You effing fat C,' he said. 'Going sticking your effing nose into other people's effing business. Proud of yourself, are you, you fat eff? Pleased with yourself, you fat, ugly, interfering effing C effing eff?'"

Patrick's lips pursed in distaste. He clutched his hands together near the top of his stomach and shook his head.

"That sort of thing."

Logan bit his lip. Something about the man's delivery, and the haunted expression on his face, was making the DCI want to laugh. Thankfully, he was able to swallow the urge back down.

"That must've been distressing. What did he do then?" Logan asked, moving the conversation on from all those 'effs' and 'Cs'.

"Well, he buggered off, didn't he?" Patrick said. "Up the street. Off he went. Hands in his pockets, head down, tail between his legs." He looked along the road in the direction the other man had gone, then tutted. "Bastard that he was."

"Could you describe him?" Logan asked.

Patrick turned back to the detective and looked him up and

down like he'd just said something ridiculous. "Describe him? Why would I need to describe him?"

"To help us identify him."

"But you saw him," Patrick said. "Not ten minutes ago."

Logan frowned. "Wait. So you're saying...?"

"The bastard must've gone round the back or something. Or snuck past when I wasn't looking," Patrick said. "But yes, the man I saw was the same man that young lady chased down the street earlier."

CHAPTER NINETEEN

"SHE WAS SCARY," whispered Nidds, as Hamza closed the door to Albert Hall's private room.

The nurse had not been pleased to see them, and had made no attempt to hide that fact. She actually seemed to revel in it, and took great pleasure in letting them know what an unwelcome inconvenience they were.

Albert, however, didn't seem to mind. Then again, he didn't appear to notice their arrival, or so much as acknowledge their existence.

Instead, he just lay there, partly propped up, the only sound in the room coming from the machines monitoring all his various life signs.

"You alright there, Mr Hall?" Hamza asked. He spoke slowly and with extra volume, and backed it all up with a warm, friendly smile. "I'm Detective Sergeant Khaled. You can call me Hamza, if you like. This is Constable Niddrie. She's going to help me ask you a few questions. Is that alright?"

Albert didn't respond. Didn't so much as twitch. If it wasn't for all the machines telling him otherwise, Hamza would've sworn the guy was dead.

He looked it, too. Not just in the fact that he was immobile, but in the way that age had taken such a toll. He still had hair, but it was so thin and transparent it looked like tiny strands of tracing paper had been dragged across his scalp.

His eyebrows, on the other hand, were thick, and wild, and completely out of control—two caterpillar generals about to go to war over the wrinkled No Man's Land of the old man's forehead.

The knuckles of his arthritic hands were swollen and bloated, and his fingernails were being steadily erased by the grey, papery skin growing over them.

"Will we take that as a yes?" Hamza asked, looking back over his shoulder at Constable Niddrie. He was surprised to see her carrying a chair, and watched as she planted it next to the foot of the bed, directly in Albert's eye line.

"Right, let's see if anyone's home," she said, planting herself in the seat. She smiled thinly up at Hamza, then motioned for him to stand back. "Better to keep it just the two of us. You might want to take notes, though, in case we get anywhere."

Hamza did as he was told, and scuttled back out of the old man's line of sight.

"This feels like we're doing a séance or something," he said. He mumbled the remark, worried that Albert might hear him, and completely forgetting that he couldn't.

Nor, for that matter, could Nidds.

"Sorry, Sarge?" she asked, aware that he'd spoken. She watched his mouth as he replied.

"Nothing. Doesn't matter. Sorry. Carry on."

Nidds nodded, then turned her attention back to the old man in the bed. Albert's expression hadn't changed, but the machines insisted he was still in the land of the living.

"OK, then," she said, speaking brightly and with an emphasis on her mouth movements. She gave the man in the bed a wave with a flat, open hand, then pointed to herself. "Hello. I'm Beatrice."

Hamza watched as her hand gestures became more complex and difficult to follow. The man in the bed continued to stare blankly through her, and didn't appear to register what was going on.

"I'm with the police," she said. She tapped an index finger to the side of her head, close to her ear. "I'm deaf. Like you," she explained, continuing to sign. "I'm so sorry about what has happened. I want to help find out what happened to..."

She hesitated.

"Greta," Hamza whispered. Then, he remembered, and said it again more clearly.

"To Greta," Nidds said, signing out the letters of the name. When it got no response from the man in the bed, she tried a different approach. "About what happened to your wife."

There was, if you used a bit of imagination, a slight decrease in the length of the gaps between the beeps from the heart monitor, but there was otherwise no response from Albert.

Nidds glanced over to Hamza. "I don't know if this is getting through to him," she said.

Hamza blew out his cheeks and scratched his head. He flipped his notebook closed like he was ready to give up, then a thought struck him.

"Granny," he said. "Everyone called her Granny."

Nidds turned back to Albert, lined herself up in his sights again, then tried again, hands moving in time with the words coming out of her mouth.

"We want to find out what happened to Granny," she said. There was no direct translation for the word in BSL, so she went with the sign for 'Grandmother'—a G and an M in quick succession.

Nothing.

No response.

"I think we might be flogging a dead horse here," Hamza said, and then a sound from the bed stopped him in his tracks.

The noise was difficult to identify. It was sort of a groan, maybe a gasp, and partly some kind of wheeze. Whatever the make-up of it, the sentiment was clear.

It was the sound of a man in pain.

"Albert? Are you OK?" Nidds asked, signing the question for him. "Does something hurt?"

Propped up in the bed, Albert's bottom lip trembled, like he was suddenly suffering the effects of the cold. His gnarled hands twitched as if slowly coming back to life.

Hamza watched in silence as the old man raised his frail arms and clumsily signed out a short response.

"Oh. Oh, Albert," Nidds whispered. She didn't sign the words, and angled her head so he couldn't read her lips.

"What? What is it?" Hamza asked. "What did he say?"

"He asked if Granny's alright now," the constable replied. "He asked if she's feeling better."

"What? Oh. Shite," Hamza said. "He doesn't know? He has to know. He saw her. He was there." He looked down at the man in the bed. "Although, the stress of it, I suppose. The shock. And at his age. Maybe... Maybe he's forgotten."

Nidds drew in a deep breath. When she spoke to Hamza, she kept a hand in front of her mouth so Albert couldn't read her lips. "I'm going to have to tell him. Amn't I? I'm going to have to tell him she's dead."

"I, eh..." Hamza grimaced. "I'm sorry. But... aye. I think you have to."

"Great." Nidds looked down at her lap, quietly composing herself.

"You OK? You sure you're alright with this?" Hamza asked. "We could try and get someone else. I could..." He clicked his fingers, perking up. "I could write it down for him."

"Bit brutal that," the constable pointed out.

Hamza shrunk an inch or two. "Yeah. Suppose it is a bit," he conceded.

"It's fine. I've got it," Nidds said.

She raised her head and met Albert's eye again. This time, there was more of a sharpness to the old man's gaze. He was looking *at* her now, not through her.

And he was waiting for her response.

"Albert," she said. She paused, for just a moment, before continuing to sign. "I'm sorry. I have some very bad news..."

CHAPTER TWENTY

IT WAS WELL after dinner time when everyone reconvened back at the police station in Wick. Nobody had taken the time to stop to eat, so pizzas were ordered in from a local takeaway. Everyone sat munching while they watched Sinead on the big screen, which made her whole briefing feel even more like a trip to the cinema.

A lot had happened at her end. She'd phoned up about some of it, and it was already stuck up on the Big Board. For the benefit of those who hadn't yet heard or had a chance to look, she was recapping the main headlines.

"So, they were minted," she said. "Greta and Albert. Proper minted. Palmer's team found a bank statement at the house showing they have..." She leaned off-screen for a moment to retrieve the scanned copy of the statement. "One point six million quid."

Tyler almost choked on a piece of pepperoni. "Jesus Christ!"

"And that's just one account," Sinead said. "The bank's confirmed there are multiple accounts, but won't give us any more details without Albert's permission."

"Where the hell did all that come from?" Logan asked. "They win the bloody lottery or something?"

"We don't know yet," Sinead told him. "Looking into it. Definitely a windfall from somewhere, though. Only income coming into the account is their pensions. And interest, of course."

"They don't live rich," Tammi-Jo said through a mouthful of her Hawaiian pizza. "Their house, I mean. It's not exactly fancy."

Logan didn't look at her, but raised an index finger like a teacher administering a telling-off. "You're eating pineapple on a pizza. You don't get to contribute anything to this conversation until you've apologised."

Tammi-Jo forced down a swallow, looking horrified. "Oh. God. I'm sorry. Is that...? I didn't..."

"He's winding you up," Ben assured her. "Ignore him. Just you enjoy your pizza." He flicked his gaze down to it in an exaggerated show of disgust. "Absolute bloody abomination though it may be."

"Don't listen to them," Sinead said. "There's nothing wrong with pineapple on pizza."

"Said the woman who was craving tuna jam," Logan said.

Sinead's eyes widened, and she shifted her gaze to a different spot on her monitor. Because of the position of her camera, her eyes on the screen didn't exactly turn on Tyler, but he got the impression that he was being glared at, all the same.

"Um, sorry." He coughed. "Might have mentioned something..."

"Anyway," Logan said, cutting in before any arguments or spontaneous divorce proceedings had a chance to kick off. "They're rich. That's interesting. Potential motive there somewhere. Do we know if people knew?"

Nobody in the meeting had anything to say on that, so

Logan pointed to Tyler with his pen. "Get onto that constable who lives next door to them when we're done. See if she knew."

"Will do, boss," Tyler said. He wiped his hands on his trousers to get the grease off, then made a note on the lid of his pizza box.

"And the carer," Logan said, remembering one of his conversations from earlier. "Gary Hawthorne, the guy who called it in. His wife was Granny's carer. She'd be a prime candidate for knowing."

"Want me to talk to her, too, boss?"

Logan considered this, then shook his head. "No. I want to talk to her myself for a bit of background. I'll bring it up then."

"Someone definitely knows," Sinead said, and everyone turned back to the screen. "There were a few different prints on the statement that Scene of Crime hasn't been able to identify. Someone had touched it. Someone who wasn't Greta or Albert, I mean."

"The bank, maybe?" Ben guessed. "When they were putting the letter in the envelope?"

Hamza shook his head. "Doubt it, sir. All automated now, isn't it? Don't think they've got actual people folding the letters and licking the stamps."

"Well, no, because you don't lick stamps these days, son. Keep up," Ben said, then he rocked back in his chair a little, enjoying the feeling of knowing something about the modern world that DS Khaled apparently did not.

Hamza chose to gloss over the fact that the DI had completely missed the point he was making, and just conceded with a nod. "Got me there, sir."

Ben smiled magnanimously, while simultaneously interlocking his fingers behind his head, so he was giving off quite a mixed message, body-language-wise.

"Happens to the best of us, son," he said. "Happens to the best of us."

"Anything else, Sinead?" Logan asked, cutting Ben's moment of glory short.

"Yes, actually. Couple of things. Firstly, turns out Albert's been married before. Nine years before he married Greta. Well, eight and a bit."

Ben returned all four legs of his chair to the floor. "What happened?" he asked.

"Don't know yet. Got Uniform trying to get hold of the Registrar to see what we can find. Can't see anything about a divorce, though. Looked for the ex on HOLMES, but couldn't find anything."

"You do a Google search for her?" asked Hamza.

The moment of hesitation from Sinead did the answering for her. She knew it, too.

"Sorry. Should've done that, too," she admitted. "I'll do it after the call. It's just been... It's been a day."

Tyler stopped chewing on his slice of pizza. "You alright?" he mumbled, the words having to find a way to fight past the food.

"I'm fine," Sinead assured him. "It's just been busy."

"Nothing's happening on the baby front, is it?" Tyler asked.

This time, Sinead was conscious not to hesitate. "No," she insisted. "Nothing like that."

"I can send him back down the road," said Logan.

"No, sir. You're short-handed."

"We'll be fine," Logan said. "If anything, you'd be doing me a bloody favour."

"Cheers for that, boss."

Sinead smiled, and even though it was artificially blown up to several times its actual size, it seemed real enough.

"Honestly, I'm fine. If anything starts, I'll get right on you. You'll hear about it. Believe me, you'll hear about it!"

"Aye, but are you sure? Like, are you *sure* sure that nothing's—"

Tammi-Jo interrupted before Tyler could protest any further.

"I mean, I'd imagine if anyone would know, it would be her," the new DC pointed out. "I've never been through it myself, but I'd imagine I'd have a pretty good sense of whether something the size of a melon was about to come shooting out of my vagina or not."

"Two melons," Tyler corrected, with perhaps just a smidge too much gleeful enthusiasm for Sinead's liking.

Tammi-Jo winced, but at least made an effort to quickly disguise it. "Even more so, then. If that was going to happen, I'd be the first to know about it." She looked directly at the camera fixed above the smart screen, and offered a supportive smile. "Right?"

"Right. Yes. Exactly. Thank you," Sinead said. It must've come out sounding a little more curt than she'd intended, because she followed it up with a smile of her own. "You'd hear me shouting about it from here. So, I'm fine. I'll look up the ex-wife's name after we're done here, and I'll get back to you with anything I find. It was back in the seventies, though, so I wouldn't hold out too much hope."

"Aye. Understood," Logan said. "What else do you have for us?"

The only other noteworthy development from Sinead's end had also come from Palmer's team. Knowing it would take a while to get the phone network to hand over their records, one of the SOC bods had made note of the incoming and outgoing numbers on the Hall's house phone, and on the large-screened, giant-buttoned mobile that they'd taken from the cabinet on Greta's side of the bed.

The mention of bedside cabinets made Tyler's top lip crease in distaste, but the thought of the bright green phallus he'd found wasn't enough to stop him reaching for a handful of the chips that had come with his pizza.

"And?" Logan prompted. Sinead wouldn't have brought it up if there wasn't something to report.

"She made two calls to the same number the night she died, both from the mobile. One for about an hour at half-seven, the other about forty-five minutes later. That one just lasted a few minutes."

"We know who the calls were to?" Hamza asked.

"We do," Sinead said. "Friend of hers in the village. Similar age. A..." She checked her notes. "Lois Dunlop. I was going to give her a ring and arrange for one of you to go chat with her."

Logan glanced around to make sure somebody was writing that down, then turned his attention back to the screen.

"Aye. Grand. Let us know what she says," he replied. "Any incoming calls?"

"Not sure yet, sir. That information hasn't come through from the network yet."

"Chase it up," Logan instructed. "Ask Mitchell to put some pressure on."

"She's, uh, she's not here, sir."

Logan checked his watch and sighed. "No. I bet she isn't. Leave it 'til the morning, then. Ask her to get on it when she gets in."

"She's, uh, she's gone away, sir. To Glasgow. Urgent business, by the sounds of things."

Logan groaned. "Heather."

"She didn't say. But... Yeah. I'd reckon so."

"Great." The DCI's sigh practically filled the room. "Right, well, whenever you get the list of incoming, fire it over to the shared inbox."

"Will do, sir."

"Speaking of the inbox," said Ben. "Preliminary report's in from Shona, I see."

"Is it?" Logan frowned. "She didn't let me know."

"Well, it's there," Ben assured him. "I haven't had a chance to read through all of it yet, but she was definitely strangled. Shona reckons maybe a dressing gown cord. She gave Palmer some fibres he's looking at now."

"There were dressing gowns in the house," Tyler said. "In the bedroom. Hanging up on the cupboard door."

It suddenly occurred to him that he hadn't shared his big news with his wife.

"A guy jumped out at me," he said.

Sinead frowned. "A guy jumped out at you?"

"Out of a cupboard, aye," Tyler said. "In the victim's house."

"What was he doing in the cupboard?"

Tyler shrugged. "Dunno. He didn't hang around long enough to say."

"He got away?"

"Aye," Tyler said. Then, worried this might reflect badly on him, he added, "From all of us, like, not just me. And then, DC Swanney went and—"

"*At-at-at-at-at-at-at!*" Tammi-Jo interrupted, drowning him out. "Let's not get into what DC Swanney may or may not have done. I'm not the one he pushed over."

Tyler smirked. "Aye, well, I'm not the one who arrested the wrong guy, so..."

She laughed, just a little, then flicked him the V-sign.

Tyler placed a hand on his chest in mock horror, but before he could respond, Logan very quietly but deliberately cleared his throat.

On-screen, Sinead said nothing.

"Eh, sorry," Tyler said, though it wasn't immediately clear who he was apologising to. He clasped his hands together on the desk and turned to Ben, suddenly appearing very interested in what the detective inspector had to say. "So, the pathology report. You were saying?"

"It's in there for you all to read," Ben said. "But two things jumped out."

"Was one a man in a cupboard?" asked Hamza, but a stern look from Logan warned everyone to stay on track.

"No. She had cancer. Greta. Lungs and liver. Nothing on her medical notes about it. She wasn't getting treatment. As far as we're aware, she didn't even know," Ben explained. "Although, it was pretty advanced, so she would've known something was wrong."

Tyler nodded sagely. "Aye. You do. You just sort of know."

Everyone in the room, including his wife on the screen, turned to look at him.

"What are you talking about?" Logan asked. "You didn't know you had it until the hospital told you."

"You had cancer?" Tammi-Jo asked.

Tyler nodded. "Aye. I did."

The new DC put a hand on her chest, but with a sincerity that had been missing when Tyler had made the same gesture a few moments before.

"Oh, I'm so sorry. I didn't know."

"I don't really talk about it much," Tyler said.

"Aye, just you keep telling yourself that, son," Logan said.

Tyler ignored the jibe. "But, it's not quite true, boss, that I didn't know. I mean, I didn't *know* know, obviously. But, I had a sense of it. Know what I mean? I mean, on the one hand, I had no idea. Absolutely no clue whatsoever. *But,* on the other, looking back, I had this sort of, you know, like... Like a premonition about it."

"Did you hell," Logan countered. "Unless that ball you had removed was a crystal one, you're talking out your arse, son. You had no idea."

"The point is," Ben said, cutting in, "that she'd have known. The husband, too, almost certainly. The stage she was at, there'd be signs. Coughing up blood. Abdominal pain. That sort of thing."

"A mercy killing then, maybe?" Tyler suggested. "Euthanasia, sort of thing?"

Hamza frowned. "What, battering her face off a table then throttling her to death? Doesn't exactly scream 'mercy,' does it?"

"No," agreed Ben. "I'd be surprised if that's how they go about it at Dignitas."

"I think a mercy killing's unlikely," Logan said. "I'd say not to rule it out, though, if it wasn't for the state of the husband. I doubt the poor old bugger can pull his laces tight enough to keep his shoes on these days. No way he had the strength to strangle her, whether he had a motive to do it or not."

Hamza sat forwards in his chair. "Speaking of the old man, sir. Constable Niddrie and I went to the hospital and—"

"Eh, whoa, whoa. Hold your horses there, folks," Ben said, raising his voice and his hands to draw everyone's attention. "Let's not move on quite yet. I've no' had a chance to do the big reveal. You've no' heard the really interesting news. You're going to want to pin back your ears and brace yourselves for this one."

"Is it the caesarean scar, boss?" Tyler asked.

At the other end of the room, Ben's face fell. "Oh, well, thanks a bunch, son. Thank you very much. Really blew my big moment there."

Tyler smiled sheepishly. "Sorry, boss." He indicated his laptop screen. "I was just scanning through the report."

"Caesarean scar?" Logan asked. "What, you mean...?"

"Aye. She'd had a baby," Ben confirmed. He held a hand up to Tyler, as if to stop him talking. "And no, not recently, before you ask."

"I wasn't going to ask that!" the DC protested. "It says in the report that the scar's an old one."

"Aye," Ben said. He gave Tyler a moment of grace, in case he should have anything to follow up with. It appeared that he did not. "And she's in her eighties."

"Oh, aye. Aye, and that," Tyler said, and he almost managed

to bluff his way through the fact that this had clearly not occurred to him.

"But aye, you're right," Ben continued. "It says in the report that the scar's old. No saying how old, though."

Logan looked to the screen, where Sinead appeared to be just as surprised as any of them. "Take it this is news to you?" he asked.

"Um, yes, sir. Sorry," she said, her eyebrows all but bumping together above the bridge of her nose. "I haven't seen anything about that. I'll dig into it, though."

Logan checked his watch again, then shook his head. "Give it to the Uniform dealing with the Registrar's office, then away and get home for the night."

"I don't mind carrying on a bit longer," Sinead said.

"Aye, well, I do," Logan said. "You need to get your rest while you can. And I'm sending your lesser half back to you."

"Honestly, I'm fine. You need him there," Sinead insisted.

"It's not up for discussion," Logan said. "See how you're doing in the morning. If you're alright, and you want him out from under your feet, send him back. If you need to hang onto him, do that. Somehow, I'm sure we'll find a way to struggle through without him."

It didn't go unnoticed by Logan that Sinead didn't look particularly delighted by the prospect of having her husband home, but she fixed on a smile and thanked him, all the same.

"Should, eh, should I shoot off then, boss?" Tyler asked. "Long drive down the road, and that. Some of us don't get to zip around in helicopters."

Logan thought back to the last time Tyler had been in a helicopter. "I'm sure it can be arranged," he said.

Tyler's face paled. He shook his head with near super-human levels of conviction. "You're alright, boss. I'll just drive it. It's not that bad."

"Whatever you think yourself, son," Logan said. "You could

maybe give that constable a lift back down the road when you're going. Dave's mate."

He looked around the room, realising for the first time that neither of the uniformed constables was present. Given that there was a whack of pizza on the go, this was highly unusual for Dave.

"Where the hell is she, anyway?"

CHAPTER TWENTY-ONE

NIDDS SAT on a low wall out the front of the police station, swirling a chip around in a blob of salad cream. She was deep in thought, and as the chip squeaked along the bottom of the Styrofoam tray, it sounded like the cogs of her brain slowly turning.

"I don't think I will, no," she said, then she popped the hot chip in her mouth and bounced it around on her tongue to stop it burning her.

Dave had hoisted himself out of his chair so he sat on the bench beside her. The rain was off, but the cold had stuck around. They'd grabbed an old blanket from Dave's car, and wrapped it across them both as they ate.

"You should. School reunion. Do you not want to see what everyone's up to?" he said, reaching into the tray and taking one of the chips for himself. He was careful to take one at the opposite end of the tray to the salad cream.

Or, as he'd dubbed it, the Devil's Spunk.

Nidds wrinkled up her nose. "Aye, but they were all arseholes in school. Why would they be any different now?"

Dave shrugged. "People change, don't they?"

Nidds shot him a sideways look. This close, and with so

little background noise, she didn't have to look at him to follow what he was saying. Her implants did most of the work for her.

"We've known each other, like, ten years. Have we changed?"

Dave laughed. "Aye, proper people, I mean. They change." He shrugged his broad shoulders. "Anyway, we don't need to change. We're ace."

Nidds picked up her can of *Coke Zero* and raised a toast to that remark.

"We are," she agreed. "Though, mostly me."

Dave laughed again, louder this time. "Obviously."

"But a bit you," Nidds finished. She took a drink. "Did you go to yours?"

"Did I fuck," Dave said.

Nidds nodded sagely. "Everyone in your school an arsehole, too?"

Dave fidgeted under the blanket, adjusting his seating position. "No. No, they were fine. Had some good mates."

"Why didn't you go, then?"

Dave shrugged. "Didn't fancy it."

"Well, obviously, or you'd have gone. But how come you didn't fancy it?"

"I just didn't," Dave said, and there was a harshness to it that he immediately regretted.

Nidds pulled a face at him. "Alright, alright. Keep your hair on. I was only asking."

Dave watched as she plucked another chip from the tray and swirled it in the sauce. Chips and salad cream should've been a red flag. It should've scared him off.

And yet...

"I didn't want them to see me," he admitted. He shifted position again, like the weight of the confession was pressing down on him. "Like this, I mean. In the chair. I didn't want them to see me as I am."

"What? An absolute legend?" Nidds said. She shook her head at him. "Fanny."

Dave blinked a couple of times, then chuckled. "Aye. Probably."

"What were they going to say? 'You're in a wheelchair'? Did you not know that yourself, like? What were they going to do, make you *more* paralysed?"

"Ha. No. Suppose not," Dave conceded. "I just... I suppose I didn't want them feeling sorry for me, you know? Like, I didn't want that to be the big topic of discussion on the night. 'You see Dave? Poor guy. He's got a disability now.' I couldn't have been doing with that."

"Here. Nothing wrong with having a disability," Nidds replied. "Disabilities are very in right now."

"True," Dave conceded. He took another chip, blew on it, then shoved it in his mouth.

They sat there in silence for a little longer, dunking and avoiding dunking their chips in equal measure.

"I probably will end up going to mine," Nidds announced. "I've just got this feeling that I won't be able to avoid it."

With the rain off, the sky had cleared a bit. The lights of Wick lit up the east, but things were darker out west, and they saw glimpses of stars through the gaps in the clouds.

"You know what it feels like?" Nidds continued, her gaze fixed on the sky. "The reunion, I mean. You know what it feels like?"

"A massive pain in the arse?"

"Jaws."

Dave turned away from the stars long enough to frown at her. "Eh?"

"It's like Jaws. The reunion. It's somewhere out there now, swimming about, an eating machine. And I'm Roy Scheider. The Sheriff, you know? Sheriff Brody."

Dave nodded to confirm that he understood that part, but

his expression suggested he was struggling to keep with the analogy as a whole.

"Right now, I'm here on land. This is Amity Island."

"This bench?"

"No. This... time period. This moment," Nidds said.

Dave nodded. "Gotcha," he said, though he didn't really.

"Here, I'm safe. But that doesn't matter, because the warning signs are there, and I know he's out there somewhere. Out there in the water. Swimming about."

"The reunion shark?" Dave asked.

Nidds nodded. "The reunion shark. With his big teeth, and cold, black eyes. I know that he's waiting for me out there. I know I have to face him. I know that it's inevitable."

"You know that he ate a bunch of kids..." Dave added.

Nidds grinned and nudged him with her elbow. "I know that I'm going to end up going out there to face him. Because I have to, don't I?"

"Probably."

Nidds turned to look at him. "You know what else I know?"

Their faces were quite close together now. The clouds of their breath in the cold evening air entwined, becoming one.

"What?" Dave asked, and he winced on the inside when he heard the squeak in his voice.

"That sooner or later," Nidds murmured, leaning in just a little closer. "Somewhere down the line..." Their eyes met. The smell of chips encircled their heads like a wreath. "We're going to need a bigger boat."

"What do you need a boat for?"

Both constables leaned apart and sat up straight when Tyler appeared from the station entrance. He had his jacket on, and his hands buried deep in his pockets to fend off the cold.

"You going fishing or something?" he asked, apparently completely oblivious to the moment he'd just interrupted.

Constable Niddrie brushed her hair back over her ear. It

signalled some mental change in her, as she switched back into full professional mode.

"School reunion. Long story," she said. She held up the Styrofoam tray, half wrapped in its greasy white paper. "You, eh, you want a chip?"

Tyler patted his stomach. "No, you're alright, thanks. I've just packed away half a bag. And a twelve-inch pizza." He thought for a moment, then reached for the chips. "Mind you, it's quite a long drive. I'll take a couple for the road."

"You heading off, are you? Drive safe," Dave said, keen for the DC to piss off again.

"Aye. I've to take you with me," he told Nidds. He adopted a commanding sort of tone that didn't suit him in the slightest. "Your work here is done!"

"Oh. Right. Uh... fair enough."

Nidds didn't look at Dave. She couldn't bring herself to. Instead, she placed the chip tray down on his lap, then slid out from under the blanket.

"I've, eh, I've got a bag in the station," she said. "I thought I might be staying for..."

Tyler raised an eyebrow, smirked, and held up her hold-all like he was presenting some sort of gift from the gods. "Thought I'd save you a trip," he said.

"Right. Well... right. Um... thanks," she said, taking the bag from him.

She did turn to Dave then. He didn't look particularly happy, but he returned the smile she fired his way.

Nidds pointed down at him and winked. "Just when you thought it was safe to go back in the water," she said.

Dave nodded. "Aye. Just when you thought it was safe," he agreed.

Then, as Nidds and Tyler headed for the DC's car, he picked up a chip from the wrong side of the tray, stuck it in his mouth, and then immediately spat it back out again.

"Bloody Devil's Spunk," he mumbled, but his smile only broadened further. "How the hell does she like that stuff?"

Dave arrived back in the Incident Room in time to hear Hamza's retelling of everything Nidds had learned from the old man in the hospital. The screen that Sinead had been on was now just a glowing white panel, and provided the only light in the otherwise darkened room.

Albert, Hamza said, had been reasonably talkative, once he got going, though his arthritis made some of the more intricate signing difficult. Nidds had been patient with him, though, and together they'd found ways for him to get across everything he wanted to say.

He had gone to bed just after half nine. It was his usual routine. Albert was an early riser, while Granny preferred to burn the midnight oil. It had always been that way. She used to use that time to knit, or bake, or do word searches. Or, if she'd had a busy day, to re-read an old Agatha Christie novel for the umpteenth time.

In recent months, though, she hadn't the energy to do any of that, but the habit of staying up late hadn't left her, and she'd sit there watching any old rubbish on TV until her eyelids grew heavy, and she dragged herself through to her bed.

Unless she fell asleep in her chair, she always had the same sort of arrival window in the bedroom, between half twelve and one. Albert would inevitably wake up then, and his bladder wouldn't let him go back to sleep until he'd emptied it.

Last night, it was the bladder that had done the waking. It had roused him urgently from a deep slumber, and he'd shuffled through to the bathroom to relieve the building pressure before the whole system could spring an unfortunate leak.

It was only when he returned to the room that he discovered Granny's bed was empty.

Assuming she'd nodded off in the chair again, he hauled himself through to the front room, but the chair had been empty, too.

He was about to head through to the kitchen to check there, and that was when he saw it.

That was when he saw the hand.

It lay on the floor, the only part of Granny that was visible from the living room door, the rest of her hidden by the coffee table and side of the couch.

She'd fallen, he'd assumed. He'd gone to help her up, moved as quickly as his old bones would allow.

And then, he'd seen her. All of her. And though his brain was fogged by old age and the lateness of the hour, he'd known, right away, that she was gone.

"What did he do?" Logan asked. "Obviously, he couldn't call it in."

"Not easy when you're deaf, no. And he struggles with technology, between his arthritis and, well, age."

"I know that feeling," Ben muttered.

"So, he doesn't text, either. He relied on Greta to do most of his communication with the outside world."

"Why didn't he go wake a neighbour?" asked Tammi-Jo. "That's what I would've done."

"We asked him that," Hamza said. "He said he didn't want to bother anyone at that time of night."

Logan sighed. "Poor old bugger."

"As far as he knew, she'd just fallen. Or maybe had a heart attack or something. He didn't think it was foul play," Hamza said.

Ben raised an eyebrow. "And now?"

Hamza looked over at the DI, then shook his head. "I didn't feel it was the time, sir. Sorry. I, eh, I just couldn't."

Ben sniffed, and nodded. Of all the people in the room, he was the only one who didn't have to imagine what it would be like for Albert to hear that his wife had been murdered. Hamza had been the one to break the news to Ben about Alice, and the pain of that moment—the rawness of it—still surrounded them both all this time later.

"Don't worry about it, son," Ben told him. "Did you do what you felt was right?"

Hamza nodded. "I did, sir. Aye."

"Then you've got nothing to apologise for."

"Thanks," Hamza replied, and he sounded genuinely relieved. "So, anyway, he didn't want anyone seeing her like that, so he cleaned her up as best he could. Got her dressed and up in her favourite chair."

"Couldn't have been easy for him that," Ben said. "Old boy like that, dragging her dead weight."

"There wasn't much of her, to be fair," Logan said.

"He said it was hard," Hamza confirmed. "Said he wanted to give up a few times, but he couldn't. He couldn't let anyone see her there, half-dressed on the floor. So he kept going until he'd got her changed, and got her in the chair."

"What then?" Logan asked.

Despite his best efforts, Hamza couldn't hide the little crack in his voice. "And then he, just, I don't know. He just held her, he said. He just sat with her. Said they talked about things, the two of them. Things they'd done. Places they'd been. Places they never got to go. Just, you know, reminisced." The DS shrugged and tried his best to sound unaffected by the whole thing. "I mean, I'd imagine it was pretty one-sided, as conversations go. But he made it sound, I don't know. Nice. Like they were together at the end, sort of thing. Like she wasn't on her own."

Logan and Ben both sat back. Either one could've launched

into a tirade about compromising the scene, contaminating evidence, or hindering an investigation.

But they didn't. Some things, they knew—though their tightening throats wouldn't let them admit it out loud—were more important.

"That's lovely," croaked Tammi-Jo. She sniffed. "I mean, not the bit about her being dead, obviously, but the rest of it. Them being together. *Wanting* to be together like that. After all those years. Can you imagine? I can't think of anyone I'd want to spend more than, like, a month with living in the same house."

At his desk at the back of the room, Dave said nothing.

"You'd have to see their feet!" Tammi-Jo said, like this was the worst possible thing that could ever happen to anyone. Her face contorted in horror and she shook her head. "Aw. Nut. Not into that. I'd end up panning their head in with a shovel." She noticed that everyone was looking at her, and gestured to Hamza. "But, you know, your story was really nice, though."

"Did he hear anything?" Logan asked, trying to steer the conversation back onto more relevant ground. He tutted, annoyed at himself, then shook his head. "Obviously not. Did he see anything? Or, I don't know, notice anything out of the ordinary?"

"Constable Niddrie asked if anything was taken, but he didn't think so. He hadn't really checked, though. He said they didn't keep much money in the house."

"He didn't mention the millions in the bank, no?" Ben asked.

"Not a cheep, sir, no. Maybe we shouldn't have sent Constable Niddrie away yet."

Dave perked up in his chair. "We could call her back," he suggested.

Logan checked his watch. "Not tonight. I want Tyler back home with Sinead. I don't want her popping with him not there, or I'll never hear the bloody end of it from either of them."

He rose to his feet and reached for his coat. This was the cue the others needed to start packing up, and they didn't wait to be told twice.

"Normally, DC Swanney, as you're new to the team, we'd have a wee celebration down the pub. A Christening, of sorts, anointing you as one of us. But, since we're not all here, we don't know where the decent pubs are, and I'm bloody knackered, I reckon we postpone for now."

Dave, however, was quick to offer a counterargument. "Or, we could just stop at the first bar we come to and all get absolutely smashed off our tits," he suggested.

"Aye, well, your call," Logan said. "But I'm out. And we're all back here first thing, bright and early, and raring to go. Keep that in mind when you're downing your fifth jelly shot, or whatever the hell it is people do these days."

"Jägerbombs all the way!" Dave replied, which made all the features on the lower half of Logan's face bunch together in shared distaste.

"Thank Christ I'm off the drink," the DCI grunted. "I couldn't keep up with the bloody lingo."

"There's, eh, there's just one other thing, sir," Hamza said, reading something on the screen of his phone.

This drew an audible groan from Logan, as the prospect of getting to bed within the next couple of hours suddenly felt like it was in jeopardy.

"And what's that?"

"Lois Dunlop, sir."

It took Logan a moment. "The pal? The woman she phoned? What about her?"

"Sinead's emailed. She called her up like she said. Lois is happy to talk to us, but she's heading off early tomorrow morning to visit her son."

"Can she no' delay it?" Logan asked.

"Well, it's in Queensland. Australia. So, probably not, no."

Logan grunted. "Bollocks."

"Aye, boss," Hamza said. "If we want to talk to her, we're going to have to catch her tonight."

"Ugh. Bugger it. Fine," Logan said. "What's the address?"

"I could do it," Tammi-Jo suggested. She fought the urge to shrink back under the looks the others gave her. "I'd be fine. It's just talking to an old woman, isn't it? I can handle that. I'm good at talking. Talking's like my thing."

"Aye," Ben conceded. "But the point is you need to give her a chance to talk, too."

"Oh, I mean, yeah! Obviously! Course. I'm not just going to sit there rabbiting on at her at a hundred miles an hour, just *yack-yack-yacking* at her, not letting her get a word in edgeways or sideways, or whatever it is people say. No, don't you worry, sir. I'm not going to do that. Definitely not."

"You're doing it now," Logan pointed out.

"Am I?" Tammi-Jo looked around her, like she might be able to see the words hovering in the air. "Oh. Yeah. So I am. Sorry."

She managed to keep her mouth shut for all of two seconds.

"But I can do this, though. I can. Absolutely not a problem."

Logan sucked in his bottom lip, considering the suggestion. His objection, in the end, was a practical one.

"You don't have a car."

"Aye, she does," said Ben, picking up his keys from Logan's desk and holding them out to her. The detective constable beamed from ear to ear as she took them from him. "Just, you know, make notes. Be careful. And, if you need help..." He smirked as he patted Hamza on the shoulder. "Well, you've got DS Khaled's number."

CHAPTER TWENTY-TWO

TAMMI-JO SAT in Ben's car, just along the street from Lois Dunlop's house. She'd been sitting there for a few minutes now, her phone pressed to her ear. Now that the engine was off, her breath was slowly fogging up the inside of the windscreen as, outside, the rain beat a drumbeat on the metal and glass.

"No. No, I know, Dad," she said. A flicker of regret flashed across her face. "Daddy, I mean. Sorry. And no, I'm not."

She listened for a while, her head lowered, gazing down at her free hand as she picked at the skin around her thumbnail.

"I'm trying not to. I'm being careful," she said. "I think it's going OK, actually."

She listened again. Her fingernail kept working away at her thumb.

"No, I can do it. I can. I am doing it. It's going fine."

She forced herself to stop picking.

It lasted all of three seconds before she started again.

"No, I know I do. I know I can be. But I'm trying not to," she said. "And I think... I mean, it's early days, obviously, and I can't say for sure or anything, but... I think they like me."

The sharp staccato of laughter made her flinch. Her head lowered further while she endured the reply.

"OK, well, I don't think they hate me, then. How's that? Is that—"

The voice on the other end became raised and harsh. The skin around her thumbnail turned white as she shredded the top layer.

"Sorry. I wasn't shouting. No. No, I know. I know you're just looking out for me. I understand."

Tammi-Jo raised her head, but it seemed too heavy for her neck to cope with, so it immediately fell backwards so it was against the headrest.

"I know you do. I know you just worry. But they're nice. And the DCI, he said I was part of the team. He said he thought—"

She closed her eyes, then swapped the phone from one side of her head to the other before she could rip right through her nail bed.

Almost at once, she started to pick away at the other thumb.

"No, I know that. I know people can say things they don't mean. I'm in the police. That's basically everyone we meet, but I think he..."

On the other end of the line, her father spoke over her, forcing her back into silence until he decided it was her turn to speak again.

"No, I don't think I know best," she said. Her eyes opened. She lifted her head. "Although... maybe I do," she said, after pausing for a breath. "Maybe I do know what's best for me."

She bit her lip and braced herself for the response.

None came.

"Dad?" she said, before correcting herself again. "Daddy?"

Silence.

She braved it out. Stood her ground.

But not for long.

"I'm sorry, I shouldn't have said that," she told him.

Only then, did he respond. As she listened, her eyes closed again, her head rolled back, and—without even noticing she had done it—her fingernail broke the skin at the base of her thumb, drawing a droplet of blood.

"No. I won't. I won't get ahead of myself, I promise," she said. "And yes, I'm taking my tablets. I always take them. You don't need to keep... I know. I know you do, but you don't have to. I'm fine. I'm keeping on top of it."

Sitting up, she looked along the street to Lois Dunlop's house. The porch light was on, welcoming guests at even this late hour. The silhouette of the old woman herself was visible against the blinds, as she peered out into the night, no doubt impatiently awaiting the detective constable's arrival.

"But I have to go now. There's someone waiting for me." Tammi-Jo sighed, but quietly, so he wouldn't hear. "No, not a man. It's a work thing."

She listened to the response in silence. There was a lot of response to listen to, so it took some time.

Finally, with one last pick of her bloodied thumb, she said, "I know. I won't. And, I love you, too," and then quickly pressed the button that ended the call, and dropped the phone into the passenger seat beside her.

Chastising herself, she sucked the blood from her thumb until it stopped flowing. Then, she arranged her expression into one pitched midway between friendly and professional, picked up the phone she'd thrown away, and opened the door.

———

Lois Dunlop was something of a contradiction. She was seventy-eight—she'd announced this fact to Tammi-Jo almost as soon as the detective constable was in the door—but simultaneously seemed too young and too old for her age.

It was the mind that was too young. She spoke quickly, but with an air of authority like she not only knew precisely what she was doing, but that it was unequivocally the correct course of action. She appeared sharp and on the ball, with none of the fogginess or confusion someone Tammi-Jo's age might equate with the over-seventies crowd.

Or, for that matter, the over-fifties.

While the brain was firing on all cylinders, it was the body that was letting her down. She was painfully stooped, her spine curving from the centre of her back so her natural standing position would leave her staring at her own feet. This meant she was forced to angle her neck awkwardly in order to look straight ahead.

Tammi-Jo was glad she'd been the one to come out to visit the old woman, and not Logan. Unless Lois could rotate her whole head like an owl, there was no chance she'd be able to look the DCI in the face.

She walked with two sticks, each as ancient and knobbly looking as she was. They acted like extra limbs, and she moved them individually—leg, stick, leg, stick—before repeating the process all over again, so her gait was like that of a very slow-moving insect.

Lois had offered Tammi-Jo her choice of tea, lemonade, or gin, and when the DC had hesitated, the old woman had assured her that she'd be helping herself, and not, "waiting on me to drag this sorry bloody carcass around."

Tammi-Jo had settled for lemonade. Lois had said that was fine, then had informed her where to find the gin and the glasses.

When Tammi-Jo insisted she was working, and that she couldn't possibly drink alcohol, Lois realised she wasn't picking up on the hint, and the instruction became much clearer.

"Yes, but *I'm* not working, am I, dear? And I'd like a gin."

There were, it turned out, quite a range of gins to choose

from in the compact kitchen. Most of them were liqueurs, flavoured with pomegranate, or toffee, or whatever else the makers had knocking around in the pantry.

She'd settled on something red and berry flavoured, poured a generous glug into a glass with some ice, then topped it up from a bottle of flat, fizzless lemonade, as per Lois's instructions.

That done, she returned to the living room with the gin and her lemonade, and found the old woman already settled into her chair, enjoying the warmth of the fire roaring away in the hearth.

An old vinyl LP crackled away on a record player, and Lois tapped her fingers in time to the crooning of a man who was, presumably, long since dead.

"There we go, Mrs Dunlop," the detective constable said, as she carefully set both drinks down on the coffee table.

"Oh, now, let's not stand on ceremony, dear. Call me Lois." She watched appraisingly as Tammi-Jo took a seat on the couch across from her. "You're quite beautiful, you know? Those blue eyes and all those blonde curls. You're really quite striking."

Tammi-Jo swept a strand of hair back over her ear. "Uh, thanks," she said. Then, because she didn't know what else to say, she added, "You, too!"

"Oh, my backside! I'm nothing of the sort. I'm like a slice of apple left on a bloody radiator. But you... You must have men lining up around the block to take you to the dancing."

"Ha! Not quite," Tammi-Jo replied. "Not the right men, anyway."

"Ah. Well. I know that feeling," Lois replied. "I had a few belters after me, back in the day. Proper entitled they were. Thought they were God's gift. Thought they could do what they pleased to whomever they liked."

With some difficulty, she shuffled forwards in her chair and beckoned the younger woman to lean closer. Tammi-Jo did as she was told, partly humouring her, and partly because she felt a pearl of wisdom might be about to drop.

"You know what I found was the best way of dealing with them?" Lois whispered.

Tammi-Jo shook her head. "No. What?"

"The toe of a pointy shoe right up between their legs," Lois said, then she laughed so suddenly and so uproariously that Tammi-Jo jumped in fright.

This only made the old woman laugh harder, until her top teeth fell down over the bottom set, and she had to scramble to put her smile back together.

While bent forwards, she retrieved her gin from the table, raised it in a toast, then necked half the contents in one gulp.

"So, you're really with the police? Good looking girl like you?" Lois asked. "I find that hard to believe."

She sat her glass on the crooked palm of one hand, and turned it around and around with the fingers of the other hand, like she was trying to slowly drill through her own flesh and bone.

"Um, yes," Tammi-Jo confirmed.

"I bet the boys like it when you arrest them. I bet they don't object to being handcuffed," Lois said. She screwed up her face and smacked her lips together, like she'd tasted something unpalatable, but which she couldn't quite place. "Some of them like that sort of thing, don't they? Getting handcuffed and tied up, and whatnot. Slapped around."

Tammi-Jo sat with her smile fixed in place.

"Um. So I'm told."

"Getting spanked. Clamps on their nipples, things up their bums, and what have you. Some of them like all that sort of thing."

Lois sat her glass on the arm of her chair, then crossed her hands across her stomach, her expression becoming more disgusted with every word she said.

"And they like to watch their wives getting it from other men. Some of them. Some of them do. In vans, sometimes." Her face, which had been wrinkled to start with, was now so puckered with disgust that she looked like a raisin. "I mean, you can't imagine that, can you? A man, just standing there, watching his wife getting it from other men at all angles? Two, three, four of them sometimes. In a van? Touching himself, probably. While he watches them all pounding away. You can't bloody imagine it."

Thanks to Lois' description, the detective constable could, unfortunately, imagine it quite vividly.

"No. No, no. I mean, call that a man? What sort of man is that?" the old woman continued. "I'll tell you what kind. The kind that's probably rubbing himself off on all fours with a hairbrush up his back end, that's what kind."

Hands shaking, Lois picked up her gin, and polished off what was left in the glass. The dead man on the record player continued to croon.

Lois shook her head, her eyes slowly moving left and right, a frown troubling her brow.

"How the hell did we get onto talking about that?" she wondered.

"Not sure. Can't remember," Tammi-Jo said, then she railroaded the pensioner into the conversation proper. "Thanks for seeing me at such short notice. I know this must be a difficult time for you, with what happened to Greta."

"Granny. We all called her Granny," Lois said, and the horror that had been etched across her face gave way to a weary sort of sadness. "We all did. Even me. Even Albert. How is he, by the way? You know he's deaf?"

"We know that, yes," Tammi-Jo confirmed. "And he's fine. He's in the hospital getting looked over, but we think he's going to be OK."

"OK." Lois snorted and shook her head. "How can he be

OK? How could anyone be OK after something like this? Poor, poor Albert."

She let out a long, heavy sigh, then frowned as a thought hit her.

"It wasn't him, was it? He didn't kill her?"

"No. No, we don't believe so."

"Good. I mean, I didn't think for a second, but... Good." Lois nodded, satisfied, then repeated her sigh from a moment before. "Poor, poor Albert."

"He's being well looked after."

"Oh, I have no doubt, dear. No doubt. That's our NHS for you. Envy of the world. Angels, that lot. Angels, the lot of them."

"We're very lucky," Tammi-Jo agreed.

"You don't know the half of it, young thing like you. Probably barely have need for them. But you wait," Lois warned, waggling a crooked finger. "Just you wait until you're my age, and you'll be thanking God every day for them."

Tammi-Jo didn't really know what to say to that, so she just smiled instead, and opened her notebook in the hope the old woman understood.

Fortunately, unlike the detective constable herself, Lois was very quick to pick up on hints.

"You'll be wanting to know about the phone call. That other woman said so on the phone."

"That would be great, thank you. Granny called you yesterday evening, I believe. Twice. Is that right?"

"Twice?" Lois looked sceptical for a moment, before the penny dropped. "Oh. Yes. She called back to wish me well for my trip. That's what she'd phone for in the first place, but we got chatting, so she forgot."

Tammi-Jo smiled. "You were having a good chinwag, eh?"

"We were having a blether, aye. Happens every time we get on the phone. It can be for the quickest thing—something that should take just a minute or two to say—and half an hour later, we're still going."

"Sounds nice. Must be good to have a friend like that."

"Oh, it is. It is," Lois confirmed. "It is. Just someone you can pick up the phone to. Someone you can just be yourself with, you know what I mean? No airs and graces. No pretending. Just be yourself."

"That's lovely."

"It is. Oh, it is. I mean, I'm sure you've got friends like that, too, dear. Lovely girl like you."

Tammi-Jo smiled, but said nothing.

"We just talk on the phone these days, though. I don't go round much."

"Oh? That's a shame. Is that... health-related, or...?"

"Honestly? Vanity, probably. I see her, and I'm reminded about how old I'm getting. I love our chats, but when I see her, I come away feeling... I don't know. Anxious, maybe? That time's running out."

Lois fell silent for a moment, drew in a big breath, then gave herself a shake.

"Also, she's had a few stomach issues lately and, well, the house doesn't half fucking stink sometimes! Lord Almighty. It's like being under chemical attack, sometimes. You could cut slices out of it."

Tammi-Jo's smile fell, just a fraction. "Right."

"So, we stick to the phone. Safer all round," Lois told her. "That way, we have a lovely chat, and I'm not left questioning my own mortality, or trying not to be sick."

"Well... good!" said the DC, rallying well. She blurted out the next question almost as soon as it popped into her head, without bothering to couch it in niceties. "Do you know how they were doing financially?"

"Financially? What's that got to do with anything?" Lois asked.

"Eh, no. I was just..."

"They were doing about the same as any of us. Getting by. I think Albert had a decent pension—aye, from his old job, I mean —and that helped. But the price of everything's going up, isn't it? It's a struggle." Lois pursed her lips. "But that's not the sort of thing we talk about. That's their business, not mine."

"Right, yes, I see. And what was the big topic of conversation last night, if you don't mind me asking?"

Lois's defences dropped again almost immediately. "Oh, everything and anything! This, that. The other!" She laughed. "We're a right old pair of gossips when we get started. A right old couple of busybodies!"

"Haha! I bet you are!"

The old woman shot her a look. "What's that supposed to mean?"

"Oh. Um. No, I was just, you know, agreeing with..." Tammi-Jo looked down at her pad. "So, Granny didn't mention anything she was worried about or anything? Or mention... I don't know, seeing anyone around that she didn't recognise?"

Sitting in her armchair, Lois said nothing. She glanced away, and the lines on her throat bunched together as she swallowed.

"Lois? Did she say something? Was there something worrying her?"

"Well, I mean... Not worrying, exactly. But she did say that she'd had a few things go missing."

"Oh? Like what?"

"Her music box, for one."

"Music box?" Tammi-Jo thought back to the shape in the dust on the mantelpiece. "From the living room? Above the fire?"

Lois's eyebrows dipped, like she was witnessing a magic trick and couldn't quite figure out how it had been done. "Yes. That's right. How did you know that?"

"I'd just, um, seen where something wasn't. If you know what I mean?"

Lois shook her head. "Not really, no."

"What else was taken? Did she say?"

"Nothing big. Bits and bobs. Nothing that valuable. She'd have thought she'd just misplaced it—she was always doing that —if it hadn't been for the music box, which she swears she didn't touch."

"What did it look like, the music box? Do you know?"

"Yes. Lovely wooden thing. Walnut, I think. There was a little scene carved on the outside. Done by hand, I believe. So the salesman told her, anyway. And this was back in the sixties, or something, when people told the truth."

"Right. Thanks for that. But couldn't her husband have done something with it?"

"Albert?" Lois snorted. "He's deaf, dear. What would he want with a music box?"

"No. Right." Tammi-Jo scratched the centre of her forehead and looked down at her still-empty notebook page. "Not a lot, I suppose."

"If you ask me, I think it's that new lad that's taken it," Lois said, her nose threatening to crinkle up in distaste again.

"New lad?"

"Sandra's replacement. While she's been away." The look of disdain gave way to a smile. "Now, talking of NHS angels, there's one right there. I don't know what I'd do without Sandra. Granny and I were both saying that last night, actually. We were saying we wouldn't know what to do without Sandra."

"Sandra?"

"Yes. Sandra. From down the road. She pops in. Aye, but officially, I mean. She's a nurse. Or, not a nurse, exactly, but she's something," Lois explained. "Comes and sees us. Checks in." The old woman's smile became so wide that Tammi-Jo was concerned her teeth might fall out again. "*Makes sure we're behaving ourselves*, she says, and that we're not off gallivanting around the town. Can you imagine? At our age! *Behaving ourselves!*" Lois sighed happily and shook her head. "She's a gem, is Sandra. She's just a bloody gem."

"She's your carer?" the detective constable asked.

Lois shuffled around in her seat, like she wasn't comfortable with the word. "Oh no. Well, yes. But she's more than that. Much more. She's a friend. God, she's like family, that's what Granny always said. She keeps an eye on us. Any health problems, we ask her first, and she sorts it out if we need to see someone. Ask anyone round here—any of us old buggers—and we'll tell you the same thing. She's worth her weight in gold."

Tammi-Jo smiled. "She sounds like a big help."

"Oh, she is, dear. She is. We've missed her terribly these past few weeks. The new lad—the one filling in while she's been off—just isn't the same." She beckoned Tammi-Jo closer again, and lowered her voice to a whisper. "He's a man, for one thing. So you don't like to tell him too much, do you? I mean, different if he's a doctor—you don't mind with a doctor—but he's not. He's just some man."

Tammi-Jo nodded sympathetically as she brought her lemonade glass to her mouth. "I'd imagine that must take a bit of getting used to, yes."

"It does. It really does." Lois ran her finger around the inside of her glass, then licked the last few traces of gin off it. "Especially what with him being a darkie."

Tammi-Jo coughed, choking on her drink and spluttering it all down her front. "Jesus," she wheezed.

"No, no, now, don't get me wrong, dear. I'm not one of them racialists. I've nothing against the darkies. Some of them are lovely fellas. I mean, look at Johnny Mathis. *When a Child is Born*. That's a beautiful song, and I'll defend it to the death. To the bloody *death!*"

She pulled the face she'd previously reserved for men who put hair brushes up their arses.

"But you don't want them in your own house. Not poking around in your things, or your private business. Because most of them, well, they're thieves, aren't they? I hate to say it, but they are, they're bloody thieves, the lot of them. And that's not racialist, that's just a fact. You look it up."

"I'm, um, I'm sure that he isn't," Tammi-Jo replied.

"You're sure he isn't what? A darkie? He is! Black as coal, he is. Black as the bloody night sky. Can hardly understand a word he's saying, with that accent of his, neither."

"A thief," said the DC, raising her voice to stop the old woman saying anything more. "I'm sure he's not a thief."

Lois frowned in confusion. "Oh? And what makes you so sure about that?"

"What makes you so sure he is?" Tammi-Jo asked, flipping the question back at her. "Is there any evidence that he's stolen anything? Have you noticed anything missing?"

"Well, I haven't, thankfully, but where's Granny's music box, if he didn't take it?" Lois shot back.

"It could've been anyone. Or maybe it was just misplaced..."

Lois shook her head and looked over at the living room window, her liver-spotted hands wringing together, an expression of dread setting up camp on her face.

"No. He'll have been checking my place out. You mark my words. He'll have been casing the joint, knowing I'm going away. Seeing what he can get his hands on once I've left."

She took a wadded-up ball of tissue from the sleeve of her cardigan, and dabbed at her nose with it.

"I bet you'll find it was him that killed Granny, an' all, if you look into it. But, oh no, you won't, of course. Will you? You can't be seen doing that. Not in this day and age. You can't be accusing a darkie of something like that, in case everyone thinks you're a racialist. So, you'll turn a blind eye. You'll let an old woman's murderer go free because you're worried about how it might look." She shook her head, her wrinkled lips pursing. "It's disgusting what they've done to this country, that lot. It's absolutely—"

Tammi-Jo held up a hand. "Shut up, you mad racist!" she cried, then her eyes went wide and her mouth clamped itself shut, like the proverbial stable door.

Lois stared back at her, aghast. "I beg your pardon?"

"Sorry." Tammi-Jo winced. "I didn't meant to... Sometimes my inner voice just sort of..." She concluded that this explanation wasn't going to help much, and quietly cleared her throat. "What I meant to say was..."

"You told me to shut up!"

"I know. I'm sorry. It wasn't deliberate."

"What's that supposed to mean? How do you *accidentally* tell someone to shut up?" the old woman demanded. "And you called me a mad racialist."

"Racist. The word is 'racist,'" Tammi-Jo corrected, then she winced again. "That's not the point. I shouldn't have said it. I'm sorry."

There had been a real change in the temperature of the room. Despite the fire beside her, a wave of cold seemed to be radiating from the old woman.

The detective constable moved quickly to try to repair the damage.

"I assure you, Lois, we're going to do everything we can to find out who killed Granny. Whoever they may be. If you give me the details of your carer, I'll make sure he's interviewed."

Lois sat there, hunched in her chair, staring at the DC with her beady, shrunken eyes.

Then, she reached for her walking sticks.

"It's Mrs Dunlop," she said. "And I have an early start in the morning, so I think it's time you left."

The detective constable smiled apologetically. "I'm really sorry for what I said, Mrs Dunlop. I'm sorry if I offended you."

Lois tutted. "That's typical of you young ones. Always think it's all about you, don't you? Always think you're the centre of the bloody universe, with your blue eyes and your blonde hair, and your perfect fucking skin."

It took her a few attempts to get to her feet. Tammi-Jo stood and tried to help her, but was angrily shrugged off.

"I can do it. I'm not an invalid," Lois snapped.

She pointed with one of her sticks to the door, and then started picking her way forwards, using her frail, stooped body to usher Tammi-Jo out.

"I understand that you're angry with me, Mrs Dunlop," the DC said, allowing herself to be escorted across the room. "I have a... a condition. Sometimes, I say things that I don't really mean. Honestly, it wasn't my intention to—"

"Again, with the *me, me, me*," Lois barked. "It's nothing to do with you. I have a lot to do. I'm tired. It's time to go, that's all. Now, out."

Tammi-Jo let herself be guided into the hall, then opened the door and sidled out onto the top step. By the time she turned, Lois was already holding the door and doing her damnedest to block the entrance.

"Um, OK, well, thank you for your time," the DC said. She fished in a number of pockets until she found a card with her contact details. "If there's anything else you think of, please give me a call. But on the mobile. The other number's in Aberdeen, and I won't... I'm not there."

"Well, obviously you're not there. I can see that," Lois said. She didn't even look at the card to acknowledge it. "And you can hang onto that, thank you. I won't be needing it. I've told you everything I know. I've even told you who done it, but you're not interested."

"Like I said, Mrs Dunlop, we'll be sure to interview your carer if you could just give me his..."

She raced through those last few words, trying to get to the end of the sentence before the door was closed in her face.

She almost made it, too.

"...name."

She heard the *clack* of the door being locked. The porch light above her head clicked off, plunging the front step into darkness. Behind Tammi-Jo, the wind nudged the drizzle towards her until it found the back of her neck.

She sighed.

"Great work, TJ," she whispered. "You really nailed that one."

She looked down at the business card in her hand, started to pocket it, then thought better of it and posted it in through the letterbox.

And then, with one final lingering look at the door, she turned away from the house and ran, head lowered against the rain, back to her car.

———

On the other side of the door, Lois Dunlop stood with her hand still on the light switch.

The nerve of that bloody girl, coming in here, accusing her of being a racialist when nothing could be further from the truth.

It probably was him. It was probably the new lad who'd killed Granny. She wouldn't put it past him.

And yet...

There *had* been something else. Something Granny had said on the phone. Something she'd told her.

Lois had been sworn to secrecy, though. The information

had been given on the understanding that it would be held in the utmost confidence.

And yet...

What good were secrets if they cost you your life?

She opened the door and looked out, but there was no sign of the policewoman now, and so she quickly closed it again to keep the heat in.

Looking down, she saw the business card sticking out of the letterbox. She plucked it out, squinted at the numbers, then fished in her cardigan pocket until she found her mobile.

With some difficulty, she keyed in all the numbers, listened to the phone ringing, then grimaced when it went to an answering machine.

Paying little heed to the message, she waited for the inevitable beep, then spoke a single short sentence, before hanging up.

Lois stood there in the hall for a moment, fretting over what she'd done. She'd broken her best friend's confidence. She'd betrayed her trust.

But she consoled herself with the thought that, given the circumstances, she'd had no other choice.

She slipped the phone back into one pocket and the card into another. She locked the door with a *clunk*, then reached for the sticks she'd leaned against the wall.

And behind her, at the top of the stairs, a shadow moved, and a floorboard gave a low, solemn *creak*.

CHAPTER TWENTY-THREE

TO LOGAN'S IMMENSE SURPRISE, the phone was answered on its third ring. This, in recent years, was something of a record, and the sudden, "Hello," from the other end caught him on the hop.

Had she just not seen his name, maybe? It was late, so had she just grabbed her mobile and answered it without checking the screen?

"Dad?"

Apparently not, then.

"Eh, aye. Aye. Maddie. Hello. It's, uh, it's Dad."

"Aye. I know," came the reply. "That's why I said, 'Dad,' a second ago. Be a bit weird if I hadn't known."

Logan leaned back against the headboard of the hotel bed. Was she...? No. Surely not. If he didn't know better, he'd have sworn she sounded like she was smiling.

"Aye. Aye. Of course," he said. "I just... I'm surprised to hear from you."

"You called me," Maddie pointed out.

"What? Oh. No. No, I know. I just... I'm surprised you answered."

There was a pause.

"You and me both," his daughter said, and this time he was *positive* he could hear her smiling.

She was joking with him. She was *teasing* him. This felt like a seismic shift in their relationship. Like its whole structure was being rearranged around him into something new.

He had no idea what it was going to look like when it had finished transforming, but whatever the new dynamic was, it couldn't be any worse than the old one.

No doubt he had Shona to thank for it. She'd been the one to bring Logan and his daughter together for a makeshift 'peace summit' over ice cream down in Largs.

Aye, Maddie's new husband had been there, too, but he hadn't turned out to be the absolute fud of a man that Logan had built him up in his head to be. He'd been working with Shona behind the scenes to make the whole thing happen, in fact, and while Logan hadn't been impressed by all the plotting and treachery at the time, he'd quickly come around.

Something else that Dr Shona Maguire had done for him, then. Some other positive impact she'd had upon his life.

"You OK?" Maddie asked, and Logan realised he'd gone silent on her again.

"Eh, aye. Aye, I'm fine," he assured her. "How about you? You alright?"

Maddie sighed, but for once, he got the impression that it wasn't aimed at him. "Yeah. Yeah, not bad, I suppose."

"You want to try that again, but with a bit more conviction this time?"

Maddie laughed. It wasn't long or loud—barely audible at all, in fact—but Logan knew he'd hold on to the thought of it for a long time to come.

"Oh, yeah, I forgot. You're a detective. You eat bullshit for breakfast."

It was Logan's turn to laugh, though there was much more gusto behind his.

"You remember that, then?" Maddie said.

He did. It was something he'd said to her when he'd accused her of lying about something or other during her wilder teenage years. He couldn't even remember now what it had been, but he remembered wincing as he'd heard the words coming out of his mouth, and seeing the look of glee on her face.

'I'm a detective. I eat bullshit for breakfast.'

She'd used it to take the piss out of him for weeks. Months, even.

Years, as it now turned out.

"Aye, aye, very good," he told her. "You ever going to let me live that one down?"

"Absolutely not," Maddie assured him. She let out a little groan, like she couldn't believe what she was doing. "It's work. If you must know. It's just... It's stressful at the minute."

He opened his mouth to reply, but she quickly jumped in and shut him down.

"And I know, I know, it isn't dealing with murderers and kidnappers, or any of that stuff. It's not as stressful as yours."

"I wasn't going to say that."

In fact, he had been about to say more or less exactly that, so he was glad she hadn't given him the chance.

"You want to talk about it?" he asked.

Maddie thought for a moment, then replied with a pretty definitive sounding, "Nah. You're fine."

Logan sat forward long enough to plump up one of the pillows behind him, then pushed himself a little higher up the bed and kicked off his shoes. They landed on the floor with thumps so loud the people in the room below probably thought the ceiling was coming down on them.

"Aye, well, if you ever need to moan at someone..." he ventured.

"Thanks. But it's alright. That's what husbands are for," Maddie replied.

Logan still wasn't entirely used to the idea of his daughter being married. Yes, he'd met the man face-to-face, but he hadn't been invited to their wedding, so the whole thing still didn't feel quite real to him.

"How is he, anyway? *The Husband*?"

"Anderson, you mean? He's fine, thanks for asking."

Logan grunted. It sounded good-natured, even if it wasn't *entirely* meant to be.

"Good. That's... Aye, that's good," he said. "And, eh, anything else exciting? Any holiday plans or anything?"

Just like when she smiled, he could now hear Maddie frowning. "What is it, Dad?" she asked. "What's wrong?"

"What? Nothing's wrong. Can I no' just give you a call?"

"Are you dying? Is that it?" Maddie asked, and he couldn't quite tell if she was teasing him or not.

"No. Of course I'm not bloody dying!"

"Are you sure?"

"Well, if I am, no bugger's said anything to me about it," Logan replied.

There was a pause then. And, if he tried very hard to imagine it, perhaps just the tiniest little exhalation of relief.

"Right. Good. So, what's the matter, then? You never just call without a reason."

"Well, maybe I'll start!" Logan protested.

"Aye, maybe you will, but that's not what this is," his daughter shot back. "Come on, Dad. Spit it out. I know when you're lying. I eat bullshit for breakfast."

Logan pulled a face that was half-grin, half-grimace.

"No, well, it was nothing really," he said. "I just... I had a question."

"Here we go. If it's, 'Can I use you as bait to catch a serial killer again?' then I'll give you three guesses what the answer is," Maddie said. "And the first two don't count."

That one hurt. It had been delivered as a joke—a bit of father-daughter banter—but it was too close to the bone not to sting.

"Eh, no. No, nothing like that, you'll be glad to hear," he said, skimming quickly over it. "I was just wondering, when you were growing up—when you were a kid, I mean—did you ever feel like you were missing out on having—"

"A reliable father figure?" Maddie asked, jumping in. "Funny you should say that..."

"Haha. Hilarious. But, no," Logan said. "Did you ever feel like you were missing out on having a sibling?"

There was a pause from the other end of the line.

"A sibling?"

"A brother or sister," Logan clarified.

Maddie tutted. "No, I know what a sibling is. I just don't understand why you're asking about—"

She gasped, and Logan heard a sudden *creaking* of sofa springs as she suddenly sat forward. Something clattered onto the floor, but it was impossible to tell what just by sound alone.

"Wait a minute, wait a minute," she cried, her voice developing a shrill, sharp edge to it. "Is Shona pregnant? Is that what this is?"

"What?! No. No. *No*. No," Logan said, and each repetition of the word was given an entirely different emphasis. "No. She isn't pregnant. She definitely isn't pregnant."

"Are you sure?"

"Yes!"

"Oh, thank *God*!" Maddie wheezed. "Don't do that to me."

Logan laughed, but it felt as forced as it probably sounded. "Aye. No. No, don't worry about that. She's definitely not pregnant," Logan said. "I mean, can you imagine? At my age."

"I'd definitely prefer not to," Maddie told him.

Logan chuckled. "Aye," he said.

He adjusted himself on the bed again, then reached for the bedside table, and the cup of tea he now realised he hadn't got around to making.

Damn.

"Although..."

He felt the silence growing heavier down the line.

"I mean, would it really be all *that* bad?"

"Yes," Maddie answered, without a moment's hesitation. "I'm an adult woman. I'm married. I don't want a baby brother or sister."

"Well, no," Logan conceded. "I mean, I suppose it would be—"

"Mental. It would be mental."

"I mean—"

"Completely, totally mental. And even if I did want one then, no offence, but I'm not sure I'd want them brought up by you."

Logan grimaced. "Bit harsh."

"Come on. You've got many strengths, but being a dad isn't exactly one of them," Maddie said, twisting the knife that she'd plunged into his chest with her previous remark. "There are enough absentee fathers on the planet. We don't need another kid to be lumbered with one."

She must've realised then quite how harsh she was sounding, because her tone softened.

"Besides," she said. "Imagine the hassle. Sleepless nights. Dirty nappies. School concerts. Parents nights."

"I suppose that's true," Logan conceded.

"All those things you didn't bother with last time," Maddie added, but he could hear her smiling again, which took some of the edge off the jibe.

"I did some of that," Logan protested. He sat forward long

enough to punch his pillow into shape. "I mean, maybe not all the time, but—"

"I know, Dad. I was joking," Maddie said. "But a baby? That's a terrible idea. That bit, I'm not joking about."

Logan should've been relieved. She was talking complete sense. She was giving voice, almost word for word, to the thoughts rattling around inside his head.

And yet, he was disappointed by her response, he realised. He thought he'd been calling so he could be reassured that he was right. But was it possible that he'd been hoping she'd talk him into it?

"Don't worry. I wasn't actually considering it," he said.

Logan heard a mumbling from elsewhere in the room that Maddie was in. A male voice. The Husband, no doubt.

"Coming, babe," Maddie said. "Just be a minute."

Her voice was muffled, like she'd pressed the phone to her shoulder, or covered it with her hand.

When she spoke again, she was back to her usual volume.

"Listen, Dad, I need to go."

"Aye. Aye, of course. You'll have stuff to do. Don't mind me."

There was silence from the other end, just for a second or so.

"You're sure you're alright?"

"Ach, you know me. I'm always alright."

"OK. Well... alright. If you're sure," Maddie said. "So, uh, goodnight then, I guess."

"Goodnight, sweetheart," Logan said, and he felt his throat tightening around the words, like it was trying to hold onto them. To cherish them. "I'm, uh, I'm glad you answered."

There was another silence, and this time it went on for a little longer. He could still hear her, though, hanging on the other end of the line.

"Me too," she said.

"Good luck with work," Logan began, but the texture of the sound from the phone changed, and he realised that his daughter had ended the call.

He watched her name and her picture vanish from his screen, to be replaced by the text he'd received from Shona.

At first glance, there was nothing unusual about it. She'd been replying to one he'd sent, just asking how she was getting on. She'd written back that she was fine, but tired, and told him her report was in the group mailbox, though there wasn't anything exciting in it beyond what she'd already revealed.

She'd ended the text—and the conversation—with a simple, 'Night!' Which, to the casual observer, may have seemed perfectly normal. But the suddenness of it had caught Logan off guard. He'd been expecting a bit of back and forth, then a call to chat about how their days had been, during which they'd both completely ignore the elephant in the room.

But she'd shut all that down with that one-word sign-off, leaving him to respond with a, 'Night, then,' and an X that had gone unanswered for over twenty minutes now.

His thumb hovered above the text box on the screen as he contemplated whether to write something else.

It was possible, of course, that he was overthinking it all. That he was imagining a tension between them that didn't actually exist.

Everything might be fine. He may well be worrying about nothing.

"Bugger it," he said, and he tossed his phone onto the duvet beside him.

Getting up from the bed, he took his laptop from its case, and opened it on the room's small desk-slash-dressing table.

The dark wood was ringed with the circular marks of a hundred hot mugs, and Logan rubbed his hands together as he waited for the computer to boot up.

"Right, then. Tea," he announced to the empty room.

And with that, he reached for the tiny kettle and headed for the sink in the bathroom.

———

Sinead's eyes were dry. She rubbed them, massaging them with her thumb and the knuckle of a forefinger until colours swam across the walls of the darkened Incident Room.

She'd drawn the blinds to shut out the night, and the only light in the room came from her computer screen.

How long had she been staring at that screen now? How many hours had she been sitting there in front of the computer, clicking, and scrolling, and searching?

Too bloody many, if the state of her eyes were anything to go by.

It wasn't just today, either. Her bump had left her tied to her desk since Christmas. She hadn't even been able to join in with all the excitement at the Eastgate Centre.

The biggest thing to happen in the Highlands in years—a full-scale hostage situation right in the centre of the city—and she'd been stuck here manning the phones.

It was important work, Logan had assured her. She might be wedged into a chair all day long, but what she was doing was vital to the smooth running of the whole *blah, blah, blah*.

She'd tuned him out at that point, having had quite her fill of being patronised on that particular day.

She wanted to be out there, right in the thick of it, making a difference, like a proper detective. Not sitting here. Like a balloon.

Shona had been and gone, and had taken Taggart home with her, robbing Sinead of even that responsibility.

The pathologist had offered her a lift home, even suggested they go grab a bite to eat on the way, but Sinead had politely declined. She was too busy, she'd said. She had too much to be getting on with.

And that was partly true. That was part of the reason for her hanging on here as long as she possibly could.

But it wasn't the real reason. Not by a long shot.

"Please tell me my eyes are deceiving me and you're not still here, Detective Constable."

Sinead shimmied her chair around, and tried to look upbeat and full of energy, yet suitably contrite. The results were mixed, at best.

Mitchell leaned in the doorway, one shoulder resting against the frame. It was the first time Sinead recalled seeing the detective superintendent leaning. It was so out of character, in fact, that Sinead had to peer through the darkness to make sure it was really her.

"Sorry, ma'am," she said, when she was sure she had the right person. "I'm just waiting for Tyler to pick me up."

Mitchell stepped further into the room. She was still wearing her uniform, but she'd shed her tie, and opened the top button of her shirt. This was, for the usually immaculate detective superintendent, practically slovenly.

"Tyler? Isn't he...?"

"DCI Logan sent him home for the night," Sinead explained. "He should be here any minute."

"Ah. Good."

Mitchell picked up the same stapler she'd fiddled with earlier, and turned it over in almost exactly the same way.

"You're back earlier than expected, ma'am," Sinead remarked.

"Yes." Mitchell looked up from the stapler, smiled thinly, then went back to studying it like it was some fascinating historical artefact. "Yes, I am. All went a lot quicker than I thought."

"That's..." Sinead wasn't quite sure what it was. It was hard to judge Mitchell's mood at the best of times, let alone while exhausted, annoyed, heavily pregnant, and in near absolute darkness. "...good?"

"Well. That remains to be seen," Mitchell said. She returned the stapler to the desk. A face on Sinead's screen caught her eye, and she came closer. "Who's that?"

Sinead had absolutely no recollection whatsoever of what was currently on her monitor, so she shuffled around until she could see it. The mugshot of a dark-haired man with sunken eyes and pockmarked skin stared back at her.

"Oh, that? That, ma'am, is David Bowie."

Mitchell frowned. She looked from Sinead to the screen and back again, like she was aware there was a joke somewhere in the vicinity, but couldn't for the life of her figure out where.

"He's let himself go," she finally remarked. "Mind you, he is dead, isn't he?"

"Ha. Yeah. He's not that one. It isn't his real name. Well, technically it is, he had it legally changed," Sinead explained. "But he was originally Malcolm Hall."

"Hall? Isn't that the victim's name?"

"It is, ma'am, yes." Sinead motioned to the screen. "He's her son. Her and her husband's. Uniform got his details from the Registrar's office, and I managed to track him down."

Mitchell stopped at Sinead's desk and leaned in closer, reading the information on the screen. She'd looked pretty downbeat from the moment she arrived, and the list of offences laid out below the photograph did nothing to perk her up.

"Oof. He's a bit of a waste of space, then."

"He's certainly got a colourful background, ma'am."

"And an addiction problem, by the looks of it. Does he know? About his mother, I mean?"

"I'm not sure, but I doubt it. We weren't aware of him until... well, about ten minutes ago."

"Do we have an address?" Mitchell asked.

"We've got several," Sinead replied. "Looks like he moves around a lot. I can try and find a current one."

Mitchell turned to look at her. The glow of the screen gave her dark skin a sickly greenish sheen and highlighted how blood-shot her eyes were. The detective superintendent looked almost as exhausted as Sinead felt.

"You'll do no such thing. You'll pass it on to someone else, and you'll get yourself home, where you should've been hours ago."

"It won't take long, ma'am. I can just do a bit of digging and—"

"That's not a request, Detective Constable. It's an order."

Sinead's mouth snapped open, then she closed it again, reconsidering her response.

"I just... I want to be useful, ma'am. While I can."

"You are being, Sinead. Of course you are," Mitchell said. She put a hand on the DC's arm. "*And*, you're helping ensure the future survival of the entire human race. What could be more useful than that?"

Sinead smiled. She didn't really want to, and she didn't really feel like it, but she forced it. "That's true, I suppose. I just—"

Mitchell wasn't allowing any further discussion on the matter.

"Go home. Rest. Come back to it tomorrow. Or, you know, don't. See how you're feeling. Play it by ear. I'm off to Aberdeen for meetings first thing, so I'm not here, but you have my full blessing. Whatever you decide, you can do so safe in the knowl-edge that you've done enough. It's time to let someone else take the strain. Just for a while."

The smile didn't change, but perhaps now felt like it was a little less effort to maintain.

"Well, if you insist, ma'am."

"I do," Mitchell said. "I really do."

"Alright, gorgeous? How's it going?"

DC Neish clicked on the lights, threw his arms wide like he was presenting himself to an appreciative audience, then stopped dead when he saw Detective Superintendent Mitchell staring back at him.

"Not bad, sweet cheeks," Mitchell replied. "How's yourself?"

"Shite," Tyler said, then he grimaced, let his arms drop to his side, and stood up straight. "I mean *whoops*. Sorry, ma'am. I'm, eh, I didn't think anyone else would be..." He swallowed. "I'm, um, I'm here for Sinead."

A smirk tugged at one corner of Mitchell's mouth. "Relax, Detective Constable. We're so far beyond office hours now that, you know what? I don't even care. In fact, despite not being the intended recipient, I'll take that compliment. Lord knows I could do with it tonight."

Tyler nodded a little too keenly. "Of course, ma'am. By all means, you should take it. You *are* gorgeous."

Mitchell's eyebrows twitched downwards. Wedged in behind her desk, Sinead lowered her head to hide the laughter that threatened to erupt out of her.

Tyler shifted his weight from one foot to the other. "I, eh, I made that weird, didn't I?"

"Yes. Yes, you did a bit," Mitchell told him. She stopped beside him on her way to the door. "I think you should take your wife home. Run her a bath, make her something nice to eat, give her a massage, maybe. I think she's earned that. Don't you?"

"Absolutely, ma'am," Tyler said. He saw a chance to redeem himself and leapt for it. "You both have."

Mitchell's eyebrows dipped again. "Well," she said. "Massages aren't really my thing." She patted him on the shoulder as she passed. "But if I change my mind, you'll be the first to know."

Both DCs watched as the detective superintendent left the

Incident Room, then Tyler squirmed so hard his head almost sunk right down into his chest.

"Jesus. That was a bit embarrassing."

Sinead giggled. "A bit? Looked like total humiliation from where I was sitting."

He walked over to her desk, grabbing his chair on the way and rolling it up next to her.

"She seemed weird," he remarked, flopping down into the chair.

Sinead looked over at the door again. "Yeah. She did a bit. Something's happened, I think. Something about DCI Filson."

"Sacked, probably," Tyler said. "Wasn't sounding good for her, from what I heard."

"Oh? What did you hear?"

Tyler hesitated. "Uh, just that... it's not sounding good for her," he said. "Not really heard anything more than... Holy shit, that's him!"

Sinead blinked, taken aback by the sudden handbrake-turn Tyler's sentence had made. He was staring at her screen now, his mouth open, the mugshot on the display reflected in his eyes.

"Who?" she asked.

"Him! That's him! That's the guy!" Tyler cried. He pointed to the screen, and the dead-eyed face staring back at him. "That's the bastard who jumped out at me from the cupboard!"

CHAPTER TWENTY-FOUR

IT WAS FAR TOO EARLY in the morning for this.

Logan sat in the corner of the booth in the hotel restaurant, sipping on his coffee and silently trying to talk down the headache he could already feel building.

Ben, Hamza, and Dave were eating their breakfasts, though Dave lacked the gusto and enthusiasm he usually showed for a Full Scottish. There was a croak to his voice and a heaviness to him that suggested a lot of drink had been consumed the night before.

Not happy drink, either. Sad drink. Angry drink. Logan recognised the signs well enough to have spotted them the moment the constable joined them for breakfast.

Wedged in next to Ben, DC Swanney was talking. She had been talking a lot since they'd all met up again that morning. In fact, Logan was struggling to recall a point when she hadn't been talking.

She was like a cross-country train, thundering on and on.

Except... no. She wasn't like that, because that suggested a clear route from A to B. A train went in one direction, following the tracks. It didn't flit from point to point without warning or explanation, before eventually circling back around to close to where it had started.

And all this was without having had any coffee. Granted, she'd knocked back five big glasses of apple juice—three of them one after the other at the buffet table itself—but a jolt of caffeine had yet to pass her lips.

"That was the weird thing, though," she babbled, waving a crust of toast around like it was a conductor's baton. "She was nice to start with. Lovely. Said she found me attractive. Kept going on about it, which felt a bit weird, but she was just friendly. Offered me lemonade. Offered me gin, too. I mean sure, yes, I had to go and get it myself—the lemonade, I mean, not the gin. I didn't have gin. I was working. Also, even if I hadn't been, I don't like gin."

Dave let out a low, pained groan at the very thought of the stuff, and shoved a chunk of square sausage in his mouth.

He chewed it slowly and miserably.

"But, yes, I had lemonade, and she had a gin. She had lots of gins, actually. In her cupboard, I mean. She didn't drink them all. Peach, toffee, um... orange something. There was, like, a unicorn one."

Ben looked up from his plate and blinked. "What are you talking about? What do you mean 'a unicorn one'?"

"I don't know. That's just what it said," Tammi-Jo explained. "Unicorn flavoured something or other gin. I don't know."

"But..." Ben looked around the table, checking to see if he was the one who'd lost his mind. "Unicorns don't exist."

Logan massaged one side of his forehead, still trying to fend off the headache. "I don't think any unicorns were harmed in the making of the product, Benjamin. It's just a, you know..."

"Gin?" Tammi-Jo guessed.

"No. Gimmick. It's just a gimmick."

"Oh. Right." Ben pronged a bit of sausage with his fork. "Bloody weird gimmick."

"There were others, too," Tammi-Jo continued. "Coffee. Candy cane. Marshmallow."

Logan had heard enough. "Can we skip on a bit?" he asked. "Or I think Dave's going to bring up his breakfast."

Dave didn't look up from his plate, but he managed to raise a grateful thumb for Logan's benefit.

"Right. Yes. So... things she told me. Useful things." Something about the way the DC said the words suggested she was searching through some internal database or spreadsheet for the requested information. "She said the call with Granny wasn't about anything in particular, really."

She took a swig of her apple juice then. It was Logan's turn to glance around at the other detectives, before turning his full attention back to DC Swanney.

"What? That's it?"

"Yes. Well, no. Mostly. She said it was a music box. On the mantelpiece. Or, you know, not on the mantelpiece. Missing. The thing we didn't see in Granny's house. The thing that wasn't there."

A movement on his left caught Logan's eye. Hamza was munching on a slice of toast, but had now started rubbing his temples in much the same way the DCI was.

"*And*," Tammi-Jo continued, sensing Logan was about to press for more information. "She reckons she knows who the killer is."

Around the table, heads were raised and forks sat down. Logan took a moment to dab at his mouth with a paper napkin before replying.

"I'm sorry?"

"Lois. Mrs Dunlop. She reckons she knows who the killer is."

"And?"

"Who does she think it was?" asked Ben.

Tammi-Jo shrugged. "I didn't get a name. But she said it was the new carer. The one filling in while the normal one was away."

"Should be easy to find," Hamza said. He had wiped his hands, and was already reaching for his phone.

"I don't think it was him, though," Tammi-Jo said. "I mean, maybe it is. It might be. But I wouldn't jump the gun."

She glanced around the hotel restaurant. It was mostly empty, partly because it was still early, but mostly because nobody in their right mind came on holiday to Wick in January.

Once the DC was sure nobody was listening in, she continued, albeit in a whisper.

"She was a bit racist."

"Ah, now. I'm sure she wasn't," said Ben. "What you've got to appreciate is that some of us older folks, we don't necessarily know all the right lingo. And, aye, maybe occasionally we'll use an outdated term or two, but—"

"She said all black people are thieves."

Ben hesitated. "Oh. Right." He spent a moment processing this. "All of them?"

Tammi-Jo shrugged. "Well, maybe not Johnny Mathis." She knocked back the last of her apple juice. "Whoever he is."

"OK. Aye," Ben conceded. "That does sound a bit racist, right enough."

"Still, racist or not, we need to check it out," Logan said. He gave Hamza a nod, and the DS left the table to go make some calls. "She say anything else?" Logan asked, before quickly adding, "Relevant, I mean? She say anything else relevant?"

Tammi-Jo thought for a moment. "Not really. I said we didn't think it was Albert that killed Granny, which she agreed on. She clearly felt sorry for him. Didn't seem that sad about Granny, to be honest, but I think it was maybe a stiff upper lip type thing, because they were clearly close."

"Anything else?" Logan prompted.

Tammi-Jo's brow furrowed in concentration. "She said young people are very self-centred these days, she didn't seem to know anything about Granny and Albert having a million quid in the bank, and she said she had a stomach problem. You know, that she was... gassy. Granny, I mean, not Lois. Although, I have to say, when I first went in I could definitely smell something. So you know, people in glass houses, and all that."

"She didn't know about the money?" Logan said. "That's interesting. So, they kept it secret."

"Don't blame them," Dave said, finally summoning the energy to speak. "People come crawling out of the woodwork if they get a whiff of cash. Happened to me when I got my payout for my accident. People I hadn't heard from in years suddenly popped up, wanting to be my best pal. And that was nowhere near a million. Don't blame them wanting to hide it from people."

"Or maybe not *people*," Logan mused. "Maybe one specific person."

"Who?" asked Ben.

"The caesarean scar," Logan said. "Someone came out of that. Hopefully we'll find out more on that today." He turned back to DC Swanney. "What time's Mrs Dunlop heading off?"

"Um, not sure exactly, sir. Think she got a bit fed up of me and kicked me out," Tammi-Jo confessed. She clutched her glass in both hands and rolled it between her fingers and thumbs. "But early, I think. Why? Do we need to talk to her? Did I miss something? Is there anything else I should've asked?"

Logan shrugged. "I don't know. You tell me. Is there?"

The detective constable stared at him. It could've been taken as slightly confrontational, but Logan was getting enough of a handle on the new team member now to know that the only battle she was locked in right now was with her own urge to look away, which she was wildly overcompensating for.

"No, sir," she eventually said. "No, I think I covered everything."

Logan nodded. "Well, there you go, then."

A quick look around at the plates confirmed that everyone had finished, or at least eaten their fill. Logan rapped his knuckles on the table, and gave Ben an encouraging nudge with his elbow.

"Right, let's get a shifty on. DC Swanney, until Tyler gets here, you're with me. We're going to go see the carer."

Tammi-Jo looked along the bench of the booth, past the sideways shuffling Dave, in the direction Hamza had gone.

"Isn't DS Khaled still trying to—?"

"The other one. The woman. The one they usually had."

"Sandra?"

"If you say so," Logan replied. "We'll go talk to her. Hamza can go talk to the other one when he gets a name. You pair head back to the station."

"Will do, Jack," Ben confirmed.

"But, eh, we'll be taking your car," Logan told him. "Which means..."

"Christ!" DI Forde spluttered.

"That you'll be going with Dave. Assuming he's no' still over the limit."

"Should be fine. Stopped drinking well before midnight," Dave said. He pointed to his own face, clearly only too aware of the state of it. "This is mostly just tiredness. Didn't sleep much."

The expression of fear that Ben was currently wearing gave the constable his first reason to smile all morning.

"Don't worry," he said, sliding himself off the end of the bench and into his waiting wheelchair. "I know it's your first time riding with me. I promise I'll be gentle."

"No, but, I feel like I shouldn't be going," Tyler said. "I feel like I should be staying here."

He slid two slightly burnt Scotch pancakes onto a plate in the middle of the table. Sinead made no move to take one, so Harris swooped in from his seat and pinched them both.

"Why? I'm fine," Sinead insisted, for the fifth or sixth time that morning.

She watched her brother getting stuck into one of the pancakes, and felt her stomach—or that part of it not currently compressed by two unborn infants, at least—twitch unsettlingly.

"Are you not going to put something on them?" she asked. "You're not just going to eat them both dry?"

Harris paused with his mouth half full of pancake. He had shot up in height in the last year, so he was almost as tall as Sinead was. After a wee wobbly stage where he could never be certain of the sounds that were going to come out of his mouth, his voice had deepened dramatically.

He was a teenager now. On his way to becoming a man.

Just one more thing for her to worry about.

"What?" he asked, spilling crumbs onto the table. "I like them like this."

Sinead's face puckered in disgust. "Clarty bastard," she said.

Harris smirked. "Yeah, yeah, Tuna Jam."

Sinead rolled her eyes, turned her attention back to her husband, and reiterated what was fast becoming her catchphrase. "I'm fine. It's not happening today."

Tyler tore his eyes away from the batter bubbling in the pan long enough to look back over his shoulder. "How do you know?"

"Because I won't let it happen today," Sinead told him through slightly gritted teeth.

When it was clear that this answer wasn't holding water, she forced a smile and tried again.

"Believe me, if I thought it was happening today, you

wouldn't be going anywhere. But it isn't. I've got a couple of weeks left to go. It's not happening today."

"Aye, but how do you—?"

"I just know, Tyler. Alright?" she snapped. "I just know."

A battle raged on Tyler's face, as he tried to work out the right thing to do. "What do you think?" he asked Harris. "What do you think I should do?"

Harris shrugged his shoulders, shook his head, and made a sound that was somewhere in the region of, "I dunno."

"I think you should turn that pancake," Sinead said.

Tyler frowned, like he had no idea what she was on about, then suddenly remembered the pan.

"Shite!"

Grabbing the handle, he gave the pan a jerk, and then watched helplessly as the half-cooked pancake flipped end over end through the air, and landed wet side down on the floor.

Sinead pushed back her chair and, with some difficulty, rose to her feet.

"Here, I'll clean it up," she said, unravelling some kitchen towel from the roll on the worktop.

"No, no, I'll do it. I've got it!" Tyler said, trying to snatch the paper from her hands.

She pulled it out of his reach, and smiled at him. "It's fine. Honest. I can do it. Away you go and get on the road. If anything changes, if I feel even a twinge, I'll let you know. Alright?"

Tyler almost ran a hand through his hair, before remembering he'd already styled it that morning, and thought better of messing it up. He swept the hand down his face, instead, then let out a sigh of resignation.

"Right. OK. If you're sure," he said, then he immediately talked himself out of the idea. "But I don't like it. No. I think I should be here."

"I'm going to be in the office. I'm not going to be on my own.

There'll be people around if anything happens." She could see the uncertainty was still there, so she leaned forward and planted a kiss on his lips before spelling it out for him once again. "I. Will. Be. Fine."

Tyler drew in a breath, then reluctantly nodded. "OK. OK. You'll be fine. You will," he said, like he was trying to convince himself. "You'll be fine. I'm not *that* far away. I can get back quick."

"You could use the siren and the flashy lights," suggested Harris from the table.

"I could use the siren and the flashy lights!" Tyler exclaimed. "Exactly. And you'll have people with you. You're not going to be on your own."

"I'm not," Sinead confirmed. She smirked, but it looked a little forced and unnatural. "Besides, poor Tammi-Jo needs your wisdom and expertise. I hear she's *very* impressed by all your accomplishments."

Across the kitchen, Harris paused mid-chew of a pancake. "Accomplishments? Are you sure she's thinking of the right guy?"

"Oi! Cheeky bastard!" Tyler cried, pointing to the grinning boy at the table. "I nearly got hit by a train!"

"That's not an accomplishment," Harris countered.

Tyler tutted. "OK. I *avoided* being hit by a train, then. That better?"

Harris shrugged. "I mean... just, I suppose," he said, then he went back to filling his face.

"Seriously, though, Tyler. I'll be fine," Sinead said, bringing him back on topic. "I've got people around, you can get here quickly. Even if I do go into labour—which I won't—then it's going to take a while. These things aren't quick. You'll have ages to get back."

Tyler looked deep into her eyes, then nodded. This time, unlike before, there was conviction behind it.

"Aye. Aye, you'll be fine. I'm overthinking it. I'll head up the road," he said. Then, like a striking cobra, he plucked the kitchen towel from his wife's hand. "But first, at least let me clean this up."

"Well, if you insist," Sinead said, stepping back while her husband recovered the smooshed-up pancake from the floor.

He deposited it in the bin, turned off the hob, then gestured around at the absolute carnage he'd left the area around the cooker in. Pancake batter had spattered across the worktops, three different mixing bowls and a selection of utensils were steeping in the sink, and a partially melted spatula was still lightly smoking beside one of the cooker top's rings.

"You, eh, you want me to get this before I go, too?" he asked.

Sinead dismissed him with a wave. "It's fine. Go get ready," she told him. "Harris can get this."

Behind her, her younger brother almost choked. "What?!"

"Cheers, gorgeous," Tyler said. He leaned in for another quick kiss, then turned and scurried out of the kitchen.

Sinead's smile faded as she watched him go.

Unseen by anyone, her hand slipped down to her belly, and she cupped it as the pain came again.

CHAPTER TWENTY-FIVE

THIS TIME, Tammi-Jo meant business.

Yesterday, she hadn't been properly equipped for the situation. They'd caught her off guard. Today, though, she was ready.

"Seventeen, eighteen, nineteen—ooh!" She lunged for the ball and got enough of a foot on it to make it count. "Twenty!"

The detective constable thrust both arms above her head, then jogged in circles around the garden, cheering triumphantly. Rory laughed and clapped, while seventeen-year-old Edgar continued to blush, like he'd been doing since DC Swanney arrived with the other detective.

He smiled when she met his eye on the way past, then swallowed and immediately looked away again, for fear that his little brother might see and take the piss out of him.

"Twenty. Two zero," Tammi-Jo announced, slowing to a stop. "Not bad, eh?"

"I've done over two hundred before," Rory declared. It didn't come across as arrogant, just a statement of fact. "Then I got bored."

"Alright, alright, don't rub it in," the detective replied. "That's impressive, though. You'll be going pro at this rate."

Rory nodded enthusiastically. "I know. I got offered a place with Rangers. In Glasgow. Playing for the junior team."

Tammi-Jo leaned back and looked him up and down, making a show of being impressed. "Check you out! A star in the making! Don't forget about me when you're rich and famous."

Rory's enthusiasm waned, and he shrugged. "Can't do it," he said. "Too far away. It's like..." His lips moved as he attempted a calculation. "Ten hours."

"It's not ten hours," Edgar corrected. "It's five hours."

"Duh." Rory pulled a face that suggested his brother had some developmental difficulties. "Both ways I meant. Total. Five and five is ten."

He dodged away just in time to avoid a dead arm from Edgar, and cackled with glee.

"Counting's not his strong point," Rory announced. "We don't know what his strong point is yet. We're still looking."

"Shut up," Edgar hissed, though this time he stopped short of swinging a punch. "I'm better at football than you."

Tammi-Jo couldn't resist teasing him. "Well, *he* got offered to play for Rangers, so..."

"So did I," Edgar told her. "Well before he did. Years before."

"Oh. Right." DC Swanney put her hands on her hips, looked from one brother to the other, then flicked the ball up into Edgar's arms. "Let's see you beat twenty, then." Her blue eyes twinkled with mischief. "Unless you're worried you're going to get beaten by a girl..."

Logan sat on Gary and Sandra Hawthorne's couch, watching DC Swanney keeping the boys busy in the garden. They'd tried to nosy in on the conversation between their parents and the detectives, so he'd suggested that Tammi-Jo take them outside while the grown-ups talked.

Now, Gary sat perched on the front of a sofa cushion across from the DCI, his hands flat together like he was praying. His smile was a strained, awkward thing, all his reserves of small talk now completely depleted.

"She, eh, she shouldn't be long now," Gary said, shooting a glance at the living room door. "She'll be getting biscuits out. She won't make tea for anyone without putting out biscuits. She's a feeder, I suppose. The boys burn it off, but me..." He gave his stomach a couple of hearty slaps. "Well, I could probably do with some of their energy."

"Aye, I know that feeling," Logan said.

Silence fell again. The only sounds were the ticking of a clock, and the *thud-thud-thud* of a football being juggled from foot to knee out in the front garden.

"Least it's dry," Gary said, really scraping the bottom of the barrel now. "Been raining a lot. I mean, about the same as usual, I suppose, but that's a lot."

"Aye," Logan agreed. "Still, that's January for you."

"Right. Yeah. That's January for you," Gary agreed. "Well, I mean, that's October through to April for you up here."

Logan smiled politely at the comment. "Aye. You're not wrong."

Tick-tick-tick.

Thud-thud-thud.

Gary slapped his hands on his thighs. "I'll go see if she needs a hand," he announced. He rose to his feet, then immediately sat down again when the living room door opened and his wife returned carrying a tray.

Sandra Hawthorne could best be described as 'sturdy looking'. The scales would probably tell you she was overweight, but they wouldn't give the full picture of a woman who clearly knew her way around a set of dumbbells.

She was tall for a woman, but not remarkably so, and her physique suggested she worked out regularly—not for appearances, but for strength.

Sandra might be a woman in her mid-forties, but Logan reckoned that, if it came down to a straight scrap between them, she'd give him a run for his money.

"Shift that stuff," she ordered, nodding to the table, where a bowl of random odds and ends and a couple of back issues of *Match* magazine were blocking the tray's safe touchdown.

Gary sprang into action, shoving everything aside to clear a landing zone. Logan's eyes were immediately drawn to the plate of biscuits sitting front and centre on the tray.

Rich Teas. Plain *Digestives*. Something oaty and dry looking. He hadn't really been too worried about a biscuit, given he'd not long finished his breakfast, but this meagre offering came as a disappointment, all the same.

"Sorry," Sandra said, as if reading his mind. "Gary and the boys must have polished off all the chocolate ones while I was away, and not bothered to replace them."

"It was them, don't blame me!" Gary protested, but a stern look from his wife quickly silenced him.

Logan couldn't quite tell if the look was a serious one, or something light-hearted. It didn't look all the way like a legitimate telling off, but nor did it look entirely jokey.

"It's never him. It's always the boys," Sandra declared.

Once again, it came across as quite cutting, and the distance between them when she sat on the couch only added to the feeling that her husband was not currently in her good books.

She gestured to the lacklustre spread. "Anyway. Tuck in."

Logan, not wishing to appear impolite, helped himself to a couple of *Rich Teas*.

And, to be on the safe side, one of the *Digestives*.

"I'm guessing you've been brought up to date about what's

happened?" Logan asked, dunking the first of his biscuits in his mug of tea.

"I have. Gary phoned me yesterday to tell me. Couldn't believe it," Sandra said. She kept her hair short, but it was just long enough for her to sweep it back over an ear. "Poor Granny. I haven't had a chance to check in with Albert yet, but I've called the hospital a couple of times, and they tell me he's doing alright. Or about as well as can be expected, at any rate."

"You know them well?" Logan asked.

"Very. Yes. I mean, I'm in there most days. Four times a week at least, but usually more," Sandra said. "Checking in on them. Making sure they're eating properly. Helping with personal care. Doing a bit of tidying. Whatever they need, really. Lovely couple, they are. I don't know what Albert's going to do."

"But you haven't been in recently. That right?"

Sandra nodded. "Yes. That's right. I've been over at my mum's, giving her a hand while she's been ill. I got back early yesterday evening."

"And where is she?" Logan pressed. "Your mum?"

"Across in Thurso." Sandra jerked her head to her right. "She's had a cold. Although, to be honest, her health's been failing in general since my dad... Well, since he passed away a couple of years ago."

"I'm sorry to hear that," Logan said.

"Thank you. It's hard, obviously, but it was for the best. He was suffering towards the end. Wasn't nice to see him like that. For any of us." Sandra let out a big sigh, shook herself, then plastered on a thin, unconvincing smile. "But, such is life, eh?"

"Such is life," Gary said, but from the way his wife's eye twitched, his agreement only seemed to irritate her.

She took her own mug from the tray, but didn't so much as glance at the biscuits. "You got any, you know, leads, or what have you?" she asked.

Logan dunked his *Digestive* in his tea. "Enquiries are ongoing," was as much as he was willing to say on the matter. "Which is why I wanted to talk to you."

Sandra froze with her mug almost to her mouth. She looked at the DCI over the top of it. "Oh? That sounds ominous."

Logan smiled. "It isn't. Don't worry. Just really trying to get a bit of background."

Gary laughed. It sounded a little desperate. "Haha. So, we're not suspects, then?"

He suddenly found himself the centre of the DCI's attention, and shrunk back a little into the couch, clearly regretting his choice of words.

"No," Logan said, after an uncomfortable pause. "No. You're not suspects. Like I say, just after a bit of background."

Gary laughed again, and this time the pitch was even higher. "Haha! Well, you've come to the right place. Nobody knew Granny like Sandra. Right, babe?"

"Babe?"

Logan didn't know if Sandra looked more disgusted or confused by her husband's use of the word. She fired him a look with heavy *shut the fuck up* vibes, then turned back to Logan.

"I knew her pretty well, yes. You get to know them all well. Hard not to when you're cutting their toenails or washing their backs," she said. "Anything I can help with, just ask, and I'll do my best. Obviously, we all want whoever did this to be caught."

"Obviously," Gary agreed. He frowned deeply and nodded with a level of sincerity that almost tipped all the way over into sarcasm.

"She was popular, I believe. Locally, I mean," Logan said.

"She was, yeah. Everyone used to love her."

Logan raised an eyebrow. "Used to?"

"Before she died," Gary said, jumping in.

If looks could kill, the one his wife gave him then wouldn't just have ended him, it had erased him from time.

"Before she became completely housebound, I meant," Sandra said. She shook her head. "That's harsh of me. I'm sure people did still love her, it's just... They didn't think about her as much. People would stop for a blether with her when she was out and about, and talk for ages, but once she wasn't able to get around, very few of them took the time to visit."

"I see. But, she didn't have any problems with any of them?" Logan asked. "She didn't have any what you might call *enemies*?"

"Enemies?" Sandra almost laughed. "No. Of course she didn't have *enemies*. She's an old woman, not James Bond."

Logan smiled. "No. I assumed not, but I have to ask," he explained. "Can you think of any reason anyone might want to kill her?"

"No. No, of course not!" Sandra shook her head emphatically. "There is no reason. Granny's lovely."

"Was lovely," her husband corrected.

"Shut up, Gary!" Sandra snapped at him. "Just... just stop."

Gary shrunk further into the couch, flinching a little at his telling off.

"Granny—well, Granny and some of the others—they're the whole reason we're even still here," Sandra explained.

Logan frowned. "How do you mean?"

"We thought about moving. You know, going somewhere more central? Not quite so arse end of nowhere. But Granny and the others, they've come to rely on me. And, you know what? I've come to rely on them, too. The boys are growing up, they don't need me as much, so, with Granny and the others, it's..." Sandra stopped and sighed, like she'd realised she was saying too much. "It's just nice to feel appreciated, I suppose."

"I appreciate you," Gary protested.

Sandra nodded, already trying to backtrack a bit. "No, I know you do. I know. It's not that. It's just... I don't know.

Having a purpose. I think that's important. And that's what they give me, my ladies and old boys. They give me a purpose."

Logan jotted a quick note in his pad. Both the Hawthornes eyed his pen as it scribbled, like they could work out what he was writing just from the movement of its end.

"So, you don't know of any reason why anyone might want to kill Granny?" he asked again.

Again, the answer was a resounding *no.*

"What about the money?" Logan asked, and he watched their reactions very closely.

"Money?" asked Gary. "Granny had money?"

Damn. Logan had been hoping Sandra would be the first to react. She was the one most likely to know about the funds in the Halls' bank account, but if she did, then her husband's blundering in had given her the time she needed to structure her denial.

"What money do you mean?" she asked.

"There's a substantial sum in an account in their name," Logan said. "We found bank statements."

Gary shuffled forwards, suddenly interested. "How substantial a sum are we talking?"

"A *very* substantial sum," was as much as Logan was willing to clarify. "You didn't know about it, then?"

"No," Gary said. "Didn't have a clue."

Sandra sighed. "He wasn't asking you, Gary. Jesus, what bit of shut up don't you understand?"

She hadn't so much as glanced his way while addressing him, her attention fully owned by the detective sitting in the armchair across from her.

"No. I didn't know," she replied. "I didn't know anything about that. Granny never discussed money. I knew they were doing alright. Albert had a good pension, so they were on a solid footing. But that's all I could really tell you about their financial situation."

Logan nodded slowly, then made a note in his pad. Sandra and Gary both watched again as he wrote.

Outside, the regular *thud-thud-thudding* of the football continued.

"And what about family?" Logan continued. "What do you know about that?"

"How do you mean?" Sandra asked.

Logan pulled a face that suggested he didn't understand where the confusion lay.

"I mean what can you tell me about Granny's family," he said. "Any relatives you're aware of? Sisters? Brothers?" He left a pause. "Children?"

Sandra's brow furrowed as she thought. She fidgeted a little in her seat, making the cushion beneath her give a little creak.

"There was a sister, I think, but she's long gone. She was a few years older, I think. Sissy, maybe? Sally? Something like that. Granny didn't talk about her much. I think it upset her."

Logan sat with his pen poised, not yet writing. "Nobody else?"

"Not that I know of."

Logan kept his gaze fixed on Sandra. She'd said herself that she'd bathed the woman. She must've at least seen the scar.

"We have reason to believe that Granny had a child," he said.

The reaction was one of surprise. A blink, then a widening of the eyes, and a slight dropping of the jaw.

Textbook.

"I had no idea," Sandra said. For the first time since she'd sat down, she turned to her husband for his input. "Did you know?"

"Why the hell would I know?" he asked. "No. Not a clue. Are you sure?"

"We're still looking into it," Logan said. "But we believe so, yes."

"Wow." Sandra blew out her cheeks and shook her head.

"That's shocked me. What happened to him, do you know? The baby?"

Logan didn't look at his pad, but his pen scribbled something, like his hand was working on auto-pilot.

"Like I say," he told them. "We're still looking into it."

"Good. Well... I hope you find something useful," Sandra said.

She made a show of checking her watch, and an even bigger one of looking shocked.

"Blimey. Well, I should really start getting ready..."

"Of course. You need to get off," Logan said.

Then, since no other bugger was bothering with them, he leaned over and retrieved one of the oaty biscuits from the plate. He dunked it in his tea a couple of times, then removed it before it lost all its structural integrity.

"So, just a few more questions, Mrs Hawthorne," he said. "I promise, I won't take up too much more of your time..."

"Hundred-and-six, hundred-and-seven, hundred-and-eight."

Tammi-Jo sat on the front step with Rory, both watching as Edgar showed off his keepie-uppie skills. He counted each kick, flick, chest, and knee, whispering below his breath, his gaze fixed on the ball like some advanced laser targeting system.

"He's good," the DC remarked.

Beside her, sitting shoulder to shoulder, Rory didn't look that impressed.

"He's just showing off because he fancies you," the boy said.

Tammi-Jo smiled. "Aye? He show off to all the girls, does he?"

"Probably," Rory said. "But I don't think he knows that many. He mostly just hangs out with me."

"Aw. That must be nice. Having a big brother around," Tammi-Jo said.

Rory shrugged. "Suppose."

"I'm the oldest in my family. I sometimes think I'd have liked a big brother or sister," the DC said. She leaned in closer and whispered in the boy's ear. "And then, sometimes I think they'd just be a pain in the bum."

Rory grinned at that, and gave a little giggle.

"You're right. They are!" he whispered back.

They sat quietly for a while, watching Edgar juggling the football.

"Hundred-and-fifty-two. Hundred-and-fifty-three."

He really was good.

It was Rory who eventually broke the silence, albeit with some trepidation in his voice.

"Are you going to catch them?" he asked. He glanced at her, just briefly, then went back to watching his brother. "The one who killed Granny? Are you going to catch them?"

Tammi-Jo weighed up her options—brutal honesty, or complete reassurance.

"We are," she said, plumping for the latter.

"Good." Rory let out a shaky sigh. "And they're not going to come back?"

"What do you mean?"

"They're not going to come after anyone else, are they?" Rory asked. He fidgeted on the step.

"You've got nothing to be worried about, Rory," Tammi-Jo told him. "You're perfectly safe."

"You promise?"

The detective constable nodded. "Definitely. There's nothing to be scared of. And, even if there was—which there isn't—you've got your mum, and your dad, and your big brother to look after you."

Rory smiled, but it was a thin and unconvincing thing. He

kept his gaze trained on Edgar's display of football skill, but Tammi-Jo could practically hear the cogs whirring away inside his head.

"It's just..."

The sentence disintegrated into silence. Tammi-Jo waited a moment before prompting him.

"It's just what?"

"My dad didn't come the other night." He shot her a furtive look, then quickly averted his gaze again. "I had a bad dream. I shouted, but he didn't come."

"Oh. Right. Well... maybe he was asleep. But if there was anything *really* wrong, he'd be there." She noted the look of hurt on his face and rushed to clarify. "No, I mean, I know nightmares are rubbish. Believe me. They're the worst. I have this one about Bugs Bunny, only he's dressed up like Jacob Rees-Mogg. The politician. You know who that is?"

Rory shook his head.

"Right. Well, imagine the ghost of an accountant. But, like, an evil accountant. From the eighteen-hundreds. And that's—"

"He wasn't in."

Tammi-Jo's babbling ended abruptly.

"What?"

"My dad. After he didn't come. I went to his room." Rory shook his head, just once. "He wasn't there."

Tammi-Jo glanced at the living room window. She could see Gary in there now, sitting beside his wife, who was replying to one of Logan's questions.

"Maybe he was downstairs," she said.

Another head shake. Rory still wasn't looking at her. Across the garden, Edgar continued to kick the ball around.

"Hundred-and-eighty-one. Hundred-and-eighty-two."

"He wasn't. He wasn't anywhere," Rory said. "So I just got some sweets and went back to bed."

"Midnight feast. Nice!" Tammi-Jo said. She kept her next

question as natural sounding as possible, despite the fluttering in her stomach. "So, eh, what night was this?"

There was no hesitation from the boy. "The night before last. The same night Granny died," he said. Finally, he turned to look at her, and his eyes were wet with tears. "So, if the killer had come to our house that night, he wouldn't have been there to stop him!"

CHAPTER TWENTY-SIX

SINEAD LOWERED herself halfway into her seat, counted to five to see if anything unpleasant was going to happen, then allowed herself to collapse all the way into it. Her weight made it shriek in protest, but she tried her best not to care.

Once safely touched down, she booted up her computer, then sipped on her tea while she listened to the processor and hard drive grinding away.

She looked around the office, clutching her mug in both hands to warm them up while she waited for the heating to kick in. Not that she'd set it high, of course. She got too hot very easily these days. Just another benefit of being pregnant that no one had thought to mention before.

Still, it was January in the Highlands, and the room was large and high-ceilinged. Even in her current state, she needed a bit of warmth about the place.

Her computer sprung to life, and she set down her mug. A quick poke around in the inbox produced a few new nuggets of information that had come in overnight.

The up-to-date pathology report was there, albeit without the toxicology stuff, which would take longer.

There were a handful of addresses for Greta and Albert's son, the man calling himself David Bowie. They seemed to be scattered across the country, though there was one near Loch Glascarnoch, about forty miles north-west of Inverness. That was the most recent, so the most promising. She made a note of it in her pad, then went back to checking what else had come in.

She soon found a death certificate for Albert's first wife. It was in an email from one of the CID DCs, who mentioned they'd been 'asked' to look into it by Mitchell in a late-night message the evening before.

In the email, the detective constable suggested she check out the cause of death, so Sinead double-clicked the attachment, and drummed her fingers impatiently on the desktop while she waited for the file to open.

As soon as it loaded, she sprung for the mouse, and dialled the scroll wheel until the relevant section of the document appeared on-screen.

"Bloody hell," she ejected.

She read the words again, knowing she couldn't possibly have made a mistake, but wanting to be sure.

They hadn't changed. Of course they hadn't.

Albert Hall's first wife had died due to complications during childbirth.

Sinead felt a little twinge of panic, which she immediately stamped down again. This wasn't about her. This was about the investigation.

She sent the file to the printer, then closed it. The obvious question that the cause of death implied was answered there and then, when she saw the email's second attachment. She'd caught a glimpse of it before, but the filename hadn't made sense until now.

'Birth Certificate.pdf'

Tammi-Jo started talking the moment she and Logan closed their car doors. She was aware that they were clearly visible to anyone watching from the house, so she kept her head lowered a bit, just on the off-chance that Sandra had picked up any lip-reading skills from Albert Hall.

"Gary was out. The night Granny died," she announced. "Rory, the younger brother, he woke up after a bad dream. He went looking for him. Couldn't find him. He wasn't there."

Logan's eyebrows arched, but he otherwise remained as impassive as possible. "Aye? What time was this?"

"About half eleven, Rory reckons. He's not sure when he came back, because he fell asleep, but after one, he thinks. He remembers still being awake then."

"Right. OK," Logan muttered, the cogs in his head all spinning into action. "So, no alibi, then. Motive?"

"Money?" Tammi-Jo guessed. "If he knew they had cash in the bank..."

"His wife insists they didn't," Logan said. "And why would they stand to benefit?"

Tammi-Jo's shoulders sunk a little, then immediately popped back up again. She clicked her fingers. "Ooh! Lois Dunlop! Last night, she said Granny thought of Sandra like family. A lot of them did. Maybe she's in the will?"

Logan rolled his tongue around inside his mouth, like he was searching for any stray biscuit crumbs. He tapped his fingers on the steering wheel. "Maybe," he said. "We'll have to check that. But, last time I checked, Albert was still alive and kicking, and I'd imagine most of it's going to him."

"And there's the son, I suppose," Tammi-Jo conceded.

"Son? We know it's a son, do we?"

"Yeah, sir. It's all in DC Neish's report. I had a look last night."

"Tyler?"

"Oh. No. Sorry. Forgot, she uses her maiden name, doesn't she? His wife. Sinead."

Logan nodded. That made more sense. He turned his attention to the house. There was a figure standing watching them through the living room window, but they were too far back for him to be able to see who it was.

"She said, 'him.' Or 'he,' maybe. Can't remember which."

"Sir?"

"Sandra. The carer. When I said that Granny'd had a child, she knew it was a *he*. I didn't pull her up on it at the time, because I wasn't sure she was right."

"She knows about him, then," the DC surmised.

Logan shook his head. "She says she doesn't."

"Lucky guess, then?"

"Maybe. Maybe not." Logan opened his door again. "Follow my lead. Alright?"

"Sure thing, boss!" Tammi-Jo said, grabbing for her door handle.

Logan gave a shudder. "Please. Don't call me that," he told her. "One of you doing it is bad enough."

"Right, sir. Sorry, sir."

"Better," Logan grunted, then they both got out of the car, and Tammi-Jo fell into step beside him as he went marching back up the path, past the two boys, and raised a fist to knock on the door.

It was opened before he had a chance. Sandra reacted in surprise, almost dropping the jacket and handbag she was clutching in her arms.

"Oh! Sorry. Didn't see you there!" she said. "Was, eh, was there anything else? Did you forget something? I'm just on my way out the door..."

"Sorry, Sandra. Couple of things. I'm going to need the two of you to come down the station for me."

Sandra's grip tightened on the door, like she was contemplating slamming it shut in their faces.

"What?" she asked after a moment. She laughed, but it came from too far forward in her mouth to be convincing. "Why? What for?"

"Just a formality," Logan said. "We've got a lot of prints in the house. Obviously, with you being in there regularly, and Gary having been the one to find the body, we need to discount you both. For that, we need to take your prints. It's a pain in the arse, I know. Shouldn't take long, though."

"I was just about to go to work."

"Aye. But, like I say, it won't take long," Logan reiterated.

Some internal war waged inside Sandra, and the effects of it were written all over her face.

Finally, she sighed. "OK. Yes. Of course," she said. "What was the other thing?"

"This one's a bit more embarrassing," Logan said. "DC Swanney here has a bit of a... bladder issue."

"I do?" Tammi-Jo blinked. "Yes! I do! That's right."

Logan put a hand on the detective constable's shoulder, and smiled at the woman in the doorway. "I don't suppose she could nip in and use your bathroom?"

CHAPTER TWENTY-SEVEN

TWO MINUTES LATER, Tammi-Jo stood outside the Hawthorne's bathroom at the far end of the upstairs landing, wondering what she was supposed to do.

DCI Logan clearly hadn't *actually* wanted her to use the bathroom.

Or had he?

No. She shook her head. No, that would be stupid. She wasn't a child. She could make her own calls vis-a-vis any sort of bathroom situation.

Not that, then. So, what?

Surely he didn't want her to poke around up here while he was talking to Gary and Sandra downstairs about the finger-printing procedure?

Did he?

That seemed unlikely, given that it broke a number of rules.

And yet, from what she could hear of his conversation, it did have a certain 'keep them talking' feel about it. If you wanted to keep someone distracted, then boring them into a coma with the ins and outs of Police Scotland's internal processes was certainly one way to go about it.

But how could she snoop around? How much time did she have? As it turned out, she had actually needed to use the bathroom, though she put that down to nerves as much as anything else. She'd had the foresight not to flush when she was done, though, as that would've signalled the end of the whole thing, and she'd have been forced to return downstairs, empty-bladdered, yes, but empty-handed, too.

This was a test, she thought. This was DCI Logan assessing how she performed in the field. Working out if she had what it took to be a copper on his team.

She couldn't let him down. She wouldn't.

There were four doors on the upstairs landing, including the bathroom she'd just been using. That was the only one that was marked with a little sign, and the other three were each identical.

That didn't help matters.

She picked one at random, hoping it was Gary and Sandra's bedroom. That was where the good stuff would be. That's where she would find all the intel. The info.

Assuming, of course, there was anything like that to find.

Tammi-Jo listened at the door for a moment, then cocked her ear towards the stairs. Logan was still in full flow, explaining to the couple exactly—*exactly*—what would be involved in getting their prints taken, and filling them in on the details of all the relevant privacy laws surrounding the capture and storage of their personal data.

She still had time, then.

Gritting her teeth, she pushed down the handle and opened the door.

She almost screamed when she saw the man standing there, grinning at her, one thumb raised like he was welcoming her in. Fortunately, she was able to bite her tongue in time to stop the cry of fright escaping.

The cardboard cutout of some fella in a *Glasgow Rangers* strip continued to smile unnervingly back at her.

This had to be one of the boys' rooms, then. Rory, probably, going by the number of posters and soft toys, almost all of which were football themed, and most of them in the red, white, and blue of his favourite team.

It was unlikely she was going to find anything here, but she leaned her head inside and took a quick glance around, just in case.

Sure enough, all she saw was a small stack of clothes waiting to be put away, an overflowing laundry basket, and a small TV with a *PlayStation 4* plugged into it.

The empty case of a game sat on the floor beside the console. The latest *FIFA*, unsurprisingly enough.

She quietly closed the door, looked across the hall to the one opposite, then stopped with her hand still clutching the handle.

An itch spread through her brain like a fast-moving rash. There had been something wrong. Something out of place. Something she'd seen that was only now starting alarm bells ringing.

She rapped her knuckles on her forehead, trying to distract herself and refocus, but she knew she was wasting her time. Now that her subconscious brain had picked up on something, it wouldn't give her peace until she'd figured out what was wrong about the room.

After another pause to listen at the top of the stairs, she returned to Rory's room, and let her gaze wander idly across all his things.

The cardboard cutout was still watching her. Like any great work of art, his eyes followed her as she poked around the room.

Posters. Teddies. Toy cars.

No, it was none of that.

The telly? The games console?

Nope. Nothing there that worsened the tingling in her head.

What, then? The clothes?

She looked at the pile of clean ones, then at the sprawling laundry basket. Neither one raised any concerns.

But there was something. She was sure of it. Something she was overlooking.

Something she had seen.

Something out of place.

She could almost feel her brain chastising her, berating her for not seeing the obvious, for being *such a bloody idiot*.

It reminded her a bit of her dad.

But there was nothing in the room that she could pinpoint as being wrong. Nothing she could see.

Or nothing she could see from where she was standing, at least.

She retraced her steps out of the room, but this time walking backwards, head twitching as her gaze swept the bedroom.

Something...

Something...

Bingo.

She saw it then, though a part of her wished that she hadn't. Not here, at least. Not in Rory's room.

There, mostly hidden among the junk and shadows below the bed, was a carved wooden music box.

Rory Hawthorne sat in the middle of the couch, his head down, his hands clasped between his trembling knees. He looked guilty as sin, despite his protestations to the contrary.

He'd clammed up as soon as Logan had started to talk, and the DCI had quickly concluded that neither his questioning nor

Rory's parents' increasingly irate-sounding demands were going to get them anywhere.

Instead, he'd tagged in DC Swanney, who now sat on the chair across from him, smiling warmly as she tried to catch his eye.

Edgar had been instructed by his mother to wait outside, but Logan could hear him hanging around out in the hall, listening in.

"You're not in trouble, Rory," Tammi-Jo told the younger boy. "We just want to know why it was under your bed."

Her voice was like a soothing melody, proving that, when push came to shove, she was able to keep a lid on her wittering instincts.

"I don't know," Rory whispered. A tear ran down his cheek.

"He's bloody lying!" Gary snapped.

His wife glared at him. "Gary!"

"Well, look at him! He is! He's talking shit!"

Rory's father took two big marching paces, making the boy flinch in fear. He pointed to the music box, now sitting on the coffee table, safely wrapped in an evidence bag.

"Where did you get it, Rory? Why is it here?"

"Mr Hawthorne," Logan intoned, but Gary pressed on.

"They could arrest you. You know that? They could sling you in the bloody jail!"

This time, Logan's words came as an angry bark. "Mr Hawthorne, that's enough!" He pointed to the door. "Maybe you should leave the room."

Standing in the shadow of the towering DCI, it took Gary a moment to build up the courage to respond.

"This is my house. He's my son. You can't just come in here and order me around."

Sandra jumped in before Logan had a chance to respond.

"No, but I can. Get to the kitchen," she said.

Logan had said those exact same words in that exact same

tone just a few nights ago, after catching Taggart chewing the leg of the living room table.

The way Gary slunk out of the room, head lowered and eyes wide with a sort of shameful, guilt-ridden sadness, reminded the detective a lot of how the dog had reacted, too.

Once Rory's father had left, Logan gave DC Swanney a nod, urging her to continue.

"You sure you don't know how it ended up under your bed?" she asked.

Rory shook his head. He sniffed—all burning and snot-filled —as another tear went cascading down his cheek and hung precariously from the point of his chin.

"Did Granny maybe say you could borrow it?" Tammi-Jo asked, throwing the lad a possible lifeline. "Did she give you it, maybe? As a present?"

There was no denial this time. Not right away. Instead, Rory sniffed again, and wiped his eyes on his sleeve.

From the kitchen, Logan could hear muttering, and the sound of cupboards being slammed.

"Come on, Rory, tell us, for God's sake!" his mum cried, but it was more pleading than angry. "Just tell us how you got it. Please!"

Rory's legs shook. His shoulders hunched. His voice was a rasping croak, like he'd been crying for hours.

"I just... I didn't..."

"I took it."

Everyone in the room, Rory included, turned to the living room door. Edgar stood there, tall and confident, his shoulders back and his head held high.

"What?" Sandra gasped.

"I nicked it. Last week," her older son said.

"You did *what*?!" Sandra cried.

Rory rose to his feet. "What? N-no."

"It's OK, Rory," Edgar said, shutting down his little brother's objections. "It's fine. You shouldn't get into trouble for something I did."

Logan stepped between the boys, blocking their view of one another. He glowered down at Edgar, who did an admirable job of not immediately shitting himself in fear.

"Where was it?" Logan asked. "In the house, I mean. Where did you take it from?"

He saw the moment of uncertainty, and saw through the charade at once.

"Doesn't matter where it was. I took it."

"It was in Rory's room," Tammi-Jo said.

"Yeah, and we're always leaving stuff in each other's room. All the time!" Edgar told her. "Aren't we, Roar?"

Logan eyeballed him for a moment or two longer, then turned and looked back over his shoulder at the younger boy.

"Rory? Is this true?"

Rory tried to look at his brother, but Logan continued to block his line of sight.

"I... I was going to bring it back," Rory whispered.

Sandra reeled, like her legs were about to give out from under her. "Jesus Christ, Rory!"

"I wasn't going to keep it. I just... I wanted a proper look at it, and I didn't think they'd notice."

He collapsed onto the couch and buried his face in his hands, too ashamed to look at anyone, or to be looked at in return.

"I'm sorry! I'm sorry!" he sobbed, the words coming between big shaky gulps of breath. "I was going to put it back, and then... and then... Granny died, and I didn't know what to do, and I wished I hadn't done it, and I shouldn't have, and I'm sorry. I'm sorry!"

Tammi-Jo glanced up at Sandra, like she was expecting the boy's mother to offer him some comfort. Instead, she just stood there, her hands on her hips, her head shaking in disapproval or disbelief.

It was Edgar who eventually elbowed his way between his mum and the DCI, muttering as he passed.

"For God's sake. Someone check him."

He sat down beside his brother and put an arm around him. Rory tried to pull away at first, then buried himself in against Edgar, shaking them both with his sobs.

"It's alright. It's alright," Edgar soothed, patting the smaller boy on his shoulder.

It was a little stilted and awkward, but Logan put that down to the judgemental gaze of the audience. The care and affection, that bit was real.

Edgar looked up at Logan without even making eye contact with his mum.

"It's just a stupid music box. It's not a big deal," he said. "It's not like he killed her, is it?"

"That's not the point, Edgar!" Sandra shot back.

"Then what is the point? What's the big deal? Look at what you're doing to him. Look at the state of him. He's sorry, alright? He made a mistake."

Sandra's face was turning a troubling shade of red. It wasn't embarrassment, if her expression was anything to go by, but a rapidly rising rage.

"You're too bloody protective of him! That's the problem!" she barked. "He needs to stand on his own feet. He needs to take responsibility for his own—"

Edgar, whose jaw had dropped open when his mum had started shouting, now shouted back.

"Too protective? Someone has to be! Someone has to be here for him. Someone has to look after him when you're off out with—"

His mouth snapped shut so suddenly that the *clack* of his teeth rang around the room. Logan followed the boy's gaze, and saw Gary looming in the doorway again, his eyebrows shaped in a shallow V above his nose.

"Ah, forget it," Edgar said, getting to his feet. He pulled Rory up with him, then faced the detectives. "Is he in trouble? With the police? Is he in serious trouble, I mean?"

Tammi-Jo answered before Logan had a chance. "No. We might need to talk to him, but no." She smiled supportively, and Logan watched the older boy's ears turning red. "He's not in trouble."

"Yes, he bloody is!" Sandra said, but Edgar was already leading the way out into the hall, barging past his dad and pulling his still-sobbing brother along behind him.

The adults all stood in silence, listening to the boys thumping up the stairs.

Eventually, the pressure of it became too much for DC Swanney to bear.

"Tch. Boys," she said. She smiled, quite goofily, and rolled her eyes. "Am I right?"

CHAPTER TWENTY-EIGHT

ALISON DUNLOP TRIED NOT to be worried as she pulled onto her mother's street.

She tried to remain calm when she unbuckled her seat belt and hurried up the path, noting the closed blinds.

Tried to convince herself that there was a perfectly good reason why her mother wasn't picking up the phone. Assured herself that, despite the big day of travelling Lois had ahead of her, she'd probably just overslept.

Yes. That was it. Her mother would have been so up to high doh about the trip that she would've been sitting up for hours the night before.

She'd still be asleep, that was all. And Alison had left them plenty of time to get to the airport, suspecting that this was a possibility.

Strange of her not to hear the phone, though. There was one right next to her bed, after all.

Fishing in her pocket for her keys, Alison dismissed the concern. She tried the key in the door, but found it already unlocked.

"Mum! Wakey-wakey!" she called, wiping her feet on the mat. "We need to get off!"

She pressed on into the silence of the house, but didn't close the door behind her.

The lights were on in the hall, and through in the kitchen. Alison checked that room first, and felt a wave of relief when she saw a bottle of gin sitting on the countertop.

Aye, that felt like her mum, right enough. She felt a gin or two steadied the nerves, and she'd been worried about flying all the way to Australia on her own since the ticket had been booked, even though she was being taken right to the security gate at one end, and met by Alison's brother at the stopover in Singapore.

They'd forked out for a business class seat for her, too, so she was going to be well looked after.

But yes, one too many gins the night before went some way to explaining the lack of response this morning.

The stairs were across from the kitchen. Alison sidled past the stairlift chair, and thudded up the steps, making as much noise as possible.

"Mum! Rise and shine! Time to get..."

She stopped on the seventh step, and looked back towards the ground floor.

The stairlift. The chair was down at the bottom.

There was no way her mum could've climbed up to bed on her own.

Alison suddenly became aware of her heart moving inside her chest. It fluttered like an injured bird desperately trying to take flight.

One by one, step by step, Alison descended the stairs.

"Mum?" she called, her voice wobbling off into all the rooms of the house. "Mum, you there?"

She headed for the living room, but stopped at the door to

the downstairs bathroom. It had been a cupboard once, but as Lois's health had deteriorated, Alison had arranged for it to be converted.

Nudging it open, she saw only the toilet, the compact sink, and the little ballerina figure with the big dress which hid the toilet roll on top of the cistern.

Her heart beat faster as she pressed on down the hall towards the living room. As she got closer, she could hear a sound. Rhythmic. Repeating. Over and over. Slow and steady.

Click-click-zzzpt.

Click-click-zzzpt.

Alison pressed her hand on the door and eased it open. Her gaze was pulled in the direction of the sound, and landed on her mother's old record player. The record was still spinning on the turntable, but the arm had been knocked so it bumped against the middle spindle before bouncing back a half inch or so across the vinyl.

Alison's voice, when it came, was a shrill whisper of fear.

"Mum?"

The door creaked open the rest of the way, and this time Alison's gaze was dragged down to the shapeless, motionless form on the floor.

Alone in her mother's house, Alison Dunlop stumbled back out into the hallway, and screamed.

Logan glanced in his rearview mirror, making sure Sandra's car was following them as they pulled away from the Hawthorne's house, headed for the station in Wick.

In the passenger seat beside him, Tammi-Jo shook the tension from her fingers, and performed some quite complicated breathing exercises.

Neither of these things went unnoticed by the driver.

"What are you doing?" Logan asked.

"Just exhaling the stress," the young DC replied. "All the tension, you know? Just shaking it off and breathing it out."

"Right," Logan said. He continued on for just thirty or forty yards, then shot her a sideways look. "Could you maybe not do that, though? It's quite distracting."

"Oh. Sorry."

"Aye, no, it's just... It's right in the corner of my eye," he said. "Just... when I'm driving. It's a bit—"

"Look out!"

Logan's eyes snapped to the front. There, right ahead of them, a middle-aged woman in Alice Cooper makeup came stumbling into the road, arms frantically waving.

The DCI's big boot stamped down on the brake pedal. The detectives' seat belts snapped tight across their chests, while everything that had been sitting in the back seat of Ben's car slid forwards before being unceremoniously dumped on the floor.

"Hang on. I know this house," Tammi-Jo said, but Logan had already unfastened his seat belt, and thrown open his door.

"Jesus Christ, what are you doing?" he cried, marching over to the woman.

Behind them, back along the road, Sandra's car rolled to a stop.

It was only when Logan was approaching the woman who'd run into the street that he realised she hadn't styled herself after a glam rock icon. Or not deliberately, at least. Instead, she was crying so hard that her mascara was painting itself all the way down her cheeks.

"Hey. It's OK. What is it? What's the matter?" he asked, dropping the confrontational tone. "I'm with the police. Has something happened?"

The woman babbled incoherently, then pointed a shaking

finger back in the direction of the nearest house. Both the front door and the garden gate stood wide open, and Logan was already halfway up the path when he ordered Tammi-Jo to stay with the woman.

He slowed at the door, just long enough to loudly inform anyone inside that he was with the police, and that he was coming inside.

There was nobody waiting for him in the hall. Another shout, louder this time, brought no response from elsewhere in the house.

He picked a door and barged straight through into the room beyond, fists clenched, ready for anything. Logan knew real, genuine panic when he saw it, and he'd seen it in the eyes of the woman outside.

Something in here had terrified her. Something so awful that she'd run blindly into traffic.

That was when he saw it.

Not *her*. The thing on the carpet was no longer a *her*. It hadn't been a her for some hours now, judging by the colour of the skin.

There was a clattering out in the hall as DC Swanney came running in.

"Is everything alright? Are you— Oh!"

She let out a gasp when she saw the body on the floor, and hung back behind Logan, not yet fully entering the room.

"I told you to wait outside," Logan intoned, not looking at her.

"Sandra and Gary know her. They're keeping an eye," Tammi-Jo said. "I didn't... I just thought..."

She took another short series of breaths, flexed her fingers, then tried again.

"I thought, because I'd spoken to her last night, I might be able to help," she explained.

Logan did look back over his shoulder then. "Spoken to her? So... what are you saying? Is this...?"

"Yes, sir," Tammi-Jo replied. She stole a lightning-quick look at the body on the floor. "That's Lois Dunlop. That's the woman I was here speaking to last night."

CHAPTER TWENTY-NINE

"OOF!"

Hamza raised his eyes from his laptop screen and looked across the room to where DI Forde was staring at his mobile phone.

"Everything alright?" the DS asked.

"Aye. Well, I mean, no. I mean... fine for me, aye," Ben said. He pointed to his phone. "It's Moira. Corson. You know, from the station in—"

"I know the one, sir, yeah," Hamza confirmed.

They all knew Moira. Only too well, in fact. She was the guardian of Fort William Police Station, and ruled the front desk with a fist of iron. She and Ben had been having some sort of relationship for a few months now, but nobody on the team was entirely clear on the details of it.

And nor, to be quite honest, did they have any desire to be.

"Right. Aye. Well, we've been texting." Ben looked up over the rim of his reading glasses. "You know, messages?"

Hamza nodded to confirm he'd grasped the concept.

"We weren't great at it at first. I mean, I'm no' the best when it comes to technology, but she's like a bloody dinosaur. So, it took us a while, but we're getting the hang of it."

"That's good," Hamza said, and he tried not to make it sound like a question.

He turned his attention back to his screen, satisfied that he'd done his bit.

Ben, however, wasn't finished. "Aye, well, she's just sent me one saying she's had a rough time at physio today. She had that stroke, mind? She's saying she's really suffering the day."

He lowered his phone, removed his glasses, and chewed on the end of one of their legs.

"I mean, what do you say to that?" he wondered. "I can't exactly just say, 'Chin up,' can I? It needs something a bit more... sensitive."

"Eh, aye," Hamza said. "I suppose so. I'm sure you'll think of something."

He tried once again to get back to work. The clicking of Ben's tongue against the back of his teeth made that more of a challenge.

"Any ideas?" the DI asked.

Hamza removed his fingers from his keyboard and sat back. There was no way he was getting anything done until he'd helped Ben come up with a response.

"Maybe just, *hope you feel better*, or *get well soon*, or something," he suggested.

Ben nodded, but he didn't look impressed. "I mean, aye. Could say that. But it's a bit impersonal, isn't it? I might as well just say, 'kind regards,' or something. It needs to be something a bit less... You know? And a bit more..."

He made the same hand gesture twice, and neither went any way towards clarifying what he was trying to say.

Hamza crossed his arms, cupping his elbows in his hands. "Right. I get it. So, what is it she's saying?" he asked. "Maybe, if I hear her message, I'll get a better idea of what to put."

Ben nodded again, but with much more enthusiasm this time. "Yes! Good idea. I'd messaged to ask how she was doing, and she's replied to say..."

He pulled his reading glasses back on, and squinted at the screen as he read the message.

"'Shite. Been at stroke clinic for physio. Awful. Feel old, and weak, and bloody useless.'"

Hamza winced, suddenly wishing that he hadn't asked. Moira wasn't so much a private person as an impenetrable fortress of mystery. It seemed that she'd started opening up to Ben, but the message clearly hadn't been intended for DS Khaled's consumption.

"Maybe just..." he began, trying to think of a response, but an excited cry from Ben cut him off.

"It's alright! It's alright, I've got it!" the DI announced. He tapped his screen a few times, then set his phone down, beaming from ear to ear.

Hamza didn't want to ask, but he had to know.

"What did you put?"

"I just wrote *lol*," Ben said. He picked up his mug, raised it as if toasting some sort of victory, then took a gulp of cold tea.

"Why the hell did you write that?" Hamza asked.

The tone of the detective sergeant's voice stopped Ben in his tracks. Grimacing, he swallowed down his tea.

"What do you mean?"

"You replied with *lol*? As in...?"

"As in L-dot-O-dot-L," Ben explained. "As in *lots of love*."

"Uh, no, sir," Hamza said. "As in *laughing out loud*."

Ben stared back at the detective sergeant in silence.

When he finally rediscovered his ability to speak, it wasn't really worth the weight.

"Eh?"

"That's what it stands for, sir—*lol*—it means *laughing out loud*."

Ben continued to sit there, frozen like a statue.

"Not *lots of love*," Hamza continued, trying to hammer the message home.

"Naw!" Ben laughed and waved a hand. "You're having me on. It means *lots of love*."

"It doesn't, sir. It really doesn't," Hamza insisted.

Ben's phone bleeped. He didn't acknowledge it right away, but his eyes were soon drawn down to the screen.

The worried look on his face quickly evaporated, and was replaced by a smile. "See? I bloody knew it. She's written back C!"

Hamza frowned. "C?"

"It's a misfired kiss."

Hamza's frown deepened. "A what?"

"It's next to the X on the wee keyboard. She's always hitting it by mistake," Ben explained. He chuckled, visibly relieved. "See? *Lots of love*. She's not going to come back with a C if she thinks I was laughing at her, is she?"

Hamza couldn't really argue with that one. It didn't really matter what the acronym meant, he supposed, if they'd both agreed it meant something else.

"Suppose not, sir," he said. "My mistake."

"Wait'll I tell her what you thought it stood for," Ben said. "She'll get a laugh out of that, alright."

He had just started to tap out a reply when the phone came alive in his hand. It rang and buzzed, the screen changing to display Logan's name.

"Jesus, Jack, you were almost the end of me there," Ben said, once he'd tapped the answer button and brought the mobile to his ear. "I was just in the middle of writing out a text. Here, you'll never believe what Hamza..."

His voice fell away. From his desk, DS Khaled watched the detective inspector's smile head in the same direction.

"Oh. Oh. I see." Ben rose from his chair, pointed to Hamza,

then pointed to where their jackets were hanging on hooks by the door. "Leave it with us, Jack," Ben said. "We're on our way."

———

The printer *whirred* and *clunked*, then *whirred* some more.

It struck Sinead as quite an elaborate warm-up procedure, given that she'd only asked the bloody thing to print one page of A4. At this rate, she'd have been quicker copying the information from her screen by hand.

Of course, it was also possible that she was reaching peak pregnancy impatience and irritability. No doubt the printer always took this long to get up to speed in the morning. It was just that today was the first day she'd wanted to kick the fucker to death, then throw it out the third-floor window.

She was glad that the others weren't here. She feared for what might happen to them, if they were. They'd all mean well, of course, but their fussing and concern could very well push her over the edge.

Not all the way over into violence, necessarily. She wasn't saying that.

But nor was she ruling it out.

Being pregnant, she decided—not for the first time that day —was shite.

She scratched at her neck, then ran her hands through her hair, then breathed, then repeated the whole thing again while the printer continued to piss about checking alignment, or filling the heads, or whatever the hell was so important.

"Right, bugger it," she spat, grabbing a pen from her desk, and clicking back to the screen she'd been trying to print information from.

She started to scribble down the details, the letters forming jagged, angry shapes on the paper as she jerked the pen across it.

Yes, the rest of the team were very fortunate that they weren't there to face her wrath.

"Alright, ya fannies?"

Sinead's pen jerked and pressed down so hard it tore a hole through the top three sheets of paper in her pad, and scratched an inch-long line on her desk.

"Jesus Christ. Dead in here, innit?"

Oh God.

It wasn't.

Not him.

Not now.

She heard the *thump* he made as he dropped down into a chair, then the creaking of the wheels as he rolled himself across the floor towards her.

Sinead didn't look at him, but he kept on rolling until he'd inserted himself into the hazy outer edges of her line of sight.

"The fuck is everyone?" he asked.

With a tut, and a sigh, Sinead finally turned to face Bob Hoon.

He looked better than he had the last time she'd seen him, a couple of days into the New Year. He'd still been sporting an assortment of bruises then, which had made him look like a colour chart for a new range of purple paints.

Now, aside from a black spot below his right eye, and some rawness around a couple of mostly healed cuts, he was pretty much back to normal.

Which was unfortunate, because had he still been injured, Sinead might've gone easier on him.

"They're out. And I'm busy. So, what do you want?" she demanded.

"Jesus. Cool your fucking jets," Hoon said. He raised both hands in a calming gesture, which was up there with the worst possible decisions he could've made. "Can I no' just swing in to say hello? Is that a fucking problem?"

"Yes. Yes, it's a problem," Sinead spat back at him. "We're busy here. We're doing actual police work. We can't just drop everything to entertain you. Especially since, you know, you don't actually work here, and shouldn't have been let up the stairs."

Hoon sniffed. "Doesn't look like you're busy," he said. "Looks to me like you're just drawing on your desk."

Sinead felt her hand adjusting its grip on her pen, and for a moment she enjoyed the thought of plunging it into Hoon's throat.

Sensing the danger, Hoon stopped slouching in the chair, and clasped his hands in his lap.

"Sorry, that was a joke," he said. He tapped his thumbs together. "I'm just... I just, eh, I needed out of the house. Berta's doing my nut in."

Sinead's grip on the pen loosened a little. His sudden shift in tone had surprised her.

"Keep getting the fucking press at the door. Phoning me up. Had fucking *Loose Women* on the phone, wanting me to go on and talk to them."

The absurdity of that image made Sinead snort in surprise. "What? Seriously?"

Hoon nodded. "Aye. About the whole fucking, you know, Eastgate thing? All the hoo-ha about that. Everyone's still talking about it. Apparently, I was trendy on Twitter. Whatever the fuck that means."

"Trending," Sinead corrected.

Hoon looked at her blankly for a moment, then shrugged. "Whatever. It's a bit mental."

Sinead sat down her pen. "What did you say to them?" she asked, curious despite herself. "*Loose Women*. What did you say?"

"I told them I'd sooner chew my own cock off," Hoon replied.

Much as she might have liked not to, Sinead couldn't help but smile at that. "I can't imagine they were impressed by that."

Hoon shrugged. "I'm sure it's no' the first time they've heard it," he replied. He twisted the chair and looked around the empty Incident Room. "Jack's no' here, then?"

"They're in Wick. Well, up that neck of the woods, anyway," Sinead said.

"All of them?" Hoon asked. Then, when Sinead nodded, he added, "But no' you?"

Sinead presented her stomach, flashed her teeth in what could've been either a smile or a grimace, then gestured to the screen.

"I'm here. Doing this."

"What?" Hoon squinted at the screen, his nose wrinkling and his lips drawing up over his teeth in distaste. "Boring shite? They've left you here doing that, have they?"

"Well, I can't exactly be chasing down suspects."

"Aye, well, but it's no' like it's one or the other, is it?" Hoon countered. "I'm sure there's boring shite needing doing in Wick, too. I'm sure you could be interviewing some witness or, I don't know, some fucking casual acquaintance of the victim's, or something."

Sinead's eyes widened. "Right?!" she said, then she caught herself just a little too late. "I mean, no. It does make sense, though. I've got my brother here. Hospital's here, if anything happens. It makes complete sense."

Hoon shrugged. "Aye, well, whatever you need to fucking tell yourself."

Sinead's expression darkened again. "Oh, and what should I be doing, like? Getting shot at? Getting blown up? Getting myself beaten up by Santa?"

"Here, it wasn't *actually* fucking Santa," Hoon protested. "And I didn't get beaten up! I won that fucking fight, I'll have you know. And I've got a whole fucking fan club now!

Fucking *Hoonigans*, they're calling themselves. Can you believe that?"

Sinead sadly could believe it. Tyler had shown her the hashtag on various social media platforms.

"Shower of arseholes," Hoon declared. "I can't go for a shite without one of them knocking at my door for an autograph."

"An autograph? From you?" Sinead asked, fascinated despite herself.

"Aye. I know. Mental. It's the fucking press's fault. They got photos of me on the motorbike. Made me look like a fucking action hero." He sniffed and shrugged. "Which, I suppose is fucking fair enough. I mean... come on. It was pretty fucking epic, if I say so myself."

"But *autographs*, though?"

"Aye. I don't actually sign any, obviously. I'm no' a complete prick. I just send Berta to the door, and she sends them packing."

Sinead stared blankly at him, still trying to process the idea that people were turning up at his house to try and get his signature.

Bob Hoon, a disgraced, middle-aged, foul-mouthed, border-line psychotic former detective superintendent.

And people were trying to get his *autograph*?!

She shook her head, deciding to draw a line under this whole part of the conversation.

"Whatever. I don't care," she said. "The point is, I know my place, and right now, it's here. This is where I'm needed. This is what I do now. I sit here, and I read emails, and I answer phones, and I pass messages on to whoever they need to go to. That's it. That's what I do."

While she'd been talking, the printer had finally gotten its finger out of its arse and spat out the page she'd requested. Hoon reached over and snatched it from the tray before she had a chance to reach for it.

He read the printout, his eyebrows arching.

"Oh, aye? That right?" He placed the sheet of paper down in front of her. "So, if you're so happy sitting here with your feet up," he began, "then why the fuck are you printing out directions to some address near Loch Glascarnoch?"

CHAPTER THIRTY

LOGAN STOOD in the doorway of the living room, listening to the sound of approaching sirens.

Lois Dunlop was dead. That much was obvious.

He'd checked for life signs, of course, though he'd known that finding any would've been nothing short of miraculous.

The old woman's eyes were open, like she was still staring up at the person who'd killed her, begging them, pleading with them to stop.

Her throat was like a scarf of raw red marks. Blood had oozed from her nose and down over her mouth, coating her false teeth in a red lacquer. She'd been punched, Logan guessed. Knocked to the floor, then pinned down and strangled.

From what he could tell, it had all happened here in the living room. The body hadn't been moved this time, which should keep the Scene of Crime team happy.

Logan groaned at the realisation that he was going to have to deal with Geoff Palmer again.

As if this poor woman's murder wasn't enough bad news for one day.

The sirens came screaming onto the street, and the walls of the living room were coated by an ever-shifting pattern of blue.

Logan looked out the window to where Tammi-Jo was sitting in Ben's car with the victim's daughter. The detective constable was talking—of course she was talking—but the woman in the passenger seat didn't seem to mind.

Of course, it was hard to tell, the way she was crying.

Gary and Sandra Hawthorne were still sitting in their car, directly behind Ben's. Logan had told them to shut off the engine and await further instructions, then had returned to the house and called in for backup.

Through the window, he saw the two Uniforms from earlier come clambering out of one car. They pulled on their hats while they waited for the two officers in the other car to join them on the pavement.

A little further back along the street, Logan recognised Hamza's car as it pulled up next to the kerb.

He shoved his hands deep down in his pockets, and turned to the woman on the floor.

Then, just for that moment, he allowed himself to think of the body not as an it, but as a *her* once again.

"Here we go then, sweetheart. This is us now," he muttered. "We're going to get you taken care of. We're going to make things right."

He paused then, like he was leaving space for her to reply. Then, with a nod, he left the house and went stalking along the garden path.

Hamza was already in full swing, coordinating the Uniforms, arranging the street to be cordoned off on both sides.

Ben raised a questioning thumb to DC Swanney as he passed his car, and she returned it with a nod to indicate everything was under control at her end.

"Good lass," he mumbled, then he entered the garden and met Logan halfway along the path.

"That was quick," the DCI told him.

"Aye. No' half bad," Ben said, checking his watch. He nodded past Logan to the house. "Another one, then?"

"Another one," Logan confirmed. "Same M.O."

"Strangled?"

"Aye, looks it. Old woman, too. Friend of Granny Hall."

Ben nodded slowly. "So you said. Lois Dunlop, wasn't it? The auld wifey that—"

"That DC Swanney interviewed late last night. Aye," Logan said.

Ben blew out his cheeks, and ran his hand through the wisps of his thinning hair. "That's not going to look great, is it?"

"Not perfect, no," Logan agreed.

"You did ask her if she did it, aye?"

Logan's laugh amounted to a single short exhalation through his nose. "Didn't need to. She told me it wasn't her. Several times, in fact."

"Aye, well. At least that's something, I suppose," Ben said. He gestured past Logan. "Shall we, then?"

Logan tipped his head backwards and stepped aside.

"Knock yourself out. I'm going to send Tammi-Jo back to base with the daughter. The Hawthornes can follow them down."

Ben frowned. "The Hawthornes?"

"Long story. I'll fill you in later. But, I'm sending them for fingerprinting."

"Right. To discount them?"

Logan scraped his teeth across his bottom lip. "Something like that," he said, then both men continued past each other as they headed in opposite directions along the path.

"Oh, by the way, Jack," Ben said, stopping by the door.

Logan stopped at the gate and turned back. "Aye?"

"Shona says she's having to bring the dug."

"Can she not just drop him at the office with Sinead?"

Ben shrugged. "Says she tried," he said. "But there was no sign of her anywhere."

"You want to know what this is?" Hoon spat. "This is a bad fucking idea."

His fingers drummed on the steering wheel of his car while he waited for the lights on Longman Road to go green. It was the third set to be on red since they'd left the station, but for once, he wasn't complaining. He was in no rush to get anywhere.

The same could not be said for the heavily pregnant woman in the passenger seat beside him.

"I want to see if he's there," Sinead said.

She was clutching the printout with the address on it in one hand. The other hand, Hoon couldn't help but notice, was rubbing at the lower part of her bump, just above where it met her pelvis.

"You've got a whole fucking building full of polis back there! Send one of them. Send fucking five of them, if you want. That's how many you've got going spare."

Sinead tutted. They'd already been through this. Several times, in fact.

"Like I said, I want to do it myself," she told him. "It's just checking an address. That's all. I just... I want to do something. I can't sit staring at that bloody screen any longer. I need to be doing something. And you didn't need to come. I didn't ask you to. I didn't *want* you to."

"Well, I can hardly fucking let you go yourself, can I?" Hoon shot back. "I might be an arsehole, but I'm no'..." He thought for a moment, trying to think of something worse. "*Two* arseholes."

He wasn't happy with it, but it was the best he could come up with in the heat of the moment.

The lights ahead changed from red to green. Sinead pointed, drawing his attention to them.

"Go," she instructed.

Hoon sighed as he crunched the car into gear.

"Fuck's sake," he muttered below his breath. "I should've just gone on *Loose Women*."

Tammi-Jo took Alison Dunlop by the elbow, and steered her up the steps towards the front door of Wick Police Station.

A quite cheerful sounding, "Alright?" hailed her from across the car park, and the detective constable looked over her shoulder to see Tyler and Constable Niddrie walking towards her.

Tyler had a big friendly smile on his face. Clearly, the news of Lois Dunlop's death was yet to reach him.

"What's up?" he asked, bounding up the steps. He caught sight of Alison's face, all red and puffy-eyed, and ejected a quiet, "Yikes!" before he could stop himself.

"Eh, DC Neish. Hi. This is Alison," Tammi-Jo hurriedly explained. "Her, um, her mum, she's just... She just... She just found her mum."

"Aw, nice one. Was she lost?" Tyler asked, which prompted an outburst of sobbing from the woman Tammi-Jo was currently supporting.

Tyler's face fell, as he quickly realised where he'd gone wrong.

"Oh. Shit. Sorry," he said. "Completely misunderstood. I thought... Sorry. I'm sorry for your loss."

"I was just, eh, I was just taking her in for a cup of tea. She needs to make a few phone calls."

Constable Niddrie appeared from behind Tyler. "I could do that, if you've got stuff to do," she suggested.

Then, before waiting for either DC to respond, she offered a hand and a supportive smile to the crying woman standing between them.

"Hi, Alison. I'm Beatrice. Bea." She stepped in closer, and Tammi-Jo relinquished custody of the woman's elbow. "Let's get you inside for that cuppa, eh?"

Alison accepted this change of chaperone without a word of objection. She just nodded, and allowed herself to be guided up the final few steps, then in through the station's front entrance.

Tyler waited until the doors had slid shut, before leaning back and hissing out a long, low, "Fuuuuuck!"

"Yeah. Yeah, that was a beauty," Tammi-Jo told him.

"She's dead, aye? The mum?" Tyler asked, still not *completely* sure he had the right end of the stick.

"Murdered," the other DC confirmed.

"Shit. Really? Another one?"

"Yeah. Strangled, we think," Tammi-Jo replied. "Well, DCI Logan thinks. I just sort of... I don't know. Froze a bit. Like, I could see she was dead, but that was about as far as my thought process went." She grimaced, showing her porcelain-white teeth. "Probably not great that, eh? For someone in this job."

"I wouldn't worry about it," Tyler said. "First time I saw a body, I threw up."

"What? No way!" Tammi-Jo gasped. "*You?*"

"Oh, aye. Believe it or not, I've not always been this..." Tyler hesitated, searching for the right word. Even with the young DC's oddly high opinion of him, he thought 'perfect,' might be a bit of a stretch, so he settled for, "accomplished."

"Wow." Tammi-Jo seemed genuinely shocked by the admission.

Sensing her admiration waning, Tyler rushed to reassert himself. "I mean, I got over it quick, like. It became second nature. And it will for you, too," he assured her. "It's just... The first time, it's rough. You feel a bit like—"

"Like you've made a mistake, and should've been a solicitor like your dad always said?"

Tyler smiled. "God, no. Don't be a solicitor. You'd have been a crap solicitor, anyway."

"What? What do you mean?" Tammi-Jo asked, all mock-offended. "Why would I have been a crap solicitor?"

"Because you seem like you're, you know, a human being," Tyler explained. "Like your soul's not been sucked out through your belly button in return for a criminal law degree."

Tammi-Jo's smile grew as she considered this compliment. She rocked back on her heels, which was dangerous, given she was balancing halfway up the stairs.

"You know, I think that's one of the nicest things anyone's ever said to me," she told him.

Tyler returned her smile. "Aye, well, what can I say? I'm a charming guy," he said, then a voice from behind them brought their conversation to a close.

"Uh, hello?"

Both detectives turned to see a dark-skinned man with greying dreadlocks and a bushy beard standing at the bottom of the steps, looking up at them. He was dressed in charcoal-coloured jogging bottoms and a dark blue tabard.

"I'm Chilton," he said. "Chilton Baxter? I was looking after Greta Hall?"

His accent was indeed quite difficult to understand, though it was broad Brummie, from Birmingham, which wasn't quite what Tammi-Jo had expected based on Lois' rant the night before.

Chilton looked from one detective to the other. When neither responded, he shrugged.

"I got a phone call from the office," he explained. "They said you guys wanted to ask me a few questions?"

"Oh! Yes! Sorry!" Tammi-Jo chirped. "It's just... Well, the person who'd generally be the one to interview you is a bit tied up at the moment. And so's, like, everyone else, so..."

"So, we'll do it," Tyler announced.

Tammi-Jo's eyes widened in surprise. She looked at him, and he gave her a nod which seemed to dismiss any concerns she may have been about to voice.

"Uh, yes. Sure! We'll do it," she said, smiling down at the man in the tabard. "But just give me a few minutes..."

She looked over to the car park entrance, just as Sandra and Gary's car pulled in.

"There's one quick thing I need to get sorted first."

CHAPTER THIRTY-ONE

SINEAD POINTED off down a branch in the single-track road, then consulted the map that she'd managed to download onto her phone before they'd come too far out into the wilderness for the mobile signal to find them.

"There. Down there," she cried, then she grabbed the door handle as Hoon swung his ten-year-old, clapped-out Honda CR-V hard to the left, so as not to miss the turning.

"Bit of fucking warning would've been nice." Hoon scowled. "And are you sure this time?"

"It's got to be down here," Sinead said, her grip on the door relaxing.

"Aye, I'm pretty sure that's the third fucking time you've said that," Hoon shot back. "And we're still none the fucking wiser as to where the place is."

"It's down here," Sinead insisted, peering through the thicket of trees on either side of the road. "It's got to be down here somewhere."

"No, it doesn't!" Hoon countered. "It could be fucking anywhere. You don't have a clue where we're going."

"We've got the address," Sinead reminded him.

"Aye, but it means fuck all," Hoon said, shooting the printout a scathing look. "I mean, 'Cottage Five, by Loch Glascarnoch.' It might as well just say, 'House near a bush in the arse end of fucking nowhere,' for all the good it's doing us. It's no' like there's street names. And look!" He gestured around them. "We're no' even near the loch anymore. That's half a bastarding mile back."

"It'll be down here. It has to be."

Sinead looked from her phone to the road ahead. Without a connection, she couldn't be sure that the map on-screen correlated with their actual location, but the bends of the track seemed similar enough.

"I just hope he's in."

"Who the fuck is he, anyway?" Hoon asked. "What's his name?"

"David Bowie."

Hoon snorted. "Fuck off!"

"No, it is. He changed it."

Hoon shook his head. "What a sad bastard," he remarked. "Who was he before that?"

Sinead didn't answer right away. She shouldn't really be sharing information about the investigation with anyone. But, she'd manipulated Hoon into driving her all the way out here, while making him think it was entirely his idea, so she owed him something.

"Malcolm Hall. Son of a woman murdered up near Wick."

Hoon shot her a sideways look that did nothing to hide his irritation. "What? That's it? You're coming out here to break the fucking bad news? That's Uniform's job!"

"No. He's... a suspect. Sort of," Sinead explained. "He was in the house. After the body was found, I mean. He attacked Tyler."

"Who?" Hoon asked.

Sinead rolled her eyes at him.

"Oh, Boy Band? Fuck. He didn't get his hair messed up, did he?" Hoon asked. "Poor bastard doesn't need a setback like that."

"He's fine," Sinead said, then she hissed and clutched at her stomach as one of the car's front wheels *kadunked* into a pothole.

"Fuck! What? What the fuck's happening?" Hoon cried, his knuckles going white on the wheel. "Is this it? Fuck, *is this it?*"

"No! Shut up! It's nothing. I'm fine," Sinead insisted. She opened her eyes, which she'd screwed shut when the pain had struck. "It's nothing. Don't worry about it. Just watch where you're going, and try not to... Hang on." She pointed ahead, excited. "Hang on, look!"

Hoon slowed the car to a stop in the narrow track. There, just forty yards or so in front of them, half-hidden by trees, was a ramshackle old cottage with a big number five painted on the wall beside the front door.

"Well, fuck me," Hoon mumbled. "Looks like maybe it is down here, after all."

Once Tammi-Jo had passed the Hawthornes over for fingerprinting, and checked in with Alison Dunlop and Nidds, she joined Tyler in the interview room, where he and Chilton Baxter were slurping through a cup of tea and coffee respectively.

Chilton rose to his feet when DC Swanney entered the room, and smiled politely while he waited for her to sit. Tyler, suddenly wondering if he should do the same, but not wanting to look like he was just copying the other man, leaned backwards in his chair so it rocked onto its hind legs.

A slightly confused frown troubled Chilton's brow when he

spotted this, but then Tammi-Jo took her seat, and both men returned to their previous positions without a word.

"Thanks for that," Tammi-Jo said, smiling at them as she pulled her seat in closer to the table.

"No bother," Tyler said. He pointed to two mugs on the table in front of her. "Didn't know if you'd want tea or coffee, so I got you both."

"Aw, thanks," she said. "But I don't really like them."

"What?" Tyler asked. He looked from the DC to the mugs, then back again. "What do you mean?"

"I'm not really a tea or coffee drinker."

Tyler blinked a few times, like his brain was struggling to process this.

"What do you drink, then?" he asked.

Tammi-Jo shrugged. "Juice, mostly. But, eh..." Her eyes flitted to the man sitting on the other side of the table, sipping away at his coffee.

"Oh. Aye. Right," Tyler said, filing the conversation away to be revisited at a later date. "So, eh, thanks for coming in, Mr Baxter."

"Chilton's fine. Unless... I'm not in trouble, am I? If I'm in trouble, you can call me Mr Baxter."

"Ha! No," Tyler said. "You're not in any trouble."

He realised he wasn't sure this was correct, and shot Tammi-Jo a questioning sideways look.

"No. You're not in any trouble," she stressed. "We're just doing a bit of background on Greta Hall."

Chilton sat down his mug. "Granny? Why?" He looked between them both. "What's happened?"

"You don't know?" asked Tyler.

"Know what?"

"Greta Hall was found dead yesterday."

"What?!" Chilton gasped, shock sweeping in like a cold front across his face. "Oh, God. Her heart? Was it her heart?"

"Eh, no," Tyler said. "She was murdered."

Across the table, the other man's expression changed. The look of shock from a moment ago had been a little too much. He'd over egged the pudding a bit. A woman her age, with her health issues? No way anyone would be *that* shocked, particularly someone who'd been helping care for her.

Rather than become more exaggerated still, though, it now became more subtle. More genuine. More real.

"Murdered?" he asked. "What do you mean *murdered*?"

"An intruder, we think," Tammi-Jo said. "Night before last."

"What, like a burglary?" Chilton ran a hand down his face, smoothing his grey-flecked beard. "Oh, God. That's... that's awful. Did you catch the guy?"

"We're working on it," Tyler said. "That's why we wanted to ask you a few questions."

Chilton's eyes narrowed as they ticktocked from one detective constable to the other. "Oh. Right. Yeah. I see. Bring in the black guy. See what he knows. He's probably involved."

"What? No—" Tammi-Jo began, but he raised his voice to talk over her.

"I wasn't even here. I was in Inverurie, over near Aberdeen. Left at four that afternoon, got back here this morning," he said. "Got a dozen witnesses who'll back that up. My wife and kids being four of them."

"No, no, we didn't... That's not why you're here, Chilton," Tammi-Jo insisted. She squirmed a little, feeling like maybe this was a bad idea, and that they should've waited for DCI Logan to come back, after all. "We're really just trying to get some background information. That's all. Honest."

Chilton sat back in his chair. He didn't look wholly convinced by the DC's response, but he seemed prepared to give her the benefit of the doubt.

"What about Albert?" the carer asked. "How's he doing? He alright?"

"He's being looked after," Tammi-Jo assured him.

"This is going to finish him off," Chilton said, wincing at the thought of the old man's plight. "I mean, he didn't have long left, anyway. With the cancer. But... God. This'll be the end of him."

The detectives swapped glances.

"Cancer?" Tyler asked. "Albert has cancer?"

"Yeah. Didn't you know? Stage four. Aggressive. He's not bothering with treatment. Doesn't see the point at his age."

"How do you know? Did he tell you?" Tyler asked.

"No. Sandra did. During the handover. Before she went off to look after her mum."

"Sandra? She knew, then?"

"Yeah." Chilton nodded. "She knew."

"So, Albert's dying?" Tammi-Jo looked saddened by this revelation.

Chilton smiled, not unkindly. "We're all dying, miss. But, yeah, he's getting there a lot faster than most. They gave him four to six months. That was back in October."

Tyler counted silently in his head.

"So, within the next couple of months, then?"

"Sooner now, I'd imagine. Granny kept him going. She was his whole reason for even trying. Without her..." He blew out his cheeks and shook his head. A tear may well have formed at the corner of an eye, but he moved to wipe it away before anyone noticed. "Nah. The poor old boy's not going to be with us much longer."

He took a drink of his coffee, composing himself, and washing away the croak that had been building in his voice.

"Whatever you need from me, however I can help, just ask," he said. "Whoever did this, they need to be caught. Because they haven't just killed one person. They've killed two."

Tammi-Jo cleared her throat softly. She looked to Tyler for guidance, and he gave her a nod.

"Well, Chilton. It's funny you should say that," she said.

Then, realising that her word choice might not have been completely appropriate, she hurriedly tried to course correct.

"Well, I mean, not funny, exactly. Not *funny ha-ha*. Not that sort of funny, more sort of... In fact, no." She shook her head, more at herself than anyone else. "It's not really any sort of funny, I suppose. Funny's not the right word. It's more..."

Beside her, Tyler quietly coughed. It was the prompt she needed to shunt her back on track.

"Tell me, Chilton," she said, clasping her hands together on the table between them. "How did you get along with Lois Dunlop?"

CHAPTER THIRTY-TWO

LOGAN LURKED in the corner of the living room, watching Shona examining the body on the floor.

She'd arrived in her car just a few minutes before, with Geoff Palmer's SOC minibus hot on her heels. Hamza had taken Taggart for a pee on the grass down the road from the house, while Shona had followed Logan inside to officially declare the victim dead.

"Yeah, she's a goner, alright," the pathologist said, removing her fingers from the old woman's wrist, before gently setting her arm back down.

"Good," Logan said, then he grimaced. "No, I don't mean... It's not good, obviously. I mean, thanks. For confirming."

"That's what I'm here for," Shona said, and Logan couldn't help but notice that she didn't even look at him when she spoke.

"So, eh, strangled, I'm thinking," he said.

Shona nodded. "Yep. From on top, I'd say." She stood up, but kept looking down at the body. "Looks like the same sort of material used on the other lady. Dressing gown cord. Maybe even the same one."

She mimed tying a knot in the air, like she was doing up a shoelace.

"There's a lot of bruising on the back of the neck. The cord was probably wrapped all the way around, then pulled outwards on both sides. Crossed over."

Logan came over to join her, his shoes rustling in their protective blue coverings.

He held his arms out, imagining the movement she was describing.

"That'd have brought them close together. Face to face, I mean. Nose to nose, practically," he reasoned. "The killer'd have to be leaning over to get enough of an arm's stretch."

Shona shrugged. "Not necessarily *that* far over. He could've wrapped the cord around his hands, kept them close to the neck. You'd get more strength behind it then."

Logan didn't look convinced. "You sure?"

"I'm sure. I think about this stuff a lot."

"Bit worrying," Logan said, but it didn't raise so much as a smile.

"It's my job. So, yes, I'm sure."

Logan nodded slowly, adjusting his mental picture to fit with Shona's explanation. "Aye. I can see that," he agreed. "Makes sense."

He shifted his weight from one foot to the other, building up to the non-work related question he'd wanted to ask since he'd seen her walking up the path.

She spoke again before he had a chance.

"I'd say she's been dead well over fourteen hours. Died yesterday evening at some point. Can't say much more than that yet."

"Right. Aye. DC Swanney left here after nine, so it must have been after then."

Shona nodded. "Yeah. That fits."

Logan waited until she'd finished making some notes in her

little hardback notebook, then voiced the question before she could say anything else.

"Are we alright?"

"What?" Shona flashed a smile. It didn't hang around long enough for Logan to determine its authenticity. "Yes. We're fine. Why wouldn't we be fine?"

"I, eh, I don't know. You tell me," Logan said.

Shona's mouth pulled downwards into an exaggerated frown, and she shrugged again. "Sure, I'm not the one who brought it up," she said.

"Trouble in Paradise?"

Geoff Palmer grinned at them from the doorway, then jumped back at the sheer, raw ferocity of Shona's, "Oh, fuck off, Geoff!"

"Jesus!" Palmer cried. He retreated, but the smirk didn't leave his face. "I'll let you finish up. Shout when you're done."

Logan waited until the SOC man had fully followed Shona's instruction.

"So... fine, then?" he ventured.

For a moment, it looked like Shona was going to give him the same sort of response as she'd given Palmer, but then she groaned, and rubbed at her forehead, embarrassed by her outburst.

"Sorry. I was out of order."

"Doesn't bother me," Logan said. "The more people who tell Geoff Palmer to get to fuck, the better."

Shona smiled, and this one lingered for a second or so. "Not about that. About being... you know. Weird."

"You're always weird," Logan told her. He rocked on his heels, his hands deep in his pockets. "I, eh, I like that. That you're weird, I mean."

"I just..." Shona began, talking over him, like she hadn't even been listening to his response. "I'm not even sure why I'm bothered. About, you know, the whole baby thing. I mean, I didn't even... I haven't even really thought if I even..." She looked at him imploringly. "You know what I'm saying?"

Logan started to nod, but then decided honesty was the best policy, and said, "Not really."

Shona sighed. She moved as if to lower herself on the couch, then remembered this was an active crime scene, and somehow managed to remain on her feet.

"I suppose I'm just..." She took a big breath then muttered something under it, giving herself a talking to. "I hadn't really thought about, you know, babies or anything. I mean, not for a long time. I just sort of assumed I'd end up as a mad old spinster, poking around at dead bodies, eating *Pot Noodles*, and having, like, ten-to-twelve cats, all with eighties movie character puns for names." She began to count on her fingers, starting with a thumb. "*Mr. Meowagi.*"

She waggled the next finger along for a few seconds, then shrugged and let her hand fall back to her side.

"I'd have come up with others. But, whatever, that was it. That was going to be my life. I had it all figured out."

She looked down at their matching blue shoe coverings, and wiggled both her feet, penguin-style.

"And then I met you. And everything changed," she said.

"That's—" Logan began, but she loudly *shushed* him into silence.

"Let me finish. I, um, I just... Suddenly, there were all these, you know, like... possibilities? Suddenly, I didn't have to be that mad woman with the dead bodies."

"You'll always be that, to be fair," Logan said.

Shona's smile briefly widened, humouring him.

"But I didn't *just* have to be that," she continued. "Or I didn't have to just be that on my own. Meeting you, us getting together... Suddenly, there were other doors that could be opened. Someone to spend my life with. Eight-to-ten fewer cats." She shrugged. "A family, maybe."

The word, and all its implications, hung there in the air between them.

"I'm not saying I wanted kids. I'd sort of come to accept that it wasn't going to happen. But now, suddenly, it was an option, you know? Suddenly, for the first time since... Well, for the first time ever, really, it was a thing that was on the table. *They* were a thing. And now... Well, and now they're not."

Logan had no idea what to say to that, but he opened his mouth in the hope that the right words would magically appear.

Shona, however, wasn't yet finished, and spoke before he could come up with anything.

"And you're right. I know you're right. I'm heading towards forty. You're nearly fifty."

"I'm no' *that* bloody near," Logan objected.

"And they're hard work. I get that. And we've got our careers to think about. And just, you know, they take up so much time. And they're expensive, too," Shona said, working her way through some mental list she'd clearly been compiling. "Like, I'm not saying you're wrong. I'm just saying..."

She let out a long, drawn-out sigh, then shook her head.

"I have no idea what I'm saying, to be honest," she admitted. "I just... You know, it was an option, now it's not, and I just have to close that door again. That's all. Or, like, put a padlock on it, or something, because I hadn't actually opened it in the first place. Does that make sense?"

Logan nodded. "Aye. Aye, it does," he said. "And I'm sorry. We should've had a proper discussion. It shouldn't have been something I brought up standing over an old woman's corpse."

Shona's gaze flitted down to the body on the carpet.

"You're making a bit of a habit of it, right enough," she said. "I hope all our discussions aren't going to have to be done like this, or the mortality rate's going to go through the roof."

Logan chuckled. "Aye. Maybe best to just chat over coffee or something next time. But, eh, but we're good? We're alright?"

"Ah, sure, nothing that dinner and a trip to the cinema won't fix," Shona replied.

"Do I at least get to choose the film this time?" Logan asked.

"Ha. Good one." The pathologist snorted. "And, sure, people say you've no sense of humour..."

"What do you think you're doing?" Sinead asked.

Hoon paused with his car door half open. "The fuck does it look like I'm doing? I'm going to get your man."

"Eh, no you aren't," Sinead said. "You're not in the police anymore."

"I'm a paid fucking consultant," Hoon fired back.

"Maybe, but that doesn't mean you can go knocking on doors or arresting people."

Annoyingly, she was right, Hoon knew. The paid consultant gig was pretty sweet, since it was basically free money for doing nothing, but he'd have loved some of his old polis powers to have been thrown in as part of the deal.

Sadly, it wasn't to be, though. He was a civilian advisor, and that was as far as it went.

"You can't go in there on your own," he objected. "He could be violent. You said yourself, he attacked Boy Band."

"He pushed him over," Sinead countered. She huffed and puffed as she dragged herself out of the car and onto the soft, marshy ground outside the cottage. "And I'm not an invalid. I can do this. I've got it."

"He's probably a fucking psycho," Hoon said. "I mean, he's changed his name to *David Bowie*, for fuck's sake. How's that normal? That's no' the actions of a man who's right in the fucking head."

"I'll deal with it," Sinead said. "I've handled people like that before, and I can handle them now."

Hoon glowered at her. One of his really impressive ones, too. Sinead just stared back at him, unblinking and unflinching, until he finally shrugged in acceptance of his defeat.

"Fine. Aye, fine, whatever," he said, slamming his door closed. "On you go. Go for your fucking life. Just don't come crying to me if he shoots you, or headbutts you, or whatever the fuck he decides to do. Don't say I didn't fucking warn you."

"Cool," Sinead replied brightly. "Just stay here, don't do anything, and I'll be back in a few minutes."

And with that, she shut the door, and went waddling through the broken down gate of Cottage Five.

"Trouble in Paradise?" Geoff Palmer's pudgy red face grinned out from within the elasticated confines of his hood. He looked like a particularly unpleasant and painful spot that was desperately in need of squeezing.

"That's twice you've made that joke, Geoff," Logan told him. "You need to get working on some new material."

Palmer's eyebrows, which had been hidden above the line of the hood, now lowered into view. "It's not a joke. It's a thing people ask."

"It's a thing tedious nosy bastards ask," Logan corrected. "And not that it's any of your business, but everything's just dandy, thanks."

He and the Scene of Crime man were standing on the front step of Lois Dunlop's house, the canopy above them sheltering them from the January drizzle that had been off and on all morning.

The rest of Palmer's team were already either inside, or hurriedly erecting tents in the garden to protect any forensic evidence from the rain.

Palmer himself, as per usual, appeared to be doing very little in the way of actual work.

"Didn't look dandy to me," he persisted. "It looked like a wee lover's tiff from where I was standing."

Logan drew in such a long, deep breath through his nose, that had they been standing inside, Palmer would almost certainly have passed out due to lack of oxygen.

"It may have escaped your notice, Geoff, but I don't really care what you think, beyond the very narrow parameters of our working relationship. You said you had something you wanted to tell me. If it's relationship advice, you can feel free to ram it up your hoop."

Palmer really shouldn't have been surprised by any of that, and yet he managed to look hurt, like he'd previously believed the two men shared some sort of friendship.

He sucked in his bottom lip, which made him look a bit like a frightened tortoise, then replied in a flat, ever so slightly croaky monotone.

"We ran the prints. On the bank statement. This 'David Bowie' fella that your DC found." He made the air quotes, which made Logan dislike him even more. "His were on there. And one of the recent ones, too."

Logan stared down at him in confusion. "Recent ones?"

"Yes. The husband and wife. They got processed up here and the prints were sent down the road, so I had one of my team down there run them through the system. Because, like me or not, Detective Chief Inspector, I care about my job. I want to do my best for your investigation."

"Alright, alright, very good. Well done," Logan said, brushing all that aside. "And?"

"And we got a match."

"On the bank statement? One of them had touched the bank statement?"

Palmer nodded. "The wife. Sandra, was it?" he said. "Both hers and Mr Bowie's prints were all over it."

CHAPTER THIRTY-THREE

THE PASSENGER SEAT of Hamza's car *the-thunked* as Logan slid it all the way backwards, giving himself more legroom and stopping his knees being pressed right up against the glovebox.

They had left Lois Dunlop's house behind, driven past Gary and Sandra's, then headed south towards Wick once they'd seen that the Hawthornes' car wasn't yet back.

"Nah, they're not here, boss."

Tyler sounded slightly breathless as his voice chirped out of the car's speaker system.

"I checked the car park, but they must've already left."

"Damn it," Logan muttered. "We'll keep our eyes peeled on the way down, then circle back if we don't find them."

"How come, boss?" Tyler asked. "Something come up?"

Logan told him about the fingerprints, and how Sandra had lied when she'd said she had no idea about Granny and Albert's secret riches.

"Aye, well, that's not all she knew, boss," Tyler explained. "We spoke to that other carer. Me and DC Swanney. He popped in, and since no one else was here, we thought we might as well—"

"Skip to the end, son," Logan urged. "What did he say?"

"Albert's dying. Got weeks left. Well, maybe even less than that now, he reckons, what with Greta being dead."

Logan ran a hand down his face as he added all the various components together.

"So, she knew about the money, she knew Albert was on the way out, and there's a very good chance she's named in the will," he said. "Get rid of Granny, and there's potentially a big whack of cash headed her way in the immediate future."

"Sounds fishy to me, boss," Tyler said.

"And didn't you say the husband disappeared on the night of the murder, sir?" Hamza added. "Could well be in it together."

"Want me to put out a shout and get them brought back in?" Tyler asked.

"No need for that, son," Logan replied.

He pointed ahead, and Hamza turned on the blue lights and the siren, catching the attention of the car heading towards them on the opposite side of the road.

"Looks like we've just spotted them. Prep us up a couple of interview rooms," Logan said. "We're bringing the bastards in."

There was no answer from the front door of Cottage Five, not even when, with some difficulty, Sinead leaned down to the letterbox and shouted to anyone who might be lurking inside, identifying herself.

A look through the grimy windows confirmed that the house looked lived-in. Although, that was actually quite a generous way of saying it was a bloody tip. All the mess—from the dirty plates on the coffee table to the piles of clothes on the floor—looked relatively recent, though.

Even if nobody was in there right now, they hadn't been gone for very long.

Gritting her teeth, Sinead picked her way around the side of the house, one hand leaning on the wall, the other cupping the underside of her stomach.

Right now, there was no pain. That was a bonus.

There was discomfort, of course, but that was hardly new. She'd basically been nothing but discomfort from the shoulders down for a few months now, and today was no exception, but the electrical stabbing sensation she'd been experiencing back and forth since yesterday was not currently causing her any concern.

She was fine. This was fine. She was a police officer doing police work, and the little nagging voice in her head insisting that she'd lost her mind could, quite frankly, quit with all its bloody whinging.

And then, as if to prove her wrong, her foot slipped on a wet, mossy rock. She hissed through her teeth as one leg shot out from under her, and only a frantic scramble and grab at a window ledge stopped her falling all the way.

Once fully upright again, she took a moment to just stand there, to just breathe, to just wait and see if the sudden movement had done any damage, or kicked anything off.

The pain grumbled at her, but then settled down, like a sleeping dragon half-opening one eye before nodding off again.

That nagging voice redoubled its efforts, though, and for a moment, she contemplated turning back.

But it was just that. It was just a moment.

Being more careful about where she put her feet, Sinead pressed on around the side of the house until she came to the back.

It had been half-consumed by the forest behind it, and the spindly winter branches seemed to claw at the windows and walls. A little lean-to woodshed was attached to the wall, its sloping corrugated iron roof all pitted with rust.

Beside it stood a weathered porch, with a door that was more bare blackened wood than it was paint.

The little voice in her head raised some concerns again. Valid ones, too. She ignored them, ducked under a few of the claw-like branches, and waddled her way to the back door.

She'd come too far. She'd done this much. If this was going to be her last act before starting her Maternity Leave, then she was damn well going to see it through.

The door didn't look capable of standing up to a proper polis knock. Of course, she wasn't really capable of doing one, either —not in the same way DCI Logan did, at any rate—but she gave it her best shot.

The dampness of the door deadened the sound but she was sure, just for a moment, that it prompted a brief flurry of movement from inside.

Sinead bent closer to the rotten wood and listened. The noise could've been a bird, or a big rat. Some sort of non-human life form, anyway, that she'd startled with her knocking.

But it could just as easily have been someone else.

"Hello?" she called. Then, unable to bring herself to call for, "David Bowie," she settled for the more generic, "Anyone there?" and listened again.

This time, the movement sounded heavier. More cautious than panicked.

A floorboard creaked.

Sinead felt a bit like an outside observer as she watched herself reaching for the rusted handle. It turned without a problem, and the ironmongery *clunked* as the swollen door was released from the frame and swung inwards.

"Hello?" Sinead said. Her voice wobbled as it explored the dirty kitchen just beyond the door. Half a dozen pots and pans hung from a rack on the ceiling, and the word seemed to bounce around inside them, before echoing off into the rest of the house. "Is anyone there?"

She heard another creak from beyond the kitchen door, like someone was trying to tiptoe away.

For a moment, she hesitated. She had no right to just barge in there. She had no legal argument for entering the house.

But she'd come too far, and if she went back to the office now, she'd be sitting at that desk, staring at that screen.

Terrified for the moment that would forever change her life.

Steeling herself, Sinead stepped over the threshold and into the kitchen. The smell of it assaulted her—old grease and rotting food, and the sour damp stench of a washing machine in desperate need of cleaning.

It all proved quite challenging for her already hair trigger gag reflex, and she hurried to the door with a hand clamped over her nose and mouth, trying desperately not to breathe.

With a gasp, she threw herself out into the hallway, where damp and mould had made the wood chip wallpaper come buckling away from the walls.

The front door stood at the opposite end of the hall, directly across from her. A door on her right stood open, revealing a bathroom she'd rather not think too much about. On her left, another door led into what she guessed was a bedroom, and then...

She stopped when she saw the man standing tucked in against the wall right beside her. Their eyes met, and she recognised his face from his file.

Malcolm Hall.

David Bowie.

Greta and Albert's son, and the man who had attacked Tyler in his rush to get away.

He lunged, his eyes wide, his arms thrusting forwards, shoving her in the chest. Sinead stumbled backwards, crying out. She fell against the bedroom door, which flew open behind her.

Malcolm, or David, or whatever his name was, saw his opening. He sprang towards the front door, his skinny arms and legs pumping like a sprinter.

But Sinead had come too far to let him get away that easily. Catching onto the door frame, she kicked out a foot, just above floor level.

It caught him hard across a shin. He let out quite a high-pitched scream, and as his legs tangled up around the foot, his bottom half had no choice but to stop running. His top half didn't get the message, though, and his arms continued to swing even as his direction of motion suddenly shifted from *forwards* to *downwards*.

The *thump* he made when he hit the floor was reassuringly solid-sounding. He lay there groaning for a moment or two, then suddenly remembered where he was, and what he'd been doing.

Placing his hands flat on the floor, he tried to raise himself up in a push-up position, but a foot between his shoulder blades reintroduced him to the threadbare carpet.

There was a sudden *crack* from along the hallway, as a foot that had been meant to throw the front door wide open instead came straight through the rotten wood.

"Oh, for fuck's sake," Hoon muttered, and Sinead could just make out the shape of him through the dirty, frosted glass, hopping up and down as he tried to free his leg. "You alright? The fuck's happening?"

"I'm alright," Sinead called back.

So much for the cavalry.

But then, she hadn't needed his help. She had it all under control.

Sinead pressed down harder with her foot, and fixed her

most Logan-esque glower on the man pinned to the floor beneath it.

"Malcolm Hall, or David Bowie, or whatever your bloody name is," she said a little breathlessly. "You, sunshine, are nicked!"

CHAPTER THIRTY-FOUR

DC NEISH STOPPED JUST outside the door to the interview room. He was carrying a cup of tea, a can of *Coke*, and a cheeky plate of biscuits, and now couldn't for the life of him figure out how the hell to open the door.

"Shite," he muttered, looking around for somewhere to offload some of the items he was carrying. Finding none, he drew back a foot to dunt the door and get Tammi-Jo's attention, but stopped when he realised she was talking to someone inside.

Tyler, being a nosy bastard, leaned in a little closer and listened.

"No. No, I know, Daddy," she said. "No, it's fine. It's all good. Nobody's thinking that." There was a pause then, and an almost imperceptible sigh. "Because they're nice. They're not... No, they're not like that."

Tyler suddenly felt a bit guilty about listening in, but not quite guilty enough to stop.

"No, I do know what I'm doing," Tammi-Jo said. The hurt in her voice was tangible when she continued, "Please don't laugh at that. I do. I know. If they don't like me, they don't like me. So what? I'm doing my job."

The guilt, combined with a healthy dose of second-hand embarrassment, proved too much for Tyler to cope with then. He kicked the bottom of the door a couple of times, and announced his presence with a, "Hey, Tammi-Jo, can you let me in?"

The other DC's voice lowered as she whispered a few final words into the phone. Tyler stepped back from the door and fixed a big friendly smile on his face while he waited for her to appear.

It took her a little longer than he'd expected, and his cheeks were really starting to feel it by the time she opened the door.

He saw right away the hint of red around her eyes, and the similar colouring of her cheeks.

"Cheers!" he said, ratcheting the smile up a notch or two as she held the door wide for him. "I just came back with this now," he said, ducking past her. "Just got here this second and knocked."

He'd over egged the pudding, and he knew it. And, judging by the way her face turned a shameful shade of scarlet, she knew it, too.

"For what it's worth," he said, passing her the can of *Coke*. "I like you. Pretty sure the others do, too."

Tammi-Jo swept a strand of hair back over an ear and looked down at the floor, like she couldn't physically bear to maintain eye contact.

Tyler was well aware that he wasn't particularly good at this sort of thing. The last time he'd tried to offer anyone advice, he'd ended up announcing that *one man's case is another man's custard.*

Or was it *cucumber?*

Either way, it wasn't exactly wisdom for the ages. Sinead was much better at this than he was. Or Hamza. Or Ben.

Or any of them, in fact.

But, he knew he had to say something.

He racked his brains for some sort of appropriate idiom or saying that would fit the situation, but when he drew a blank, he did the only thing left he could think of.

He spoke from the heart.

"Listen, it doesn't matter what anyone else thinks. You're doing fine," he told her. "You're doing *great*. It's not easy fitting into a new team. Especially when everyone knows one another. But you're doing it. You were brilliant in that interview."

"Was I?" Tammi-Jo asked. She sounded younger than her years. Much too young.

"Aye, you totally nailed it. I could barely even tell it was your first one!"

DC Swanney glanced up, just for a moment. "It wasn't my first one," she said. "I've done others."

Tyler fought to keep his smile in place.

"Oh." He swallowed. "That'll be why you were so good at it, then."

He offered her the plate of biscuits, then glanced at her phone, which was sitting on the desk beside her. "Was it your dad? That you were talking to?"

Tammi-Jo took a chocolate digestive from the plate, then nodded glumly. "Yeah. He's still going on about me going back to uni."

"And do you want to?" Tyler asked.

"No." DC Swanney's head shake was emphatic. "No, I want to do this. I want to do what we're doing."

Tyler chuckled. "Aye, standing around eating biscuits, you can't beat it," he said.

Tammi-Jo finally managed a smile at that. "You know what I mean."

She slumped down so she was sitting on the edge of the desk and cracked open her can of *Coke*.

"But, I mean, maybe he's right," she said. "Maybe he knows best."

She slurped down a drink, then burped in a very unladylike manner. Tyler's eyes widened in surprise and he looked her up and down, as if just seeing her now for the first time.

"Do you really think that?" he asked.

"I don't know," she said. She seemed to be miles away, and completely oblivious to her recent gaseous outburst. "I just... I don't know what to do. Maybe I am too young. Maybe he does know best."

"Who knows best about what?" Logan's voice was a sudden bark in the hush of the Incident Room. He barged in, shrugging off his coat. "What're we talking about? What's happened now?"

"Nothing, boss," Tyler said.

Beside him, Tammi-Jo jumped to her feet and hurriedly smoothed herself down. Logan regarded them both in a suspicious silence for a second, his eyes narrowing.

"Aye, there is. Something's up," he said. "Out with it."

"It's, eh, it's nothing, sir. Just a... family issue," Tammi-Jo said.

For a moment, it didn't look like this would be enough to satisfy the DCI, but clearly he had too much else on his mind to dwell on it right now.

"Fine. Tyler, you got hold of Sinead yet?"

It was Tyler's turn to frown. "What do you mean, boss? I texted her to let her know I was here."

"Did she reply?" Logan asked.

Tyler plunged a hand into his pocket and whipped out his phone. "No. No, not yet. Why?" he asked, panic stirring up his insides. "Is something wrong? Has something happened?"

"No," Logan said, reassuring the lad. Then, deciding that honesty would be much kinder, he grimaced. "Maybe. Not sure. Shona took a swing by the station this morning, and she's no' there."

"Not there? Why isn't she there? She should be there!"

Tyler said, the pitch of his voice rising like someone was pushing a slider all the way to maximum. "Where is she?"

"I don't know," Logan admitted. "Maybe she was just down at the canteen."

"The staff canteen? At the station?" Tyler shot back. "She's pregnant, boss, not mental."

"Well, maybe she stayed at home, then," Logan reasoned. "There's no point getting worked up until we know more. So, get on the phone and get hold of her before you have a bloody stroke."

Tyler was already tapping away at the screen of his mobile, concern creasing his usually smooth brow.

"Right. Good. DC Swanney," Logan intoned. He raised an index finger and pointed to the young detective constable. "You're in the interview room with me." One corner of his mouth was tugged upwards into the beginning of a grin. "And guess which one of us is going to be playing the Bad Cop..."

CHAPTER THIRTY-FIVE

"SORRY TO KEEP YOU. Gary, wasn't it?"

DI Forde offered his hand across the table, and smiled broadly as Gary Hawthorne met him halfway.

"I'd blame the hold-up on traffic, but then you'd know I was lying," Ben said, taking his seat next to Hamza. "Roads are quiet up here, eh?"

"Sometimes. Right now, aye," Gary confirmed. "Not so much in the summer. North Coast 500, and all that."

Ben grimaced at the thought of all those tourists clogging up the narrow roads. "I bet that's a pain in the arse, is it? Worse because it's so quiet the rest of the year, I'm sure."

He shuddered, like the very thought of it chilled him to the bone, then fixed Gary with another big beaming grin.

"I'm Detective Inspector Ben Forde. Just 'Ben' is absolutely fine, though. No need to stand on ceremony." He turned to Hamza. "Have we started the doodah?"

The detective sergeant nodded. "Recording's underway, sir."

"Good. Good." He met Gary's eye and tried to reassure him with another smile. "Just to keep everyone in the right. It's for your benefit as much as anyone else's, Gary. Can I call you that, by the way? Gary? Do you mind?"

"I, eh, I don't mind, no," Gary said, his gaze flitting from detective to detective. "But what's this about? The other guy, DCI Logan, was it? When he flagged us down, he seemed..."

"Concerned. That's all," Ben said. "After everything that's happened, we want to make sure we're asking all the right questions, getting all the information we can. We appreciate you taking more time out of your day to help us out, we really do."

He took a pen from his top pocket, clicked the button on the end a few times, then twirled it around between his fingers.

"Did you want a solicitor?" he asked, keeping his tone light and his smile in place. "I know, it seems a bit excessive, but we have to ask," he continued, before the other man could reply. "Totally up to you, though. Your call."

"I, eh..." Gary considered the question, and the slightly incredulous way in which it had been asked. "Do I need one?"

"When does anyone ever *need* one of those buggers?" Ben chuckled. "And I can't advise, unfortunately. All I can do is ask. We can get you one, no bother at all. But, obviously, it'll mean you waiting around a while, when I'm pretty sure we could get this all squared away in no time."

He clicked the pen again.

He twirled it around his fingers, drawing the other man's eye.

"Your call, though, Gary. Totally up to you."

"Uh, I'll be fine," Gary decided. "Seems a bit excessive, like you say. It's not like I'm in any trouble."

Ben continued to smile. He clicked his pen one more time, retracting the point, then set it on the desk beside the fresh, clean notepad Hamza had brought for him.

"No, you're not in any trouble, Gary," Ben said. He steepled his fingers together on the desk in front of him. "At least, let's hope not..."

"Why does she keep shouting at me?" asked Sandra, staring pointedly past Tammi-Jo to where Logan was lurking near the door.

The DC slapped both her hands down on the desk and stood there, leaning over, glaring at the woman on the other side of the interview table.

"I'm not shouting!" Tammi-Jo snapped. "Believe me, when I'm shouting, you'll know about it."

Logan was forced to look down at the floor, biting his tongue to stop himself smiling. He hadn't expected Tammi-Jo to throw herself into the Bad Cop role with such gusto and enthusiasm.

She'd already announced that she was going to go through Sandra "like a dose of the shits," and Logan was just grateful that the interview room didn't have a staircase, or poor Mrs Hawthorne would likely be lying in a crumpled heap at the bottom of it.

"Just answer the question, Sandra!" urged the detective constable. "Answer the question, and save us both a lot of hassle."

"What question?" Sandra shot back. "You haven't asked a question. You told me you know I'm lying, and that's it! You haven't even said what I'm supposed to be lying about!"

Tammi-Jo slammed her hands down again. At the rate she was performing the move, her palms must surely have been red raw.

"There's an implied question, though, isn't there?"

The suspect frowned. "Is there? What?"

"Why are you lying, Sandra?" DC Swanney demanded. "Why aren't you telling us the truth?"

"The truth about *what*? What am I supposed to be lying about?"

There was yet another *bang* as the hands came down once

more. This time, however, Logan spoke before Tammi-Jo could get a word in.

"We know you know about the money, Sandra," Logan said.

He leaned against the wall by the door, his sleeves rolled up, his arms folded across his bear-like chest.

"What money? I don't know what you're on about," Sandra said, but her protests were fooling no one.

"Your fingerprints were all over the bank statement," Logan told her.

Sandra's brow creased in concentration. "Bank statement?" she whispered. "Bank statement, bank statement, bank... Oh!" She sat up straight, raising a finger in the air. "In the paperwork in the drawer? I probably picked it up to tidy it away at some point."

Tammi-Jo all-but sneered at her. "What part of *all over it* don't you understand?" the DC demanded. "You didn't just touch it, you *fingered* it." A flicker of doubt troubled her face. "Not like *that*. I don't mean you... Not in a sexual sense."

Sandra stared at her in silence for a few moments, then turned her attention back to Logan.

"What's she on about?"

"We don't care about your prints being on the bank statement, Sandra," Logan said, ignoring the question. "I'm sure there are a hundred and one reasons they might be there."

He stepped away from the wall. Sandra's gaze followed him all the way until he was sitting in the chair across from her.

"Yes. Yes, exactly! I tidied up a lot of their stuff. That's probably half my job, sorting out clients' mess. Putting stuff away for them. That's what I do."

"Right. I see," Logan sat back, folding his arms again. "So, even though you'd picked up the bank statement and got your prints all over it, you didn't actually look at what it said at any point?" he asked. "Is that what you're saying?"

"Ha! No chance!" Tammi-Jo cried. "She's looked at it. She knows."

"Do you, Sandra? Do you know how much money Granny and Albert had in the bank?" Logan pressed. "Because, I can't see how you couldn't know. It's all over the bank statement, all the way down that right hand column."

It was early in the interview, but Sandra was already starting to squirm. That was a good sign. With a bit of luck, they'd have this wrapped up in no time.

"Right. Yes. I did see," she admitted. "Just recently. I had no idea before then."

Logan interlocked his fingers and sat forward. "How come you lied to us?" he asked.

"Because she killed her," Tammi-Jo said. She jabbed a finger at the suspect, practically foaming at the mouth. "Because she's a *fucking murderer!* Aren't you, Sandra?"

Logan coughed, gently clearing his throat. He caught Tammi-Jo's eye, and gave a little tilt of his head to suggest she might want to dial it down a bit.

"Or, you know, maybe you aren't," the DC said, all the confrontation in her voice suddenly evaporating.

She sat back down in her seat and flashed a smile that was far more disconcerting than the shouting had been. "Sorry," Tammi-Jo said. "Continue."

"What the fu...?" the woman across the table muttered. She looked from Tammi-Jo to Logan. "What is this? What's her problem?"

"Why did you lie to us about the money, Sandra?" Logan asked again.

"Yeah, Sandra! Why did you lie to us?!" Tammi-Jo demanded, getting herself riled up again.

This time, though, she managed to restrain herself from slapping the desk and leaping to her feet, and settled for some high-grade glaring action, instead.

"I just..." Sandra began. Logan could see her desperately trying to come up with an answer, and then watched her expression change as one suddenly came to her. "Data protection."

"I'm sorry?" the DCI asked, though he could already see where this was going.

"Client confidentiality. Data protection. I can't just go shouting about that sort of thing," Sandra said. "It's illegal."

"Not if the person's dead," Tammi-Jo countered.

Sandra looked quite pleased with herself then, and Logan knew exactly what was coming next.

"Joint account, isn't it?" she said. "Still in Albert's name."

"And is he a client?" Logan asked.

"Technically, no," Sandra conceded. "But, I'm not sure how that works, legally. That's why I couldn't say anything about their financial situation, just in case. It could get me sacked."

"Oh, believe me, getting sacked is the least of your worries right now," Tammi-Jo warned.

"Are you in the will, Sandra?" Logan asked. The sudden change of subject was designed to keep the suspect on the back foot, and from the look of shock on her face, it seemed to do the trick. "Do you know if Granny wrote you in before she died?"

"I'm not... I don't..." Sandra swallowed, then shook her head. "No. No, I doubt it. I mean, why would I be? I'm not family."

"Oh, come on, Sandra. I think you're selling yourself short," Logan told her. "The help you've given them? The years of care and support? Don't you think that maybe they're planning on leaving you a bob or two?"

Sandra folded her arms. "Like I said, I doubt it."

"Well, I've got good news for you, then," Logan told her. He tapped a folder that lay closed on the desk between them. "Because I've checked, and your name's in there. Quite a tidy wee sum, too. Do you want me to spoil the surprise? I'll give you a clue, it starts with a three, and it ends in five zeros."

She knew. He could see it in her face. He could tell by the movement of her hands, and the angle of her shoulders. She knew. To the penny.

"That's a lot of money," Logan said. "Life-changing, some would say. Would you say that, Detective Constable? Would you call it a life-changing sum?"

"I would, sir," Tammi-Jo confirmed. "That's exactly what I'd call it. You could buy a house with that. Go on a nice holiday."

Logan started to speak, but the DC hadn't finished.

"Buy a car. Or a camper van, if you wanted. Start a business."

"Aye. Any of that," Logan agreed.

"Or buy a boat," Tammi-Jo added, then she shot Logan a quick sideways look. "That's me done."

"Good. Right. Well. Congratulations on your upcoming cash bonanza, Sandra," Logan said. His chair creaked as he leaned forwards. "Which leads me nicely into my next question..."

"Where were you the night Greta Hall was killed?"

Gary Hawthorne's next breath came whistling out of him, like he'd just been punched in the stomach. He frowned, but it was such an exaggerated caricature of a thing, that Ben didn't even need to put his glasses on to see right through it.

"I was at home."

"All night?" Hamza asked.

He sat with his pen poised above his notepad. He was already on the third page, and every word he wrote seemed to make the man on the other side of the table a little more nervous.

As a result, most of the stuff he'd written had been random

word salad, scribbled solely to push Gary Hawthorne ever further into a state of panic.

"Yeah," Gary said. He swallowed, his eyes darting to Hamza's pen as it moved across the page. "All night."

"But that's no' true, is it, son?" Ben said. "You went out, didn't you? The night she was killed, you left your house."

Gary made a show of thinking. "Um..."

"Lying to us is not going to help you, Gary," Hamza told him. "We know you went out. We know you left the house. And, honestly? That doesn't look good for you."

"It looks bad for you, Gary," Ben added. "I mean, think about it from our perspective. A woman is killed just down the road from you. A woman whose house your wife has a key to. A woman who, as we've just established, planned to leave you and your family a substantial sum of money after she died."

He leaned closer, like he was sharing a secret.

"And you're no' in your house when it happens? And not only that, you won't tell us where you were?"

"Smells fishy," Hamza said.

"Fishier than a trawlerman's Welly boot," Ben agreed.

"I told you already, I have no idea about any money," Gary insisted. "I don't think Sandra knows, either. She's never mentioned it. And I'd never kill anyone! Never. Especially not Granny, of all bloody people!"

"Good. So, where were you?" Ben asked. "And if you say you were at home, then I'm afraid this conversation is going to go downhill fast."

Something between a groan and a whine emerged from deep inside Gary Hawthorne. He squirmed in his uncomfortable chair, like there was a wrestling match going on down in the very guts of the man.

"We didn't..." he began, then he hurriedly backtracked. "*I* didn't go anywhere special. Just for a wander."

"Back up there a moment, Gary," Ben said. "*We?*"

Gary ran both hands through his thinning hair, fingers splayed into claws like he was tearing at his scalp.

"Just tell us the truth, son," Ben urged. He smiled kindly. "Don't get yourself all worked up about it. Just tell us what happened, and we can all go about our day."

Across the table, Gary's face screwed up, his mouth clamping tightly shut, like his mind was willing to talk, but his body was having none of it.

Finally, though, with a gasp of breath, his willpower won out.

"We, uh, we have a thing," he said. His shoulders heaved, and his face contorted again, but it was impossible to tell if he was laughing or crying. "We have a thing we do."

"Who?" Ben asked.

Gary cleared his throat. He looked at both detectives, then directed his gaze down to his hands instead. He'd picked away the skin around his fingernails, exposing a layer of raw, shiny pink below.

"Sandra and me."

Ben and Hamza swapped glances. Both men clicked the ends of their pens, extending the nibs.

"I thought Sandra was away that night?" Hamza asked. He checked back through his notes. "Off seeing her mother."

"She, uh, she was. I mean, she had been," Gary said. "But... she... Well. She came back."

Ben frowned. "Home?"

"Not exactly, no," Gary said. "Not home."

"Come on, son. Spit it out," Ben urged. "Get it off your chest."

Gary groaned again. He laughed, a series of short, frenzied breaths that disintegrated into sobs.

Finally, with a nod, he pulled himself together enough to reply.

"OK. OK, I'll tell you everything," he said. He winced. "But you're going to think it's a bit weird..."

Five minutes later, Logan, Ben, Hamza, and Tammi-Jo stood together in the corridor outside the interview rooms, swapping notes.

Technically, only one note had been swapped so far.

But it had been a belter.

"He watches her getting pumped?" Logan asked in an incredulous whisper.

Ben, whose face was currently fixed in a rictus of disbelief, could only nod dumbly.

"It's a regular thing, apparently," Hamza said, keeping his voice low. "Couple of times a month, she meets a different guy at a hotel here in Wick. Same room every time. Ground floor, window looking out onto the car park."

Logan's face was now almost a mirror image of Ben's. "And he stands outside?" the DCI asked. "He watches her getting pumped by some randomer?"

"Aye, sir. Films it, too," Hamza confirmed.

"He showed us," Ben muttered. His thoughts on the footage were written all over his face. "Dirty bastard."

Hamza shot Tammi-Jo a slightly awkward glance before continuing. "Apparently, he stands outside the window and, well, you know..."

"He doesn't crack one off!" Logan said, surprise cranking up the volume of his voice. He dropped it back to a whisper before continuing. "No way. Surely not? Surely he doesn't stand out there..."

"*Wanking*," said Ben, for the sake of clarity. His grimace tightened further, pulling his features in, like they were all bunching together for comfort and safety. "Right there in the car park. Bold as you please. Camera in one hand, his old lad in the other."

"Watching his wife getting pumped," Logan added with a shake of his head.

"Dirty, *dirty* bastard," Ben muttered.

Tammi-Jo, who had so far remained tight-lipped about the whole thing, finally offered an opinion.

"Men are bloody weird."

"Here, no' all of us!" Ben protested. He looked around at the others. "I mean, can you imagine me up to that sort of thing? Standing there in a bloody hotel car park, bashing one out at a downstairs window? At my age? No! No, you cannot!"

"Well, now I'm very much trying not to," Logan said, his lips drawing back in distaste. "So, thanks for that."

Before any of them could dwell on that mental image any further, Tyler's voice called from along the corridor.

"Boss! There you are!" He sounded out of breath as he jogged up to meet them. "It's Sinead."

"What about her?" Logan asked. "What's happened?"

"I don't know, boss. I still can't get hold of her," Tyler said. "She's not at home, not in the office, her mobile's off, and she hasn't checked in at the hospital. I don't know where she is."

His panic was palpable. He was dancing on the spot, his eyes wide with terror.

"Right. Calm down, son. This is Sinead, she'll be fine," Logan said. His hands clamped around Tyler's upper arms, pinning the young DC in place. "But you head down the road. Find her, then stay with her. You're done here now. It's time to go."

The gratitude swept across Tyler's face. "You sure you don't need me here, boss?"

Logan laughed, then it fell away into silence.

"Oh. You were being serious?" he teased. "Aye. It's fine. I

reckon we'll cope. You get going. It's going to take you a couple of hours to drive down there and..."

He stopped, his eyes darting left and right, like he was silently scanning a proposal that had suddenly been presented to him.

"Actually, hang on," he said. He raised a finger. "I think I've just had a better idea..."

CHAPTER THIRTY-SIX

MALCOLM HALL SAT with his hands cuffed in front of him in the back of Hoon's Honda, complaining loudly about the treatment he'd received at the hands of the heavily pregnant Detective Constable Bell.

"It's no' right," he grumbled. His voice was slurred around the edges from years of substance abuse. "That was my house. You shouldn't be allowed into my house. That's no' right."

"The back door was open, Malcolm," Sinead replied, glancing back over her shoulder at him. "I was concerned for your wellbeing."

"My name's no' Malcolm. It's David. I'm David Bowie."

"Are you fuck," Hoon spat.

"I am so. I'm the Starman," Malcolm insisted. "That's my name. David Bowie. It's on my library card."

"Aye, like you can fucking read," Hoon retorted. "I've seen more brains in a tub of fucking margarine."

He tapped the car's SatNav, like this might prompt it to suddenly find a signal it could connect to. Instead, it continued to show a featureless map of the whole of the north of Scotland, overlaid with a spinning circle.

"You're polis. You can't talk to me like that," Malcolm whined.

"No, I'm no' polis, actually," Hoon said, glowering at the prisoner in the rearview mirror as the car rumbled along yet another single track road. "So, I can talk to you any way I like, you spangle-eyed fountain of horse shit."

Malcolm's lips moved silently as he tried to figure out if this was an insult.

It didn't take him long to come to the correct conclusion.

"You can't do that! You can't say stuff like that. I know my rights!"

"Rights?!" Hoon barked. "You've no' got any fucking rights, pal. No' in my car. In my car, I'm the fucking Lord Almighty. I set the fucking rules, and the only right you've got is the right to button your fucking lip and—"

Beside him, Sinead let out a sharp, sudden hiss. She'd already been rubbing her stomach with one hand, but now the one she'd been using to grip the door handle joined it.

Hoon shot her a sideways look, and saw the pain registering on her face as she huffed out a low, guttural grunt.

"What? What's happening?" he demanded.

"Is she going into labour?" asked Malcolm from the back. "Is she going to have a baby?"

"You fucking stay out of this!" Hoon spat.

He hit the brakes, which forced Sinead to hurriedly brace herself with her arms, and drew a yelp of pain through her gritted teeth.

"Watch what you're doing!" she yelped. "Why did you slam on the brakes?"

"Because I thought you were about to pop out a fucking wean!"

"So, what? You thought you'd try firing it out of me, instead?!" Sinead cried. She drew in a deep breath, shook her head, then pointed to the road ahead. "Just go. I'm fine."

"Are you sure you're fine, pet?" Malcolm asked, his glassy eyes sharpening just a fraction. "You look really, really pregnant."

Sinead rolled her eyes, whispered a, "Jesus," to herself, then pointed ahead again. "Come on. Go. I'm fine."

Hoon studied her face for a few moments, then shifted his feet around on the pedals.

"Far be it from me to agree with Bonzo the Talking Fucktrumpet back there, but you don't look fine."

Sinead's teeth clamped together again. This time, though, it was more through anger than pain.

"I'm. Fine," she stressed. "People don't need to keep asking me. I'm OK. Nothing's happening yet. I'm not going to let it."

"I'm no' sure you get the final say on the matter," Hoon told her. He tapped at the screen again, but the SatNav was still refusing to cooperate. "I'm taking you to the hospital."

"No, we're going back to the office," Sinead insisted. "I need to bring Malcolm in."

"It's David," the man in the back reminded them.

"Shut up!" Sinead snapped, then she let out a cry and almost doubled over as a jagged lightning bolt of pain tore upwards from her pelvis.

She shook her head, her face pale, tears welling up in her eyes.

"No. No, no, no, no. It's not happening. I'm fine. I'm fine," she said, but the words weren't meant for Hoon, or for the drug-addled prisoner sitting handcuffed in the back.

They were aimed at herself, as she tried to stay calm by denying reality itself.

"I'm fine. I'm fine. It's not happening yet. There's plenty of time."

Another cry of pain begged to differ.

When it passed, Hoon was speaking in an urgent whisper. "Breathe. Breathe. Just remember to breathe, for Christ's sake."

"I *am* breathing!"

"I wasn't fucking talking to you!" Hoon retorted. "I was talking to me!"

He slapped the flat of a hand against the SatNav screen, shot a series of rapid-fire expletives in its direction, then the car weaved from side to side as he dug around in his pocket for his mobile.

One glance at the signal strength icon confirmed his worst fears.

"Fuuuuuuuuck!" he roared, so loudly that birds in the trees on either side of the road took to the air in fright.

"It's fine. Just drive. It's not happening yet. I'm not—"

She gasped, her eyes widening, her hands clamping onto the curved underside of her belly.

"What?" Hoon demanded. "What's the matter?"

"Nothing," she replied.

"Bollocks! There's something," Hoon spat. "What is it?"

Sinead swallowed. Her tongue darted across her lips and found them suddenly dry.

"I, um, I think my waters just broke."

Hoon's face became a mask of horror. "What? On my fucking seat?! It's no' leather! It'll soak in, for fuck's..."

The stark, awful reality of it hit him then. The seat, and its condition, were the least of his worries.

"Wait. Wait a fucking minute," he said. "Your waters broke? Does that no' mean—?"

Another contraction gripped Sinead, forcing her to stamp her feet and grab the dashboard while she waited for the pain to pass.

From behind them, the slurred tones of Malcolm Hall offered some insight.

"Looks to me like someone's got a wee baby on the way!"

"Shite." Logan groaned when he saw the name flashing up on the screen of his phone.

Mitchell.

There were a very limited number of reasons why she might be calling him, none of them particularly good.

Standing at the edge of the windswept field, he leaned on a fence post, and braced himself for a bollocking.

"Ma'am?" he said. "To what do I owe the—"

"Don't bother with the buttering up, Jack," Mitchell said.

Logan winced. The detective superintendent sounded more annoyed than he'd been expecting.

And he'd been expecting her to sound really quite annoyed indeed.

"Why isn't there cover for DC Bell?" she asked. "I've had a report handed to me by CID because they couldn't find anyone on your team to deliver it to."

"I'm sorry about that, ma'am," Logan said. He pulled his coat tighter around himself, then jammed a finger in his ear so he could hear her more clearly above the growing background noise. "We didn't actually know that Sinead wasn't coming in."

"She didn't call?"

"No, ma'am."

"What, nobody? What about DC Neish? He must know."

Logan looked over at Tyler. He was sitting with his seatbelt on and his eyes closed, his lips moving in silent prayer.

"He's been trying to get hold of her, but no joy," Logan said.

There was a moment of silence from the other end of the line, while Mitchell processed this. "I'll get feelers out for her," she finally said. "Send someone to the house."

"That's much appreciated," Logan said. "We're, eh, we're sending Tyler down now. I thought that might be what you were calling about, to be honest. The transport arrangements."

"No, I'm calling about this report. Albert Hall's son. The

one to the wife who died during childbirth. He lived. He was adopted out. We found him. We have a name that..."

Her voice tailed away into silence. Logan pressed the finger deeper into his ear canal, blocking out the ever-increasing racket.

"Hold on," Mitchell said. "Why would I be calling about Detective Constable Neish's *transport arrangements*?"

"Well," Logan began. He raised a hand and waved to the terror-stricken Tyler as the helicopter the DC was sitting in lurched upwards into the air. "There might be one or two cost implications for you to sign off on..."

CHAPTER THIRTY-SEVEN

ONCE TYLER HAD BEEN WAVED off, Logan returned to Wick Police Station, where the remainder of the team was gathered in the Incident Room.

He'd taken a bit of a bollocking from Mitchell on the whole helicopter thing, but it had been fairly subdued, and he suspected that, in his shoes, she'd have done the same thing. For all her cold, stern exterior, Logan reckoned she was a big softy underneath.

Of course, he had very little evidence to back that theory up, yet he was convinced of it.

It took one to know one, after all.

The Hawthornes' stories had matched up, even if their perspectives on them didn't fully align. Gary clearly took real pleasure in, as Logan put it, "watching his wife getting pumped."

Sandra herself, however, seemed to be doing it more out of spite, or to prove some sort of dominance over her husband. The fact that he clearly got off on it had apparently almost put her off the whole arrangement, until she realised that, when push came to shove, she quite enjoyed having sex with strange men.

It kept their own relationship fresh, Gary insisted. On the nights following Sandra's clandestine hotel-based pumping, the husband and wife would apparently, "Go at it like rabbits," he claimed.

Then, over the next couple of nights, the potency of the high would fade, and neither would so much as touch the other until the following month, when it would all happen again.

"You probably think it sounds a bit sordid," Gary had said, to which DI Forde had replied resoundingly in the affirmative.

Their timings matched. They were both able to show their phone's GPS history, which tracked Gary from his house to the hotel and back again, and marked Sandra as having driven over late in the evening from her mother's to the hotel, where she stayed until check-out the next day.

Both of them had plenty of video evidence on their phones that showed what they'd been up to. The murder of Granny Hall hadn't featured in any of the footage, although Ben may well have been less horrified if it had.

Hamza checked through the GPS data and the time-stamped footage, and confirmed that they all appeared to be legitimate. Around the time that Granny was being strangled, Gary Hawthorne was beating his meat outside a hotel window, while his wife was being hammered from behind by a man half her age and twice her size.

As alibis went, they were both pretty solid. Messages on Sandra's dating app further backed up their story, and a quick call to the guy she'd been with in the hotel room confirmed that she hadn't left the room all night.

The next evening, while Lois Dunlop was being murdered, Sandra and Gary were having frantic, mostly-clothed sex in the shed in the back garden, away from the prying ears of their children. They had been kind enough to film this interaction, too, and while the angle hadn't been particularly flattering, their faces appeared in shot long enough to confirm it was them, and the time-stamp went some way to exonerating them.

Logan didn't like it, but he'd had no choice but to let the couple go. He'd warned them not to leave town, but as they'd headed out to their car, he knew that, in reality, the investigation was back to square one.

He wasn't alone in that. He felt the sombre mood as he returned to the Incident Room, and even his description of Tyler's terror during the helicopter take-off only barely lightened it.

"Right. Where are we now, then?" he asked, dumping his coat across the back of a chair. "What's the latest?"

"It's still a bit early to have anything back on Lois Dunlop," Ben said. "Shona's away back down the road. Palmer's lot are still here, but packing up."

"Early indications?" Logan asked.

Ben deferred to Hamza, who checked his notes. "Strangled, like Greta. Shona reckons the same dressing gown cord was used on both. Or similar, at least. Friction burn marks on the skin match."

"Don't suppose Lois Dunlop has a few million quid sitting around in the bank, does she?"

From the back of the room, sharing Dave's desk, Constable Niddrie piped up. "Not unless she's been hiding it from the family, sir, no. I spoke to the daughter, Alison, and she has no idea who'd want to kill her mum. Said she was well-liked."

"Neighbours say the same," Hamza added. "Uniform checked, but nobody heard or saw anything. That street's pretty sheltered. No houses across the road." He shrugged, and shot a quick look at Tammi-Jo. "Well, there was one thing a neighbour saw. Guy from two doors down says he saw a 'fit-looking lassie' leaving the house yesterday evening, sometime between nine and ten."

"Hang on, he couldn't have. I was there then, and I

would've seen..." Tammi-Jo began, before the penny dropped. "Wait. Gotcha. Right. 'Fit-looking,' eh? What's he like?"

"About sixty years old and twenty-four stone," Hamza said.

Tammi-Jo nodded. "Aye. That sounds about my luck." She raised both hands, like she was surrendering. "And, just to make clear again, in case anyone was wondering, I didn't kill her. She was definitely alive when I left. She even locked..."

The detective constable frowned, as she realised the significance of this.

"She locked the door. After she threw me out, she locked the door behind me. How was it found this morning, do we know?"

It was Nidds who replied. "Unlocked. Alison has a key, but she said she just walked straight in."

Logan walked over to the Big Board, and rubbed a hand across his jaw. "No other forced entry, so either someone had a key, she let someone in after you'd gone—"

"Or they were there the whole time," Tammi-Jo added, her face paling at the thought. "They could've been in the house when I was there, just waiting for me to leave."

"No saying that's the case, but aye. Maybe," Logan admitted. "Try and no' think about it too much, though. That way madness lies."

They went through the rest of the information they had, trying to fit the pieces together. The alibi of Chilton, the other carer who'd stepped in for Sandra while she was on her compassionate leave, checked out, so he was in the clear.

They combed over Sandra and Gary's statements, trying to find some discrepancy between the lines of those that they might have missed.

They'd both been quizzed about the music box in Rory's possession, but both maintained the boy must've taken it in the days before Granny's death, like he'd claimed. Both had seemed angry about it, though Sandra admitted she'd been impressed at how Edgar, the older brother, had thrown himself into the line of fire.

"He'd do anything for his little brother," she'd said, and she'd smiled proudly as she'd spoken the words.

Gary had been more concerned about the boys—or anyone else, for that matter—finding out about the couple's monthly *sexcapades*. If their friends and neighbours knew the truth, he'd said, then they'd have to move away out of shame and embarrassment. And they couldn't do that, what with Sandra's clients and her mother in such poor health.

Ben had assured him that nobody was going to find out from the police, but had pointed out that it was only a matter of time before word got out some other way. Masturbating in a busy hotel car park wasn't exactly a low-key activity, and someone was bound to spot him sooner or later.

"Best knock it on the head, son," the DI had urged. Then, he'd clarified that he'd meant the whole activity, and not any particular part of Gary's anatomy—an activity which the man already seemed to have well in hand. Literally.

Malcolm Hall, aka David Bowie, was still an unknown quantity. He was definitely at the house the day after the murder, and he knew about the money. With the Hawthornes now sliding down the list of suspects, the junkie, repeat criminal son of the victim now sat at the top of the pile of potentials.

Unfortunately, his whereabouts were still a mystery. Logan instructed Hamza and Tammi-Jo to put out a shout for him, both internally and in the press and social media accounts. Finding him was high on the list of priorities.

Although, following Logan's call with Mitchell, there was someone else in joint first place.

The others listened as he brought them up to date. Albert Hall's first wife had died during childbirth. The child had survived, but Albert had been so stricken with grief that he

305 ONE FOR THE AGES

could barely bring himself to look at his newborn son, let alone care for him.

The baby had been taken into the system. He had been adopted soon after by an older couple who'd never been able to have children of their own, and had been brought up south of the border under his new name.

Patrick Parkes.

"Wait, wait, wait," Tammi-Jo said. "Hold on. That's that guy, isn't it? The shouty man from across the road. The one who told us to *pee off*."

"Hell of a coincidence if not," Logan said. He looked across the faces of the team. "So, hands up who thinks we should pay him a visit?"

CHAPTER THIRTY-EIGHT

"IF YOU EVEN FUCKING think about running, I'll wrap your fucking legs in a bow, and tie them round your fucking neck!" Hoon warned, after dragging the still-handcuffed Malcolm Hall out of the back of the Honda. "Just stand there, shut the fuck up, and if you see any cars passing, flag the fuckers down. Alright?"

"How am I meant to flag them down with my hands cuffed together?" Malcolm asked, his brow furrowing with the effort of working that out.

"For fuck's..." Hoon clamped his wrists together, then raised both hands and waved. "Like that. It's no' fucking rocket science, pal.

Malcolm studied the movement, then sniffed. "Aye, but I've got a gammy shoulder. If I do that, it'll hurt."

"It'll hurt a lot fucking more if you don't," Hoon warned. "Now pay attention. Eyes peeled. And not a fucking word unless you see someone coming."

Malcolm blinked slowly, like all these instructions were overloading his brain. He didn't turn and look at the road, but instead peered past Hoon to where Sinead was now sitting in the back of the car, both front seats shoved all the way forward to give her room.

"Is she alright?" Malcolm asked. "She looks like she's upset."

"Just watch the fucking road," Hoon said, shoving him out into the middle of the single-lane track.

Malcolm grumbled as he stumbled along, but then he stood with his back to the car, looking in both directions for any signs of movement.

With him out of the way, Hoon took several steadying breaths, then walked over to the car, smiling a little too broadly at the detective constable sprawled in the back.

"You, eh, you doing alright?" he asked.

Sinead raised her eyes and glowered at him. There was something bordering on the demonic in that look, and it stopped Hoon dead in his tracks.

"Does it look like I'm alright?" she hissed, then a contraction twisted her mouth into a grimace, and she gripped the headrest of the chair in front of her, breathing heavily until it passed.

"Well, alright or not, I think we need to prepare for the possibility that this is fucking happening," Hoon told her.

"It's not happening!" Sinead protested. The sentence started angry, but ended with a sob. She shook her head. "It can't. I need to get to the hospital. I can't do it out here. What if something goes wrong?"

"I'd say we're two klicks north of 'Gone Wrong' as it is, and headed deep into 'Royally Fucked' territory," Hoon replied. He saw the panic in her eyes and changed his tone. "But you can power through this. You've fucking got this. Everything's going to be fine."

Sinead's head shaking became even more emphatic. "No! It can't happen. I'm not ready. I'm not ready!"

"Aye, look, it's no' ideal. Believe me, I'm no' exactly jumping for fucking joy about it, either, but it is what it is. And what it is, is two sprogs about to come sliding headfirst out of your—"

"For any of it!" Sinead cried, cutting him off. "I'm not ready for any of it. I don't... I don't know what to do."

"I think you just push," Hoon said.

"*After that*, I mean! It's not this bit that I'm worried about. It's all of it. It's everything that comes after. It's being a mum." She was shaking, her eyes swimming with tears. "What if I can't do it? What if I'm no use? What if I'm a bad mum?"

Hoon shrugged. "Dunno. Sell them on the black market?" he suggested.

Then, when a glare from Sinead almost cut him in two, he sighed.

"Look, no offence, but you're being a fucking idiot. You'll be a great mum," he told her. "I mean, look at the practice you've had. And I don't mean with your wee brother, I mean with Boy Band. That's a full-time fucking mothering role right there. And, to your credit, you've managed to stop him drinking bleach, or chasing a ball into traffic, or whatever else the clueless fucking dunderheid would have done without you around. This'll be a fucking walk in the park compared to dealing with him. Trust me, you've got this in the bag."

Sinead laughed through her sobs—a single, half-hearted snort that was immediately swallowed again by another fear rising to the surface.

This one, she'd never mentioned to anyone. This one, she'd barely even been able to admit to herself.

"And what if I don't like them?" she whispered, and she winced at the sheer awfulness of the thought. "What do I do if I don't like them?"

"Like them? What are you talking about? *Of course* you won't fucking like them," Hoon told her. "They'll be a couple of wee bastards. They'll make your life a living fucking hell, morning, noon, and night. And because there's two of them, they'll pair up on you. They'll join forces so they can be sure they've really ruined your life forever. You'll rue the fucking day they were born."

"How is this helping?!" Sinead hissed, burying her head in her hands.

Hoon dropped into a crouch at the side of the car so that he was looking up at her.

"Because none of that'll matter," he said, his voice losing much of his usual venom. "I don't have kids, but I've spent enough time with people who do to know that none of that makes any difference. They'll get right on your tits. They'll drive you up the fucking wall, twenty-four-seven. But, pains in the arse or not, you'll do anything for them. You'll be ready to die for them. Every fucking time."

He took her hand and gave it a squeeze. She looked down at his rough hand as it gripped hers, and for the first time ever she thought that maybe, just maybe, she'd had the man pegged all wrong.

"So, how about we face facts that, like it or not, this is fucking happening, you squeeze them two weans out of your vag, then we hightail it to the fucking hospital before I throw up, shit myself, pass out, or some fucking combination of the three?" He gave her a smile of encouragement, and she saw a softness there that he usually kept well-hidden. "What do you say to that, eh?"

Sinead let out a big, shaky breath.

"Jesus Christ," she muttered, wiping her tears with the heel of a hand. "I can't believe this is happening. Out here. With you of all people!"

"Aye, well, I can't believe that you're about to completely fucking ruin the back seats of my—"

"Car!"

Hoon and Sinead both looked over to Malcolm, who stood in the middle of the road with his hands raised above his head.

Turning further, Hoon saw a vehicle rounding a corner along the road. It was a white car.

A white car, with a set of blue lights fixed to the roof.

"Oh, thank *fuck* for that!" he cheered. He spun back to Sinead and pointed between her legs. "Change of plan. Put a fucking cork in that!"

Sinead's smile of relief didn't quite make it all the way across her face before a cry of pain wiped it away. She shook her head, gripping the back of the chair in front of her.

"No. Too late. No time."

"No. No, no. You can do this. Just fucking hang on!" Hoon urged.

Behind him, a police car drew to a halt beside the Honda. A male constable who looked two sizes too small for his uniform peered through the passenger side window, then recoiled in horror at the scene playing out in the back of Hoon's car.

He opened the door to get out, then did a double take when Hoon came marching over. The levels of terror on his face were ratcheted up a notch or two. Clearly, he recognised the former detective superintendent. "Is, eh, is everything alright?" he asked, before adding a hesitant questioning, "Sir?" at the end.

"I'll give you two fucking guesses, son!" Hoon barked. "You stay where you are in that fucking car. I'm loading her into the back. We're getting her to the—"

Sinead screamed, and something about it—about the urgency of it—made him abandon the plan before he'd even finished explaining it.

"Right. No. Clearly, that's no' fucking happening," he muttered. "Call an ambulance. Get them here on the fucking double. If they've got teleportation technology they've been saving for a rainy day, then now's the fucking time for them to crack it out."

"I've got no signal," the constable said. "I need to drive a couple of miles down the road to get one."

"Then why are you still fucking sitting there?" Hoon bellowed. He stabbed a finger back along the road in the direction the car had come. "Go. Get a fucking signal, and call it in!"

Sensibly, the man in the car chose not to argue. He pulled his door closed, and Hoon pulled Malcolm aside so the constable could pull a seven-point-turn in the narrow road.

"And hurry the fuck up!" Hoon bellowed, as the car went speeding off.

He watched it go until it was nearly at the corner, then ran a hand down his face.

"Right, then," he muttered. He turned back to Sinead, who was now lying almost flat in the back seat of the Honda. One by one, he rolled up his sleeves. "Here goes fucking nothing!"

CHAPTER THIRTY-NINE

PATRICK PARKES' face fell when he opened the door to find Logan and Hamza standing on his front step. Considering his face seemed to be fixed in a permanent fallen state, this was quite a feat.

"We meet again, Mr Parkes," Logan said. Both detectives held up their warrant cards, in case the bushy-eyebrowed gentleman standing in his hallway needed a reminder as to who he was dealing with. "Mind if we come in and have a few words?"

"You can't, no. I'm very busy," Patrick said. "You'll have to make an appointment."

He started to close the door, but Logan pressed the flat of a hand against it, stopping it moving any further.

"We know, Patrick," he said. "We know who you are."

Inside, Patrick stopped trying to push the door.

"Either you let us in, or we take you to the station in Wick," Logan continued. "Your call."

Patrick chewed on his bottom lip for a moment, shot a look back over his shoulder, then relented.

"We can sit in the kitchen," he said. "But I really am busy. I don't have long."

"Well, then," Logan said, stepping past him into the hall. "Here's hoping you're a fast talker, eh?"

Patrick shut the door behind Hamza, then ushered both men towards a door at the far end of the hall. It led into a decently sized kitchen with a small dining table tucked in below the back window. There were three chairs pushed in under the table, with a fourth sitting in the corner ready to be called into play should it be needed.

A box of recycling sitting on top of the chair suggested its services weren't often required.

Logan and Hamza took a seat at the table, then the DCI shot a meaningful look at the kettle, which Patrick failed to pick up on. Instead, he pulled the third seat out from under the table, planted himself on it, and placed his hands on his knees like he was bracing himself.

"What do you want?" he asked.

Realising that tea wasn't going to be on offer, Logan got right down to business.

"So, old Albert's your dad, eh?"

Patrick shook his head. "No."

"I'm sorry?"

"He isn't my dad. You're wrong."

Logan folded his arms. "Well, I've got some paperwork back at the office that begs to differ. Maybe we should head down there, after all, so you can see it for yourself?"

"He's my father," Patrick continued, his lips pursed. "He's not my dad. He'll never be my dad. My dad was a good man, and he's sadly no longer with us. Biologically, Albert provided half of my genes. That was where his input started and ended."

"So, you do know, then?" Logan asked.

"Of course I know! Why would I be here if I didn't know?

Why would I be here, living across the road from him? That would be some coincidence."

"Why are you here?" Hamza asked. "You spying on him?"

"Yes. Exactly that," Patrick snapped. "No law against that, is there?"

"Yes," Hamza said. "Plenty."

Patrick grimaced. "Oh, OK, well I'm not *spying*, obviously. No more than anyone else on any other street in any other town is spying on one another, anyway. I'm just..."

"You're just what, Patrick?" Logan pressed. "What are you just?"

"I just... I wanted to..." He tutted, rolled his eyes, then shrugged. "When my parents died—my proper parents, I mean, the ones who didn't abandon me—I just... I wanted some answers."

"Did they tell you that you were adopted?" Logan asked.

"Yes. Early on. It wasn't a secret," Patrick said. "We had no secrets. Not really. They didn't want me to find out down the line, and think it was some sort of shameful thing to be hidden. They celebrated it. They called me..." His throat tightened. His fingers gripped his knees. "They told me I was a gift. They said they were the lucky ones. They always made me feel like I was *more* loved, not less. Like, with all the kids in the world needing homes, they were blessed to have ended up with me."

A short, sarcastic little laugh escaped through his nose, and he turned to look out of the window at a back garden that was mostly stone chippings and weeds.

"The way they spoke, it was like they'd won the lottery. Some prize I turned out to be, though, eh? Never married. Never left home." He swallowed, his gaze still lost somewhere out the window. "Never dared."

"When did they pass away?" Hamza asked.

"Just over two years ago. Well, that was Mum. Dad was about nine months before then."

"Must've been rough," the DS continued.

Patrick smiled, but it was a sad, empty sort of thing. "You can say that again. They were my only family, you know? When they went, I was on my own. For the first time ever—well, for the first time since I was abandoned—I was on my own. And I *hated* it."

"So, you came looking for your father?"

Patrick shook his head. "No," he said, then he relented. "Maybe. In my head, I came looking for answers. That was all. After they died, I was a mess. Not sad. Well, I was, but mostly angry. Like... I don't know. Like I'd been cheated. But on purpose. Like someone had deliberately dealt me a bad hand."

"And you wanted someone to take that anger out on?" Logan guessed.

"Albert," Hamza said.

"Yes! Exactly! I wanted to find him, and I wanted to hurt him. I'm not hiding that fact," Patrick said. "I was suffering, and he wasn't. After everything he'd done, after blaming me for what happened and casting me aside, he'd started again. New wife. New life."

"So, you decided to make him pay? Is that it, Patrick? You decided to kill Greta to, what? To get your own back?"

"I didn't kill Greta," Patrick said. There was no shock or outrage in the reply. Clearly, he'd been anticipating the question. "Of course I didn't. How could I? She was... nice. They both were. That was the worst of it. I came up here to confront him. I came up here to tell him exactly what I thought of him, but... I don't know. When I saw him, he was just so... *old*."

He ran a hand through his thinning hair, then scratched the back of his head. Some of the bitterness that had been woven into his words petered out as he continued.

"I'd built him up to be this cruel, heartless bastard. This monster. And then, when I saw him, and he was so frail... And then, I spoke to him. I just made an excuse and went to the door.

Took a clipboard, and told them I was doing a census survey. They invited me in. Made me tea. Offered me dinner, would you believe? I mean, who does that?"

"Did you tell them why you were really there?" Logan asked.

"No. How could I?" Patrick said. "I mean, Albert... He's, you know? It's not easy for him to communicate. And Granny, she was... I couldn't just put her in the middle of it, could I? I couldn't just have her translate, or whatever? She'd done nothing wrong. She didn't deserve that."

He jabbed a finger back in the direction of his front door, and his voice cracked with emotion.

"And she *certainly* didn't deserve *that*."

"How did you end up living here?" Hamza asked.

Patrick's hand dropped back onto his knee. He shrugged. "The day I came round to talk to them, the first thing I saw when I stepped out was the estate agent's notice in the front garden there. It was a literal sign, as far as I was concerned. So, I put an offer in, sold up the house down south, and I was living here three months later."

"Did they no' think that was a bit weird?" said Logan. "Some random stranger who'd just been to see them suddenly moving in across the road?"

Patrick smiled. Once again, there wasn't an ounce of genuine happiness to be found in it.

"They didn't remember me," he said, and a tear skiffed down one of his cheeks. "They came to the door to welcome me to the area. Brought tablet and scones. Albert had made me a wee key hook."

His voice broke again on those last two words, but he forced his way through it.

"He'd made it himself. It's rough as hell." He laughed, just for a moment. "I mean, it's bloody awful! But he made it. He made that. For me. First and only present my father ever made me."

"Did you tell them then?" Hamza asked. "Who you were?"

"No. No, I couldn't do it. They were too old for the drama of it all. So, I thought, if I can't be his son, I'll be his neighbour. You know? I'll be a good one. I'll do his bins. I'll get the shopping in, if he's stuck. I even started learning BSL. Sign language. From YouTube. I thought that would let me talk to him. And, in the meantime, I'd keep an eye on him."

He brought his hands from his knees and wrung them together, more tears starting to fall.

"Fucked that up, didn't I? So much for keeping an eye."

Logan ran his tongue across the back of his teeth, considering the other man's big speech. He seemed genuine enough, but by his own admission the man had been living a lie for the last couple of years. He'd had practice at hiding the truth.

"Where were you the night Greta died?"

Patrick had been ready for that question, too. "I was here. All night. On my own."

"Right. So, no one can corroborate that, then?"

"I'm sure the game logs can."

Logan immediately shot Hamza a sideways look, deferring this one to the detective sergeant.

"Gaming logs?"

"Online poker. It's how I make my money," Patrick explained. "Texas Hold 'Em, mostly. I use various sites, but *Poker Facial* had a tournament on that night, so I was playing on there. Came away with three grand. The player and chat logs will back me up, and I was camming at the time, too. For my elephant."

Logan suddenly knew how Ben Forde felt when talking about any form of post-1990s technology.

"For your elephant? What are you talking about?" he asked.

"Not a real elephant. It's the site, it's one of its gimmicks,"

Patrick explained. "To play, everyone needs a camera on, and the face tracking is overlaid onto their avatar. Mine's an elephant in a wee hat."

Logan considered this for a few moments, then asked, "Why?"

Patrick shrugged. "Well, it was between that and an ostrich with a bow tie."

"No, I meant why is it even a thing?" Logan asked, then he shook his head, dismissing his own question. "Doesn't matter. So, you're telling us that there will be a record of you playing poker at the time that Greta was murdered?"

"I don't know what time she was murdered," Patrick said, neatly side-stepping the trap, either by accident or design. "But I went online about seven that night, and played through until four or so the following morning. I got up for a couple of pee breaks while everyone was shifting tables, but two or three minutes, max. I was doing well, I didn't want to miss any hands."

"What did you say the name of that site was?" Hamza asked.

"*Poker Facial*," Patrick said. "They're based in Malta, I think. If they're playing hardball and need my permission to share information, or whatever, I'm happy to do that."

He stared intently at both detectives in turn.

"I didn't kill anyone. I wouldn't. Whatever happened in the past, whatever happened with Albert and me, it doesn't matter. Not now. They're good people. They didn't deserve this."

"No. No, you're right. They didn't," Logan said. "But then, very few people do."

"What about last night?" Hamza asked.

"Lois? I heard about that, yes. It's bloody scary. I don't have any alibi for that, I might as well tell you now," Patrick admitted. "But, I didn't really know her other than to sort of pass in the street. She didn't get out much, and I never went to see her. I know roughly where her house is, but I'm not sure I'd be able to tell you exactly which one's hers. I've certainly got no reason to kill the poor woman."

He shrugged. "And even if I did, even if I was capable of that, with you lot around, it'd take a much bolder man than me to even try..."

CHAPTER FORTY

"YOU ALRIGHT THERE, BUDDY?"

The words crackled over Tyler's headset, the suddenness and closeness of them jolting him in his seat. He raised a thumb, but kept his eyes closed, so as not to see the distant ground rolling by beneath him.

"Oh aye. Tip-top," the DC replied.

"You sure?" Tyler could hear the smirk the pilot was wearing on his face. "You look a bit peaky."

"Don't you worry about me," Tyler urged. "Just you worry about staying in the air."

"It sort of does itself, really," the pilot said. "I mean, I can take my hands right off the controls if I want..."

"Don't!" Tyler cried out, his eyes flicking open.

The pilot sat holding the yoke, grinning back at him.

"Calm down, buddy. I've been doing this for years," he said. Then, he shrugged. "Well, *a* year. Almost. Over six months, anyway."

Tyler emitted a shrill squeak of panic, before realising that the other man was royally taking the piss.

"Funny guy," he said, swallowing back the rising knot of panic and nausea.

Since his eyes were now open, he risked a look out the side window at the ground far below. It was mostly trees at this point. He could see part of a loch, too. From up here, the water looked so dark it was almost black. It made Tyler think of a hole leading deep into the Earth's core, and he was suddenly gripped by the fear that something huge and snake-like might emerge from it and swallow the chopper in one big bite.

This, of course, was idiotic. He knew that. And yet, worrying about that helped take his mind off his much bigger and more pressing worry.

Where the hell was his wife?

There was a hiss of static in his ears, then a crackly voice spat out what sounded to him like gibberish.

"What was that?" he asked, once the racket had passed. "Was that foreign?"

The pilot shook his head. His voice filled Tyler's ears in stereo.

"Nah. It's English, believe it or not. It's like they try and make these bloody things as unintelligible as possible. You get used to it, though. I get maybe eighty percent of it these days."

Tyler looked at the radio. Or rather, he looked at part of the control panel that he guessed might have something to do with the radio. He was struggling to believe that anyone could understand the garbled nonsense he'd just heard.

"What was it saying?" he asked. He sat up straighter then, a thought occurring to him. "Shite. Is there something wrong? Is that it? Are we on fire, or something?!"

"Why would they radio us to tell us we're on fire?" asked the pilot. "If anyone would know we're on fire, it would be us. You tend to notice that sort of thing. We're not on fire. We're fine. It was just radio chatter. It wasn't for us."

Tyler relaxed a little. Although, considering he was still several hundred metres in the air, he didn't relax all *that* much.

"It was for the air ambulance," the pilot continued. "Call out."

"Oh. Right. Fair enough," Tyler said.

He shut his eyes again and tried to pretend he was somewhere else, much lower to the ground.

"Some lassie's gone into labour in the arse end of nowhere."

"Right."

It took three full seconds before Tyler's eyes opened again, and almost thirty more before, against his better judgement, the pilot begrudgingly altered the helicopter's heading.

Bob Hoon wasn't cut out for this.

He'd led a life more interesting than most folk's. He'd been shot at, stabbed, blown up, tortured, and beaten. He'd been smashed around in high-speed crashes, watched friends die face down in the Gulf sands, and had the shite kicked out of him by a giant albino.

What he had never done—and what he'd had no desire to do —was look straight down the barrel of a woman's vagina as the top of a human head emerged from it.

And yet, this was precisely the position he found himself in, squatting beside the open back door of his car at the side of a single-track road, while a squeamish police constable knelt in the front passenger seat so as to remain as far from the business end of proceedings as possible.

"Fuck! I can see the wee bastard!" Hoon cried. "Push! Push!"

"I... can't..." Sinead cried.

"Well, I'm no expert, sweetheart, but it looks like we're out of fucking options," Hoon told her. "It's coming, whether you like it or not."

Up front, the constable's face contorted in pain as Sinead tightened her grip on his hand. He'd driven a few miles until he found a signal and then, to his credit, had come zooming back to help.

Hoon had tried to hand the whole process over to him, but the constable almost passed out at the thought of it, and Sinead insisted that Hoon—God help her—was the best man for the job.

The constable had readily agreed to this, and on Hoon's instruction had scoured his car for something they could use to wrap the babies in. The best he could come up with was a hi-vis jacket. Hoon's own jacket was dumped on the parcel shelf above the boot, so between the two of them, both twins would be covered.

All they had to do was get the buggers out. And now, going by the horror-show of stretching, distending flesh that Hoon was currently eye-to-eye with, that time was very much upon them.

"Atta girl," said the constable. "You're doing very well."

Sinead stopped straining just long enough to shoot the man a fierce look, then gritted her teeth and pushed in time with the latest contraction.

From over Hoon's shoulder, a slurred voice offered some commentary.

"Bloody hell. Look at that. Her fanny's like the top of a welly," Malcolm Hall remarked. "Is nature no' fucking amazing?"

"Shut the fuck up and get ready with that coat!" Hoon barked.

He'd released Malcolm from his cuffs, on the understanding that any attempt to escape would lead to him sustaining a number of harrowing, life-changing injuries.

In his defence, Malcolm hadn't tried to run, and had mostly just followed Hoon's orders.

"Got it here," he said, displaying the bright yellow hi-vis jacket. He had it over both hands, ready to grab and wrap. "Whatever comes shooting out of there, I'm ready for it."

"Nothing's going to come *shooting out* of any—" Sinead began, then she wailed in pain, threw back her head, and squeezed the constable's hand until he was sure he felt the bones start to crack.

Aye, there was no doubt about it. Hoon's upholstery was ruined.

"Fuck, fuck, fuck, fuck!" he said in a hissing whisper. He continued to say it, too, getting faster and faster, until the word just ran into itself and become one constant undulating sound wave of swearing. "*Fuckfuckfuckfuckfuckfuckfuck!*"

He grabbed the jacket from Malcolm, flipping it so the softer lining was facing upwards. Sinead screamed. Hoon's swearing reached fever pitch.

And, as a helicopter crested the trees behind them, the piercing cry of a newborn baby rang out through the cold January air.

Tyler ran. The trees clawed at him, their spindly fingers tearing at his clothes and his skin as he went barrelling through the trees in the direction the pilot had pointed.

"Sinead! I'm coming! I'm coming!" he cried, each word a wheeze as he thundered onwards through the forest.

Tyler ran. His legs trembled and his head spun, his fear of flying now superseded by the terror of not knowing what awaited him when he eventually reached the car.

The air ambulance wasn't here yet. Tyler had caught just a

fleeting glimpse of the car sitting up on a verge at the side of the road, with a police car parked nearby.

There had been a couple of men gathered by the back doors of the car, though one was half-inside, so Tyler could only see his legs.

The other one had waved at the helicopter as it soared above them, hunting for a landing site, and Tyler in his terror-stricken stupor had waved back.

Tyler ran. Try as they might, neither the trees nor his own legs were going to stop him.

Tyler ran. And, with a final big burst of speed, he exploded from the woods, collided with the bonnet of a clapped-out old Honda CR-V, and performed a clumsy forward roll right over the top of it.

"Where the fuck did you come from?!"

Tyler twisted on the ground and found himself staring up into the frowning face of his former detective superintendent.

"Hoon?!" he ejected. "What the hell are...?"

He sprang to his feet, deciding the question could wait, and raced for the back of the car. The man who had come leaping out of a cupboard at him the day before stepped into his path, offering out a hand to shake.

"Hiya. I'm David Bowie," he announced, then he yelped in complaint when Tyler barged past him.

"Sinead? Sinead? Is she in there, is she...?"

He stopped when he saw his wife, and the bright yellow bundle wrapped in her arms. Sinead's face was shiny with sweat. Her hair was practically standing on end. There was a smear of blood on her cheek. With a bit of imagination, it was the shape of a tiny handprint.

She had never in her life looked more beautiful.

Tyler's voice box suddenly failed him. He faltered to a stop, his throat tight, his eyes prickling with heat.

The bundle in Sinead's arms wriggled. A hand patted Tyler

on the back. Hoon spoke, but right there and then, words had no meaning.

Then, after a few strained squeaks, Tyler finally found some words of his own.

"Is that...?"

Despite her obvious exhaustion, Sinead managed to smile.

"Tyler," she said. She turned the bundle towards him, and Tyler looked down into the eyes of perfection itself. "Meet your daughter."

"Daughter?" The word escaped him as a sob of disbelief and joy. "I've got a... We've got a... That means I'm a..." He tore his eyes away from the baby just long enough to steal a look at his wife. "And you're a..."

"Aye. It does," Sinead confirmed.

"Uh, hello, by the way," said the constable in the front seat. He smiled, somewhat awkwardly. "I wasn't sure when to say hello there. Felt a bit wrong to just jump in, but I was starting to feel a bit uncomfortable just kneeling here and not saying anything."

"Here, button it, son," Hoon snapped. "This is a beautiful fucking moment here, and you're ruining it with your fucking chit chat."

"Aye. Gonnae shut up, man?" Malcolm agreed.

"See? Even he knows the score," Hoon said, jabbing a thumb back over his shoulder. "And he thinks he's David fucking Bowie."

Neither Tyler nor Sinead had paid the slightest bit of attention to any of this conversation. Instead, Tyler had half-clambered into the back of the car to be nearer his wife and newborn child.

"Are you OK?" he asked, whispering the question like he was afraid what the answer might be.

"So far, yeah," Sinead assured him. "I mean, the midwife's bedside manner's not up to much..."

"I fucking heard that!" Hoon objected.

"But I'm fine."

Tyler's whole face crumpled. Tears of relief cascaded down his face, but he made no attempt to hide them.

"Is... is *she* OK?" he asked, looking down once again at their daughter.

"She's fine. She's perfect," Sinead said.

"Are you sure?"

"I'm sure," Sinead promised. She adjusted her grip on the hi-vis bundle. "Do you want to hold her?"

"Hold her?" Tyler gasped. His eyes widened in terror at the thought of all that responsibility. "But, I might drop her."

"What, on purpose?" asked Malcolm, lugging in.

Sinead and Tyler continued to ignore him.

"You won't," Sinead said. "Here."

With a few panicky deep breaths from Tyler and some shuffling from Sinead, the baby was passed from mother to father. Her eyelids fluttered open, her eyes swimming, not yet able to focus.

"Alright, sweetheart?" Tyler whispered. "I'm your dad."

Hoon leaned in, appearing over Tyler's shoulder. He nodded down to the infant, like he was passing an old acquaintance on the street.

"And I'm your Uncle Bobby."

"And I'm your Uncle David Bowie," Malcolm chipped in.

Once again, he was completely ignored.

"Should we get her in the car?" suggested the constable. "I've got the engine running and the heating on. Air ambulance should be here any minute."

Tyler looked to Sinead for her approval, and she nodded. "Go get her warm," she urged. "It's freezing out here."

"Right. Aye. OK!"

Tyler carefully backed out of the Honda, his daughter nestled in his arms. He picked his way carefully over to the squad car, like he was crossing a minefield, whispering as he went.

"You're OK. We're alright. We're just going to get you warmed up."

Hoon plodded along behind him, unrolling his sleeves as he walked. "Trust you to rock up after all the fucking hard work's done. Well fucking timed, son. You played a blinder there."

"Guys!"

The shout from Sinead made them both turn back to the Honda. She motioned to her stomach with both hands.

"There's still another one."

Hoon's mouth became a little circle of shock. "Oh fuck, aye! So there is!" He stabbed a finger at the constable, beckoning him over. "You, take the wean into the car," he ordered.

His hand slapped down on Tyler's shoulder, and he grinned.

"No way Daddy here's getting off *that* easily!"

CHAPTER FORTY-ONE

CONSTABLE BEATRICE NIDDRIE clicked out a tune on her fingers, tapped a fist into the open palm of the opposite hand, then said a slow, drawn out, dripping with meaning, "So..."

Dave Davidson smiled up at her from his chair. It wasn't his usual big beamer of a grin. It was something much smaller. Less confident. More real.

"So."

"How you doing?" Nidds asked.

"Not bad, ta," Dave said.

"Still paralysed?"

Dave nodded. "Still deaf?" he asked, though he mouth the words in complete silence.

"Funny guy," Nidds replied.

She took a seat across from him. Her mouth, unsure of what else to do, opened into a yawn. This immediately set Dave off, too. He'd been struggling to stay awake as it was.

"Late night?" they both asked at the same time.

Nidds shrugged. "I didn't really want to fall asleep in Tyler's car. "I snore like a chainsaw. So I'm told, anyway."

A pang of jealousy flitted across Dave's face. "Oh aye? By who?"

"This app I've got. Tracks your sleep. Records your snoring."

Dave's smile widened.

"First time I heard it, I thought a wild animal must've got into my bedroom," Nidds continued.

Dave resisted the urge to make any jokes. All the ones he was thinking of came across as a bit presumptuous about their future together.

"I just hit the hotel bar and got smashed," he told her.

"Nice!" Nidds held up a hand, and they swapped a quick high five. "Them chips were good, eh?"

"Aye. Aye, they were," Dave agreed.

"And then I nearly snogged the face off you."

Dave choked on nothing but air. He had to wait until the subsequent coughing fit had passed before replying.

"Did you, aye?"

"Aye. Totally," Nidds said. "So, you know, sorry for nearly taking advantage of you."

"No bother. Anytime."

Nidds leaned in a little closer. "And, just to be clear, it's the 'nearly' bit that I'm sorry about. Not the rest of it."

Dave released his wheelchair's brake and rolled an inch or two nearer to the desk.

"Right. Well, that's good to—"

The door to the Incident Room was thrown wide, announcing the arrival of DCI Logan, who stormed in with a face like thunder, and with DS Khaled hurrying along behind him.

Logan stopped when he saw the almost empty room.

"Where the hell is everyone?"

Nidds sprang to her feet and away from Dave's desk.

"DC Swanney's at the shops, sir. DI Forde is phoning home."

"Home?" Logan's brow furrowed, first in confusion, then in dismay. "Christ. His fancy woman." He shuddered, then shrugged off his coat. "Right, well, let's get set up for them coming back, because as of now, we are officially back to square one."

Hamza's phone buzzed in his pocket, and after a quick glance at the screen, his breath caught at the back of his throat.

"Tyler. It's Tyler," he announced, then he thumbed the icon to put the call on speakerphone. "Tyler? Alright? You're on speaker. Is everything—"

"I'm a dad."

He said the words like he didn't quite believe them himself. Even without the benefit of the visuals, though, Logan knew the daft bugger was grinning from ear to ear.

"Aw, mate. Nice one!" Hamza said.

"Congratulations, son," Logan said, leaning in. "Is everyone alright?"

"They're great. They're perfect! A girl and a boy," Tyler replied, and his voice wobbled like he was about to burst into tears. "So, I'll be able to tell them apart! I was worried they might, like, do tricks on me or something, you know? Like pretend to be one another, and I'd have no idea!"

Logan rolled his eyes. "Aye, I'd imagine that must be quite a relief for you, son."

"So, was she in the hospital after all, then?" Hamza asked.

"No. Was she hell! She went looking for Granny and Albert's son!"

"What?!" Logan boomed. "On her own? What was she thinking?"

"Not exactly on her own boss, no," Tyler said. "She had Hoon with her."

"Hoon?!" Logan stared in confusion at Hamza, who could only shrug. "Why was Hoon there?"

"Don't know yet, boss," Tyler said. "But thank God he was. He delivered them. Side of the road, middle of nowhere."

Logan massaged his temples with the forefinger and thumb of one hand. "Christ. You'll never hear the end of that," he muttered.

"Aye. He already says we've to name them after him. Both of them. First name Robert, middle name Hoon."

"What are you going to call them?" Hamza asked. "That's the first thing I'm going to be asked when I phone home to tell them."

"Not sure yet. Still working on that," Tyler replied. He laughed. "They won't be Robert Hoon, though. That one's out the window. But, eh, there was something else I had to tell you. Work stuff."

"You shouldn't be thinking about work stuff," Logan told him.

"Well, I can keep it to myself if you want, boss..."

"Very funny. Out with it," Logan said.

"Sinead wanted to make it clear that this was all her doing. I had to start with that," Tyler said.

"What's all her doing?" Hamza asked.

"Malcolm Hall. David Bowie. Greta and Albert's son," Tyler said. "We've got him. Uniform's bringing him up to you now."

While they waited for their chief suspect to be brought in, Logan and the others went over everything they'd found so far.

Lois Dunlop was the problem for them. Granny Hall's death made a certain amount of sense. She had a whack of money, and a husband on his last legs. Whoever stood to benefit from that was the most likely suspect, and since Gary and Sandra Hawthorne had alibis, that only left Malcolm Hall and, if he chose to contest things after Albert eventually passed, Patrick Parkes.

That said, there was comparatively very little actually set aside for Malcolm, with Greta and Albert leaving their son the grand sum of thirty-five thousand pounds. Most of the rest of their money—excluding the three hundred grand going to Sandra—was earmarked for a variety of children's charities, with a few grand here and there to friends and neighbours.

But, wherever the money was going, there was motive there. Someone stood to benefit. In its own twisted way, Granny Hall's murder at least made sense.

The same couldn't be said for Lois Dunlop.

She hadn't been well off, she wasn't a particular pain in anyone's arse, and she wasn't mixed up in anything dodgy. At least, not to the best of anyone's knowledge.

There was no apparent sexual motive for it. Neither of the bodies had been interfered with after death, and there was nothing to indicate sexual assault while they were still alive, either.

So, what did that leave? A burglary gone wrong was an obvious answer, but just like in Granny's place, nothing appeared to have been taken.

Like Patrick had pointed out, killing Lois had been particularly risky, given that there was so much police attention on the area. So, why chance it? Why kill her now? Why did she have to die then, and not later, when it was safer?

Was it her trip? She was leaving for Australia. Was that the deadline? Had the killer known about the holiday, or was there some other reason for the urgency? Some reason they didn't yet understand?

"Anything from Palmer or Shona?" Logan asked.

He was half-sitting, half-leaning against the edge of the desk closest to the Big Board, a cup of coffee clutched in one hand.

Tammi-Jo had been sent by Ben to get some biscuits, and had come back with a disappointing selection of the non-chocolate variety in a tin shaped like a snowflake. It was leftover stock from Christmas, reduced to just 99p. Based on the taste of them, she'd been well and truly ripped off.

Still, they were quite addictive, and Logan dunked his fourth or fifth in his coffee while he waited for a response.

"Just estimated time of death and confirmation that they were both strangled by the same thing," Hamza said. "Dressing gown cord. Dark blue. There were fibres on the body."

"Probably a man's, then," Ben reasoned.

"Not necessarily," Logan countered. "And even if it is, there's no saying the killer was using the belt from their own dressing gown. Could've come from anywhere."

He turned his attention back to the board, and fished another of the biscuits from the tin.

The deaths weren't random. They couldn't be. There had to be a connection. There had to be a reason behind them both.

"Oh!"

All eyes turned to Tammi-Jo, who had stood up suddenly, and was now staring at her phone.

"Oh," she said again, her eyes scanning the message she'd received. "Oh!"

"It's *maaagic*..." sang Dave. This made Nidds laugh, even if nobody else appeared to hear him.

"What is it?" Logan asked.

"It's a voice message. Well, it's a message about a voice message. It's not the actual voice message itself," Tammi-Jo babbled. "Because that would be audio, and not..." She took note of all the impatient looks and cleared her throat. "Sorry. Someone checked my old answerphone up in Aberdeen. There was a message on it. A message from Lois Dunlop."

"Bloody Hell. Was she calling from beyond the grave?" Ben asked.

"She must've left it just after she kicked me out," Tammi-Jo explained. "It doesn't say much. Well, there aren't a lot of words, but it might actually tell us a lot."

"Well?" Logan promoted. "What did she say?"

"She said, 'Granny was scared, because her boy's been coming around, acting a bit aggressively.'"

"That's it?" Hamza asked.

Tammi-Jo glanced down at her screen again, then nodded. "That's all it says she said, yeah. I could call up the road and see if they can send it down for us to listen to, but that's apparently the full text."

"Sounds like her son's been making a nuisance of himself," Ben said.

Logan checked his watch. It was dark outside, but at this time of year, this far north, that meant nothing.

He was a little surprised to discover it was after six o'clock.

"Where's the bloody day gone?" he muttered, as he reached once again for the snowflake shaped tin.

They should've been stopping for dinner, but Malcolm Hall would only be minutes away, so a handful of discounted biscuits would just have to do.

CHAPTER FORTY-TWO

LOGAN HAD MET Malcolm Hall before.

Well, maybe not him specifically, but he'd seen hundreds like him. Thousands, maybe.

Guys who'd taken the wrong path early on in life. Who'd fallen prey to some dealer or other in their teenage years. Whose addictive personalities meant they were never quite able to claw their way free.

There was no saying what the other Malcolm Hall would've been like—the one who had taken a different fork in the road. Doctor? Mechanic? Family man? Whatever he was, he would almost certainly look a lot better than the ragged husk of a human being currently sitting across the table from Logan and Ben.

He was agitated, scratching at his scrawny arms and neck, chewing over and over on his bottom lip, itching for another fix of whatever the hell he'd last ingested, smoked, snorted, or injected into his veins.

That was good. Not for him, obviously, but for the detectives. They'd seen that plenty of times before. They knew how to use it, how to weaponise against a suspect until they sang like a bloody canary.

Still, Logan couldn't help but feel a wee pang of guilt. Word from down the road was that he'd tried to help with the whole Sinead situation.

On the other hand, he'd also assaulted her. Tyler, too. So, any chances the guy had of Logan going soft on him were right out of the window.

"You alright there, Malcolm?" Ben asked. "You're looking a bit antsy there."

"I'm sorry. I don't answer to that name," Malcolm said. The words were slow and soft, like an out of shape boxer. "I'm David Bowie. I'm the Starman."

"Fine. I don't care," Logan said. "You know why you're here, *David*?"

Malcolm shrugged. "Cause of what I done."

Logan nodded. Maybe this was going to be easier than he thought. "Aye. Cause of what you done."

"I didn't mean it. It was an accident," Malcolm slurred. He scraped his fingernails down his neck and winced. "I just sort of panicked, and it just happened. She was just there, you know? She was just... I just... I just saw her, and I panicked. It was an accident. Honest."

"An accident?" Logan asked. "That's a new one. How do you accidentally strangle someone?"

Malcolm blinked. The signals from his brain weren't firing properly, though, so each eye shut in turn, one after the other.

"Strangle someone? Who strangled someone?"

"You did," Logan stated, matter-of-factly. "And you know it."

Across the table, Malcolm's ravaged, acne-pitted brow creased into deep furrowed lines. "Naw. Naw, I don't think I did. My memory's no' that good, but I'd mind doing something like that."

Ben chimed in. "So, what do you think you're here for?"

Malcolm shifted his gaze towards the DI, and seemed mildly surprised to see him there, even though it wasn't the first time that Ben had spoken.

"Pushing that pregnant lassie," the suspect said. "I just panicked, you know? I thought maybe she was with the Russians." He wiped his nose on his arm. "Thought maybe they'd come for their money."

"The Russians? You mean your dealers?" Ben asked.

Some alarm bell went off in Malcolm's head. He shifted around on his chair, then shook his head. "I don't touch drugs. I don't do that stuff. That's a crime."

"Fine. Whatever you say, David," Logan said. They could circle back to this, if they needed to. Right now, he wanted to press on. "Well, that's not why you're here. You're here because of what you did to your mum."

Like everything going in Malcolm's ears, it took a moment for the words to register on his face. His features sharpened a little, like this sentence, more than any so far, had managed to penetrate the fog inside his head.

"My mum? What are you on about?" he asked. "What about my mum?"

"Don't try my patience here," Logan warned. "You know exactly what I'm talking about."

"I don't," Malcolm replied, and there was an urgency to him for the first time since he'd entered the room. "I don't know what you're on about. What about my mum? What happened?"

Logan caught the sideways look from Ben. The same terrible thought that had struck Logan had obviously occurred to the DI, too.

Malcolm Hall had no idea what they were talking about.

It wasn't so much in his words, but in his body language. His eyes were in focus. He'd stopped scratching. He was just sitting there, holding his breath, motionless, waiting for an explanation.

But, no. He must know. He had to. If he didn't, then they had nothing. If he wasn't their man, then the investigation had hit a brick wall.

"She's dead, David," Logan announced. "But you already knew that, didn't you? Because you killed her."

The word came as a croak from some well of pain deep down within Malcolm Hall.

"Dead?"

His head shook. His fingernails went back to tearing at his skin.

"Naw. Naw, naw, naw. What? What? What do you mean?"

The words fell out of him. Spewed out onto the table. Tumbling together into one garbled mess of syllables.

"What do you mean she's dead? How's she dead? How's my mum dead? What are you on about? She's no' dead. She can't be dead! Not my mum. Not my wee mum!"

Ben raised a hand, trying to calm him, but Malcolm shot to his feet and stumbled backwards.

"You're lying! You're lying! Don't lie to me! Don't say that!"

His back slammed hard against the wall, pummelling the air out of his lungs. He slid to the floor, arms wrapping around his knees, his face a knotted mess of tears, and snot, and pain.

"Not my mum," he whispered. "Not wee Granny."

As Malcolm Hall sobbed on the floor, Logan felt Ben's eyes on him again.

"Aye. I know," he muttered. "*Shite.*"

"What do we do now?" Ben asked.

Logan ran a hand down his face, leaned back in his chair, and sighed. "I reckon we start by sticking the kettle on," he said. "And we'll play it by ear from there."

There was less persuasion required this time to get past the scary nurse. Nidds' visit had brightened Albert up a bit last time, and she'd been able to help the medical staff ask the old man a few questions of their own about his needs, and his care.

"Besides," the nurse had said, as she'd waved Nidds and Tammi-Jo through. "I'm sure he won't complain about having two young lassies at his bedside."

The fact that Albert had genuinely looked pleased to see Constable Niddrie spoke volumes about his recovery. Gone were the dead, lifeless eyes and the thousand yard stare. He smiled gummily at the officers as they entered, and even had a bash at shoving himself a little higher in the bed.

Not that it came to much, but it was the thought that counted.

"Hey, Albert!" Nidds said, signing a hello. "You're looking well."

Albert signed a response, and Nidds laughed.

"Flattery will get you everywhere," she replied.

"Hello, Albert," Tammi-Jo said. She had a bash at the sign that Nidds had taught her on the way up in the lift, but seemed embarrassed by her attempt.

The gesture almost brought the man in the bed to tears, though. He touched a hand to his chin, signed a, "Thank you," then pressed both hands against his heart.

Tammi-Jo had completely exhausted her knowledge of BSL, though, so settled on a double thumbs up in response, which she reckoned was pretty universally understood.

She took a seat near the bed while Nidds stood at the foot of it, directly in Albert's line of sight. The constable spent a few moments buttering him up, telling him how much better he was looking, how worried everyone was about him, and how the whole of the village was sending its best wishes.

Through it all, he became visibly more impatient, and when

he struggled through a series of agitated-looking signs, Tammi-Jo could guess at the meaning without it being translated for her.

"Not yet," Nidds signed back. "But we're working on it. We're going to find them, Albert. We're going to get the person who did this."

Beside the bed, Tammi-Jo spoke in a whisper. "Ask him about Malcolm. What did he want?"

Nidds nodded, then put the question to the old man in the bed. Albert's face seemed to sink inwards a little at the mention of his son, but then he shook his head and replied with a series of short gestures.

"What's he saying?"

Nidds shook her head. "He says he hasn't seen Malcolm in months."

"Lois Dunlop said he's been bothering Granny. Has he called, maybe?"

Nidds signed the second part, but left off the first.

She waited for Albert to struggle through a response, then shook her head again. "No calls. No letters. Nothing."

Tammi-Jo frowned. "But Lois said... And the bank statement. His prints are on the bank statement. He must've been around."

Nidds turned to the detective constable, angling her face so Albert wouldn't be able to read her lips. "Maybe he doesn't know. Maybe Granny didn't tell him."

Albert may not have understood what was being said, but he saw what they were up to. His gestures became sharper, angrier, demanding they tell him what they were discussing.

"Just tell him," Tammi-Jo said. "He needs to know."

Nidds took a moment to sign an apology to the old man in the bed, then filled him in on the message Lois had left on Tammi-Jo's old answering machine.

"She said that Malcolm had been coming to see Granny.

Said that Granny had told her he'd been acting a bit aggressively."

Albert shook his head emphatically, and signed out a rebuttal. There was no way that Granny wouldn't have told him, he insisted. No way she'd have been meeting with their son behind his back. There were no secrets between them, he insisted.

Tammi-Jo took a deep breath then. There was a question she knew she needed to ask, but she didn't want to. It felt too personal. Too invasive. Too raw.

And yet, she reminded herself, that was what she'd signed up for. If she couldn't ask questions like these of nice old men like this, then her dad was right—she wasn't cut out for this.

"Ask him if Granny knew about the son he had put into care."

Nidds hesitated.

But only for a moment.

She asked the question, as instructed. Tammi-Jo watched the way Albert's expression shifted. The colour that had returned to it faded away once more. His eyes lost much of their sharpness again, and the muscles of his face seemed to lose all their strength at once.

He signed something short and to the point.

"Always," Nidds said. "He says she's always known."

Albert signed some more. Nidds nodded along, smiling encouragingly at him, as if feeding him the strength to keep going.

"He says they spoke about him all the time. Wondered how he was doing. Granny never judged him for it. Even after what he did, she loved him, all the same. That's why he knows she wouldn't have hidden Malcolm's visits from him. They told each other everything."

Tammi-Jo sat back in the uncomfortable hospital chair. She got the impression there was no point in questioning him further on that particular topic. He firmly believed that Granny would've told him about Malcolm's visits, so insisting that he was wrong was unlikely to yield any positive results.

She looked down at her notes. The next question on her list was about Patrick Parkes. That was going to be a belter to ask. Albert currently had no idea that the man was his son.

Tammi-Jo decided that there would be no harm in skipping that one for now, and coming back to it later. She moved onto her next question, which had far less potential to devastate the poor old bugger.

"The, eh, the music box. On the mantelpiece. Ask him if he knows what happened to that, will you? Might as well get that squared away."

Nidds signed out the question. Rather than replying, though, Albert's hands wrung together on top of the blanket. He pulled a face that suggested the question was more painful than Tammi-Jo had anticipated.

"What is it? What's wrong with him?" she asked.

"I don't know," Nidds said. She asked him if he was OK, and he eventually nodded to confirm that he was.

Nidds translated as the old man began to sign.

"He says there was nothing meant by it. They didn't steal it, they just borrowed it. They would've brought it back. They're not bad kids."

Tammi-Jo nodded. That fit, then. She was halfway through making a note when Nidds translated another burst of gestures from the old man in the bed.

"They're good boys. They're *Granny's boys*. That's what she called them."

Tammi-Jo's pen stopped dead on the page.

She felt her stomach flipping all the way over like a pancake.

"Wait, what? Who's he talking about?"

"Not sure," Nidds said. "That's all he said. They thought one of Granny's boys must have taken them."

"Oh," Tammi-Jo said, rising suddenly to her feet. "Oh God, no."

CHAPTER FORTY-THREE

A PIPING hot cup of sweet, milky tea may not have been what Malcolm Hall was itching for, but he was working his way through it, all the same.

It had taken a good ten minutes for the news to finally sink in, and for him to stop insisting the detectives were lying to him.

After that, though, he'd become something of an open book. Whether this was for altruistic reasons, or because he suddenly realised he might be in much deeper trouble than he'd thought, Logan couldn't tell. Then again, as long as the man was talking, he couldn't care what the reasoning behind it was.

He hadn't spoken to either of his parents in months, he claimed. That wasn't to say he hadn't been around, he'd just waited until one of the few times they were both out, or timed his visits for when they were sleeping.

There was always food in the freezer. Soups and stews, mostly, all in individual bags, ready to be reheated.

Sometimes, there'd be a wee tub of tablet, taped shut so Albert didn't get tempted by it.

Malcolm always returned the tub, though he didn't always remember to wash it out first.

And there had been money, too. Not much—forty or fifty quid, maybe, depending on whether or not he'd washed the tub before bringing it back last time. Enough to help him out, but not enough to get him into any more trouble.

None of this had ever been spoken about, and Malcolm couldn't remember when it had started. Probably after he'd snuck in and cleaned out his mother's purse one night, he thought.

The next time he'd snuck in, her purse and Albert's wallet had both been empty, but an envelope had been sitting on the kitchen table with the cash inside.

He'd grabbed some food from the fridge then too—a packet of ham, half a block of cheese, and some milk.

Next time, the fridge was well-stocked for him. The freezer, too.

And so, without a word passing between them, it had continued.

"You knew about their money, though," Logan said. "What they've got in the bank."

"Aye. I saw that. Mental. Saw a bank statement when I was looking for more cash. Think they must've won the lottery, or something," Malcolm muttered. "They never said, though. Kept it quiet. Probably so I didn't find out."

"That's a big old whack of cash, David," Logan said. "That'd get your Russians off your back, I'm sure. You must be desperate to get your hands on it."

Malcolm shook his head. "That sort of money'll be the end of me," he said. "I know if I've got that sort of cash to splash around, I'll be dead in a day. I don't want it. I'll no' take it, if they try and give me it." He screwed up his face. "I hope I don't, anyway. It'll do me in, that much money. Know what I mean?"

Logan, to his immense annoyance, found himself believing the man.

"What were you doing in the house yesterday?" asked Ben. "When you attacked DC Neish?"

"Hiding. In a cupboard," Malcolm replied.

Logan sighed. "No, we got that bit. It's the *why* we're wondering about."

"Oh. I was round to see if they'd left anything out for me. Things have been a bit hard going, an' that, you know? I can't afford to put the heating on. Price of food's through the roof. Thought that maybe she'd have left me a wee something to help me get by. Know?"

"Still doesn't explain why you were hiding in a cupboard, or why you assaulted one of my officers," Logan said.

"I thought it was the Russians again," Malcolm explained. "Thought they'd followed me. I heard voices, an' that. So I hid. And then, he came upstairs, and I thought he was going to do me in, so I pushed him, and I ran. I ran right down to the harbour. Jumped in the water."

"You jumped in the water? In the North Sea? In January?" Ben asked.

"Aye. It was cold, right enough. But I thought, you know, maybe Russians can't swim. I just waited there for a wee bit, right in close to the edge, so no one could see me. Then, I got out. Freezing, it was. Thought my willie was turning inside-out."

Logan sat back, his arms folded like he was in the huff.

The guy was so affected by addiction that, intellect-wise, he was only a few notches above the average cabbage.

And yet, his story was plausible. Ridiculous, aye, but plausible. Maybe Russian drug dealers *were* after him. Some of Bosco Maximuke's old cronies were still active across the Highlands, and Logan couldn't imagine they were the types to offer flexibility when it came to payment arrangements.

Everything the bastard was saying was within the realms of

possibility. And, more importantly, Logan had no evidence with which to counter any of it.

The one bit of evidence that he'd had—the fingerprints on the bank statement—Malcolm had owned up to and explained away.

What else did they have on him? Nothing. Nothing but a cryptic phone message from a dead woman that didn't even mention him by name.

Even if you took the money as a motive, Logan got the impression that Malcolm genuinely didn't want anything to do with it. His brain might've shrunk to the size of a walnut, but he had enough self-preservation left to know that he couldn't handle a lump sum of cash that size. It'd be up his nose, or in his veins in a matter of hours. He'd be dead in a matter of days, if he even lasted that long.

The man was a cockroach, and like all cockroaches, he was nothing if not a survivor.

Before Logan could start picking away at the threads of Malcolm's statement, there was a knock at the door. For once, he was grateful for the interruption. It'd give him a chance to think. A moment for him and Ben to regroup, and swap notes on the performance of the man they were interviewing.

Hopefully, the DI would've picked up on something that Logan had missed. Though, from the sombre look on Ben's face, this seemed unlikely.

Logan suspended the interview and paused the recording, then he and Ben stepped out into the corridor to be met by Hamza and a breathless DC Swanney.

"What's up?" Logan asked. "There a problem?"

"Eh, not exactly, sir," Hamza said, then he stepped aside, giving the floor to Tammi-Jo.

"It's not him. Malcolm. He's not the one. In the message, I mean. It's not him. It wasn't about him," Tammi-Jo gushed.

ONE FOR THE AGES 349

"Albert's not seen him in months. Doesn't reckon Granny had, either. She'd have said. They had a very honest relationship."

Logan looked from Tammi-Jo to Hamza, but the DS just nodded encouragingly at the babbling detective constable.

"Skip to the end..." he suggested.

"Granny's boy. That's what Lois said on the message. 'Granny's boy's been coming round and acting a bit aggressively.' That's what she said."

"Aye. I know. You told us," Logan confirmed. "So?"

"So..." Tammi-Jo pointed past the DCI to the door at his back. "Granny didn't mean him. She didn't mean Malcolm. She meant a *literal* boy."

Logan started to frown in confusion, but then stopped as piece by piece, bit by bit, everything began to click into place.

"*Granny's boys*," Tammi-Jo said. "That's what she called the Hawthorne brothers!"

CHAPTER FORTY-FOUR

SANDRA AND GARY HAWTHORNE stood shoulder to shoulder at the door, a united front of a barricade designed to stop the detectives going any further.

"What now?" Sandra demanded. "What do you want?"

"We're not talking to you without a lawyer," Gary added. He looked proud of himself for standing up like that, but ruined it a bit by adding, "So there!"

"We're not here to see you," Logan said. Tammi-Jo stood behind him, Hamza and a couple of Uniforms gathered down at the bottom of the path.

"What?" Sandra took in the activity down by the gate.

A couple of the Uniforms were following Hamza's instructions, and heading around the block towards the back of the house.

"What do you mean?" Sandra asked. "What's going on, then? What do you want?"

"Are the boys in?" Logan asked.

It was Gary who answered. "The boys? What have the boys got to do with anything? What do you want them for?"

"The night Granny died. Rory, your son, he shouted for you, but you didn't come," Logan said.

Gary winced and looked around, worried one of the neighbours might be earwigging in.

"No. And I explained why that—"

"Nobody came," Logan continued, cutting him off. "He was terrified, shouting his head off, and nobody came to help him. Not you, Gary. And not his brother, either."

He gave that a moment to sink in.

Sandra worked out what he meant a split-second before her husband.

"No. No, don't even say that," she said, snapping at the DCI. "Don't you *dare* even suggest that."

"Can we maybe come in and talk?" Tammi-Jo ventured. "Rather than do this out here, where people can see? I think that's in all your best interests. Edgar's especially. Don't you?"

"Or will we just talk about your weird sex thing?" Logan asked at the top of his voice.

At that, Gary's head shrunk down into his chest and he hurriedly retreated, beckoning them into the house.

Logan didn't wait to be told twice. He barged in, forcing Sandra to flatten herself against the wall.

He pointed up the stairs, and Tammi-Jo took them two at a time, calling Edgar's name, ignoring the shouts of protest from Sandra down below.

Logan went charging around the ground floor, checking in the rooms there, searching for the boys.

"I don't understand what's happening!" Gary cried. "What's going on? What are you saying?"

"Where is he?" Logan demanded, brushing off the question. "Edgar, where the hell is he?"

"Sir."

Logan returned to the hall, and saw Tammi-Jo standing at

the bottom of the stairs. She had a dark blue Rangers FC dressing gown hooked onto one finger.

"No belt," she said, pointing to the loops where the cord should be.

Bollocks.

Sometimes, Logan really hated to be right.

He spun back to Sandra and Gary, any suggestions of doubt he might have had now gone.

"You need to tell me where he is. For his sake. You need to tell me, and you need to tell me *now*."

Sandra squared up to him, all bluster and defiance. Her husband, however, wasn't made of the same stern stuff.

"We sent them away. Just until all this was over and done with," the boys' dad explained. "Just until everything was sorted."

"Away where?" Logan demanded. "Where are they?"

"They're in Thurso," Gary told him. He shot his wife a worried look. "We sent them to stay with Sandra's mum."

"You, get on the phone to her," Logan barked, stabbing a finger at Sandra. For all her defiance of a few moments ago, she ran to the living room where the house phone was. Logan turned to Gary. "You, give me her address."

Gary began to recite the address from memory, then stopped when he realised that neither detective was ready. Tammi-Jo whipped out her notebook and pen, then gave a nod, and Gary rattled off the details again.

"She's not answering," Sandra said, returning to the hall with the phone pressed to her ear. "Landline or mobile. She's not answering either."

"How long to get there?" Logan asked.

Gary looked to his wife for confirmation, then shrugged when she failed to respond.

"Twenty minutes, maybe? It's actually outside of Thurso, this side, so..."

He was already talking to an empty space. Logan was racing down the path, shouting orders to Hamza, instructing him to recall the Uniforms and get onto the station at Thurso.

"Wait a minute! Don't you dare!"

Shoving her husband aside, Sandra ran out into the garden after Logan and Tammi-Jo, the phone still held to the side of her head. "I'm coming with you!"

"No, you're not," Logan bellowed back over his shoulder. "Stay here. Keep calling. We'll keep you posted."

He climbed into Ben's car, drummed his hands impatiently on the wheel while he waited for Tammi-Jo to jump in beside him, then went screeching off, tyres spinning, the moment the DC's door was closed.

Sandra reached the gate too late to stop him. The phone, too far from the house now to hold onto the signal, sputtered into silence. She threw it onto the grass as Hamza and the Uniforms sped off, lights flashing, sirens wailing.

"Keys, Gary!" she screeched. "Don't just stand there! Go and get the bloody car keys!"

"Where the hell is Uniform?" Logan barked at the world, as he threw open the door of the car and went charging for the front gate.

"I, eh, I don't know, sir," Tammi-Jo told him, hurrying to catch up.

From not too far away, they heard the screaming of approaching sirens. Those belonged to Hamza and the officers who'd come with him, though. There was no sign of any contingent from Thurso.

Logan raced up the path of the compact semi-detached house the address had led them to. He didn't bother to knock, and instead just barged on inside, already shouting at the top of his voice.

"Edgar? Edgar, it's over!"

From the living room, there came the cheering of a crowd. Logan headed for it, and found Edgar perched at the very front of a couch. A football match was playing on an old TV, but the lad was facing the door, his eyes wide in panic, one hand clutching the telly remote like it was a weapon to be wielded.

When Logan came striding in, Edgar jumped to his feet, the fear in his eyes spreading like an infection across the rest of his face.

"What? What? What's wrong?" he cried, holding his hands up to protect himself.

"Where is she, Edgar? Where's your gran?"

Edgar swallowed, then flicked his gaze up to the ceiling. "She's up there. Why?"

"Have you hurt her?"

"Hurt her? My gran? No! Why would I hurt my gran!"

"Same reason you killed Granny Hall and Lois Dunlop."

"*What?* No. No, I didn't!" He shot an imploring look at Tammi-Jo as she entered the room, like he was begging her to intervene. "Of course I didn't!"

"You were out the night before last. When Granny died. You weren't home," Logan told him. "They were holding him back, weren't they? Like they'd held you back. All these old folks, like anchors around your mother's neck. Keeping you here. They stopped you moving down to take up that offer with Rangers, didn't they? They made you miss your chance. And, when you saw the same thing was going to happen to your wee brother, you couldn't just stand by and let that happen, could you?"

Edgar shook his head emphatically. "No. What? No! No, no, no. I wouldn't... Why would I...?"

"Same reason you were going to take the blame for nicking

that music box," Logan said. "Because in your own twisted way, you were looking for him. You were being his big brother. That's why you did it, Edgar! That's why you killed them!"

"I didn't kill anyone!" the boy insisted. His voice cracked. Tears rolled from his eyes and down his cheeks. "I didn't! I didn't! I wasn't out. I was home. I was in bed!"

"Oh, aye? Then how come you didn't hear Rory shouting?"

Edgar shook his head again, dislodging a few more tears. "Shout? He didn't shout. I didn't hear him."

"We found your dressing gown, Edgar," Tammi-Jo said, her voice like a soft, silken blanket in comparison to Logan's gruffness. "The belt was missing."

Edgar stared at her in silence for a few moments, like he'd been hypnotised by her again. Then, confused, he asked, "What dressing gown?"

"The bloody dressing gown, son. The blue dressing gown. You know full well what bloody dressing gown we're—"

"Wait! They're always leaving stuff in one another's rooms," Tammi-Jo said. "That's what you said, wasn't it? When we asked about the music box!"

She slapped the heel of her hand against her head a few times.

"Argh! It's too small. Think about it. Picture it. It's too small. It's not his. It can't be his. It was in his room, but it's not his. Stupid, stupid, stupid!"

She appeared to be saying all this to herself, like it was some internal monologue that had accidentally slipped out.

"What are you—?" Logan began, but then he understood.

Finally, at last, he understood.

"Shite! Where is he, Edgar?" the DCI demanded. "Where's your brother?"

Again, just like a few moments before, Edgar's eyes crept up towards the ceiling.

They hadn't come down. Neither the boy, nor the old

woman. Despite all the shouting, they hadn't come down to see what the noise was about.

Logan allowed himself just one solitary shout of, "Bollocks!" then he ran out into the hall, almost collided with DS Khaled at the door, and took the stairs two at a time.

Sandra Hawthorne's mother fell limply onto the bed, her face red, her eyes bloodshot, a tangle of blue fabric wrapped around her throat.

"No, no, no, *no!*" Rory screeched, stumbling backwards until he collided with the old woman's dressing table.

The word may have been the same, but the tone was very different to his brother's desperate denial downstairs. He spat it out with venom, outraged and angry that someone had dared to interrupt.

Hamza hurriedly unwrapped the dressing gown cord from around the old woman's neck, and she wheezed in and out, as her lungs refilled with air.

"You shouldn't be here!" Rory roared. "You're ruining it!"

Logan didn't know if it was the shock of seeing the boy, barely a teenager, throttling his grandmother with such demented glee, or whether he was still trying to deal with the fact that he'd gone for the wrong brother, but for the first time in a while, he was lost for words.

"Rory. Calm down," Tammi-Jo soothed. "It's alright. It's alright. It's OK."

"How the *fuck* is it OK?" he screeched. "You've ruined it! You've all ruined it!"

The DC took a step closer. Rory's hand fumbled furiously through the perfumes, powders, and assorted other items on top of the dressing table, then came back holding a long, thick knitting needle.

"Stay back!" he screamed, brandishing the sliver of metal like a tiny sword.

"It's over, son," Logan said, finding his voice again. He put a hand on Tammi-Jo's shoulder to stop her getting any closer. "Put that down, eh, and let's go talk about this."

"Talk about it? What's there to talk about?" Rory shot back. He looked older than his thirteen years. Sounded it, too. "You want to put me in jail. But I'll kill you all if I have to."

He thrust the knitting needle forwards in a series of stabbing motions. It wasn't a particularly sharp thing, but with enough force behind it, it would do damage.

Logan almost made a grab for it when Rory's eyes were drawn to his grandmother. The Uniforms were helping her out of the room, getting her away from danger.

Before Logan could move, though, the boy's gaze returned to him.

"You've ruined it. You've ruined everything. Like they did! Stupid old bastards! Always ruining everything!" He raised his voice to a screeching bellow, like he was addressing the two women he had killed, and the one he had tried to. "You ruined my life!"

His hand shook uncontrollably, waving the knitting needle around like it was a magic wand.

"I shouldn't be here. I should be down there. In Glasgow. I should be playing for Rangers. That's all I wanted. That's all I've ever wanted. Me and Edgar, we should both be there." His fury boiled over inside him again, and he hissed the rest out through gritted teeth. "But these fucking old bastards just wouldn't die!"

"Rory?"

Edgar appeared in the doorway, standing on his tiptoes to see past the detectives.

"Stay out there, son," Logan barked, but Edgar slipped past him and approached his younger brother.

"What the hell are you doing?" Edgar asked. He stopped moving when the knitting needle was whipped around to point at his chest. "What's this all about?"

Rory just stared at him, eyes so wide they were bulging, his hand trembling.

"They're saying you killed Granny and Mrs Dunlop," Edgar said. "And I saw Gran. She's hurt. What the fuck's going on?"

"I did it for us," Rory squeaked.

"Edgar. Get back," Tammi-Jo urged.

Logan sized up the distance. He could grab the older brother with one big lunge, but Rory was closer. If he panicked and lashed out, there was no saying how this was going to end.

"We should've been famous," Rory whispered. "We could've been playing together. For Rangers. For Scotland. The World Cup! I did it for us, Ed. For us."

Edgar stared at his younger brother for a long time before replying.

"What are you talking about? It's just football, Roar. That's all. It's just a game."

"It's not! It's life changing!" Rory insisted. "We'd get to play at Ibrox. Hamden. All over the world, Ed! We'd be in sticker books. Us! Me and you! That's why I did it."

"Aw, Rory." Edgar shook his head. "You didn't do this for me. I don't want this. *You* don't want this."

He held a hand out for the weapon. Rory's gaze flitted to it, but didn't hang around.

"So, quit being a wee dick. Give me that. We can sort this out," Edgar urged. "We can fix this."

Suddenly, from the hallway, came a frantic cry from the boys' mother.

"Edgar? Rory?"

Rory looked to the door. Edgar saw his chance. He lunged, grabbing for the pointed metal rod.

"No!" Logan boomed, throwing himself forward.

Edgar's breath caught in his throat. He gargled.

Rory raised his hands, the panic he'd been managing to fend off now fully taking control.

"No, no, Edgar! No! I didn't mean to! I didn't mean it!" he wailed. "It was an accident! An accident!"

Logan caught the older brother as he staggered backwards, the knitting needle buried in his stomach, blood oozing around the edges.

"You're alright, son. You're alright!" Logan promised, easing the boy down onto the bed.

Edgar managed to nod. His cheeks bulged then deflated again, like his lungs were malfunctioning, forcing out air then sucking it back down again with no discernible pattern or rhythm. His eyes darted left and right, like he was marvelling at the ceiling in his grandmother's room, seeing things there that no one else could.

Logan raised his eyes to Hamza. "Ambulance," he said.

The DS, already on the phone, nodded to confirm it was in hand.

Without a word, Rory made a run for the door, but Tammi-Jo caught him by the arm. He turned, features all knotted with rage, and swung a clenched fist at her.

She caught the wrist, twisted it up his back, then pressed him against the wall.

"Don't," she warned. "It's over. It's over."

And, with his brother gasping on the bed, and his parents shouting from where Uniform was blocking them at the bottom of the stairs, thirteen-year-old Rory Hawthorne finally began to cry.

CHAPTER FORTY-FIVE

"GET AWAY! You're not welcome here! We don't want you!"

Sandra Hawthorne clasped her hands together, so as to stop herself assaulting the towering detective in the doorway of the hospital room. Logan wasn't entirely surprised by her reaction, but before he could say as much, the young man in the bed called her off.

"Mum. It's fine."

Still glaring at Logan, Sandra retreated a few paces, then lowered herself onto the chair beside her son's bed.

Edgar raised a hand just a fraction off the blanket, acknowledging the DCI. Then, when a bob of blonde hair appeared from behind Logan's back, the lad hurriedly tried to push himself up the bed.

A yelp of pain burst from his lips, and he decided that even DC Swanney wasn't worth all that effort.

"Hey! Check you out! You're looking great!" the detective constable told him, dazzling him with her smile and her sparkling blue eyes.

"Cheers," he said, casting his eyes down to his blanket as he blushed.

"What's happening with Rory?" Sandra demanded. "Nobody's told me anything."

"His dad's with him," Logan said. "Rory will need to come to Inverness. Because of his age, and the nature of what he's done, a specialist team will be brought on to deal with him. They'll take care of him, though. But, it's going to be hard. On all of you. You've all got a rough road ahead."

"Oh, don't patronise me! You think I don't know that? You've accused my son of murder!"

"Your son has confessed to murder, Sandra," Logan reminded her. "What happens next... Well, I'm afraid that's going to be out of my hands. But, he's going to need you."

He looked down at the young man lying in the bed.

"Both of you. And, I know that might be hard, son, but—"

"It won't be," Edgar said. He glanced at his mum, then back at the detectives. "Whatever he's done, he's my wee brother. We'll figure it out."

Logan nodded. "He's lucky to have you," he said, then he checked his watch. "I've got another appointment, I'm afraid, so I'm going to have to leave you in DC Swanney's company for a minute or two."

"Sorry!" Tammi-Jo said, her smile broadening.

From the look on Edgar's face, he had no objection to the detective constable waiting behind.

"You can tell me what the food's like," Tammi-Jo said, planting herself on the end of the bed. "I did mean to bring you a box of chocolates, but first I forgot, then I nearly left them in the car, then I ate them. But don't worry, I've got someone bringing in some more any minute. And I won't eat these ones. Well, not all of them. Totally having the strawberry creams, though."

"That's fine, I don't like strawberry creams," Edgar said. Ironically, his face had turned the colour of that particular chocolate's gooey insides.

"What do you mean? How can you not like strawberry creams?!" Tammi-Jo asked. "Are you an alien or something?"

Logan nodded and smiled grimly at Sandra. She rolled her eyes, crossed one leg over the other, and folded her arms, making her opinion of him very clear. He may have saved her mother's life, but she was blaming him for ruining her son's.

And, chances were, she always would.

He caught Tammi-Jo's eye, tapped his watch, and held up all five fingers of one hand. She was still talking about chocolates, and didn't pause for breath, but tilted her head towards him to confirm that the message had been received and understood.

With that, Logan slipped out of the room, strolled back through the busy corridors of the hospital, and stopped at the small waiting area near the front door.

Patrick Parkes closed the book he was reading, tucked it under his arm, and rose from his chair.

"There you are. What is this?" Patrick asked. "What's this about?"

Logan looked around the waiting area, checked his watch again, then tutted. "Late. Aye. Of course he bloody is."

"Who?" Patrick asked, following Logan's gaze towards the front door. "What are you talking about? Who's late? Late for what?"

And then, Logan spotted him through the hospital's front doors, trying to cadge a cigarette from the people passing by.

"Wait here. Be right back," Logan said, striding off.

Patrick watched in befuddled silence as Logan stepped outside, grabbed the man out front by the scruff of the neck, and dragged him back inside.

"Here, easy! Calm down, big man! I was just coming!"

It was only when Logan and his wriggling captive were almost upon him that Patrick recognised the other man.

"Wait! I know you!" he gasped. "You're the one who called me an *effing C!* What is he doing here? What is this?"

"Patrick Parkes, meet Malcolm Hall."

"David Bowie," Malcolm protested.

"Shut up," Logan told him. "You two are brothers."

"Brothers?" both men said, looking each other up and down.

"I've no' got a brother," Malcolm said, confusion practically radiating from him.

"Aye, you do," Logan told him. "You both do, in fact. And your old man's just down that corridor, last door on the right."

Patrick, who had been staring in a mix of horror and shock at Malcolm, tore his attention away long enough to spit a response at Logan.

"They won't let me in. I've asked."

"Aye. I know. *Family only,*" Logan said. "I've had a word with the nurse. She's going to let you through. Both of you. How much you decide to tell Albert, that's up to you. But, my advice? You might want to tell him the truth."

Patrick's throat tightened. He blinked, pushing back the tears that threatened to come.

"Thank you," he said, bowing his head. "I appreciate you doing that."

"You know what I don't get?" Malcolm asked, his voice carrying across the waiting area like a foghorn. "Where did I get a brother from?"

Patrick smiled. He put a hand on the other man's arm. Logan watched as they walked off together in the direction of their father's room.

"I'll explain later," Patrick said. "I think you and I are going to have a lot of stuff to talk about..."

Logan was halfway across the car park, headed for Ben's car, when his phone rang. He stopped dead in his tracks when he saw the name on-screen.

Heather Filson.

It wasn't like her to call him. Not without a damn good reason. He pulled the collar of his coat up against the rain, and pressed the phone to his ear as he resumed his stride.

"Heather. To what do I owe—?"

"What did you say to them, Jack?" Filson asked. There was an edge to her voice. A sharp one, at that. "When you were being a *character witness* for me, what did you actually say?"

"The truth," Logan replied. "I told them that you were a stubborn bastard, a massive pain in the arse, and one of the best DIs I ever had working with me. Why? What are they saying?"

Heather ignored his questions. "Aw, great. Well, that's just fucking marvellous, Jack! Good job. Well done! Good for you!"

"What's happened?" Logan asked.

He reached the car. Ben was sitting in the driver's seat, tapping his fingers on the steering wheel in time with music playing from the radio. When he saw that the DCI was on the phone, he turned down the volume.

Logan didn't open the car door, though. Not yet.

"Heather? You still there?" he asked.

"Aye. I'm still here," Heather replied, after a pause.

"What's happened? What did they say? You're not losing your job, are you? They're not sacking you for this, surely?"

"Your 'best DI' speech must've given them ideas. They're demoting me. Bumped back down to Detective Inspector."

"Oh. Shite," Logan ran a hand down his face. "Still. That's... I mean... It could be worse."

"Easy for you to say," Heather told him. "Still, at least we'll get to work together again."

Logan glanced into the car at Ben, then turned away, swapping the phone from one hand to the other.

"What?"

"Haven't they told you yet, Jack?" Heather asked. "They're moving you back down here. We're going to be a team again."

"What? No. They can forget that." Logan shook his head. "I'm not going anywhere. I'm staying where I am."

Heather laughed. It was a dry, shrivelled sounding thing. "Aye, since when did we ever get a say in these things?" she asked. "So, here's to us, Jack!"

He heard the *chink* of a glass hitting a bottle, then the sound of something being glugged from the latter.

Heather burped.

"I'm looking forward to picking things up where we left off."

The mobile *beeped* in Logan's ear as the call was disconnected. Logan stared at it for a few moments, waiting for it to ring again.

When it didn't, he returned it to his coat pocket, swore under his breath, then climbed into the front passenger seat of Ben's car.

"Everything alright?" asked the DI.

"Aye. Aye, just peachy," Logan said.

He looked out through the rain slicked windscreen at the lights of the hospital. Two figures—Hamza and Tammi-Jo— were walking towards the car through the rain. Hamza was trudging ahead with his hands in his pockets, while Tammi-Jo scurried along beside him, her arms flailing around, her mouth flapping up and down.

"Is she coming with us?" Ben asked.

Logan ran his tongue across the front of his teeth, then shook his head. "That wouldn't be very fair, would it? Me and you, Dave and Constable Niddrie. Wouldn't be right to leave Hamza all on his own, would it? It's a long journey. We can't deprive the poor bugger of a bit of company."

Ben smirked. "You're a bad man, Jack Logan."

Logan feigned innocence. "Honestly?" he said. "I don't know *what* you mean..."

A few miles down the road, Constable Dave Davidson's car cruised sedately around a bend. He indicated left, letting the buildup of traffic behind him pass when they reached a straight, then he flashed his lights to acknowledge their thanks.

The car, for its part, had no idea what was happening right now. For once, the engine wasn't roaring. For once, the brakes weren't screeching whenever they reached a sharp turn. For once, the hand operated lever that controlled the accelerator wasn't jammed all the way forwards.

For once, Dave Davidson was in no rush to get anywhere.

Beside him, Nidds looked out of the side window at the passing gloom.

"There's bound to be a chippy somewhere along the way." She turned to him, one eyebrow raised suggestively. "Isn't there?"

Dave smiled. "Aye," he said. "Bound to be."

And together, side by side, they drove onwards into the dark.

They were, Logan was forced to admit, about as close to perfect as they could be.

Which was frankly a bloody miracle, given where they'd got half their genes from.

"You got names for them yet?" Shona asked.

She was sitting in a high-backed chair with one of the twins swaddled in her arms. It was the boy—his full head of jet black hair was a dead giveaway. His sister was as bald as a coot, and though she had come into the world a good twenty minutes before him, her brother's hair easily made him look a few months her senior.

"Not yet," Sinead admitted.

She was breast feeding her daughter. Logan suspected she was only doing this to stop him having a go at her over the whole running off into the middle of nowhere thing. And, if so, then fair play to her, because he was yet to say a word about it.

She wouldn't be able to escape the conversation forever—or the bollocking, for that matter—but now wasn't the time.

Tyler, who stood hovering at the bedside like a butler waiting on orders, shrugged a little self-consciously.

"We, eh, we thought about naming them after Sinead's mum and dad."

"But they were called Isa and Ivor," Sinead said. She wrinkled her nose. "And we thought that those were maybe a bit..."

"Crap."

All eyes went to Harris, who sat in the corner, eyes glued to his *Nintendo Switch* and very much not looking in his sister's direction, so as to avoid accidentally catching sight of something he *really* didn't want to see.

"*Old-fashioned* is what I was going to say," Sinead said. "So, we're still working on it. They won't be called Bob Hoon, though. We've settled on that much."

Logan nodded his approval. "Aye, good. One of that bugger's quite enough."

He looked down at the chair, where Shona was cooing over the baby in her arms. Standing there, watching her, he felt... something. A twinge. A pull.

An urge that caught him unaware. An urge he'd thought long gone.

"You want to hold him?" Shona asked, looking up.

Logan shook his head. "No. No, best not. I'll only drop him or something. I'm not great with kids."

"Course you're not going to drop him," Shona said, rising to her feet. "The size of your hands, you could juggle the two of them."

"Maybe don't do that, though, eh, boss?" Tyler said, a look of genuine concern on his face.

Shona presented the lad to Logan. He grimaced, then accepted him into his arms. Swaddled in his blanket, with tufts of hair poking out at the sides, the infant opened both eyes. He looked up at Logan, his lip petted, then he gave a tiny grunt of effort.

"He's just shat in my hand," Logan said, matter-of-factly.

"He's got a nappy on," Sinead assured him.

"Well, it's no' on very well," Logan countered. "Because I can tell you now, he's shat in my hand."

"Tyler put it on him," Sinead said.

Logan nodded. "Aye," he said, forlornly. "I thought that might be the case, right enough."

"It's a crazy system, boss!" Tyler explained. "It's all Velcro straps, and tear-off coverings, and God knows what else. It's far too complicated."

Logan ignored the DC's wittering, and the hot, liquid effluent currently pooling in the palm of his hand. Instead, he just stared down into the wide, brown eyes of the tiny human being currently nestled in his arms.

The baby squirmed, wriggling around in the blanket like he was already trying to break free. Aye, this one was going to give his parents a run for their money. Rather them than him.

And yet...

Would it be so bad, he wondered?

He might not have the energy of youth on his side, but he had the wisdom of age.

Well, maybe 'wisdom' wasn't the right word. He had the *experience* of age.

There were no two ways about it—he'd made an arse of being a father the first time around.

But maybe history didn't have to repeat itself.

He wasn't the man he used to be. This team, these people, they'd made sure of that.

He tore his attention away from the baby. Shona stood just on the other side of the boy, holding one of his hands between her thumb and forefinger, completely transfixed.

Logan felt that pull to her again. That urge.

"You know, maybe these things aren't *that* bad, after all," he said.

He watched the realisation spreading across Shona's face. She looked up until her eyes met his. A smile spread across her face, but before she could reply, there was a knock at the door that heralded the arrival of three enormous silver balloons.

Ben entered right behind them, with Hamza following hot on his heels. The detective sergeant had a teddy bear in each hand, and one tucked under each arm.

"Alright, stop hogging the bloody place!" Ben cried.

He thrust the balloons out to Tyler, who accepted them with a, "Cheers, boss!"

"Oh, will you look at the size of them!" Ben continued, pointing to each of the babies in turn. "They're like wee dolls, are they not?"

"They are," Sinead said. "Thanks for coming, sir. Nice to see you."

"Och, you can save that 'sir' shite for when you're back in the office," the DI declared. "Hamza's brought the kiddies some toys." He urged the DS towards the bed. "Hamza. The toys. Show them the toys."

"Eh, they're just wee teddies. Amira and Kamilla picked them," Hamza said, placing the two he'd been holding down at the foot of the bed. "One's a rabbit, and the other one's... I don't know what it is. A badger? It's pink, though. I don't know if you get pink badgers."

"They're lovely," Sinead said.

"Ah, damn!" Tyler muttered. He'd accidentally let go of the helium-filled balloons, and could only watch as they rose quickly towards the ceiling and stayed there.

"And these are from DC Swanney," Hamza continued, taking the teddies from under his arms. "She thought you probably wouldn't want her coming in, so she asked me to give them to you."

Sinead glanced at the door. "Where is she?"

"She's waiting downstairs," Hamza said. "I'm going to give her a lift home."

"You might as well bring her in," Sinead said. She glanced around at the packed room. "I mean, the more the merrier at this point."

"You sure?" Tyler asked. "You're not going to get tired out?"

"I'm exhausted already. I hardly think one more's going to make any difference," Sinead said. She shrugged, and the baby on her breast grumbled her complaint. "Besides, she's part of the team now. Can't leave the poor girl out in the cold."

"I'll go get her," Logan said. "Ben's about to tear this wee bugger out of my arms, anyway."

"Aye, well, you've been hogging him enough!" the DI said. He rubbed his hands together, then held them out. "Give him here."

Once the handover was complete, Logan stole another look at the smitten Shona, then headed for the door.

He found Tammi-Jo in a corridor downstairs. She stood with her back to him, her phone pressed to her ear. It was only when he got closer that he heard her whispered protests.

"No, Daddy. No, I'm not just being difficult. I like it here. I like them. I think... I think I actually fit in." She rubbed her eyes as the sound of tinny laughter bounced around in the narrow corridor. "Please. Don't. Don't laugh."

The laughter stopped. It was replaced by a sharp-sounding outburst that made Tammi-Jo lean her weight against the wall and sigh.

"No. I know. I know what usually happens, but I think it's different this time. I feel like I'm... I don't know. Like I can make a difference. I feel like they might actually want me to be..."

She stopped when she saw the shadow falling over her, and turned to see Logan standing there with a face like thunder.

Slowly, without a word, he held out his hand.

Tammi-Jo stared at it, saying nothing. Then, with the sound of her father's laughter hissing from the speaker, she handed Logan the phone.

"Mr Swanney?"

The laughter died away. The voice on the other end was a nasal whine, exactly as unpleasant as Logan had imagined it to be.

"Yes. Who is this?"

"I'm Detective Chief Inspector Jack Logan."

Tammi-Jo picked at the skin around her fingernails, eyes wide with terror at the thought of what might happen next.

"I just wanted to congratulate you," Logan continued. He and Tammi-Jo's gazes were still locked, eye-to-eye. "Your daughter is a very talented detective. We're all very impressed here by her performance."

The reply down the line wasn't even in words, just a series of confused, spluttering noises.

"She's been instrumental in cracking a major murder investigation today. There's no saying how many lives she's saved. She's a remarkable young woman, and I can tell she's going to be a great addition to the team."

Tammi-Jo couldn't hold Logan's gaze any longer. She looked

down at her hands, saw what she was doing to the skin around her fingernails, and stopped picking.

"We're all a bit in awe of her, so I can't imagine how you must feel," Logan continued. "You must be proud."

"Um, yes. Yes. Well, of course," Mr Swanney replied.

Logan nodded. "Mind you, there's no point telling me that, is there?" he said. "Hold on, let me put you on speakerphone, and you can tell her yourself."

He thumbed the button and held the phone closer to the detective constable.

"That's you now, Mr Swanney. In your own time."

The voice on the phone was hesitant. "Um... I'm..."

"Maybe a bit quicker than that, though," Logan urged. "We haven't got all day."

"I'm very proud of you, Tammi-Jo," her father mumbled.

"Uh, thanks," she said, leaning a little closer to the mobile.

"There we go. That wasn't so hard, was it?" Logan said. "I'm going to get your number off Tammi-Jo, so I can personally keep you up-to-date with her progress."

He let all the implications of that sink in.

"So, I'll be in touch, Mr Swanney," the DCI said. "You'll be hearing from me soon."

With that, and before Tammi-Jo's father had a chance to reply, he ended the call and gave the detective constable her phone back.

"Um... Um..." she said, squirming on the spot. "You didn't have to say that stuff."

"Aye, I did. It's all true."

This only made her more uncomfortable.

"Oh. Well... Thanks. Thank you." She smiled self-consciously, then shrugged. "You, eh, you can't choose your parents, I suppose."

"No, sadly not. And don't mention it. My old man was a right miserable arsehole, too," Logan explained. He jerked a thumb up in the direction of the maternity ward on the floor above. "Now, come on. Let's go join the rest of the team. They're all waiting for you."

Tammi-Jo drew herself up to her full height, smoothed down the front of her jacket, then nodded.

"Yes, sir. Coming, sir," she declared.

Logan returned the nod, then they fell into step with each other as they headed for the stairs.

Only then did Tammi-Jo look closely at the mobile that Logan had handed back to her.

"Hang on," she said. She gave the device an experimental sniff. "How come there's shit on my phone?"

Logan winced. "Oh. Right. Aye," he said, looking back over his shoulder. "About that..."

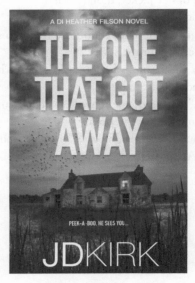

The One That Got Away

Uncover the secrets of The One That Got Away in the first in a brand new series by JD Kirk.

JOIN THE JD KIRK VIP CLUB

Want access to an exclusive image gallery showing locations from the books? Join the free JD Kirk VIP Club today, and as well as the photo gallery you'll get regular emails containing free short stories, members-only video content, and all the latest news about the world of DCI Jack Logan.

JDKirk.com/VIP

(Did we mention that it's free...?)

ABOUT THE AUTHOR

JD Kirk is the author of the million-selling DCI Jack Logan Scottish crime fiction series, set in the Highlands.

He also doesn't exist, and is in fact the pen name of award-winning former children's author and comic book writer, Barry Hutchison. Didn't see that coming, did you?

Both JD and Barry live in Fort William, where they share a house, wife, children, and two pets. You can find out more at JDKirk.com or at Facebook.com/jdkirkbooks.

Made in United States
Troutdale, OR
06/16/2024

20619813R00235